Cobra

Adrian Flanagan

ROBERT HALE · LONDON

ISBN 0 7090 6881 6

Robert Hale Limited
Clerkenwell House
Clerkenwell Green
London EC1R 0HT

2 4 6 8 10 9 7 5 3 1

Typeset by
Derek Doyle & Associates, Liverpool.
Printed in Great Britain by
St Edmundsbury Press Ltd, Bury St Edmunds, Suffolk.
Bound by Woolnough Bookbinding Limited.

For Louise and Benjamin

Author's Note

In recent years, some of the nuclear weapons laboratories in the United States have suffered major security breaches. The thefts of defence secrets are rarely publicized and, in a number of instances, the loss of technical data has been potentially cataclysmic. The theft of information relating to the United States' Radar Ocean Imaging Programme described in this book is true. The consequences are yet to be fully understood.

Adrian Flanagan
www.adrianflanagan.com

Prologue

There was nothing to suggest they would die, out here, in this vast empti-
ness. Sir John and Lady Elizabeth McGovern sat together on deck,
breathing air spiced with the tang of salt. A light south-easterly canted
Clarissa on to a beam reach, the crump of sails seeking a rhythm with the
cleaved water beneath her hull. Only the wake slipping from the yacht's
transom scarred the sapphire sea.

They had sailed 2,000 miles across the South China Sea and through
the island-spangled waters of the Banda to this place, somewhere in the
Arafura Sea that washed Australia's jagged northern coast.

The sudden screech of the radar soured the soft sounds of wind and
water. Sir John locked the helm and took the Steiner binoculars
Elizabeth handed up from the companionway. The horizons forward,
south, and to the east and west were clear. He scanned astern, to the
north, but even through the powerful magnification the other boat was a
tiny, indistinguishable speck. As he stared at it, tendrils of fear began to
slither along his sinews.

They had said their farewells to a large crowd of friends and
colleagues at the Hong Kong Yacht Club three weeks before. They had
smiled and shaken hands and hidden their pain. There was nothing left
for them but to end a corporate life stretching back thirty years.

For two months they had heard nothing. The cheap brown envelopes,
their son's blindfolded face, the demands – the routine, had stopped.
And after a while they knew there was no more need for ransom. It was
time to tell the other children.

Motoring through the choked congestion of the harbour, they had passed beneath the magnificent expanse of the Tsing Ma suspension bridge for the last time then raised the sails under an orange-dusted sky.

Sir John ducked down the four companionway steps balancing against the sway of the boat to the chart station on the port side, its instrumentation arrayed in a kaleidoscope of dials, screens and switches. He watched the steady sweep of the radar pick out the boat at twelve o'clock. Distance over elapsed time indicated the boat's speed at thirty knots.

'She's fast. Very fast, whoever the hell she is.' He waited for the radar to come round again.

'A powerboat? Out here?'

'Looks like it.'

'We're two hundred miles from Cape Arnhem.' Lady Elizabeth's anxiety crowded in deep wrinkles around her eyes. 'Call them.'

The radar confirmed thirty knots. Closing fast. Sir John snatched the radio mike, flicked the two-way switch to transmit. 'This is yacht *Clarissa*. You are to my north and approaching at speed. Can I assist?' He repeated the message.

'I'm sure it's nothin', darlin'.'

'You don't think. . . .'

'It's nothin'.'

All he heard was static and the tendrils started to grip. 'I'll see if they're flying flags.' He darted back up the companionway steps, aiming the binoculars.

The hull was maybe seventy feet. Great rust streaks trailed from her anchor holes. Her deck housing amidships was fitted with darkened glass. He could see the growth-encrusted ribs on her underside where the bow lifted out of the water, thrust forward by powerful engines. A single mast on the bridge supported navigation lights. He shifted the binoculars minutely to the boat's stern.

No flags.

Perhaps at the bow. No flags. Instead, a man, braced against the forward, port-side gunwale, hands raised, binoculars clamped to his eyes, watching. Slowly the man bent. When he straightened, the black silhouette of a rifle was clear against the deep blue of the sky.

Then a muzzle flash.

The marksman watched the man's head explode through the Kahles Helios ZF-9 scope. An instant spray of red flamed the sail. The figure stayed upright and motionless for a moment, then his legs jellied and the body toppled into the well of the cockpit.

Among his band of Malay-Chinese and Vietnamese cut-throats, Cobra was unique. A passport, had he owned one, would have identified him as an American national. A birth certificate, somewhere Stateside, showed his name as Billy-Ray Kepinski, though that name was as alien to him now as the place he'd been born, Clear Lake, Iowa.

The familiar nausea filled his bowels like smoke. He turned to face the black glass of the bridge and drew a finger across his throat. Almost immediately the vessel's bow settled back to the water. He raised the rifle again, pressing his eye to the soft rubber of the scope, anticipating the dip and rise of the boat. The shot was directed towards the dark opening of the companionway. A plume of impact dust told him he'd missed and hit the wheelhouse.

A shadow moved in his peripheral vision. He lowered the Steyr-Mannlicher SSG-69 sniper rifle.

'Radio coms, boss. Spider's got sixteen open,' Knifeman announced. 'Mayday – the woman gave her position.'

'Bad for us.' Cobra eyeballed the yacht. 'Worse for her.' He shook his head sadly. 'Any comeback?' He waited for rest of the message from the bridge.

'Cargo ship, *Endurance*.'

'How long?'

'Coupla hours.'

He nodded. 'Take it.' He held out the sniper rifle to be cleaned of salt spray and thought about the message while Knifeman retreated to the wheelhouse. The yacht was less than a hundred yards away. He bent down, picked up a Kalashnikov and waited as Spider drew up alongside nudging the yacht's starboard side with her port bow.

He leapt over the guard rail, landing on the yacht's teak deck with both feet planted, eighteen inches apart, knees bent, more out of habit than thought. A bush hat protected his face against the fierce sun, its floppy brim low over his eyes. The yacht had turned into the breeze, slowing to a drift while the mainsail flapped uselessly. He spared a cursory glance for the crumpled body in the cockpit.

As he bent into the dim interior of the yacht, he saw the woman. She was holding a knife, trembling, staring wide-eyed. A slight movement of a muscled forearm and the Kalashnikov swivelled round. Two bullets erupted, smashing the knife out of her hand, taking three fingers with it. He loosed a burst of fire into the electronic gizmos arrayed over the chart table. The stench of cordite was gagging. He loved that smell, the same way he loved the smell of grass after rain.

The woman was staring uncomprehendingly at her mutilated hand while short, rhythmic pulses of blood pumped from the mangled flesh.

He leaned his weapon against a galley cabinet, an amused smile on his lips. Behind mirrored glasses his eyes remained anonymous.

She tried to run. He blocked her, holding her arms and spun her round, smashing her face down on to the counter-top. One yank and the thin cotton of her dress shredded. He could never look at their faces. He reached into a thigh pocket and pulled out a Zippo, flicked the lighter and played the flame over the woman's breasts.

She thrashed her body sideways to escape the burning, bucking with feeble, child-like weakness. Screaming and burning.

A cat whistle bought three of his men over the side of the launch and on to the yacht.

'Anything more on the coms?' he asked simply.

Knifeman ducked his head into the cabin. 'Yeah, boss! *Endeavour*'s headed this way. Skipper's been trying to get through.'

He mounted the steps to the cockpit. 'Find it.' He glanced back at the woman. 'And finish her.' The nausea came again, stronger this time.

As he climbed back on to the launch, the muted sound of gunfire coughed out of the companionway.

1

Alan Bedale was worried. The evidence was by no means conclusive, but there was enough anomaly in the short life of this investigation to suggest something very dark, and the shockwaves were going to be unavoidable.

He was running late. All he needed was for Simon to be hanging around the arrivals hall, getting mad, and he would have had a truly awful day. Awful bloody week come to think of it. Still, what could he do? Simon. *Bugger's bound to be whinging about something.*

Alan raced across town and over the Brisbane River to the airport on the river's northern banks. Beyond the airport complex, Moreton Bay reflected the fading evening light. He deposited his Nissan Sunny in the car-park and strode purposefully into the arrivals hall, reprimanding himself for being uncharitable towards Simon. How long was it now? Five years. A lot could change in five years. And the bloke wasn't exactly here on holiday.

He scanned the flight monitor above the bar. 'Thank Christ,' Alan murmured, which was as close as he ever came to prayer. The plane was late, just landed. Time enough for a tinny. He wandered towards the bar, frisking himself for his Nokia.

'You lost somethin', mate?' The barman looked more suited to hanging out at Surfers Paradise.

'Mobile phone. Must have left the bloody thing in the office. I'll have a Tooheys, ta. Back in a mo.'

Alan called Bet from a payphone to let her know they'd be late home. By the time he returned to the bar, an ice-cold beer stood on the polished counter. He drank half the glass with an appreciative sigh.

'Got someone coming, mate?'

'Yeah. Brother-in-law. Haven't seen him for a while. Might not recognize him.' Alan finished his beer and pushed the glass towards the barman.

'Another?'

'Ta. Have one yourself.'

'No thanks, not allowed. Competition Saturday. Got to keep off the beer for a few days.'

Alan patted his belly. 'No such worries.'

The barman grinned, snapping the top of another can. 'So where's he coming from, this bloke?'

'England.'

'Right, a pom.'

'He's not so bad. Cheers.' Alan raised his second glass.

'Been to Oz before, your mate?'

'Nah.'

'Crikey! He might like it and decide to stay.'

'I've had a lot of luck in my time, most of it bad. Don't tempt fate.'

The barman grinned again and moved away.

Alan was not a handsome man, but he possessed an asset of much greater value than looks alone: his face smiled. Bet said it was his twinkling blue eyes. Although he was given to an acerbic wit, his mouth curled in a permanent expression of pleasure. He looked back at the television screen, perched on his barstool which gave him a good view over the meeting area.

Within minutes, passengers began to emerge. He recognized Simon immediately. Still the same youthful appearance, slim and fit-looking. Only the dark rings under his eyes testified to the trauma of the four-day-old news. He glanced down at his paunch and told himself he'd better do something about it, knowing he wouldn't.

Alan drained the last of his beer. He felt unaccountably nervous. He remembered his wedding and the cool reception he'd received from Simon and Ben. Contact with Simon had dwindled to an annual exchange of Christmas cards. There had been a call when Betina was born. They'd said hello and that was all. And then Ben's disappearance. Bet had flown to England while he stayed with the child, isolated and excluded. He was conscious, too, that once again he might be intruding on a family's private grief. Even after ten years of marriage he knew he'd never been accepted, not fully. And then the phonecall to Simon in Egypt.

2

Alexandria harbour was as chaotic as the bustling streets of the ancient city. Arab dhows skidded over the water, heedless of the cordon markers sited over the submerged city where once Cleopatra had made her head-quarters. The air was thick with belched diesel fumes and the stench of fish putrefying under the hot sun.

Simon McGovern appreciated all of this from a depth of fifty metres, staring up at the silhouettes of the hulls snaking silently over the reflected silver of the surface through the view dome of a Comex Remora 2000 manned submersible.

'Let's take a look over there.' Chuck Brenner, from the University of West Florida archaeology programme, pointed to what might once have been a pier.

Simon eased the F-16-type joystick towards his right knee, activating the submersible's lateral thruster. The panorama scrolled, golden stone picked out in relief by the craft's twin beams of conical light. A school of fish cast fleeting shadows over the intricate stonework.

Simon approached the point Chuck wanted to have a look at and stilled the submersible to a hover using the verticals, careful not to get too close to the seabed and disturb loose material. Beyond a mound of collapsed masonry, an apron of sugary sand separated them from a miniature mountain range forested with multi-coloured coral. An infinite variety of small darting fish played, flashing fluorescent blues, pinks and yellows. Larger moon-tailed grouper picked titbits from the rocks. An eagle ray rode the current, its fluid wing tips undulating against the movement of the sea.

They were mapping out the primary construction points of the site, Chuck operating a digital camera to build an enhanced computerized image of the ruins.

'Close enough, Chuck?' Simon asked.

The bearded American shrugged, head bent in concentration over a laptop. 'Nah, edge in a bit.'

Simon crept the vehicle forward. From the shadows he saw a white-tipped reef shark explode from cover in pursuit of some unseen quarry. The eagle ray held its station, disdainfully observing the frenetic activity of the sea.

The project, a joint venture between the Americans and the Centre for Research in Maritime Archaeology and History based at the University of Bristol had provided Simon with his first commercial contract as a professional diver.

'Got it,' Chuck exclaimed. 'Great shot.' He sat back massaging his neck. 'How long we got?'

'Main air gauge reads twenty litres at two-four-five bar. Plenty, plenty.'

'OK. Hey, you're really loving this stuff.'

'Beats having a day job.' Simon grinned. 'This stuff fascinates me, archaeology, research, finding things; you know, discovery. Couldn't get into anything since my brother disappeared a while back.'

'I remember you saying, a year, right?'

'One year. Seems like forever. Threw me a bit. Did a few drugs, lost my head.'

'Sure.'

'The hard bit's not knowing what happened.'

'It's a tough break.'

Simon concentrated on his instruments. 'Ben was older than me, four years. I always looked up to him, you know, hero-worship and all that.'

Chuck nodded snapping the laptop shut. 'South-east Asia wasn't it?'

'Yeah. Philippines was the last place he sent a postcard from. Said he was having a great time, then nothing. We think he was on a plane that went down.' The propellor revs climbed steeply. He eased back on the stick. 'It wasn't so long ago I couldn't talk about Ben without going on a twenty-four hour drinking binge.'

'Good for you. Talking about drinking binges, some of us are going out tonight, check out the nightlife. Wanna tag along?'

'That'd be fun.'

At that moment the radio crackled. The very English voice of the project controller, Roger Towers, spilled into the cockpit. 'Simon, how are you two doing down there?'

'Doing fine.'

'Sorry to barge in, but there's a call for you. Chap says it's urgent.'

'Who is it?'

'Bedale. An Alan Bedale.'

'Who?'

'*Alan Bedale*. Says he's calling from Australia.'

Chuck gave a thumbs-up sign. 'Let's get topside. I'm done anyway.'

'We're ascending,' Simon cut the radio link. 'What the hell is he calling me for?'

'Who's Alan Bedale anyways?'

'My brother-in-law. We don't talk much, so I guess it must be important. Christ! Haven't spoken to him for ages.'

'He know you were here?'

'He's a cop, good at finding people who don't want to be found.' Simon pulled back on the stick, watching the air pressure monitors as the Comex Remora began to rise.

The eagle ray, losing interest in the wrasse picking parasites from its back and disturbed by the light, flapped its wings and banked away, scattering fish like breaking glass.

3

Simon McGovern gazed out of the aircraft's small, oval window. Across 28,000 feet separating him from the ochre mass of the MacDonnell Ranges, he could distinguish the tiny details of rucked land, meandering rivers and isolated clumps of forest. Gradually, the contours, smoothed as the mountains receded, yielding to the flat lands of the Simpson Desert. Fascinating the way the earth looked so small and harmless. It seemed unreasonable that there could be pain down there, deep, inexplicable, immeasurable grief.

Business class was full, except for the seat next to his in row 5. It was occupied by his battered, leather briefcase. Inside the briefcase were some documents. He knew they were rare and some heightened sense told him they were precious, that there was a *reason* they had been sent to him.

He hated the claustrophobia of aeroplanes, and worse, the irrelevant chit-chat from strangers. He disliked the recycled air, the cramped suffocating space, the inescapability of it. So the extra seat was worth the £4,000 he'd paid. Simon checked his watch, a Rolex Explorer II. Its familiar face was reassuring. Three hours to go. Then he'd be out of this sardine tin.

His breath gathered and faded on the Perspex and, through the skin of the fuselage, the aircraft's vibrations migrated into his brain, adding to the rhythm of a thumping headache.

He'd hardly eaten since leaving Heathrow, a sandwich and a couple of

Cokes. The only interlude had been a screening of *American Beauty*. He'd watched it, couldn't avoid it, in five-second snatches. No headphones. Silent explosions, silent shouting, silent killing. But his mind remained full of the noise from the shattering news he'd received in Alexandria from Alan. Was it only four days ago? It seemed like his whole life. As though his past had been obliterated. Even the future was impossible to contemplate, existing somewhere outside this dark, impenetrable grave.

With twenty minutes to spare, he'd made it out of Alexandria to the airport across town, driven by Chuck Brenner in one of the project's Landrovers. 'My dear chap,' Roger Towers had said as he was leaving. 'I'm so very sorry. Look. . . .' – an awkward pause while the project leader shuffled his feet – 'we're almost done with the mapping . . . we'll . . . I'll call you.'

Orphaned and sacked in one afternoon.

Chuck had spent most of the ride cursing anyone who got in their way, a suitable means of avoiding conversation. *What the hell was there to say?* The viscid silence had congealed in the hot air. A brief, awkward handshake at the departure terminal. And that was that. Just the constant snapshots of the past, blinding him.

By the time Simon unlocked the front door of his apartment in London he was exhausted. Even his carefully selected French antiques, the large lamps with soft yellow shades and shelves housing his collection of books, seemed fundamentally altered and remote. Alan's words echoed in all the empty spaces: *sorry . . . mother . . . father . . . dead . . . murdered.*

Just as Ben was beginning to fade.

Now his parents. *Murdered?* Murdered! It was that word, *murder*, which tortured him, dogging him like a shadow.

Inside the cabin, the hot, metallic aroma of container food spread along the stale air. Simon pressed his face closer to the window. He watched the course of a river slide beneath the aircraft's belly. The view blurred and cracked. He cried for his mother and father. He cried for Ben and for himself and for Bet. For the terrible injustice and because the slab of dread weighing down on him had, finally, become unbearable.

The unrelenting desert had become fractured, creviced with lakes. The wide expanse of Kallakoopah Creek fed into the hundred-mile-long Lake Eyre. Simon absently sipped his wine, watching the sunlight splashing off the blue water as he roared overhead. *How long has it been since I saw Bet? Five years?* Time evaded his memory. Too long. He realized that now.

The sky remained unblemished. The light had become more golden with the passage of the afternoon. He felt his ears squeeze. Far below, the well-watered Blue Mountains north-east of Sydney framed massive, fertile canyons. True to their name the mountains appeared blue, a trick of the light refracted through the fine oil mist from the endless eucalyptus forests.

Towns and villages glimpsed among the hills merged into the western suburbs of the city. The plane swept over the harbour and on towards the Mascot district, impacting the reinforced concrete of Kingsford-Smith International with a squelch of tyres and clouds of vaporized rubber.

The airport's high ceilings and aggregate floors created a cool, airy feel. Simon was grateful for the simple pleasure of being able to stretch his legs, teasing out the ache in his knees. The herd of passengers passed a series of signs, one indicating passport control, another the transit lounge. He bought Australian dollars, checked on to the Brisbane flight then went to the bar. A television monitor told him his connection would leave in forty minutes. He ordered a cappuccino and took out a crumpled pack of Benson and Hedges from his blazer pocket. He hadn't smoked for six years, until four days ago, and already the tobacco tasted familiar on his tongue.

Announcements echoed around the hallway. He downed the last of his coffee and ordered another. He remembered Alan's wedding to his sister, the huge marquee on the lawns of McGovern Court, his father exercising all of his considerable charm while Alan toasted the bridesmaids with a pint of beer. His mother had fussed around the guests, almost apologetically. Beyond the marquee, manicured gardens swept up to the Jacobean manor. In a paddock, the automobile collection of 200 of the country's top society and business personalities was parked in a concentrated display of affluence.

4

Alan let Simon size him up, thinking, *here we go*. He found himself holding his stomach in, then thought, bugger it, and breathed out.

'Good to see you, Alan.'

Alan didn't believe him.

'Yeah, likewise.'

He shook Simon's hand and awkwardly clasped his shoulder. He felt it was an appropriate sort of gesture, in the circumstances.

'Let me take that.' Alan grabbed Simon's holdall. 'Bet's dying to see you. Car's this way.'

The drive took them north along the Gateway past the Brisbane International Centre and on to the coastal road through Brighton.

'I'm really sorry, mate, about what's happened.'

Simon lit a cigarette. 'Mind if I smoke?'

Alan noticed the order: action, permission. 'No worries.' He wound down his window.

'How's Bet?'

Alan shook his head as he steered on to the Houghton highway spanning the mud flats of Bramble Bay. 'She's taken it bad, but she's got the kiddie to occupy her.'

'Betina. That's a nice name.'

Alan ignored the sarcasm. 'Kiddie's been a bit crook.'

'Nothing serious?'

'Nah.'

They came off the highway and followed the cliff line towards Woody Point.

'To think I've never been here, never seen where my sister lives.'

'Yeah, well, I reckon you must've been pretty busy. Nearly home.'

Alan drove on to a single-track lane that led towards South Reef. Thick tropical vegetation lined both sides of the road. In the dark, it appeared impenetrable. He turned through an open gate, the headlights sweeping over a tin-roofed bungalow surrounded by wide verandas and low gables intricately adorned with Victorian trellising.

Bet stood on the porch, back-lit in the open doorway with two-year-old Betina, shoeless and tousle-haired, perched on her hip, sucking her fingers.

Simon scrambled out of the car, taking the porch steps in one leap. He hugged his sister, embracing the bewildered child at the same time. Alan watched them approvingly, coming up the steps lugging Simon's bag, but he noticed that Simon had kept a firm hold on his briefcase.

'Oh, Simon, it's so good to see you.' Bet wiped the tears off her cheeks. She looked down at her child. 'This is your Uncle Simon, Betina.'

The child appraised the new arrival with huge brown saucer eyes. As he reached out to stroke the child's cheek, she buried her face in her mother's bosom.

'You look good.'

'I don't think so, but thank you.' Bet absently stroked the back of her daughter's head.

'Alan tells me she's not been well.'

'Bad cough.' Bet smiled weakly. 'I'll put her to bed then we'll have something to eat.' She turned to Alan and kissed his cheek. She offered Betina who was rewarded with a kiss on the nose. 'I've lit the barbie, Al. I thought Simon would be hungry. And you left your mobile here, just in case you were wondering.'

'Thanks, love. You hungry, Simon?'

'Famished.'

'Come with me and I'll show you your room then I'll get on with dinner.'

While Bet was putting the child to bed, Alan shrugged out of his sports coat and tossed it over the back of a sofa. He hated wearing jackets.

The inside of the house, much like outside, was simple. Bet, like her brother was the beneficiary of a trust fund, but they chose to live off Alan's salary alone. A rug covered the parquet floor. The sofa was a two-seater, upholstered in a green, unpatterned material. There was an armchair to match. A cheap, scaled-down imitation of an Indian day-bed acted as a coffee table. The pictures on the walls were prints and Simon noticed that the books were all paperback.

Alan was already busy at the barbecue, portraying as normal a picture of domestic bliss as was possible in the midst of death. He watched Simon wander out to the front garden. Behind him glimpses of the sea winked through gaps in the bush that edged the grass beyond a small swimming pool.

'Fancy a proper beer? None of that warm, flat English stuff?'

'Thanks. What's cooking?'

'Prime Oz beef.' Alan tossed a can to Simon.

'Didn't eat on the plane.'

'This'll sort you out. Cheers.' Alan drank deeply. He prodded meat on the grill. He felt oddly intimidated by his brother-in-law.

'T-bones. Look good.' Simon swallowed some beer.

An awkward silence settled between them. Alan kept his eyes on his work. 'Bet needs you to be around, Simon,' he said, embarrassed by the sentiment.

'I know.' Simon raised his Tooheys.

Bet came out and they sat down to sizzling steaks and crisp green salad. A dose of Calpol had sedated Betina. They ate in silence, broken only by the sea breeze rattling palm fronds and the distant muffle of waves against cliff rocks.

'I want to thank you for calling me, Alan.'

Alan, unable to talk through a mouthful of meat, shrugged as if to say *that's OK*.

'I know it must have been difficult for you. By the way, how did you find me?'

'Your father spoke to Bet, before they left.'

Simon nodded. 'You said *Clarissa* was attacked. You said Mum and Dad had been . . . shot. Is there anything more? Have the police got any idea who did it?'

Alan glanced at his wife who had stopped eating and was staring down at her plate.

Bet took a deep breath. 'I haven't been able to go and see them, Simon, to identify them. I was hoping. . . .' A spasm rocked her.

Simon reached forward and squeezed her hand. 'It's OK. I'll go. Tomorrow.'

The rasping sound of a child coughing filtered into the warm night air. 'I'll go and settle her,' Bet said, getting up from the table.

Alan swallowed, touched her arm then wiped his mouth with a paper napkin. He waited until she'd disappeared into the house then said, 'Pirates.'

'Pirates? You mean as in eye-patches and cutlasses?'

'No. I mean as in murderous thugs driven by hunger and poverty, seaborne paedophiles, murderers and rapists. I mean the lowest form of the human condition where five bucks is fair exchange for somebody's life.'

'I didn't think that kind of thing went on any more.'

'Oh, believe me it does. It's common around here. Well, not around here, but further north in Indonesia, the Philippines. Private boats, yachts, are soft targets. They're getting bolder, the pirates, bandits, whatever you want to call them, straying into Australian waters.'

'What happened?'

'It's fairly clear what happened.' Alan leaned back in his folding garden chair. It squeaked beneath his weight. 'They were attacked. Isolated target, expensive boat. Easy pickings, to put it crudely.' He frowned. 'But some of it doesn't make sense.'

'What d'you mean?'

Alan could see the anxiety creasing Simon's face. 'None of the electronic stuff was taken, that's usually what these people are after, that and cash of course. The radio, radar and so on were shot up, destroyed.' Alan snapped the top of another Tooheys. 'Strange that they didn't scuttle the boat either. They usually do that.'

Simon lit a cigarette. 'You seem to know a lot about it.'

Alan sucked at his beer can then swallowed audibly. 'I didn't want to go into detail on the phone.'

'So?'

'So . . .' Alan hesitated.

'If you're wondering how to do this, Alan, just tell it straight.'

'Fair enough. I'm in charge of the case.'

'What?'

'You seem surprised. Simon, things have moved on. When I married Bet I was a beat policeman but I haven't been on the streets for more than five years. Sir John and Lady McGovern were subjected to a pirate attack inside Australian territorial waters. As such it falls to my department, P-Unit.'

'Your department? What the hell is P-Unit?'

'If you'd kept in touch with your sister you might know more about our lives.' Alan softened the rebuke with a smile.

Simon dragged fiercely on his cigarette. 'So, are you going to tell me what P-Unit is?'

'We were on holiday on the north coast, about six years ago, staying at a place near Darwin. A boat drifted into the bay, abandoned or so it seemed. It came right up to the beach, just rocking in the waves. Bet told me to go have a look, so I did. There were three bodies on board. The stench and the flies were unbearable. I called the local police in but they didn't have much of a clue. Found out later the people on board were Americans.'

'Pirate attack?'

'I didn't know that at the time. Anyway, I did some research, you know, local police records. There'd been several similar cases during the previous ten years, all unsolved, except one, a local couple cruising the Coral Sea. They were attacked. The bloke had a firearm on board and put some shots into them. They scarpered. I traced the couple to Sydney. We talked and I put two and two together. To be brief, I established P-Unit as an anti-piracy team liaising with police in Indonesia, the Philippines, Singapore, anywhere in this region where piracy is rife. Took two years to get through all the red tape, get funding and so on.'

'Jesus. So you're ambitious after all.'

Alan fluttered his fingers in the air. 'Surprise, surprise.' Then his tone became more serious. 'P-Unit gets notified of any apparent pirate attack, anywhere in Australian waters. When *Clarissa* was sighted drifting, the information was passed to my desk.'

Simon leaned forward, elbows on the table. He crushed out his cigarette. 'OK. You think there's something funny going on then, loose ends?'

'I didn't want to go into detail with Bet. Or with you on the phone. First, there was nothing to be gained; second, I've got suspicions, but nothing solid.'

Simon nodded. 'I need to know what's going on, Alan.'

'I'll take you to the office tomorrow.'

'Where is it?'

'Here in Brisbane. That way I've got access to central facilities – forensics, ballistics that sort of thing.'

'You've seen them . . . Mum and Dad?'

'Yes. It's not pretty, Simon.'

Simon was unable to speak. He rested his head on the edge of the table.

'Look, why don't you get some kip? You're bloody drained, mate. All that thinking about it on the way over and the days before, now talking about it. No bloody wonder.'

Bet came out of the house. The child's coughing had stopped, though neither of the men had noticed. She sat down with a sigh.

Alan got up. He brushed his lips against Bet's forehead, then went into the house.

'They would have liked it here.' Simon cupped his hands around a flaring match.

'I wonder if Mum and Dad are up there.' Bet looked at the stars.

'I'm sorry it's been so long. I'm no good at talking about . . . you know . . . my feelings.' He dragged heavily on his cigarette. 'Ben's disappearance did something to me. I've become a cynical prick. But Mum and Dad. I can't . . . deal with it on my own.'

Bet leaned forward, kissed his cheek. 'You don't have to, Simon. You've got me and Alan.'

'We'll find out what happened.'

'Al's been very good.'

'He's your husband.'

'They never welcomed him to the family. I think Dad was too busy to notice anyone really,' Bet said sadly.

'Rubbish. He was a great father.'

'Come on, Simon. Dad only ever had time for Mum and that bloody boat.'

'Alan took you away from home.'

'I was already away from home.'

'But not permanently. The marriage made it permanent.'

'It hurt Alan very deeply, you know. I was hoping this trip, Mum and Dad being here with us, would straighten out a lot of things.'

A door banged. Alan came across the grass carrying a tin tray. 'She's sound asleep now. Made coffee.' Alan placed the tray and three steaming coffee mugs on the table.

'Thanks, Al.' Bet picked up a cup from the tray.

'Pleasure, love.' He passed a cup to Simon. 'Here you go. And I brought you an ashtray.'

'Thanks.' Simon fingered another cigarette from the packet. 'Alan?'

'Yes.' Alan sipped the scalding coffee.

'Do you have any idea . . . any idea at all who did this?'

5

Dawn broke bright and crisp accompanied by the chorus of a million songbirds. Alan lay in bed, his hands behind his head, wondering about Simon and how the day was going to turn out. Last night's meat sat heavily somewhere in his abdomen. He watched the new day through the uncurtained window. Their bedroom was large, furnished in a curiously old-fashioned way. He liked Bet's taste for dark Victoriana. The bed squeaked whenever he shifted, a noise he found strangely reassuring. A tallboy stood against the wall.

At seven o'clock he went out to the garden for a swim. By the time Simon joined them for breakfast, Alan was bouncing Betina on his knee keeping time to the monotonous beat of S-Club 7.

'They're like a rash, those kids,' Simon joked.

Alan winked. 'Bit prettier than some of the rashes I've had! She likes them anyway.' Betina was gurgling happily, pieces of banana dripping off her tiny chin.

'I don't want to know.'

'You're coming with me to the office?' Alan guided another teaspoon of mush into his daughter's mouth.

'Question or order?'

'Both. I need you to help me with one or two things.' Alan returned his attention to his daughter.

Bet deposited eggs and bacon in front of them. 'Sleep well?' She kissed Simon's cheek.

'On and off. More off than on.'

Alan glanced up. 'If you're tired. . . .'

'I'll be fine, really . . . need to keep busy and all that.'

Alan and Simon left the house just before eight. The drive took them past the airport and through Brisbane, on to Royal Esplanade and down to Manly. P-Unit occupied a double storey, flat-roofed, white building with metal window frames close to the breakwater south of Darling Point. Out in the bay, the butterfly-wing sails of small boats flitted haphazardly over the water. Overhead, the hornet-buzz of a light aircraft descended towards Redcliffe Field.

P-Unit's offices lacked the austerity of a government facility, the desks arranged open-plan; most were already occupied. An urgent bustle infiltrated the air. Alan greeted his staff with an easy manner. His affability, the slaps on backs and the good mornings were enthusiastically returned.

'What's with the nuts?' Simon questioned. Pictures of nuts and plastic models on desks with grinning, mawkish faces festooned the place.

'Peanuts.' Alan grinned at Simon's incomprehension. 'We're called the "peanuts". P-Unit, peanut?'

'Right,' Simon said, eyebrows raised. 'It's a fun thing.'

'Some wit at HQ coined the name. It stuck. Anyway, stupid as it seems, it gives the boys and girls a sense of . . .' – he grappled for the word – 'solidarity, I suppose.'

'Proud to be called a peanut?'

Irritation bristled under Alan's skin. 'Lot worse things to be called.' He led the way up the stairs to his office on the first floor.

'Nice view,' Simon remarked.

'Coffee?'

'Sure, white, one sugar, thanks.'

Windows running the length of two sides of the corner room gave good views south over the marina to the Royal Queensland Yacht Club. To the east, Wellington Point and out in the bay, Green Island. Simon opened one of the windows. The heat was already mounting. He looked down into the yard, an area of hardstanding adjacent to the building enclosed with gated, security fencing. A yacht rested on blocks in the enclosure, covered with a grey tarpaulin slung over the boom and teth-ered to the ground like a tent. The boat's bow and stem protruded at either end.

Alan came in holding two plastic cups of coffee. 'From the machine, I'm afraid.'

'Christ, that's bloody *Clarissa*!' Simon shouted, pointing to the yard.

Alan nodded, handing Simon a cup. 'Forensics are going over her.'

Simon took the cup, placed it on the windowsill and rummaged for his cigarettes. 'Jesus! Sorry, Alan, it's a bit of a shock.'

'No worries. We'll have a look at her later. Right now I need to go over what I think happened.'

Simon blew smoke through pursed lips, glanced again at his parents' boat then came away from the window and sat in front of Alan's grey metal desk. 'Christ! It's seeing it up close, you know.' He closed his eyes and took a breath to steady himself. 'How'd she get here?'

'Towed behind a ship then a road transporter.' Alan flicked through papers in a tray, selected some stapled sheets and placed them in front of Simon.

'I can't believe this!' He looked at Alan. 'What're these?'

'Captain's statement, from the ship that found *Clarissa*.'

Simon thumbed through the pages without reading a single word.

'*Clarissa* put out a mayday call at 1416.' Alan deliberately avoided using his in-laws' names. '*Endeavour* responded at 1420, but never got a call-back.'

'Four minutes?'

'The skipper was plotting *Clarissa*'s position. It's in there. He said he wanted to give a response time, so he needed to figure out how far they were.'

'What was the mayday?'

Alan rooted out another sheet and read, 'Yacht *Clarissa* under armed attack. Require immediate assistance. Position 138 degrees, 5 minutes, 15 seconds west, 9 degrees, 12 minutes, 4 seconds south.'

'Where's that?'

Alan went over to a wall map. 'Here; the Arafura Sea, south of Dolak island in Indonesia, north of Cape Arnhem.' He stabbed the map with a stubby finger.

'That's almost in Australia!'

'About two hundred miles. But this is the danger zone.' His hand circled the islands of the Banda Sea, the Philippines and the Java Sea as far as Singapore.

'Where's the scale on that map?'

'Here.'

The key was in the bottom corner. Simon studied the map. 'But Brisbane's fifteen hundred miles from Cape Arnhem. You got the boat here pretty fast.'

'*Endeavour* towed her to Darwin, a day's sailing. Your parents were flown down here. *Clarissa* was lifted on to a road rig. Two days' drive. Got here two days ago. The forensics boys have been working on her since.'

Simon nodded. 'So how far away was this ship *Endeavour*?'

'Two hours, steaming under full power. The skipper recorded the time they reached *Clarissa*'s stated position at 1612. She'd drifted. They circled, found her fifteen minutes later.'

'And my father didn't respond?'

Alan shook his head. 'He didn't make the call. Skipper says it was a woman's voice. My guess is the pirates were already on board, or damned nearly.'

'Dad was dead?'

'I don't know. It's possible.'

'You're sure they were pirates?'

Alan nodded. 'And that's the strange thing.'

'What is?'

'The pirates, whoever, they would have known they had plenty of time. When *Endeavour*'s skipper answered the mayday, he gave his position and his ETA. But like I said last night, they didn't take any electronic gear. Either that, or they'd already destroyed the radio before *Endeavour* answered. But that's unlikely.'

'Why?'

'They'd keep the radio live just in case, or tune their own to the same emergency frequency.'

Simon squashed out his cigarette. He stood up and went back to the window, staring down at the yacht. 'I remember the last time I sailed her. The San Fernando race, Hong Kong to the Philippines, then back to Hong Kong. The harbour at night is fantastic. When was that? Three years ago, just before the handover, May '97.'

'I reckon they were on board a short time, ten maybe fifteen minutes max.'

On board *Clarissa* three men in white overalls started laying out equipment on the deck. 'How do you figure that?'

'Forensics; what we have so far.'

'Those guys down there?'

'Yep. And what I got from the pathologist. I'm waiting for the PMs.'

'Is that what these wankers usually do, hit and run, in and out, quick?'

'Depends.'

'On what?'

'The target, the area. They don't tend to linger over private yachts. Boat people, that's a different story, no radios, usually plenty of women. . . .'

Simon spun round. 'Rape, you mean?'

Alan inclined his head. 'Look, Simon, I need to know whether *Clarissa* was carrying anything valuable.' Alan's mouth turned down at the corners, his head moving from side to side in time with his thinking. 'Money, documents, jewellery, anything your father may have told some-body about.'

Simon turned his back to the window. 'A motive?'

'I suppose, yes.'

Simon thought for a moment. 'Not that I can think of, no.'

Alan picked up a pencil and started twiddling it between his fingers. 'OK. We, P-Unit that is, we're not really interested in attacks on merchant shipping. The motives are clear, money from the ship's safe or her cargo. Anyway those attacks are policed by Interpol, by the UN's International Maritime Organization, the International Chamber of

Commerce's Maritime Bureau and a whole bunch of regional bodies. For example, the States have MARAD, the US Maritime Administration. Why? Because merchant shipping equals trade and if you mess with trade you create the potential to screw with international relations. So governments make protection of merchant shipping their business. Private boats on the other hand are a pain in the arse. Investigations take up government resources and the probability of convictions is close to zero. There's also logic to suggest that the perps, as the Yanks would say, are the same blokes that hit the big ships. Bag them with international resources and the private boat problem goes away. That's the thinking. But it's not working. About two hundred private boats, fishers, yachts, you name it, disappeared without trace in the States and Caribbean alone last year. And when I say without trace, I mean the people on board as well. Here and in South-east Asia, about a hundred.'

'So Mum and Dad . . . they're just statistics?'

'Crudely, yeah. The problem's compounded because at least half and probably a lot more of all attacks on ships and small boats are not reported.'

'Why not?'

'Several reasons. Ships' masters reckon it reflects badly on them. If they make a noise and piss the pirates off, they get singled out, only next time the pirates are more likely to use violence. The owners are afraid they'll lose the confidence of their clients who then go to other shippers. Owners are also reluctant to offend foreign governments by complaining. Nigeria's a classic. And then there's money. Report attacks and insurance costs go up. Seamen's unions get wind and they're on the bandwagon, demanding protection payments for their members. Small boats have a problem with insurance, too. Pirate attacks aren't covered.' Alan tossed the pencil he was playing with on to his desk.

'So if you lose your boat in an attack and report it, no insurance?'

'That's about it. We're working with insurers to change that.'

'So what you're really saying is, you don't have a clue who did this?'

'Who or why. But whatever the reasons, it was premeditated.'

'Just because the radio wasn't nicked?'

'Not only that. The nature of the attack, the force used, the area. It's like they were trying too hard to make it look spontaneous. Why leave the evidence drifting, waiting to be found?'

'The other ship was too close?'

'*Endeavour*? I don't think so, two hours is plenty.'

'Well, what would you do if someone was coming to have a looksee? Get the hell out is what. Besides, *Clarissa*'s unsinkable. GRP sandwich. Blow her up and there'd just be zillions of bits of her floating around with a bloody great message saying, look, some prick blew me up.'

'I know the construction details. I'm talking about the ballistics patterning.' Alan spread his hands. 'Simon, I know this is tough. I know it'd be easier to accept if this was the work of some nutcase who happened to stumble over your folks, but I don't believe that was the case.'

'Yeah.'

'So, any ideas?'

'My mother might've had some jewellery with her, but no one'd know about that.'

Alan's interest piqued. He leaned forward. 'Valuable?'

Simon nodded. 'Some things, sure. You've seen her stuff. She was mugged twice in London for Chris'sake.'

'*Clarissa* was attacked well away from known pirate strongholds like Batam Island, just south of Singapore, or the Zamboanga Peninsula in the Philippines. She was sailing an unregistered route and she was clobbered out of sight of land. Important point that. These people don't like to stray far, mainly so they can get back to safety quickly. Pirates on Batam go for shipping transiting the Philip Channel only a few miles away.'

'So what're you saying?'

'What I'm saying is, she was followed. Let me rephrase that: I *think* she was followed. It's the only option that makes any sense. What I don't know is why. I also can't figure out why they left it so late, until she was almost within Australian territorial waters. If she was being followed, or tracked all the way from Hong Kong, then that's two thousand miles give or take.' Alan picked up his cup and swallowed some coffee which had gone cold. 'They used unnecessary violence.' He shook his head. 'Yachts are easy to board. They're slow, they have low freeboards. With one heave even a swimmer can be over the side.'

'What d'you mean, unnecessary violence?'

'*Clarissa* was pretty badly shot up, not just the chart station. And that's another thing. Not many pirates carry firearms, although it's becoming much more fashionable. Those that do tend not to use them except under conditions of extreme provocation.'

'Mum and Dad wouldn't have provoked anything.'

'Exactly my point. The only thing I can think of is that mayday.'

'How?'

'The pirates would know, if they'd been listening, that someone eventually would be on to them.'

'But when Mum put out the mayday they were already being threatened you said.'

'That's my guess, but the mayday may have turned them ugly.'

'And I guess your guess is as good as mine.'

Alan stood up. 'I'm sorry about the boat.'

'Meaning?'

'I left you alone in the office knowing you'd spot her. It wasn't really a shock tactic, but I figured it was the easiest way to bring the situation into focus.'

A sudden surge of anger boiled. Simon bit it back, clenching his jaw, hard. 'Why don't we go take a look at her,' Alan suggested.

Three forensic examiners crouched in *Clarissa*'s cockpit teasing bits of prospective evidence from the deck. Alan and Simon were dressed like moon men in white overalls complete with hoods, white cloth galoshes and Latex gloves. Sheets of polythene between the changing area and the yacht prevented more contaminants getting on to the boat. They clambered up the ladder and stepped over coloured chalk rings drawn on the deck, descending the companionway into the cabin. Above the chart table the radio's shattered fascia hung on broken wires. Black blood smeared the mouldings. Between their feet, at the base of the steps, a hatch had been thrown back exposing the ship's ribs. Fresh tears in the wood suggested violent removal.

Alan squatted on his haunches and peered into the black hole. 'Do you know what was in here?' He looked up at Simon.

Simon nodded. 'It was the last time I spoke to my father. The safe.'

Alan stood up. 'Are you sure?'

' 'Course I'm bloody sure.'

The blood has unnerved him, Alan thought. 'Simon, I know this is difficult for you. For me too. But I need answers.'

'Yes, I'm sure.'

'Any idea what was in it?'

'Dad called me the day before he and Mum left. He said it was a good place to put money, passports and Mum's jewellery. I guess he must have put *Clarissa*'s papers in there too.'

Alan frowned. 'Strange thing for your father to tell you, isn't it?'

'He called to say goodbye.'

Alan nodded sympathetically. 'Right. OK, that answers that. Let's have a look at the hull.'

Alan conferred with the forensics people, careful not to disturb the equipment scattered around them – precision drills, brushes of various sizes, bottles of fluid, plastic sample bags – then he followed Simon down the ladder.

The shots were raked along *Clarissa*'s starboard side, above the water-line. Alan went up close, fingering the holes.

'Ballistics are saying that these were all made by AK-47 assault rifles, several different weapons. The binnacle's smashed and there's a nick in the cabin roof. There're no other identified bullets so we're assuming AKs for that damage too.'

'What about the weapon that killed Mum and Dad?'

'We've got a match on one of them.'

'Which? Weapon or person?'

'The shots which killed your mother.' Alan watched Simon touch his forehead to the hull and close his eyes. He gave him a moment. 'We've recovered all the bullets from the hull. Rifling marks are being compared with other piracies where weapons were used, see if we can get a match, maybe pinpoint the gang.'

'Gang? How many do you think?'

'Pirates usually attack in groups of two to five. So far we've identified seven weapons.'

Simon straightened. 'If that's unusual and you can match these to other attacks. . . .'

'Then we might get an idea of where these people hang out.' Alan finished it for him. 'If we come up with anything, we'll take a radius to land from each attack site. Cross-over of the lines would indicate a possible stronghold or camp.' He rubbed the hull. 'Initial examination suggests that these shots were made as the attacking boat was pulling away. See those?' Alan pointed up to white paint flecks scraped on the aft starboard gunwale. 'My boys reckon they're collision marks from the attacking boat which means the hull was higher than *Clarissa*'s gunwale. A computer analysis of the position of the flecks can work out the angle of the bow or side at contact. From that we can estimate the size of the boat. We also found flecks of rust. So we're looking for a steel-hulled, ocean-going motor vessel with rust markings on its hull, maybe eighty feet long.'

Alan led the way back to the changing area where they stripped out of their overalls. He grabbed two more coffees from the machine.

'So, your mother's jewellery, was it insured?'

Simon nodded. 'Dad was a banker, conservative, I guess so.'

'I need descriptions. An insurance company would have them.'

'General Accident, in the UK. The cars are insured with them. I don't know if Mum's jewellery would be, but if I know my father, he would have kept everything under one roof.'

Back in his office, Alan buzzed the intercom on his desk and asked one of his staffers to come in.

While they were waiting Simon asked, 'What are you going to do with it, the insurance report?'

'Circulate it through Interpol.'

Someone rapped on Alan's door. A young, uniformed copper came in, maybe twenty-three, light-blue shirt, dark-blue trousers, ironed to perfection. He held a pad at the ready. Alan fired instructions. Find out where General Accident HQ is in England then fax them and request all insurance details for McGovern, Sir John. And draft up an authorization letter for signature by Simon. The officer nodded and left.

Simon wandered around the office. He stood by a fan and pumped the front of his shirt. 'You're certain this thing was set-up?'

'Not a hundred per cent. The evidence points that way. I need a more detailed ballistics report.'

'How long's that going to take?'

'Three, four days maybe.'

'Umph!'

'It'll take as long as it takes. The forensic blokes know the sooner I have information the better the chances of finding the culprits. At the moment it's all circumstantial.'

Simon's coffee was untouched on Alan's desk. 'Have you got a cold drink?'

'Machine, outside in the corridor.'

Simon went out leaving the door open and was back a moment later with a can of Coke. 'Want some?'

Alan shook his head. 'You OK?' To Alan's trained eye Simon seemed nervous. Perhaps it was the boat. Maybe all he had was happy memories. To see it riddled with gunfire was heart-breaking, of course. Should I challenge Simon outright? 'Can you think of anything else your father might have kept in the safe, anything at all?'

Simon swallowed more Coke, shaking his head at the same time. 'I told you, my father didn't say anything specific.'

'That's not what I asked.'

Simon squared his shoulders. 'What the fuck is this? I don't know!'

I'm going too quick. 'OK. Don't worry about it.'

Simon was about to speak when the staffer came in. 'Al, I've got those PMs you wanted.' The staffer handed a large brown envelope to Alan then looked at Simon. 'Could you sign this, sir?'

Simon came across to the desk and scrawled his signature on the authorization letter. He waited until the man had closed the door. 'My mother . . . was she. . . ?'

Alan slit the envelope and pulled out the reports. His ability to steer a conversation usually got him out of pitfalls. But the question was direct and he had no means of avoiding the answer. 'Yes, she was.' He averted his eyes. He could only imagine the fearsome images going through Simon's mind.

'How many times?'

Alan shook his head. 'I don't know, Simon.' He scanned the post-mortem reports on his wife's parents. More detailed DNA analysis was required on semen samples to determine frequency of penetration.

'Can I see those?'

'I don't think—'

'Alan!'

He handed the reports to Simon. Silence hung in the office, disturbed only by the rustling of paper as Simon turned the pages. He looked up when he'd finished. His eyes glistened. 'They burned her? Jesus! They fucking *burned* her.'

The hospital was a fifteen-minute drive away. The formal identification was quick but Simon stayed with his parents for ten minutes. The wounds raked across his mother's chest were hidden under a sheet. His father had been killed by a 7.62mm round fitted with a ceramic tip. Small entry hole, but the back of his skull and most of his brain was gone. Impossible to say whether it was one of the AKs. Probably. His head was supported in a block and the pathologist had touched up the entry wound so it looked more like a sore.

On the way back Alan suggested they stop at a bar in town. The memories would stay with Simon forever, seeing his parents' cold, grey bodies side by side on stainless-steel gurneys. He thanked whatever God was in Heaven that Bet had been spared the formal identification.

'You all right, mate?' He squeezed Simon's shoulder.

'Bloody stupid question.'

'I know.'

'I'm not going to have histrionics. No wailing or collapsing.'

Alan simply listened.

'I can tell you this.'

'What's that?'

'The fucker who did this is going to regret it.' He chased his beer with a double shot of whisky.

Alan nodded. 'The inquest will be tomorrow, then I'll ask Bet to make the arrangements.'

'Sure. Let's go home, Al.'

'Simon.'

'Yeah.'

Alan shook his head. 'Nothing,' he said. No one in the family, except for Bet, had ever called him 'Al'.

6

Cobra's face carried the scars of a life lost beyond hope of recapture – etched, chipped, burnt coarse, deeply grooved. The rock-like dome of his skull was scraped bare of hair, a bandanna impeding the slide of pearly beads of sweat funnelling up out of his hot skin. The cicatrix around his throat was red from the heat, raw in places where he'd been scratching. It was a reminder, every day, of why he was here. Maybe now he wouldn't notice it so much any more.

The camp was near Glan in the province of South Cotabato on the Philippine island of Mindanao. A dozen huts were arranged in a loose circle around a central kitchen and eating block that doubled as an 'operations' room. A separate building housed the armoury. The perimeter was bounded on all but its western side by a high, solid wooden fence topped with razor wire. Its open side looked out over Sarangani Bay. In the rainy season the earth around the huts quickly became a quagmire. Swampy marshes inland, alive with the clack and buzz of insects, prevented the unwelcome interest of casual observers. A single-lane track transecting the spongy ground provided the sole access to the camp and it, like the armoury, was guarded, twenty-four hours. General Santos City, thirty miles north, provided all the amenities that Cobra needed. A powerful Compaq connected to the Internet accessed the world beyond. His was a self-contained microcosm, intent on its criminality and policed by its own brutal law.

Cobra's hut faced the water. Beyond the hut, a grassy bank ran down to a narrow muddy beach from which a wooden jetty extended into the bay. A steel-hulled fishing trawler was moored at the end of the jetty, its high prow streaked with rust and its boxy deckhouse fluffy with peeling paint. High-performance Mercury inboards capable of powering the boat to forty knots were concealed beneath the trawler's stern deck.

The object of his obsession lay on the surface of the table. Cobra picked up the document, turning it over in his hands. The document was handwritten, the ink faded and smudged with wet spots in places, the language incomprehensible. Slowly he pulled the parchments from their protective sleeve. They were clearly old, rigid and brittle beneath his fingers. There were five pages, densely scripted on both sides. The last page provided the only other clue to their origin and age. The manuscript was signed Robert McGovern, underscored with showy curlicues and dated August 1719.

It was two o'clock. His usual time. He was, he realized, a creature of habit. The thought brought him a small sense of comfort. The door to the hut opened behind him and he knew by the softness of her footfalls that it was Mae-li.

He turned in his chair. She was undeniably beautiful. He always thought that when he saw her like this, demure before their love-making. Black, silken hair fell to her narrow girl's waist, cut straight, just as it had been the day he plucked her from the refugee boat in the Gulf of Siam.

'I missed you. Ten days with those boys makes you realize.' The words came as a rasping, strangled sound.

She clicked the door closed, sliding the crude wooden latch, fanning the heat from her face with delicate fingers.

'They all seem pleased,' she murmured. Mae-li lay on the bed, its wooden slats beneath the thin mattress creaking gently under her bird-like frame.

Aside from his table, chair and a grey steel gun cabinet the bed was the only other piece of furniture in the hut. He liked it that way. Simple. Wealth was a means to an end, not an end in itself. He reached down and scooped a handful of glittering jewels from the broken safe by his feet.

For the moment he ignored the two passports which slipped to the floor. He dropped the jewels on to the table next to the ancient manuscript and studied the pile.

The emerald necklace was the size of a baby's fist, but crudely cut in the shape of a heart. He separated it from the rest of the pile. The stone was set in gold and whichever anonymous craftsman had worked the metal with intricate filigree, the patterns were unbalanced and clearly cut without the aid of machines. A chain of gold rings tethered the emerald.

'I have something for you.' Cobra held the necklace aloft. The memory of the woman's squealing bounced around the chamber of his memory, haunting his eyes. He blinked quickly to rid himself of the image and lifted himself from the chair.

'I do not deserve—'

'*Only* a woman of your beauty deserves such jewels.' His voice was quiet, almost reverent. He knelt on the bed while Mae-li raised herself on one elbow and held her hair away from her neck so he could fasten the chain.

She glanced down touching the gem. 'You don't have to do this for me.'

'For you? You think this is for you? Maybe it's for me.' He unbuckled his belt. He could feel his tenderness melting like water falling from a stone.

She reached up and began to stroke him.

He stayed like that for a while, head back listening to the rustling sound of the hut's palm-thatch roof, feeling her hand on him and the hot little breaths of her effort. When he felt himself coming close he stopped her and lay next to her. Mae-li said nothing, just moved her limbs, shedding her clothes. Cobra's body glistened under a sheen of sweat; coarse grey hair blanketed his chest. He watched her raise her arms above her head so that her hair fanned out on the pillow. Slowly he prised her knees apart running fingertips along her sinewy limbs, over her slim body, across the skin of her belly, soft and smooth as velvet to the narrow wedge of black fur slipping down between her thighs.

Mae-li slid one leg across his torso then raised herself so she was straddling him, her back to his face, always her back to his face. Her hair fell across his thighs like rain. His hips began to rise and fall dictating her rhythm until he felt it like a rush, bucking his pelvis involuntarily while his hot liquid pumped into her.

An open window permitted the passage of a breeze that stirred the molasses-heavy air inside the hut bringing with it the tang of salt from the bay.

Mae-li stared at the roof thatch, tracing an imagined pattern among the fronds. The heat of his fingers passed through her hair. For a moment she forgot and savoured the gentleness of his caress.

She tried. 'We can stop this. . . .'

'We?'

'You can.' She drew the single sheet over her nakedness.

Cobra rolled away and pulled on his jeans and T-shirt. 'You think I haven't thought about that? Never a day goes by.' He stood still looking down at her. 'You don't understand! Why should you?' The rasp transmuted to a hiss. 'It's the only life I know, the only life I want. I saved you, isn't that enough?'

'How many died this time?'

'These people deserved to die. Believe me, they deserved it!' He shook his head. 'You will never understand.'

'No one deserves to die.'

'Is that so? And what about this?' He pointed to the wound on his neck. A puckered, pink necklace. A hanging wire. A permanent reminder of the Viet Cong.

'That was war.'

'My fuckin' war! My fuckin' revenge!'

'You were a prisoner-of-war. Does that mean innocent people have to die?'

'What the fuck do you know about innocence?'

She had learnt long ago that to argue was futile. Best to stay silent and allow the inner storm to dispel itself. She watched him return to his table and pick up the manuscript as if by handling it the paper would finally reveal its secrets to him. Her uneasiness was the same as always, a constancy that draped her like a second skin. After all these years it was the same, the subliminal acceptance of her fate. She was like him, condemned to an existence disfigured by other people in another place at another time. Maybe that's why she stayed.

'I know this hurts you,' she whispered.

Cobra turned with a small shake of his head. 'You know nothing, only what I allow you to know.'

'I want to help you.'

His Steyr-Mannlicher SSG-69 sniper rifle was resting against the table.

'Help me?' He smiled thinly, got up, lifted the rifle and stood over her. 'You want to help me?' He drew the sheet off her body with the barrel.

Mae-li closed her eyes. Despite the heat, gooseflesh prickled her scalp. The cold, steel tip of the muzzle touched her lips then traced a line between her small, hard-nippled breasts, across her belly leaving a faint white mark. With deft movements Cobra worked the end of the barrel into her.

'Don't betray me, Mae-li. I'm all you've got and I'm all you'll ever have.'

She heard him leave the hut.

Mae-li pulled the sheet up to her chin, clutching it with both hands. She stroked the emerald at her throat. Who had been sacrificed for this? Her eyes blossomed with tears. It was beautiful. A prized possession, a family heirloom? Why had she been abandoned to this hell? Why had she been ordained as consort to the Devil? She turned on to her side and drew her knees up to her chest.

The hut had cooled by the time she awoke. Outside the light was still strong but pewtered, as the sun dipped lower in the western sky. Mae-li sat up slowly, rubbing her eyes. He must have come back at some point and covered her with a blanket. The jewel had gone from her throat. With the lethargic movements of the sleep-weary she pushed back the bedclothes and wrapped a sheet around her body in the fashion of a sarong. The jewels were spread over the table. A pink-diamond ring, ruby ear-rings, a four-string pearl choker, a sapphire bracelet, a gold and emerald brooch.

Her concentration strayed to the two passports. One booklet was bound with a soft maroon cover imprinted with a proud, golden crest. The other, navy-blue, was adorned with the splayed wings of an eagle. She flicked them open. Their photographs smiled up at her. Sir John McGovern and his American wife, Elizabeth.

Cobra sat at a chipped Formica table in the operations room. Jimmy Pran stood behind him to one side, the fence in front, standing, nervous. Emmanuel Cortez had been here before, many times. Others lounged behind the fence, all armed, threatening. All tattooed with a cobra's image on various parts of their bodies, a ritualistic marking of their brotherhood. The routine was practised and deliberate.

A fan pushed ineffectually at the turgid air. Cobra dropped his head into his hand and brushed away the sweat. He pulled a small sack from the edge of the table and tipped out its contents, sensing more than hearing the intake of the fence's breath.

Cortez took an involuntary step forward, met his reflected image in the mirrored lenses of Cobra's wrap-rounds and stepped back.

'Sit!' Cobra issued the command without looking at Cortez. One of his men kicked a chair over the floor hitting Cortez behind the knees. He sat heavily.

With deliberate slowness Cobra removed his glasses, squinting against the harsh sunlight flooding through the windows. He pushed the pile of jewels towards the fence. He was still uncertain of the emerald's authenticity despite how beautiful it had looked draped around Mae-li's neck. Much as he hated the light, Cobra had to see this without impedance, see how Cortez reacted. The failure to overcome the light still rankled Cobra. Captured by the VC, he'd been subjected to white light for hours, days, weeks. White light and white noise. Constant. Endless. He hated noise too, except, strangely, the noise of firearms. The isolation of the camp was perfect. Quiet. Quiet and darkness. He felt strong in that environment. Weak and vulnerable otherwise. His nightmare would be to live somewhere like New York City. Times Square on a sunny afternoon. He understood absolutely how someone might wake up one day and take a machine gun to a bunch of McDonald's diners.

Cortez carefully spread the pieces. When they were evenly arranged over the table he reached for the emerald and turned it over in his fingers. He fumbled for his eyepiece and examined the stone more closely.

Cobra watched the jeweller. He noted the tremor in the man's hands. Had expected nothing less. Sitting here, surrounded by death, it would have taken a saint or an idiot not to be afraid. Cobra continued to study the fence, watching the small rapid movements at the corners of his mouth, reading the man's reaction on the map of his face.

Cortez removed his eyepiece. 'This is a . . . treasure!'

'It's genuine?' Cobra spoke in fluent Spanish, a language he had mastered together with Chinese, both the Cantonese and Mandarin dialects. He'd learned Vietnamese too, from his captor, while he starved. He avoided speaking gook; it reminded him. Breaking free, killing the guard and eating his heart before reason had any chance to reset the balance of his mind.

Cortez nodded eagerly.

'Treasure is an imprecise word.' Cobra rolled the words round his tongue.

'This is ancient.' Cortez held up the emerald. 'I would say between two hundred and two hundred and fifty years old.'

Jimmy Pran thrust his chin forward. 'How do you know this?'

Cortez glanced from Cobra to Jimmy.

Cobra inclined his head, an imperceptible command. His unblinking eyes never left the fence's face.

'The way the stone is cut, and the setting, hand wrought. You can see here.' Cortez leaned forward to show what he meant. Cobra brushed the man's hand aside.

'I don't think you would lie to me.'

'No . . . no. Of course not,' Cortez stammered.

'Where does it come from?' Cobra's voice was rough. He rubbed at his throat.

Cortez shook his head. 'I can check. From books,' he added to allay Cobra's fears that others may be drawn in. 'Spanish, possibly Portuguese. I can't be certain.'

Cobra accepted this. 'And the rest?'

One by one, Cortez examined each piece, scrutinizing through his eyepiece. An hour later he completed the job. Against each piece he'd given a price.

'Your prices are low.'

Cortez smiled weakly and cocked his head to one side, avoiding eye contact. 'Twenty-five per cent of the real value. The black market is demanding and unforgiving.'

'So am I.'

A drop of sweat dislodged itself from the end of Cortez's nose. A nervous giggle spasmed his throat.

'I'll tell you what, Cortez. Instead of you retaining ten per cent, you can keep five. I get thirty. I accept your prices plus twenty per cent.'

The giggle bubbled out of Cortez. 'My profit is not so great. . . .'

'We have a deal then. Good. Now get rid of the jewels quickly and discreetly.'

'It will take some time. They'll have to be broken up, the larger stones cut down and reset.'

With time frames discussed and agreed, Cobra dismissed his men. They'd been party to the negotiations, they were equals, brothers. Jimmy Pran waited until the men had shuffled out into the heat. Cobra indulged his lieutenant. A few minutes. Perhaps confidentialities would be exchanged between Cobra and his right-hand man. Privileged information. Perhaps not. The men wouldn't know, for sure. It was Cobra's way, the nature of his command. Reward loyalty, breed the concept of necessary hierarchy, but never exclude absolutely. Betrayal of any kind meant death. They respected that. After a suitable time, maybe three minutes, Cobra dismissed Jimmy.

He was alone with Cortez. The reek of fear was palpable. 'You are an educated man. You are also beholden to me. I control you.' He waited for the other man's acquiescence which came in a stuttering acknowledgement.

'I owe everything to you.' The words seemed appropriate.

'I should kill you.'

The fence's eyes widened.

'You know too much. You make me uncomfortable.' Cobra spoke softly in the clipped idiom of the Chinese that had become his habit. He peered at Emmanuel Cortez. Fat, putrid, disgusting Cortez. Cortez who could identify him, who had a hold on him, if only he knew it. He should gut him now with the hunting knife the reassuring weight of which pressed against his thigh. Instead he smiled, thinking all the fat shit has to do is come in here with a ghetto-blaster and shine a torch in my face and I'd do anything.

'I found this.' Cobra reached into the thigh pocket of his olive-green combat fatigues and pulled out a folder. 'Look at it.'

Cortez slid the folder across the table and carefully removed the pages. He studied the paper through his eyepiece. 'This is not my area, but I would guess this paper is old. The language' – he shook his head – 'I don't understand.'

'Is the document the same age as the emerald?'

'Possibly. This is not my area,' Cortez repeated.

'Look at the last page.'

Cortez dutifully flicked to the last page. He saw Robert McGovern's signature and the date. 'Yes,' he said, his voice surer. 'The emerald is definitely from the period. Now I'm sure.'

'As certain as the knowledge that your life had just moved closer to ending?'

His words produced the effect Cobra wanted, had known would come. The man's emotions were as transparent as water. Best not to have emotions. He smiled again.

'Take it,' Cobra motioned for Cortez to conceal the document. 'Find out what language this is, then get it translated. When you have succeeded, bring the document back to me and bring the translator as well. I will have questions.'

Cortez stuffed the manuscript inside his crumpled linen jacket.

Cobra shovelled the jewels into the sack, all of them except for the emerald. He tied the neck of the bag with a length of twine and slid it across the table towards Cortez. 'This is for you.' Cobra lowered his bull head and peered at Cortez from behind heavy brows, dangling the emerald from his fingers. The man's reaction was a caricature, his tongue almost drooling out of his mouth. Cobra snatched the emerald away. 'You get it when you deliver.'

There was a noise outside, a woman's stifled sobs, then the door burst open. Jimmy Pran held Mae-li by her elbow, hitching her shoulder up so that her body lolled sideways. Cortez sprang up and retreated to the back wall, knocking his chair over in the process. Cobra replaced his sunglasses, lifted himself from the table and walked out into the sunlight.

Cobra's face remained implacable. He looked down at Mae-li. *Your vulnerability enhances your loveliness.* 'Let her go, Jimmy.'

Mae-li was clutching her throat. Cobra ripped her arms away. Livid welts criss-crossed her slender neck. Shouts came from just outside the operations room and the sounds of a scuffle.

Most of his men relieved themselves with the local whores, or with each other. There were no women in camp, except for Mae-li. Deprivation was a yardstick of discipline and someone had just failed. It was another reason for Mae-li. Bait. To sort the wheat from the chaff.

'Who?' Cobra hissed.

Mae-li whimpered.

'The Leopard,' Jimmy sneered.

Cobra nodded. The scuffles. Lee Chu was dragged, face-down in the dirt to the area outside the operations room. Four men pinioned his arms and legs.

'Turn him over.' Cobra spoke quietly in Mandarin. He saw Emmanuel Cortez watching in horror from the shadows.

Lee Chu squirmed, arching his back in a futile attempt to be free of his captors, his eyes wide and glazed by fear and heroin. Spittle ran down his chin and as he looked at Cobra a wet stain spread on the front of his pants.

Cobra turned to Mae-li. 'Did he do this?'

She began to cry, shaking her head.

He slapped her hard. The blow stunned her, the sound ricocheting between the palm-thatched huts. She crawled to the doorway, past Cortez.

'Stand him up.' An excited noise lifted from the rabble. They knew what was coming. 'Jimmy,' Cobra said over his shoulder. 'Nail him.'

One of them ran off and came back with a mallet hammer and four six-inch nails. They stood Lee Chu up and pinned him against the wall of the ops room. Jimmy took the hammer, positioned a nail in the middle of the man's left hand then drove the nail through to the soft palm wood behind. He did the same to the other hand then through both feet, smashing through the bone. Lee Chu screamed. The heroin would absorb most of the pain. His scream was a realization of the manner in which death would be administered. He'd witnessed it before, been part of the jeering crowd, fuelling a bloodlust. He'd wanted to fuck Mae-li; the heroin had taken over, the dragon spirit forcing him to copulate.

Cobra was in front of him. He watched the man's eyes, understanding the fear there, absorbing the reek of the victim's shit. His hand went to the hilt of the hunting knife. The others crowded in, eager for death. Cobra raised the sixteen-inch blade, running its length slowly past Lee Chu's eyes.

'Bring her out,' he whispered. 'Make her kneel here.' He pointed to a place in the sand behind him without looking back. 'She must see what she has done.' *Women are the cause. They bring it upon themselves. Braying for sex. Fucking like animals. They have to be punished. They have to learn, to see what they are responsible for. An icy afternoon in January 1968. His father returning early from the fields with blood gushing from a wound to his hand. He had stumbled into the bedroom. His wife was naked; his son underneath her. She was pumping, up and down, bucking like a horse. His father didn't make a sound. He snatched a bottle*

*of rye to replace the courage which had long since left him, went to the
barn and ate a shotgun.*

The nausea came, quite suddenly, clogging his throat, stopping his
breath. He placed the point of his knife against the man's solar plexus, at
the bifurcation of his ribs. Mae-li was behind him. Her hair pulled back
by Jimmy, forcing her to watch, lip split, eye darkening and swelling.
Cobra leaned into the knife, applying a gradually increasing pressure
until he felt the tip of the blade part the fabric of Lee Chu's T-shirt and
bite through the outer layer of his skin. Lee Chu screamed. The sound
entered Cobra's brain, pulverizing his sanity. He rested his weight against
the knife, sliding it deeper and deeper until he felt its against the palm
wood, until his lips were touching the dying man's mouth.

7

Even on the brightest of days, sunlight, shattered into pieces by the forest canopy, fell only twenty feet down the shaft before dissolving. The well's 200-foot cylindrical wall of iron-hard rock was concealed beneath a thick, smooth layer of permanently wet algae that effortlessly neutralized even the most determined attempt at climbing. An iron grid of six-inch squares weighing two tons secured the mouth of the well. A hatch had been fashioned in the centre of the grid, looped closed with a padlock the thickness of a man's thumb. The floor of the well, like the walls, was solid rock, which wept permanently as though in sympathy for the man whose home this dark place had been for the past year.

He measured the cycle of the days by the alternate fading and brightening rhythm of the circle of light high above. Each day a bucket was lowered down the shaft by an anonymous captor. The bucket contained food, always rice and fish, occasionally cake or bread, sometimes fruit – pineapple or coconut. Other than food there was a litre bottle of water, from which the label had been carefully peeled, a daily candle and, when he requested, by attaching a note to the rope, medicine, lavatory paper, pencil, matches or more writing paper. His requests for newspapers were never granted, even though he had asked, every day, for 373 days.

When the food bucket was lowered, the routine was simple. The prisoner would unhook the bucket, reattach the hook to the handle of the latrine bucket, tug on the rope twice and the latrine bucket would be pulled up. He had learned quickly not to fill the latrine bucket more than half, to prevent his own faeces and urine, sometimes vomit, raining down on him if whoever was pulling the bucket up was in a hurry and caused it to bang against the side of the shaft.

The floor of the well measured six feet across. An old iron bedstead fitted into the diameter, just. The only other pieces of furniture were a plastic pail and a wooden tea-chest, which the prisoner had mounted on loose scree to prevent it sitting in the wet. His senses had adapted to the stench of the peaty water, the dimness of the light, the fetid mildew of the horse-hair mattress and his own odour of sweat and urine. The highlight of his existence was the monthly excursion to the surface. On the due day, when the food bucket was lowered and the latrine bucket raised, the rope would be passed down again with a black scarf tied at its end. He had learned this procedure quickly. The first time it had happened he had not tied the blind-fold until he was at the top of the shaft. The beating that followed had been savage. The prisoner had seen the dense stems of the forest in which he was hidden, but no other clue testified to his whereabouts. A newspaper was fed into his hands and he was made to stand against a tree, rough bark pressing against his back. A photograph was taken and still blindfolded, the prisoner was lowered back to his subterranean domain.

But these excursions gave him a taste of the sweetness of the air, the feel of dappled sunlight on his skin, and the sheer bliss of being able to walk with full strides the three or four paces to the tree, prodded by unseen hands, and then back to the shaft. No one ever spoke. The prisoner suspected that the newspapers were to accord dates to the evidence that he was alive, and the procedure doubled as an opportunity to allow his captors a cursory examination of his physical state.

He had become sick, often, during the early months, but knew, as he suspected his captors knew, the sickness was due to bad water rather than disease. So he was left to sweat it out, to vomit the poison from his stomach and to void the pathogens in an agony of dysentery. He would lie on his damp mattress day after day until finally his strength began to return. Eventually his body had hardened to the inadequacies. He kept himself fit by a daily series of exercises, stretching to keep his muscles limber, and power work, push-ups and sit-ups to maintain his strength. For lesser men, the dank isolation would have been enough to break the mind and the spirit, but the prisoner was resilient. He kept a diary, not of his days for they had quickly become an empty continuum, but of his fantasies, of things he regretted in the past and of his hopes for the future. He designed houses that he would one day build; he described the imaginary woman who would one day be his wife. And the children. How he would nurture them and love them and protect them. The prisoner imagined businesses that he would develop and wrote business plans in minute detail. And the prisoner meditated. He bundled the hatred and the pain and the confusion and the incomprehension into a tight ball and he stowed it in his soul. He placated the burgeoning monster and soothed it and grew it, but always he controlled it.

Each day the prisoner shaved, taking an hour to perform the task, careful not to nick the skin, for down here any wound would fester. He scraped the razor over his head in the ritual and he shaved his pubic hair and under his arms to prevent ticks from colonizing the hot damp places of his body. And he wrote and learned and recited chants that he spoke softly or screamed out depending on his mood. He would conjure memories that made him angry; he would think of jokes that made him laugh, and remember sadnesses that made him cry. For the prisoner knew that if he allowed himself to dwell in one place then madness would possess him.

The prisoner had divided the small space at the bottom of the well into sections, by laying lines of loose stones. His bed was the bedroom in which he slept or rested. Sitting on the upturned pail and using the tea-chest as a desk, became his office. The area on the other side of the bed was the exercise room. Near the foot of the bed was the meditation area. Sitting on the upturned pail but facing away from the tea-chest was his dining area. Depending on his activities, the prisoner moved slowly and deliberately from one area to another, imagining himself walking though a house many times the size of his space. In this way he maintained a routine.

The reward, after one year, was his sanity. But he wondered how long he could hold on to it, if indeed it was his to hold on to.

8

Simon McGovern was rarely ill. Chicken pox as a kid and occasional bouts of 'flu. Other than that, injuries picked up on the sports field. A dislocated shoulder playing rugby at school and a broken ankle showing off on a beach in Barbados playing volleyball with Ben. So, on his second morning in Australia, when he came into the kitchen for breakfast, he knew his appearance would worry Bet.

'You look. . . .'

'Bad dream,' he explained, but didn't elaborate. It had been a nightmare. He was a spectator, sitting on *Clarissa*'s transom while dishevelled pirates, whose faces remained indistinct throughout the ordeal boarded the yacht, tortured his parents then murdered them.

'I looked in on you at seven. Al was wondering if you wanted to go to the office, but I insisted you sleep.'

Simon grinned. 'You always looked out for Ben and me.' He sat down at the breakfast table and tickled Betina's chin.

'She likes you.'

'About time some woman did.'

'Eggs and bacon?'

Simon nodded. 'Thanks. Got any coffee?'

Bet brought the percolator across to the table and poured coffee for him. 'No point in asking about the dream, I can guess. You always did have the most vivid imagination. D'you remember as children you used to entertain me and Ben for hours with the strangest stories.'

'I remember.'

The sizzling smack of hot bacon came from the stove. 'What's happening with Victoria?'

Simon was feeding Betina. He looked up. 'How do you know about Vicki?'

'Mum told me.'

'Ah! If you want it to get around tell a woman!'

'You're a chauvinist.'

'Absolutely. Life member.'

Bet broke two eggs into the pan. 'So?' she said, turning and admonishing him with a spatula.

'So nothing.'

'Is it serious?'

Simon shrugged. 'No. I don't think so.'

'But she thinks it is?'

'Mum didn't spare the horses.'

Bet turned her attention back to his breakfast. 'She lives with you?'

'Yep. Well, some of the time. She's got her own place.'

'She works at a bank, doesn't she?' Bet slid the eggs and bacon on to a plate.

Simon buttered toast and ate hungrily. 'Some Japanese outfit.'

'She's your girlfriend and you don't know where she works?'

'No. I'm not that keen.'

'Obviously.'

Simon tucked into his breakfast. 'I think we've reached the stage of mutual indifference.'

Bet raised her eyebrows and began washing up the pan, then poured herself a coffee and sat opposite him.

Simon mopped up the last of his fried eggs, pushed the plate away then leaned back. 'I don't know how it's going to pan out with Vicki.'

'What about her family, who are they?'

Simon's mouth drooped. 'The usual. The old man's a banker, big pile in the country, rides to hounds, shoots badly. The mother's the fussy type. I've got a feeling they don't really approve. I don't see them much.'

'And your flat, it's in Battersea?'

This was cathartic. Simon wanted Bet to see that. He wanted her to be interested in his life, to cover lost ground. He was especially pleased that she'd been able to mention their mother without crumpling.

'I've always liked Battersea. There's a good mix of people. Dad's place in Kensington's nice but I somehow feel people are measuring you there.'

'I know what you mean. It's the same here, like Battersea. People take you for what you are, not what you have. It's refreshing. This place is a humble abode, but there's love here. I'm happy.'

That much was plain. He understood. 'My place is a two-bedroom flat on the top floor of a converted Georgian house. It's built around a small roof terrace and all the main rooms look on to it. Unusual and very private.'

Bet refilled their coffee cups. They sat in silence for a while, both watching Betina drumming happily with a tiny plastic spoon.

Simon leaned forward on his elbows. 'I saw *Clarissa* yesterday.'

'I know. Al told me. I haven't yet. I couldn't.'

Simon reached out and touched her arm. 'It's OK.' He waited until she'd steadied herself. 'Dad called me just before they left Hong Kong. I guess he must have called you as well.'

'Mum called, but I spoke to Dad.'

'Did he say anything to you, anything you thought odd or out of context?'

This time Bet shook her head. 'Al asked me the same thing. He spoke to them as well.'

'You remember the layout, inside *Clarissa* I mean?'

She nodded, her brow creasing with the effort of remembering.

A picture fused in his mind. 'At the bottom of the steps leading down into the cabin, the chart table is to the left.'

Bet nodded again.

Simon sat back and folded his arms. 'At the bottom of the steps there's a hatch. Under the hatch there's a safe, at least there was a safe. Not any more.'

'Stolen?'

'Yep. Ripped out. I could see where the wood had been torn. Looks like they used a crowbar.'

'I didn't know there was a safe. What are you driving at, Simon?'

Betina picked that moment to fling her Beatrix Potter bowl on to the floor. Bet cleared up the mess with little Betina chuckling at her handi-work.

Simon was trying to figure the best way of drawing his sister out, aware that often small forgotten details could be recalled with sufficient prompting. 'You remember Dad telling us about Robert McGovern when we were kids?'

Bet picked up the bowl and went to the sink. 'Stories of derring do.' She altered her voice as if reading from a *Boy's Own* comic. 'Adventures on the high seas.'

'Dad had the safe fitted in Hong Kong, before they left. That's why you don't remember. I think he had the originals of the McGovern papers on board, in the safe.'

Bet came back to the breakfast table rubbing her hands on a chequered dishcloth. 'He certainly didn't say anything about any papers to me.'

'Do you know what the McGovern papers are?'

Again, Bet shook her head. 'No. Tell me.'

'I don't know. Something to do with Robert McGovern. Letters maybe, a manuscript. Whatever, they'll be a valuable historical record if nothing else.' Simon thought for a few seconds. 'Dad didn't say anything to you about two pieces, or something coming in two parts?'

'No, Simon. He didn't say anything like that. He asked after Betina, said that he was looking forward to seeing us and that he would be pleased to retire from the bank. Usual stuff. It was all so *ordinary*, family stuff, you know.'

'Nothing unusual? An odd word maybe?'

She frowned with the effort. 'Hang on a second. Dad did say some-thing. I didn't think anything of it at the time.'

'What?' Simon pounced.

'That it was safe, that everything was safe.'

'Are you sure? Was he talking about *the* safe?'

'No, no. I remember now. Everything was fine, safe.'

'He used that word, "safe"?'

'Yes.'

Simon blew his cheeks out. 'Bloody *Marathon Man*!'

'What?'

'*Marathon Man*, you know, Laurence Olivier and Dustin Hoffman. *Is it safe? Is it safe?*'

'Does that help?'

'I don't know. Maybe.' Simon bit at his thumbnail. 'Look, Bet, do you think we could keep this to ourselves for the time being, our little secret?'

'What about Al? Maybe he should know. You obviously think it might be important.'

'That's the operative word, "might". Al's got enough on his plate right now. I don't want to add red herrings, not till I'm more certain.'

'Promise me you'll tell him if you think he should know.'

'Of course I will.'

'OK then.'

'You all right?'

She nodded. She unstrapped Betina from the high chair and sat the child on her lap. 'How were they, Simon, really?'

He thought about his answer. 'Peaceful.' That was the right word. 'They're together, sleeping.' He'd agreed with Alan that it was far better she should not know the truth of what happened in explicit and unwholesome detail. 'How much has Alan told you about what happened?'

Bet shook her head and looked away. 'Just what he said last night. They were attacked by pirates and shot. He said that was standard *modus* something or other.'

'*Operandi*.'

'Yes. Why?'

'It seems it might have been a set-up. Did he tell you that?'

'Not specifically, but I guessed from what he said, you know, about the radio not being taken. I don't really want to think about it.'

'Sure. It's just that there's no hard evidence. Alan's doing what coppers do, entertaining all possibilities. I don't put too much store by it. Too improbable. I told him that.'

'I hope you're right,' Bet sighed then asked, 'What are you going to do today?'

'Don't know. Thought I might go into town, get my bearings. What about you?'

'I have to make the funeral arrangements. Al told me to go ahead now that you're here. Take my car if you like.'

'Well . . . no. I'll help you with the arrangements.'

'It's OK, Simon.'

'I'd. . . .'

'Simon, it's OK, really. I think I need to do this.'

'You sure?'

'Positive. Now you take the car.'

'Thanks.' He looked at her quizzically. She knew that expression.

'Sally's coming round later. I'll go with her.'

'Sally?'

'Neighbour. She's got a little girl Betina's age.'

'Sounds cosy.'

'Go have a shower. I'll show you the car when you're done.' Simon hugged his sister. They stayed like that for a while, silent, reunited.

9

The low bough of a willow provided some cover. The watcher's clothes, like his face were nondescript. Blue striped nylon shirt, brown tie, khaki slacks, scuffed crepe-soled shoes, also brown. A sizeable gut, double chin and red face with blunt features identified him as a boozer. He was invisible, which made him ideally suited to this job. His car was equally invisible, a dust-covered, maroon Honda Accord complete with dents and scrapes. No one was going to take any notice of him, his car, his sweaty, bovine manner. This outward deception camouflaged a razor eye for detail, an IQ pushing the late 170s and a photographic memory. Weekends, those when he wasn't on a job, were his favourite times. There was no wife, no girlfriend, no television. All he needed was a fridgeful of beer and a chessboard, replaying past championship games of the grand masters, from memory, and improving upon their strategies.

The yellow Suzuki jeep reversed out of the drive and sped away down the dirt road. The watcher dropped the stub of his cigarette to the ground and squashed it beneath a crepe sole. He popped a vanilla-flavoured sweet then clambered behind the wheel and drove sedately away, not in any hurry to catch the Suzuki or even keep it in sight. He'd already tapped the telephones. But he radioed in anyway, unlocking detail from his memory for transcription. McGovern had left the house at 11.26 a.m. The subject had been carrying a jacket. Unusual in this heat, especially for a pom. A slight bulge in the left-hand pocket of the jacket. Something soft, deduced from the way the garment had been handled, thrown across on to the passenger seat. He suspected it was a tie. Therefore a need to impress. More important was the brown envelope. Creased. The address had been scratched out and the stamps had already been post-marked. Not for posting. The stamps were British in any case. The envelope contained something to show. It had been placed carefully on top of the thrown jacket. Something important, probably, or delicate. Even though the envelope was creased it had not been folded over or slipped into a jacket pocket. For the record he recited the jeep's licence number and described the vehicle in perfect detail down to the inch-long crack in the offside brake light.

The jeep skidded round a corner throwing a great dust plume into the still air. Haste. Always a telltale sign. Anxiety or impatience. In this case the watcher decided it was anxiety. By the time he turned the corner the jeep was gone. In town, he caught sight of the Suzuki several times, stopped at lights or moving up ahead, occasionally weaving around slower drivers. The watcher was careful to keep at least ten cars between them. Twice he was forced to pass when the Suzuki pulled over, presumably to check a map or instructions. Both times the watcher slipped behind a slow mover, waiting for the jeep to catch up. As they broke the edge of town he lost visual on the highway running towards St Lucia. Fifteen minutes later he saw it again: in the university car-park.

Simon wondered why municipal buildings seemed designed to cause maximum confusion. Were incompetent architects only ever commissioned on these places with a brief to create the most labyrinthine warrens imaginable? And no signs. There were never any bloody signs. What was wrong with a simple grid? Corridors running north-south and east-west, like New York City, then even the most delinquent navigator could manage perfectly. He'd got lost twice in traffic and now twice here on foot. Where's the Classics Department? You're in it. Which bit do you want? Professor Pedro Pereda. Then more tangled instructions.

Eventually he found it. By now his heart was fluttering in his chest. He could see the professor's secretary through a glass panel. Simon shrugged on his jacket, reached into the left-hand pocket and pulled out one of Alan's neckties. He conjured a knot, standing out in the corridor, felt the knot into place looking at his reflection in the door-glass. The secretary told him Professor Pereda was on a phonecall. Would he wait a moment? Then the click click of her fingers pecking at a keyboard.

Simon was thinking fast, going over the conversation he'd had with Bet. The McGovern papers were a mystery to her. Alan wouldn't know then. How could he? *Dad certainly wouldn't have said anything to him.* And Alan hadn't known what was under the hatch until yesterday. Best keep it that way, until he found out what this was all about.

Detachment was the key, if he was to avenge them. Circumstances, and the people that went with them, could be compartmentalized. Alan, into the policeman box: he was investigating a serious crime; dispassionate data handling. OK. No problem there. Bet, into the sister box: concern for him, an outlet for herself. The reconstitution of their relationship was therapy, for both of them. Now the McGovern papers: they went into an unmarked box. He preferred to concentrate on one subject at a time. Maybe that's why his success with girls was limited most of the time to effective openings, then getting them into bed. Beyond that there was no sustainability. It was Vicki who had finally had enough. What had she called him? Selfish, self-centred, uncaring. All true. It had been a relief.

He was fingering the envelope nervously. The secretary eventually stopped typing and led him along a narrow corridor illuminated by a shaft of dusty sunlight. At the end was a single door. The secretary knocked, opened the door without waiting for a reply and showed him into the professor's book-lined office.

Professor Pedro Pereda was short, very rotund, almost blind, judging by the thickness of his spectacles, and very ugly. Doleful, bulging eyes, squat nose, rubbery mouth. Simon stuck out his hand as the professor stood up to his full height of five foot six, realigning his bow tie. Professor Pereda waved him to be seated.

'I was hoping you might be able to help me.'

'With a translation, as you said when you called.' The professor peered over half-glasses causing deep creases to appear along his forehead.

Simon smiled. 'PPP. That's very neat.'

'I'm sorry.'

'Professor Pedro Pereda, PPP.'

The professor indulged Simon with a smile.

'My brother-in-law's a policeman, heads up a unit known as the peanuts. Seems P is quite popular down here.'

The professor's expression crackled with irritation. 'I'm very busy, Mr McGovern, so if we could get on?'

Simon felt contrite. 'I'm sorry, Professor. My parents were killed recently, murdered. I find myself becoming—'

Professor Pereda looked uncomfortable. 'Your enquiry sounded urgent, when you called.'

'. . . cynical. But identifying the problem is ninety per cent of the solution. Right? And urgent. Yes. Very.' Simon slipped stapled sheets from the brown envelope. He hesitated momentarily. Should I explain some of the background? No best let the professor come at it cold, that way his opinion would be clinical, professional.

'The only thing I would say, professor, is that these documents are extremely confidential.' He let his words sink in, then repeated, 'Extremely confidential.'

Professor Pereda sat back in his chair and interlaced his fingers on the blotter while he appraised the young man in front of him. 'It is clear that you are anxious. Your face shows your pain. I suspect that reference to your parents was no accident, more of a warning. Whatever this matter involves will be kept strictly in this office. I am a classics professor. If I can help you with a translation, then I am happy to do so. Beyond that, I consider the matter, whatever it may be, not my business.'

Simon nodded his appreciation and slipped the papers across the desk.

The watcher went through the moves of the game between Ivan Sokolov and the Dutchman, Van der Sterren. The match had been a classic opening offensive that had taken the Bosnian one step closer to the Dutch chess championship. The watcher knew the plays by heart. He'd read them in the morning paper.

The yellow Suzuki was parked thirty metres away. He checked his watch. Twenty minutes had elapsed. He decided to radio a report. Eight minutes later, the watcher noted the time, Simon McGovern came out into the bright sunshine. He observed, with considerable satisfaction, his target tugging at a necktie. The envelope was nowhere in sight. He concluded that whatever its contents, they were now with Professor Pereda. He knew this because he had walked right past the secretary's office and seen Simon McGovern anxiously fiddling with the package.

The watcher, contemplating an alternative strategy which might have prevented Van der Sterren's ultimate demise, folded away the travel chess set, the pieces arranged at move sixteen.

As the Suzuki's engine fired up and edged out of the car-park, the watcher followed, this time careful to keep the jeep in sight. It would have been a simple matter to fix a tracking device but in the circumstances he decided that was unnecessary. He could guess at where the target might be headed and his hunch was confirmed when the jeep gained the road for Manly.

10

Alan was leaning over one of his staffer's desks, a female officer called Jessie Franklin. They were both peering at a computer screen showing statistics of seaborne assaults in which firearms had been used.

'Right. Sort by weapon type, sub-sort by geographical area and let me have a print-out.' Alan rubbed his hands together briskly, pleased with the quantity and level of detail the data banks were revealing. He was aware of someone standing behind his shoulder.

'Sleeping beauty!'

Simon grumbled, 'You seem to be in ebullient mood.'

'What the bloody hell does that mean, *ebullient*?'

Jessie smirked.

'Up-beat.'

'Up-beat. Right. I am.' He guided Simon by the elbow towards his office. 'Any investigation depends on information. The more the better. And we're getting plenty.'

'But is it relevant?'

'If ninety-nine point nine per cent is junk, we've got something. Most police work is donkey work.'

'Peanuts, donkeys, you're really carving out a niche for yourself.'

Alan stopped suddenly in full view of the open-plan area and within earshot of the nearest four desks. 'Look, Simon, you can either help or you can be a smartass. Your choice.' Then he went into his office, leaving

Simon standing there while some of the officers coughed to cover their amusement. Drama was fun, especially at the expense of a pom. Simon glowered at them then followed Alan.

He was already behind his desk, feet propped, scanning papers. The message was clear: my domain, me boss, pleasantries over, put up or shut up. Simon closed the door, successfully defeating an urge to slam it.

'OK, sorry. What have you got?'

'One thousand, six hundred and seventy-three attacks in the area over the last ten years.' Alan lifted his feet off the desk and hunched forward. 'Nine per cent involved use of weapons. An analysis is being done on weapon types.'

'Nothing from forensics or ballistics?'

'Not yet. Anyway, that's what I've been doing this morning. What about you?'

'Nothing much. Breakfast with Bet, then I took her car and drove around Brisbane, you know, finding my way round a bit.'

'Where d'you end up?'

'Here and there.'

Alan nodded. 'This came in last night.' He waved a sheet of paper.

Simon scanned a copy of his father's insurance document from General Accident. 'And the descriptions of Mum's jewellery?'

Alan tapped some other documents. 'I've passed them on to Interpol. Now we wait and see what they come up with. It's a long shot, but like I said, the more information being bandied about, the better the chances of someone somewhere clicking.'

'Nothing much I can do around here.'

There was a knock at the door. Simon recognized the buxom officer Alan had been talking to earlier. Her hair was scraped back into a pony-tail and her blunt features were devoid of any make-up.

'Here's the print-out, Alan.'

'Thanks, Jessie.'

Jessie left flashing a smile at Simon.

Alan studied the print-out closely. 'One hundred and fifty attacks using firearms, forty-nine of those involved AK-47s, a third of all armed assaults, about three per cent of the whole. They've been busy.'

'If they're the same weapons.'

'True. But AKs have swamped the black market. They're cheap, reliable, deadly from range and every bugger's got one.'

'So what do we do?'

'Be a donkey. Here,' Alan handed the print-out to Simon. 'Every AK assault is indicated with a position grid. Take these,' Alan reached into a drawer and brought out a box of coloured pins. 'Mark up each one on the wall chart. Let's see if a location pattern emerges.'

'OK.'

'I'll fax the same list to the relevant forensics departments in Indonesia, the Philippines and Thailand. If they've got info on any of these cases, I want copies. Once our ballistics people come through we can compare data and see if any match. We'll also check against all the records we hold here.'

'Big job.'

'Donkey work.' Alan stood up. 'I'll be back to give you a hand.'

An hour and a half later they were done. Simon chose to use only red pins. They were scattered among the Arafura and Java seas and along the southern islands of the Philippines. No discernible pattern showed, no clustering. Alan was disappointed and he figured Simon would be as well. 'If it was that easy, there wouldn't be any crime,' Alan observed drily.

'How long will these people take to send their information?'

Alan shrugged. He was a patient man by nature, a fundamental prerequisite to good coppering. He was also used to the ways of his Asian neighbours. 'These guys aren't as organized as we are, or the UK,' he added as an afterthought. 'They don't have the budgets for a start.'

Simon grunted. 'You mean it could be days. Why d'you do that, Alan? Why d'you always take the oblique approach then let me interpret your meaning? Is that your idea of diplomacy, squirrelling potential excuses for the future in case there's a balls-up somewhere down the line?'

Alan stood back from the wall chart. 'I started out as a copper on the beat; now I have my own department. You decide the answer to your question.' He squinted at the map, head cocked to one side as if to divine a sequence among the pins. He gave up the attempt. 'I do have something else.' Alan walked back to his desk. 'I noticed it yesterday, at the morgue.'

Simon leaned against the window and rummaged for cigarettes. 'What?'

'The average height of western women is between five five and five seven, give or take.'

Simon agreed. 'So?'

'Your mother was five six.'

'I'm not with you.'

'She had a slight abrasion on her forehead, very faint. There wasn't anything about it in the PM report. I had a word with the pathologist.'

'He'd overlooked it?'

'Put it down to the rough handling. Didn't think it was important. I asked him to have a closer look. He lifted a piece of surface skin. Under the microscope the skin appeared striated, small neat grooves, shallow with constant widths.'

Simon blew smoke. 'Cut to the chase, Alan. I don't know what you're on about. I'm feeling slightly sick. It's *my* mother's skin you're talking about.'

'In short, stubble, the grooves were made by stubble. There were also tiny pinpricks, like mini stabs.'

Simon shook his head.

Alan became the benign questioner. 'What's the difference between westerners and Asians?'

'Diet, weight, size. . . .'

'Height. Westerners are taller, especially men.'

'I read something about that. Japanese, born and raised in the States after the war average six feet compared with nips in Japan. Something to do with diet.'

'Interesting. Anyway, in this kind of case, physical assault, molestation, close body contact, which we know occurred here, the woman will often show abrasions near the hairline. We can deduce that one of the attackers left the marks. It wasn't your father, he was cleanly shaven.'

'My mother was . . . you know . . . not facing them.' Simon forced the words out.

'Yes. I know. But she would have been struggling before she was. . . .'

'I'm still not with you.'

'It's a signpost to one of the attackers. He's at least six foot tall, possibly taller, six two maybe. Six foot plus is very unusual for an Asian, particularly as you say, a local mahout.'

'Christ! You're saying one of them might be European?'

'Either that or we're looking for a bloody tall Asian.'

'He might have been standing on a step. It's a narrow space between the chart table and the galley where you reckon the attack happened. Could be he was on one of the companionway steps?'

Alan watched Simon draw on his cigarette, saw the flinch when the heat of the smoke burnt his lips. Simon's dispassion surprised him. 'I thought of that, so did the pathologist. The relative position of grip marks on the arms and bruising to the thighs from the attacker's knees confirms the height issue. If the guy had been on a step the grip marks would be downwards front to back. They're not. They're level.'

'OK, two things. . . .' Simon looked around for an ashtray then gave up and flicked the butt out the window. 'If one of them's a European—'

'Westerner,' Alan corrected.

'A white man, then we are talking very small needle, very large haystack. But if you're right and *Clarissa* was followed from Hong Kong, then it might be more likely.'

Alan shook his head. 'Don't agree. A white pirate would be well known within the community, if I can call it that. And if this was a contract, why use an outsider? He'd be easier to detect and more expensive for sure.'

'Maybe money's not the issue.'

'Maybe not.' Alan flexed his fingers. 'Either way, white or yellow, we're dealing with a six footer and that is what I call a breakthrough.'

'Great. We've got a white boat and a tall pirate. How many people live in South-east Asia?'

'Wrong question. How many tall, white pirates cruising around in big, white boats live in South-east Asia? Big difference. What we need now is a location.'

11

The President of the United States was silent. His large frame seemed to sag under the weight of the demand. The typewritten sheet of notepaper on his desk in the Oval Office spelled calamity for the country and disaster for his presidency.

Abe Schulmann, National Security Adviser, sat on a Chippendale armchair in front of the President's desk.

'Shit!' The President picked up the paper and read it again. 'Five weeks or ROIP goes to the Chinese. Goddamit! Abe, what was the postmark on this?'

'Yesterday, sir. October 28th. New York.'

'Great, just goddam great! Lost a day already. Thirty-four days from date of postmark. Abe, who else knows about this?' The President flapped the paper.

'Us, the joint chiefs of staff and Bernard Levy, Mr President.'

The President considered this. It wouldn't be long before word spread. 'Could they use it?'

'The Chinese, no, not immediately, but eventually they will.'

'Eventually when?'

'Five years'd be my estimate, Mr President.'

The President stood. Beyond the bullet-proofed French doors, the White House Rose Garden was bathed in sunshine.

'Some little prick walks right into Los Alamos and takes the legacy codes for W-88, then they get the N-bomb specs. The Chinese jump their nuclear rearming programme forward thirty years, courtesy of billions of dollars of American investment. Now they might very shortly get their hands on ROIP data giving them the know-how to find our missile subs we've spent fifty years trying to hide.' He spun round. 'That about the size of it, Abe?'

'Yes, sir. That's about right.'

Abe Schulmann thought about what would happen to him if the Press got hold of this. He crossed his legs and tried to focus elsewhere.

'Techs at Livermore will need briefing, Mr President.'

'You deal with that. Go through the DoE.'

'The Lawrence Livermore National Laboratory.' Abe Schulmann shook his head and tutted. 'After the W-88 spillage you'd have thought the Department of Energy would have put more cyber security around the Radar Ocean Imaging Programme.'

'I want the labs, all of them, shut down tight as a clam's ass.'

'Done, Mr President. Security for all nuclear weapons research facilities is now with the FBI and the CIA. Every foreign visitor is being checked and logged, especially the Chinese.'

The President returned to his desk. 'If the Russians stick by START II then China could achieve nuclear parity in ten, maybe five years. That's when ROIP will really tell the difference.'

'You have another problem, Mr President.'

'What's that, Abe?'

'Trident represents all of Britain's strategic nuclear deterrent. If they can be seen, it'll compromise NATO and that'll mean massive US troop deployments to Europe, seeing as we let the cat out the bag.'

The President sighed. 'You're right. Putting a hundred thousand men in Europe doesn't bear thinking about. OK, get to it, Abe. We've got thirty-four days to isolate this wacko.'

The deep blue carpet in the Oval Office, embroidered with the presidential seal was spotless. Behind the polished desk, yellow drapes hung straight without the fuss of pelmets and the plain, beige upholstered sofas with their square no-nonsense lines bore little hint of use. The air too was polished, filtered to remove dust and other pollutants, cooled to a comfortable seventeen degrees and mildly fragranced with, what, rosehip?

Bernard Levy, Director of the FBI liked this room. He also liked the man who was its present incumbent. So when he took a look at the President and saw the bags under his eyes and the sallowness of his skin, he felt genuine sympathy.

'How you doing, Bernard?'

'OK, Mr President, but I have to tell you, I think this'll be a tough nut to crack.'

'That's not what I want to hear.'

The FBI man sat on one of the sofas while the President pulled up one of the high-backed carvers.

'Just to reassure you, Mr President, the only people at my end who know about the note are myself and Trick Goodyear, one of the forensics guys at the lab. The best.'

'Good. So?' The President spread his hands then clasped them together.

'Abe asked me to run a psychological evaluation based on the note.' He unfastened the flap of a thin, satchel-type briefcase and slipped out a blue folder embossed with the seal of the FBI. The original, anonymous message was now sheathed in a transparent, plastic envelope. Bernard Levy slipped it across the glossy surface of the coffee table towards the President.

'The psychological evaluation is not, I'm afraid, conclusive in any respect.'

'Have you got anything for me at all, Bernard?'

'Yes, I have, Mr President. The anonymity, and assuming this isn't just some kind of sick prank, means we have to mount a search, a big one. He or she'll know that, it's what they want. So we need to find out what the problem is also. There's nothing here to suggest what it might be. We figure that the originator of the note probably believes that whatever is bothering them will have more impact if we have to root around. Also, it means time'll be running down on the clock, so everyone'll be getting edgy. For the perpetrator, they're in a better bargaining position and we, the government, take the whole deal more seriously. That's on the bad side. On the good side, Mr President, the note's anonymous because it's from a nobody.'

'So we have got to take it seriously.'

'Yes, sir. That'd be my advice.' And despite everything else that had happened, Bernard Levy knew that this presidency might stand or fall on what he did or did not find.

'OK, Bernard. Anything else?'

'The perp wants us to chase, sir, so we figure it's a personal thing rather than some allegiance to a bunch of commies in Beijing – number one.' The Director of the FBI stuck a stubby finger in the air. 'Two, if it's not about politics we can discount Chinese, not absolutely but we have to widen the search area to include all ethnics and Americans too. By that I mean WASPS. Now, taken together, there's one helluva lot of folks employed between Los Alamos, Livermore, Sandia and Oak Ridge and that's just the national labs. When you take into account personnel with the corporations which support weapons research, like TWR Inc., hired by the Pentagon, the numbers start heading north big-time.'

The President sighed and slumped slightly in his chair. He had a head for figures. 'The FBI'll be looking at something in the order of fifty thousand people.'

'Thereabouts, sir, yes.'

'Can't be done, not in twenty-nine days.'

'No, sir. I figured that and the person who wrote the note'll have figured that, too. There's no handwriting to study and would you believe the typeface is from an old Corona typewriter, long since out of production. Also, the grammar and sentence structure is quite precise, old fashioned if you will, sir, so we reckon on someone over fifty. Now I could be accused of sexism here, Mr President but two things back me up – three, if I count instinct. First, this kind of personal vendetta thing is more prevalent as a behaviour pattern in women, and two, Trick's computer ID'd the writing style, vocab, grammar and so on as fifty-seven per cent likelihood of being written by a woman, forty-three per cent, a man. So that's where I plan to begin.'

'And someone with high level access to the ROIP?'

'Yes, sir. Now there's a bunch of other stuff Trick pulled up. Problem is it doesn't point anywhere.'

'Like what for example.'

'Like the paper, sir. Gestetner eighty grams. Probably some of that in one out of ten offices across the country. Also, some silica grains, sand, but nothing that indicates a particular area. Dust, fibres, but some's from contamination.'

'You seen this?' The President leaned forward and tapped five hard-bound volumes stacked on the coffee table.

'The Cox report, yes. Reckon Chris Cox'll be gunning, sir.'

Christopher Cox was the Republican chairman of the special committee of the House of Representatives responsible for producing the 900-page dossier entitled *Report of the Select Committee on US National Security and Military/Commercial Concerns with the People's Republic of China*. Another four Republicans and four Democrats had made up the numbers. Together they had conducted twenty-two top secret hearings, heard seventy-five witnesses, listened to 200 hours of testimony and reviewed 500,000 documents. The conclusions were devastating: America had lost legacy codes for the W-88 warhead and the W-70 neutron bomb. Rocket-guidance and nose cone design improvements, missile-guidance technology and high-performance computers with potential for nuclear weapons applications had also gone missing.

'Gunning's the word.'

'Plenty of folks saying it's propaganda.'

'Not enough.'

'I have to be straight with you, Mr President, 'we've only got four weeks and a day. I'm going to need resources.'

The President simply nodded. 'You got whatever resources you require, Bernard.'

'Thank you, Mr President. Now, whilst I figure we're looking for a white, Anglo-Saxon female of fifty plus, born and raised in the USA, I'm going to start with a Chinese male born in China in 1939.'

12

The house was two miles west of Livermore city centre, halfway down Fig Tree Drive, on the south side. It was a nondescript house insofar as it was identical or close to identical to most of the other houses that lined the street. There was a front porch and veranda furnished with a swing chair. The house was of clapboard construction, resting on a brick and concrete basement. It was two storeys high, three counting the warren of small attic spaces beneath the steeply pitching gables. A narrow yard to the front separated the house from the sidewalk, accessed through a small, tubular steel gate, in-filled with chicken wire and operated on a spring-back mechanism. Behind the house, a slightly larger garden, neglected and overgrown, backed on to open land where, rumour had it, plans were afoot to develop another Wal-Mart.

The front door was half glazed and behind the glass, flouncy net curtains were tied back with blue bows which matched the exterior, baby-blue paintwork, now weathered and in need of a new coat. Through the front door, a narrow hall, sharing space with a wooden staircase, led into a lounge which occupied almost half the ground floor. An archway opened on to a dining-room and next to the dining-room, overlooking the back yard, was a kitchen which might, in another context have been a mock-up to 1950s style. The bedrooms, three of them and a bathroom were upstairs. It was a comfortable house but no more than that.

Downstairs, in the basement, a trestle table stood against one wall. A small, slit window was set into the wall above the table, its glass opaque with ancient cobwebs, not that there was much need for a window. Even in summer the stone and brick kept the basement cool. It was for this reason, and for privacy, that Gertrude Ziegle had set up her computer on the trestle table.

The basement was painted white, but like the outside, it too was in need of redecoration. Aside from the table, the room was spartan – some MDF shelving, an old armchair that had belonged to her mother, a plastic clock ticking loudly, a threadbare rug rucked on the floor like a shed skin. On the far wall a cork board, five feet across by three feet high, was drilled into the masonry. Pinned to the board was an American flag, peppered with thousands of tiny holes. Nailed in the centre of the flag was an American passport – her passport. It looked as if it had been savaged by a angry dog. Scattered randomly on the flag were five darts, one impaling her passport, their flight feathers tatty with use.

Gertrude Ziegle sat at the trestle table staring at the blank computer screen, her mind elsewhere, particularly at this time, always at this time, every day. Her grey eyes, gradually taking on the rheumy appearance of age, flicked up to the three-dollar clock. The red second hand swept past twelve and the minute hand clicked a notch. Twenty-seven minutes past eleven. She always remembered the time, because when she'd taken that call fourteen years ago her watch had stopped at exactly twenty-seven minutes past eleven. Try as she might, Gertrude Ziegle was unable to convince herself that the mystery of her stopping watch was anything other than a sign from God.

She pushed herself back from the desk on the old castors of her swivel chair and, hands on knees, stood up feeling the squeak of arthritis in her joints. She clambered slowly up the stone steps emerging from under the staircase into the hallway. From a cupboard beside the television in the lounge, she removed a yellow duster, walked to the mantel and leaned against it staring down at the silver-framed photograph of a young man with over-sized ears and an awkward, toothy grin proudly wearing the uniform of the United States Marine Corps. Next to the photograph was an open box lined with blue satin. Resting on the satin was America's highest honour for valour in combat, the Congressional Medal of Honour.

Methodically and with infinite patience, Gertrude Ziegle began to polish the already gleaming photograph frame.

'If only he hadn't called,' Gertrude Ziegle said aloud to her beloved Jamie-Jake as she polished over his young face. 'I could have been happy.' She laughed, a high-pitched whine edged with hysteria. 'But he did. I told you. At eleven twenty-seven. Let me see now.' She looked away to the ceiling, her face crinkling to a frown. 'In 1986, I was only fifty then, Jamie-Jake. I could have been so happy.'

Raymond had died only last month. Pulled over to the roadside to help with a punctured tyre. Got robbed and shot in the face. Old Raymond, never wanted children. Too set in his ways she used to say. Ma and Pa before him. Neither of them ever got over Jamie-Jake. Both suffered terribly with cancer in the end and went, thankfully only weeks apart. Gertrude was certain the anxiety had caused the disease. Kitty had gone too, an American short-hair. Buried out in the yard. But Gertrude had never had the heart to replace Kitty, so she was alone now.

She set the frame gently back on the mantel and picked up the gallantry medal, testing the points of the star with her thumb, as she always did. Still sharp. She polished the medal then picked tiny bits of dust from the ribbon. 'You go back to sleep now,' she said, as she laid the Silver Star back on to its blue satin.

Out in the street, some kids whipped by the window, drumming over the kerbstones on skateboards. She watched them pass, then folded the yellow duster and returned it to the cupboard by the TV.

Gertrude Ziegle flexed her aching fingers and cursed the arthritis which plagued her more each day. She thought about old Raymond. She occasionally thought about him but not often. She had difficulty summoning any kind of enthusiasm for his memory.

'I was waiting for him to go, Jamie.' Gertrude stared after the receding backs of the skateboarders. 'You see, I promised him I wouldn't do anything until he was gone. That way he would not be implicated. Silly old fool. No one cared about him. But a promise is a promise, Jamie-

Jake.' She picked at her teeth with a blunt fingernail. 'I wonder if they'll find us Jamie-Jake.'

In the hallway, she pulled on a raincoat, despite the clear sky and warm California air. 'Going out for a while, Jamie-Jake. Maybe we'll have some lemonade later.'

From a small Victorian occasional table next to the stairs, Gertrude picked up an old Corona typewriter and dropped it into a plastic shopping bag. She'd seen a charity shop on Fitzroy, raising money for the Kosovar Albanians. Someone might buy the Corona for a few bucks.

By the time Gertrude Ziegle returned to her house on Fig Tree Drive the rain had started, only a light shower, but still, she had to be careful with her weak chest and the arthritis. She removed her coat and without announcing herself to Jamie-Jake or remembering her promise of lemonade, she went down to her basement and started throwing darts at the American flag.

13

'I need a motive.' Alan was pacing.

'Only if you're thinking it was deliberate.'

'I've been over what happened so many times I'm cross-eyed.' Wrestling with unanswered questions. Lying in the dark, with Bet awake beside him asking what was wrong until he had run out of excuses. He looked out the window.

Simon said, 'The jewels? Must have been.'

Alan shook his head. 'No. Why wait two thousand miles?' He came away from the window and sat down. 'How would they know the stuff was on board? They would've hit private boats before. Cash, yes. Some jewellery, maybe. Passports, definitely. But not a thumping bloody great horde of stuff.'

'Passports?'

'Very valuable. Smuggling people, drugs trafficking. Your genuine black-market passport is worth quite a bit.'

'And the electronics.' Simon looked away to the sky, resignation in his voice, concurring with Alan.

'And we know about those.' Alan peered at Simon. He saw a young man on the other side of his desk, slouched slightly, one leg crossed, ankle resting on knee, an element of nonchalance. Maybe arrogance. 'Can you think of anything at all? What have we missed?'

Simon sat up straighter then shrugged and shook his head slowly.

Alan leaned back, began drumming fingers. 'And they didn't sink her. Had the time, had the space, probably had the firepower to blast her out the water. But no. Just left her. *Endeavour* took two hours to reach her. They'd know that. And even if they didn't, then why behave like paranoids? Who the hell's going to see them in the middle of the ocean? That clinches it, in my mind anyway.'

'Coffee?'

'No thanks.'

Simon was back in two minutes. 'None of that's conclusive though, is it?' He closed the door and raised the steaming polystyrene cup to his lips. 'I mean it makes sense on the surface but there could be things, stuff we don't know about, that might provide some kind of explanation, other than conspiracy theory.'

Alan looked up. 'You don't believe it?'

'I didn't say that; I said we don't have all the facts, not necessarily anyway. I'm just saying there could be things we haven't thought of.'

'Such as?' He had thought of everything. Everything. Arrogant bugger.

Simon shrugged again.

Alan gave him a few more seconds. 'Fine. So much for that then.'

'I'm trying to cover all the bases.'

'No disrespect, Simon, but I've already done that. And I do have this.' He held up a buff folder. The information had finally come through, adding technical evidence to support his argument.

'What is it?'

'Ballistics report.'

Simon sat down and balanced his cup on the edge of the desk.

Alan flipped to the end of the report to refresh his memory. He read for a while, just the gentle humming of the fan and the low hubbub of telephones and office movement filtering through the partition walls..

'The bullet pattern in *Clarissa*'s hull doesn't make sense.' Alan shifted to get more comfortable. 'Bullet holes forward are bigger than amidships. That means they were travelling at a lesser velocity which means they were fired from further away.'

'And what does that mean?'

'If the pirates raked the hull, why fire forward first?' Alan scanned Simon's face to see if he was keeping pace. He saw incomprehension. 'Resistance. If there was going to be any it would most likely be from the cabin area. And the attackers wouldn't know whether the occupants on board were armed.'

Simon retrieved his coffee and sipped.

'We know from bloodstains in the cockpit and the drag marks that at least John was in the cockpit as the pirates approached.' Alan glanced at Simon again. 'Blood type matchings.' Corroboration.

Simon bit the rim of the cup. 'If my father was in the cockpit, he would be seen, so why didn't they fire there first, is that what you're saying?'

'Probably did. From the blood pattern on the sail the lab boys reckon it was a longer range shot. Anyone would go to the cockpit if they saw an approaching boat, even if there wasn't a perceived threat.' Alan nodded, agreeing with himself, eyes down to the report. 'If the hull was raked they'd have gone below for protection. Natural reaction, particularly older people.'

'What's age got to do with it?'

'Older people tend to be less aggressive.'

'My father was certainly a pacifist, outside the boardroom anyway. So where's this leading?'

Alan set the paper down. 'No shots were fired on approach. The hull was raked as the pirate boat was pulling away. If John and Elizabeth were already dead by that stage, then why bother shooting up the hull?'

'Shit, I don't know, Alan. You're the policeman. You've got the answers right there.'

'To make the attack look spontaneous. They spot a boat, shoot it up, kill the people on board, take the safe, disappear. That's what we're supposed to think. Only that's not how it happened.'

Simon frowned, grappling with the facts. 'The attack happened in daylight right?'

'Yes.'

'If they raked the hull when they left, if whoever wrote that report is right, then they weren't expecting any resistance?'

'Exactly. Pre-planned and well briefed.' Alan could see that Simon was struggling with this. He'd put on a brave face and that was commendable, but the difficult bits were yet to come. 'I chased the pathologists on the DNA analysis.'

Simon crunched the polystyrene cup and threw it in the bin.

Alan judged his moment. Saw the boy's eyes water, his jaw clenching and unclenching to control it. 'Your mother was raped once, one man. The pirates' habit is for gang rape. It's another aspect that doesn't fit the usual profile. Pirates tend to be shambolic. They'll organize attacks on cargo carriers sometimes, but not small boats. Those are usually opportunistic, in the wrong place at the wrong time.'

Simon rubbed his forearm across his eyes.

Alan got up, walked to the window, the one overlooking the yard and stared down at *Clarissa*. The forensics guys were still there. A white arm brushing backwards and forwards, appearing and disappearing under the edge of the tarp. There was more to come, then the confrontation. Bet was happier, a noticeable uplift since Simon had touched down. Simon could help him with this, then they could all get back to normal, or as normal as possible in the face of such devastation. Time would heal the scars. It always did. And Betina growing-up. Perhaps another child. Maybe now was the time. He came back from the window.

'I've had information back from my contacts in the Philippines, Malaysia and so on.'

'That was quick. Thought you said these people were all at sea.'

Alan smiled at Simon's dark humour. 'Apparently, they've improved. We've compared their ballistics data with our own. Rifling marks match in seven cases.' He went to the wall chart, beckoning Simon to follow. He checked the sheet in his hand and started pulling the red pins out of the map until only the seven remained.

They stood back and inspected the chart. This time there was a cluster. The only aberrant pin represented the attack on *Clarissa*. The other six pins showed a close radius to the southern Philippine island of Mindanao.

'Result!' Simon exclaimed.

'I asked for reports on each case, the extent of the violence. These people have a reputation bordering on being legendary.'

'Why weren't they sunk?'

Alan shrugged. He didn't know the answer. Could see immediately what Simon was getting at – if they weren't scuttled, then why should *Clarissa* have been? 'Question is how many boats that were reported missing but never found were put on the seabed by the same gang? A heck of a lot more than seven. For starters, there's more sea traffic where those pins are. The boats were close enough to land for salvage. Maybe they've got a deal going with the salvers on the resales. Could be any number of reasons.'

Simon stared at the wall chart.

Alan went on, defining the cluster. 'In all cases there was multiple rape. Three of the boats had all-male crew and one of those was a single-hander. These people don't discriminate. But your parents – there's a break in the pattern. Sir John wasn't touched; your mother, once. It's out of context. This was a hit but with one very big, very crucial difference.'

Simon spun to face him. 'What?'

'I think whoever did this *wanted* the evidence to be found.'

'You're fucking crazy, you know that!'

'Maybe. I've been round and round this. . . .'

'I don't care if you've been to the fucking moon and back.'

'Simon. . . .'

Simon thrust his face toward Alan. 'Why would they want *Clarissa* to be found? Why?'

Alan shook his head. 'I don't know.'

'You don't know. That's great. You come out with this bullshit, but you don't know.'

'I'm sending a second report to Interpol. This time I'm going to give them details of the route, specifics on *Clarissa*, MO but not the full ballistics report.'

'What for?'

'See if there's been anything similar.'

'Good! Get rid of your stupid bloody notion. You think you'll come up with something?'

Alan shook his head. 'Nope.' He buzzed on his deskcom and asked someone called Charlie to come in.

Charlie was tall, maybe six foot, fat, bald, kind of sweaty, small piggy eyes, all dressed in brown. He smelt of cigarettes and coffee. And vanilla. Even here from across the room, Simon could smell it. Vaguely familiar. Simon had a strange sense of *déjà vu*. He shook it off, turned back to the wall chart. Heard Alan firing instructions about the notice he wanted sent to Interpol. But there was no click of the door, the vanilla was still there hanging in the air while the silence thickened.

He turned back. They were both looking at him.

Then Charlie looked at Alan. 'By the way, Al, your wife's car, the yellow jeep, it's got a crack in the tail light.'

It came to Simon quite suddenly, the *déjà vu* crystallizing. The car-park at the university. The guy must have been near him at some time, near enough for him to smell vanilla.

Simon turned back to the wall map, only he didn't see it, didn't see the wall, didn't see anything. He scrolled events in his mind, fast, like snapshots to a drowning man, each being involuntarily replaced in a rapid historical sequence.

'You had me followed?'

Charlie shuffled towards the door. 'Sorry, mate,' he said to Simon's back. 'Way it goes.' Then the click of the door as he left.

OK, OK. So Alan's not so dumb. Had me followed because he can see through the bullshit. But this is my thing. Dad said it. It's yours, comes in two parts. I'm not ready to share this. I don't even know what the fuck it is! He could feel the weariness in his head, like a weight, pressing him down. He breathed deeply a few times, turned to face Alan, made his face neutral.

'Sorry, Alan.'

'So what were you doing at the university? Maybe it's none of my business, but this is a murder hunt, so maybe it is.'

Simon held up his hands. Came back, sat down. 'You're right. It is your business, at least I think it's your business.'

Alan steepled his fingers over his nose and mouth, peering at Simon, waiting for the explanation.

'I went to see a classics professor . . .'

'Pedro Pereda, University of Queensland. I checked him out. Charlie did.'

Simon grunted. He had to smile. Maybe he wasn't cut out for this. The truth needed no rehearsal. 'When Dad called me from Hong Kong, just before they left, he said something was coming to me, in two parts. I didn't know what he meant by that. It was pretty cryptic. Maybe a present. I got something in the post the next day. It was hand delivered. A guy at the bank coming to London on business brought it over.'

Alan's hands came away from his face. Scudding clouds crossed the sun, dousing them in shadow.

'The package contained a document. I guessed the first part of whatever Dad was on about. It was old, ancient. Handwritten, by my seven times great grandfather, Robert McGovern. I hadn't seen it before, ever.' Simon shook his head, eyes down, adding emphasis to his words. 'It's in Latin.'

'Is it the original?'

Simon shook his head again. 'No. But it's obviously old and the date's a give away, 1719.'

Alan slumped back, eyes fixed on Simon, body sagging as tension evaporated. 'This might be it. Might be a motive, *the* motive. Professor Pereda, you went to him for a translation?'

Simon nodded.

'You spoke to Bet?'

'You asking or telling?'

'Asking.'

'Yes I did, but Dad didn't mention it to her. And I didn't tell her he'd said anything to me. I didn't see the point of dragging her into it.'

'Good. And the original, where's that?'

'Don't know. I've got a feeling it might have been on *Clarissa*.'

'Did your father tell you that?'

'Not specifically, no.' The conversation with his sister had thrown up one or two inconsistencies. 'Bet said Dad told her everything was safe. She didn't have a clue what he was talking about. I think he was trying to tell her something, or maybe giving her a message which he knew I'd get. I don't know.'

Alan absorbed this. 'It's supposition. But it would sure explain a whole lot.' He thought for a while. 'You don't know what the document means, at all?'

'I did Latin at school but I was never much good at it.'

'And when's the good professor going to be through?'

'He said he'd call.'

'No one, and I mean no one, should know about this.'

'I made sure of that. Professor Pereda knows that my parents were killed, no details. I expressly told him that no one else was to know about the paper, no colleagues, anybody.'

Alan took him at his word.

They sat there in silence, both thinking.

Eventually Alan squared his shoulders. 'You'd better tell me what you know about Robert McGovern.'

14

The spotter was expensively dressed. Lightweight Armani suit, Piaget on his wrist, pricey haircut, Ferragamo tie, crocodile shoes, Pierre Cardin shades. Had to be, to create credibility as a rich, a very rich punter. His face was fleshy and the clothes did something, but not enough to mask the paunch. The woman with him was younger, beautiful, exquisitely attired. Her jewellery was real, as real as the Walther PPK nestling in her Christian Dior handbag. Anyone looking at the pair would think, rich guy, trophy wife, because she sure ain't screwing him for his looks. They made a perfect team.

The smog-encrusted heat of midday Manila was messing with her make-up. The woman dabbed at her face with a tissue, careful not to distort the image. Six shops so far and in each of them the manager had attended them personally. All effusive, some fawning, all disappointed at their failure to make a sale.

The woman returned the tissue to her bag, making certain the clasp was secure. Then an imperceptible nod to her husband. Ready for number seven. He held the door for her. Cold air spilled from the inside, draping them. Head up, slow walk in, aloof, arrogant. He followed her, a hand at the small of her back, guiding gently. They needed to keep in tune here. They stopped in the middle of the floor. Other customers, two couples were seated at tables, velvet display clothes supporting arrays of

jewels. Both women looked round, inspected the new arrivals, her especially, then returned their attention to spending large sums of money.
One couple he guessed to be Americans. The others, difficult to tell,
certainly European, possibly Italian.

José Remedios glanced up through the sheet of mirrored one-way
glass separating his office from the shop. The new customers were
Filipino locals, always the best with their potential for repeat business.

The spotter watched Remedios come towards them, tugging at his
cuffs, shrugging himself more comfortably into his jacket. A casual flick
of his eyes down to his 'wife'. She held her poise, mouth unsmiling, her
expression mildly disdainful, demanding attention as if life owed her a
living. She's good, he thought. First time he'd worked with her. He
wondered briefly if he'd get into her bed; the adrenalin usually allowed
him to have his way. A perk of the job, together with the clothes.

Remedios guided them to a table. The spotter had been here before,
knew the manager's name, knew his connection to the black market. He
also knew that he wouldn't be recognized. He was that good. He allowed
his wife to sit, stood behind her, watched her lay her arm on the table,
showing the exquisite sapphire on her fist, as he'd taught her. He noticed
Remedios looking at the stone, could almost hear the guy's brain clicking away, assessing how much he could take them for.

'I'm looking for a gift for my wife, something special, for our anniversary.' The spotter spoke slowly, a hand caressing his wife's shoulder, just
to show how much in love they were.

Remedios inclined his head in acknowledgement, waiting to be told
what they were after.

The spotter looked away, casting his eye over the glittering display
cases, ruminating. 'Ear-rings,' he said. 'Rubies.' He would start with a
fudge. Get the guy excited, allow him to talk up the price.

Remedios went to a cabinet, came back with a tray.

The woman fingered the ear-rings, admiring some, discarding others,
until she'd been through the tray. Then looked at her husband, slight
shake of the head.

'Do you have anything a bit more . . . substantial?'

The tray was slid home, another brought out. These were up to $60,000.

The spotter and his wife went through the same routine. Inspect, discard, inspect, discard. More trays, higher prices. Until they were at the $200,000 mark. The spotter picked his moment when he saw Remedios beginning to grow apprehensive. They'd seen every pair of ruby ear-rings. Only nothing they wanted. 'Doesn't have to be ear-rings.' The spotter stroked his chin thoughtfully. 'Something unusual, a necklace maybe, a ring.' He shrugged. It didn't really matter what the piece was just so long as it was 'different'.

The spotter turned his head, noticed the Americans had gone. The Italians were still there, but losing interest. The assistant was getting flustered, trying to make a hard sell. He was putting them off. He turned his head back, tapped his wife gently, twice, with a fingertip at her shoulder blade.

The spotter produced a pack of Dunhill and a gold lighter. Lit it for her while Remedios scurried away for an ashtray. The strategy again was rehearsed, to show Remedios they were here to stay, in no hurry to leave, prepared to wait for that special something.

Remedios was gone rather a long time. Good sign, the spotter thought. When he returned he held a blue velvet pouch. Placed the ashtray on the table. Seemed nervous. 'I do have this. It is very rare.' He spilled the ring on to the display cloth.

The ring was really stunning. The woman gasped. The spotter was careful not to overdo the reaction. He squeezed his wife's shoulder, a warning. Her inexperience had just showed, but he saw that Remedios had misinterpreted his wife's reaction.

'It's a pink diamond of ten point five carats; what we call in the trade a Fancy Vivid Pink. Flawless and extremely rare.' He let them play with it.

They played with it. The spotter held it up to the light, asked some questions, looked for the mark on the inside of the platinum band. If he hadn't known it was there he would never have noticed. His hands were sweaty and he could feel his heartbeat in his neck. There was a second mark, on one of the claws, an S-shaped scratch, barely visible to the naked eye. Remedios had missed it or hadn't had time to polish it. The woman had regained her composure and he was glad of that.

Remedios opened the bidding at $800,000.

15

Detective Inspector Filippo Santos ran his fingers through his hair repeatedly, trying to shake out the hair-spray. It made his scalp itch in the heat. Beyond the closed venetian blinds of his office partitions, the Manila Police Department consumed its daily diet of murder, blackmail and kidnapping.

His office was like a furnace despite the efforts of a mobile air-conditioning unit, but the hot air discharge meant the window had to be left open. At least it created a breeze. The jacket of his Armani suit was slung over the back of his chair. He was wearing a shoulder holster, packing a magnum. The Piaget and the diamond-encrusted signet ring had been signed back in and were in the safe in the basement together with the sapphire and other accoutrements which had adorned his *wife*.

Santos had picked an impossible target in his dealings with Remedios and suggested $400,000. Kept examining the ring, turning it over in his fingers. They were heading for the mid point at $600,000 in increments of ten thou' when he had finally shaken his head at $530,000. Remedios wouldn't budge off $550,000 and that was too hot. Thank Christ.

He reread the report sent to him by his old friend Alan Bedale in Queensland, tracing *Clarissa*'s route and the area of the attack. The ring had been part of the booty. Computer enhancements of the Interpol picture confirmed his finding. The emerald cut of the stone, the high-mount setting, eight claws. No doubt. And the mark was clear, an S-shaped scratch in one of the claws.

A scuffed Filofax was open on his desk at B. He slid his finger down the page, picked up the phone and dialled, then waited to be connected, until eventually his old friend was on the line. It was good to hear Alan's voice. One of those guys who always had a good word, always concerned about how other people were getting on. They exchanged pleasantries. Then Santos got down to business and explained about the pink diamond, how he'd enhanced the Interpol pictures and the S-shaped mark.

'You're sure?' Alan was ecstatic. It came down the wire.

'I'll send you the enhancement for your records.' Santos paused. 'What I found doesn't necessarily mean whoever did this is here, in the Philippines.'

'Go on.' Alan waited.

Santos had started out in Narcotics, then moved into Fraud and knew a thing or two about fencing stolen property.

'The ring could be a plant, a strategy to put us off the scent. It works like this. We assume these guys are smart. OK. I've got the details that you sent me about the boat. It looks like a deliberate hit to me. So we assume they knew what they were after. Valuable jewels will be missed. They know descriptions of the missing items will be posted. So they plant a piece, maybe two or three. The rest of the stuff goes overseas, Hong Kong, Taiwan, Antwerp, London, New York. They'll be watching us to see if we trawl locally. We find something, like the ring, pull in the buyer and they know we're on to them so they go to ground. If the stuff's all outside they wouldn't know. None of these people are international, not yet anyway.' He knew this was new ground for Alan.

'Like a safety net, you mean?'

'It's exactly that, a safety net. Gives them advance warning.'

'And if we leave it, they think they're safe.'

'Yep. I've put surveillance on the store. Every potential buyer will be logged so we don't lose sight of the ring.'

'On the other hand this ring could have come in from the outside.'

Santos laughed.

'What?'

'You made a joke.'

'What?' Alan repeated.

'On the other hand. . . .'

'Unintentional. Just a naturally funny guy.'

'Anyway. Did it come in from outside the country? Possibly. We've got no way of knowing,' Santos explained. 'Except I know most of the fences over here and most of the retailers prepared to deal with hot goods. I know the system. And I know that the Philippines is not a popular export market.'

'You'll let me know if there's movement on the stone?'

'Depends.' There was humour in Santos's voice. He wiped sweat off his brow.

'On what?'

'Exchange of information.' He waited, listening to the hum of silence down the line. Alan was figuring it out.

'You think they're there, in the Philippines?'

He didn't answer. 'Did you get a ballistics match?'

'Only seven!'

'There you go then.' Santos had been confident Alan would match his case with some of the stuff he'd sent over. Convinced of it since he'd spotted the pink diamond.

'So you think the ring was a, what did you call it, a plant?'

'That's what I think.' The perps were here, on his patch. He was certain.

'I was interested in the two steamers.'

Santos grinned. Seven hits, five yachts, two small steamers. The steamers broke the pattern. Always look for the pattern, then the break in the pattern, then ask why.

'Opportunism maybe. Can't say for certain.' Now was not the time to tell Alan about the *Santa Maria*, a sugar carrier. Attacked at sea with a full load. All the crew had been killed, lined up and shot. The weapon identified as a Glock, model 17. The ship had been sailed back to Manila, the sugar off-loaded. He was sure it was a racket, the cargo going back to the original owners so they could sell it again with a handsome commission going to the pirates.

'Santos, big favour to ask.'

'Go ahead.'

'I need anything unusual, homicides involving known pirates. I know it's a long list, but we can shorten it by staying current. Anything say in the last twelve months.'

'I'll check. Can't promise shit. Got one thing though, may be nothing.'

'I'm listening.'

'Had a report in from the regions. Body floated up on to a beach. Gutted like a fish. He's . . . sorry, *was*, a known pirate.'

There was silence for a moment while Alan digested the information. 'Interesting. Can you copy the file?'

'Sure, if you think it'll help.'

Santos replaced the phone, sat back and sipped some iced tea.

The ball was in play.

16

Alan watched Simon pace about the room, searching his pockets.

'You smoke too much.'

'Oh, back off, Alan, for fuck's sake.'

'Fuck nothing, you smoke too much. That's all.' But he was thinking, it must be hard for him hearing about his mother's treasured jewels being hawked about a marketplace in some flea-ridden hell-hole.

Simon stopped. Spun round. 'I've got Bet looking out for me, worried about my welfare and all that bollocks. Don't you start.'

'I never had a kid brother to look out for. Guess you'll have to do.'

Simon stepped forward, about to say something then seemingly thought better of it. Had he got it? Alan hoped so. He'd spoken with humour. These past few days he'd figured how Simon's mind worked. He was looking for something to respect in others and wanted respect from them in return. It was the substrate he worked off. Friendship was earned not given; could only work with him if there was a mutual feel-good factor. And Alan thought he'd found the key: dry humour. Humour disguised as insult. Simon liked to parry with that. Chuck it back in your face. It was like an initiation. Respect and humour disguised as insult. He'd gleaned some of it by talking to Bet at night, while the cicadas chirruped outside the window. But mostly he'd worked it out for himself. Three days before, he'd never have had the exchange, for fear that he might have provoked an explosion. Now he had the measure of Simon.

'Charlie here?' Simon asked.

'Outside.'

'Reckon he owes me one, or a few thousand.' Simon left the office door open but was back in a minute, a cigarette dangling from his lips and a grateful look on his face. He sat in front of Alan.

'So it's the Philippines.'

'Maybe,' Alan said flatly.

'What? How can you say that? My mother's pink diamond—'

'Not necessarily. Everything points that way but it's not conclusive.' Alan explained the thinking behind a 'plant' as Santos had told him earlier.

'But if Joe Snooks happens along and buys it, then what?'

'The bad guys follow Joe, satisfy themselves that Joe is not Mr Plod in disguise and go on their way.'

'Which is why your mate Santos didn't take the ring.'

'Buy it. Yes, he couldn't maintain the scam. Expensive house, chauffeured cars blah, blah. But he's got surveillance on the place. So if a buyer pitches up, the plan is he'll follow the guy following the buyer.'

'Sounds Irish.'

'You got a better idea?'

'Yeah, as a matter of fact. Get the fence, the guy who bought the ring, break his legs, force a confession.'

'You watch too much TV.'

'And you give too much goddamn advice.'

Alan grinned. 'Have a look at this.'

Simon pulled his chair closer to the desk. 'What is it?'

'One of my boffins out there did a radial fix to land on our six red pins.' The diagram was a mesh of circles, each of a radius representing the shortest distance from each attack location to the nearest land. Each landfall site was marked with a cross. That stretch of the southern coast of Mindanao was marked up with six crosses, some very close. A triangle identified the median distance between the two outer crosses.

'This is the possible pirate stronghold?' Simon pointed to the triangle.

'It's an indication.'

'So, there's ballistics matchings identifying ... sorry *indicating* Mindanao and my mother's ring in Manila. That's not enough?'

'Enough for us to concentrate our efforts on the Philippines. Not enough to commit resources.'

Alan felt as exasperated as Simon looked. Santos's call was another breakthrough, on two counts: one, the jewel; second, the disembowelled corpse of a known pirate washed up on a beach in southern Mindanao. Donkey work.

'What more do you want?'

Alan shook his head. It was the $64,000 question. 'I'll know it when I see it. Maybe Professor Pereda will come up with something.'

Professor Pereda radiated nervous energy that he was having difficulty keeping under control. Excitement seemed to fill his office like static, crackling out of his small frame. When he saw that Simon was accompanied, he seemed surprised and made no pretence of hiding his shock when Alan was introduced as a policeman.

'Relax, professor. Alan's my brother-in-law,' Simon explained.

Loose papers were sprawled over the professor's desk and numerous thick reference works were open, pages marked with small sticky yellow labels. The professor stacked the books on one side and gathered the papers on which he had made extensive notes in a thin spidery scrawl. A computer screen glowed on a side desk beneath a high window that looked out over a garden.

Alan waited while Professor Pereda made his fussy preparations. He wanted to shout at the professor to get a move on, to tell them what he'd found.

'Fascinating,' the professor said finally, peering over his glasses and tapping his bundle of notes. 'An educated man wrote this. It's very evident in the style and the fluency. There is an old English inflection in the tone pointing clearly to the author's country of origin.'

'He was Scottish.'

'Quite so, but schooled nonetheless in accurate usage of language.

Some of the translation is not literal and I've therefore made my best interpretation.'

Alan leaned forward. 'No one else has seen the translation, professor?'

Rapid head-shaking from Pereda. 'No, no. Not the translation or the original that Simon gave me. Simon was very clear about that.'

'Good. Just need to be certain.' Alan sat back and folded his arms.

'Robert McGovern starts off with a brief biography of his life. It is here that he makes the first of several references throughout the text to a diary.' Professor Pereda peered at them again. Simon and Alan glanced at one another.

'It seems that your ancestor enjoyed a distinguished career in the Royal Navy, until he was court-martialled. He is bitter. That comes through clearly. . . .'

'Is this just an account of his life?'

Alan placed a restraining hand on Simon's arm.

'No. Robert McGovern refers to the diary for a fuller account of his misfortune. He mentions it only briefly here, but I was able to get the gist of it. Another naval officer, it seems, was involved in corruption. Robert McGovern discovered this dishonesty, was set up and hounded out of the navy as a result.'

'I knew he was a pirate, became one.' Simon glanced at Alan. 'Dad told me that.'

'It appears it was not his choice. He was never able to return to England or Scotland.' Professor Pereda flicked over his notes. 'During his . . . career, he took on a band of disaffected sailors. He plundered Spanish shipping in the Caribbean.'

Alan leaned forward. The professor's voice had become tremulous, held an edge of anticipation. 'What happened?'

'He became sick. Death was a certainty. He sailed to a place he calls Paradise, "*a tempting Eden set amongst the barrenness of man, in which I will lay down my head to sleep*".' The professor glanced up. The quote had been recited with an almost theatrical note. 'It's where he went to die. He goes on to describe that he has, "*filled the belly of my worthy mistress with a happy harvest of no value to a homeless man, but to serve my king*".' Professor Pereda removed his glasses and looked directly at Simon. 'Your ancestor was a brave and dutiful man.'

Alan shook his head slowly from side to side, part disbelief, part incomprehension. Some of it made sense: '*a happy harvest of no value to a homeless man*'. He could feel his own heartbeat, thudding deep in his chest. 'What does it mean?'

'I'll give you a full translation. The key to this, and it's clear from the document, can be found in the diary. My interpretation is that Robert McGovern robbed Spanish ships of their gold. He became ill and went to this place, Paradise, presumably a tropical island, most people's idea of Paradise, to die. His mistress is his ship. The harvest, the gold she is carrying. And his reason was to help stop the Spanish from funding their military machine which might be used against England. His reference to serving the King.'

'Treasure, is that what you're saying, professor?' Alan's voice had become feathery with excitement.

Professor Pereda nodded sagely. 'That's what I think, but it is only my interpretation.' He swivelled round to the side desk, played with the mouse and clicked on the 'File' command. He then saved to the 'A' drive, removed the disk and gave it to Simon. 'That's the only copy. I don't have it on the hard drive.'

'You've been very helpful, professor. I must tell you that this information could be very dangerous . . .' Alan cautioned.

Professor Pereda was right on his line of thinking. 'That's the only copy.' That same reasonable, unhurried voice. 'I suspect there is more to this, and it is not my business, whatever that may be.'

Alan simply nodded his acceptance.

They both shook Pereda's hand. Simon turned back to the professor, his hand on the doorknob, about to leave. 'Does Robert McGovern mention the name of his mistress, his ship?'

'Oh, yes. You'll find it in the translation. He talks of her lovingly, a caravel, as if she were a woman. I suspect there probably was a woman. The writing has a certain poetry, a sense of loss.'

'And the name?'

'*Clarissa.*'

Alan was jubilant. The Nissan was like the inside of an oven. They were both sweating. Alan smacked the steering wheel. 'That's got to be it, has to be. It's the key. I think we've got ourselves a motive.' He drove away from the university. 'You knew, didn't you?' Alan glanced across at Simon.

'What? Sorry, Alan, I was miles away.'

'You knew this document was vital?'

'Vital? No. Maybe important. I suspected, that's all. You track me down to Alexandria, then the manuscript arriving from Hong Kong. Doesn't take a genius to figure there might be a connection.'

'Maybe not, but I didn't know about those papers.' The lights changed. Alan moved off.

'Fair enough.'

Alan reached across and squeezed his shoulder. 'You're miles away. What is it?'

Simon shrugged. 'Something Dad did, recently.'

'Yeah, what?'

'The boat. It used to be called *Afternoon Delight*. That's when Dad used to take her out, in the afternoons. It was his private joke. He changed the name to *Clarissa* just before he and Mum left Hong Kong. I never knew Robert McGovern's caravel was called *Clarissa*. I told Dad it was bad luck to change a boat's name. Like wearing green. You should never wear green on a boat.' Simon gave a soft, sad laugh. 'I thought it was bad joss.'

'Bad joss?'

'It's what the Chinese say. Bad fortune; something that'll upset the spirits. But Dad was an old China hand. He knew that, and he was superstitious.'

'You think it means something?'

'Yes, I do.'

Alan drove into the small car-park at P-Unit HQ. He switched the engine off. They sat there, in the heat, hot metal clinking as it cooled. Alan appreciated Simon's melancholy. The bad dream had become a reality. The facts pointed to *Clarissa*'s demise as premeditated destruction, Sir John's and Lady Elizabeth's deaths as calculated barbarity.

'Let's walk for a bit.' Simon got out of the car. Alan noticed that despite the heat, he had his jacket with him, slung over his shoulder.

They went around the marina basin. A light sea breeze brushed the air. Steel wire stays clinked against the aluminium masts of sailing boats moored along the pontoons. They stopped occasionally to admire the handsome lines of a boat, but mostly they walked in silence. Alan waited for Simon to crystallize whatever he was thinking.

'I've got something to tell you, show you actually.' Simon reached inside his jacket and drew out a large brown envelope, already torn open. He gave it to Alan.

Through the coarse paper Alan could feel the weight and substance of the envelope's contents. A book? He recognized Sir John's hand on the envelope – *Simon. In the event of my death.* He tipped out the contents. A leather-bound volume, its edges curled with age, the pages thick. Alan flicked it open. The same tidy calligraphy as the manuscript.

'Christ, this is the diary!' Alan breathed.

'Yes. I . . . I didn't know how important it might be, not until Professor Pereda said there was a diary . . . all a bit bizarre.'

'You're right!'

Simon looked at Alan. There was something in his voice. 'What is it?'

'Your father, you're right. He was . . . is . . . trying to tell you something by changing the name of his yacht. I'm sure of it.'

Simon frowned.

'He sent you a manuscript and this diary, right? The manuscript is a copy, the diary is original. Why a copy?'

'He had the original.'

'Exactly.'

'We don't know that for certain.'

'What else makes sense? My bet is whoever attacked *Clarissa* has now got the manuscript—'

'But not the diary?'

Alan held up the ancient book. 'And they're going to come for it.'

Simon sighed, air escaping his pursed lips in a hiss. 'Dad said there was something coming in two parts. I spoke to Bet about it, see if he'd said anything to her. I didn't understand at the time.'

'And did he?'

Simon shook his head. 'No. If anything had stuck in her mind she would have told you anyway, Al. You know that.'

'I suppose.'

'These are the two parts. The manuscript and the diary.'

'Makes sense.'

'There's something Dad means us to find out, something he wasn't prepared to tell us straight up.'

'Pretty clear motive.'

'Not to me.'

'Your father was being blackmailed. I suspected something like that, I wasn't sure. Now I am.' They were back at the car. 'And you know what else?' Alan put the diary on the hood of the car and gripped Simon's shoulders. 'There's no easy way to say this, and I may be wrong.'

'Al, what is it?'

Alan closed his eyes for a moment. *Ben might still be alive!* The prospect was unbelievable. It made sense of a kind. If there was a chance, just a tiny chance that Ben was alive, then finding him was the priority. Time was against them now that the killers had the manuscript. He prayed silently that whoever had attacked *Clarissa* would hold out for the diary and perhaps, so long as he had it, Ben might be kept alive.

'I think Ben was being held for ransom.'

'Alan! Shit!'

'Nothing else makes sense. Think about it.'

'Ben's dead, Al.'

'His body was never found at the crash site. When that plane hit the mountain there was a fire, sure, but every other passenger was accounted for, one way or another. Except Ben.'

'His name was on the passenger list.'

'Doesn't mean he was on the plane.'

'Jesus, I can't deal with this.' He looked up suddenly. 'This'll kill Bet.'

'Bet is not to know, not yet, not until we have some sort of proof.'

'But why doesn't Dad explain it? If he was being blackmailed and Ben was the pawn, why doesn't Dad say so? Dad was a rich guy; where's the shame?'

'There is another thing,' Alan suggested. 'The treasure.'

'If there is any treasure.'

'Aren't you curious?'

'Sure. Of course.'

'We could look at this two ways.' He lowered his voice to a barely audible whisper. 'One: a contract was put out by someone and the treasure was just a coincidence.' Alan picked up the diary and waved it at Simon for emphasis.

'Two: the treasure remains the priority. Whoever was blackmailing your folks got wind of it and thought they'd up the stakes.'

'There is a third option, if you're right about Ben: Dad could've offered the treasure in exchange for Ben and something went wrong.'

'Could be. Then again, a fourth possibility—'

'I know, Al, Ben might be dead. No more bargaining chip so kill the victims and have done.'

'Yes.'

Simon slumped against the car. 'This is all just crazy supposition, Al. There's nothing to suggest . . . look what happened to *Clarissa*. You said yourself, why was she attacked so far from land? Why not get rid of the bodies? Why leave the evidence?'

'I didn't say I had the whole picture. Maybe there's something we're missing.'

Simon rubbed at his eyes. 'OK, Al. Let's just take this one step at a time. We'll see what the diary says first.'

'Fine.'

'I'll go and see the professor now.'

'Take the car.'

'You sure?'

'Sure I'm sure. I'll get one of the guys to drop me at home this evening.'

'Look, Al, I need some time to take this in. You don't spare the bloody horses. I just want to clear my head, you know, put things into some kind of perspective.'

Alan slammed the door shut then tapped the roof and walked away. A question began to float in his mind. When to call in the FBI? He had some loose ends needed tidying up. He decided to call Bruno Denotti in Washington. No details about the case, just a 'How are you' type of call. They had met once, on a course at Quantico. Christmas cards were exchanged each year. A portrait of Betina at four weeks had been posted to a small town outside New York, and he and Bet had received two photos in return, one of Bruno Jr. and, a year later, Mabelle, with a note about a transfer to Washington. But they had never co-operated on a case. Opportunity had never arisen.

Maybe now was the time.

17

Bruno Denotti turned up his collar against the Washington chill and headed off in the direction of the Potomac. The call had come as a surprise and he was eager to get to Alfredo's and find out more.

Despite the pleasantness of his surroundings, Bruno had never got used to Washington. He felt somehow isolated, not at all cloaked and anonymous like he had in New York and, as a cop, he was constantly reminded of his vulnerability. Cop? Well, a Fed. So he was more involved in administration and politics, but hey that's where his future lay. Money was better than the NYPD and Marcia had wanted to come to Washington. Get a life, she'd said. Become president. They had laughed about it. Still, it was better than risking getting blown out the water by some doped-up freak on a street corner.

Scalini's was a fifteen-minute walk from the Washington field office. It was quarter to one when Denotti pushed through the glass door of the restaurant.

'Yo! Bruno. How's it hangin'?' Alfredo was behind the long bar that ran down one side of the narrow dining area.

'Good, Alfredo. How's business?'

'Like this, like that. You know.' The place was crammed with lunchtime trade.

'Sure.' Denotti perched on a barstool.

Alfredo Scalini leaned on the polished countertop. 'See that guy's brought out a new book.'

'Yeah? Which guy?'

'Hannibal the cannibal. Whatsisname?'

'Oh, sure. Yeah. . . .' Denotti clicked fingers with the effort of recall. 'Harris. Thomas Harris.'

'That's the guy. Gonna make a film. Make you famous all over again.'

Denotti grinned. Like he needed fame. 'Maybe they'll pay us more, huh.'

'You want somethin' to eat, Bruno, or you here on business?'

'Need to use the phone, Alfredo. That OK?'

'OK. Sure. Help yourself.'

'Catch you later.' Denotti slipped off the stool. He made his way along the bar to a door at its end. Narrow stairs led up to the floor above. At the head of the stairs a small office looked out over the yard at the back and through the small window the warm smell of kitchen refuse percolated into the room.

Denotti closed the door and sat behind the desk, picked up the phone and dialled a number. He waited a while then someone picked up.

'Alan? Yeah, Bruno. How's tricks?' He listened to the pleasantries bouncing off satellites from Australia. 'Sorry about this cloak and dagger stuff. Don't like to take calls in the station if it's not Fed business. Never know who might be tapping the wires.' He gave out a small laugh. 'So, shoot.'

Denotti stood, cradling the phone in the crook of his shoulder and closed the window to neutralize the cloying smell of the garbage. By the time he sat back down he'd got the gist of it from Alan.

'Jesus, Al, you being straight?'

The confirmation beamed into his ear.

'Sure I can help. Two things. One: there's no guarantee; two: you owe me.'

Then a question from Alan.

'I'll tell you. We've got a couple of regional computer support centres. One of 'em's located in Pocatello, Idaho and the other one's at Fort

Monmouth, New Jersey. There's also information technology centres at Butte, Montana and Savannah, Georgia. Now mostly these outfits support field ops and administration. But who knows? I mean, like the databases on these things you wouldn't believe. So we'll start there. Only thing I have to tell you, Al, is this ain't no priority at our end. I'll do what I can but it may be you just keep getting pushed to the back of the queue. Way to speed it up I guess, and I'm thinking on my feet here, is I'll put like maybe a trainee junior on it as say an exercise. That way I can authorize computer time.'

Alan spoke some more, fleshing out the detail to give the FBI man as much information as he reasonably could.

'I'll go with that, Al. If what you're saying holds water then we might be talking indictable offence, kinda makes it our business. Comes to it we got fifty-five field offices and four hundred resident agencies spread all over. If need be I can call in some heavy-duty muscle. But we'll keep it contained just for now.

'Al, anytime you want to talk leave a message on my cell phone and I'll come back to you. Unless it's a real emergency, I'd appreciate it if you didn't call the office.' He recited his cell phone number.

They exchanged information about the next generation of Bedales and Denottis.

'I'll talk at you, Al. Ciao for now.' Denotti put the phone down, spun the chair round and hitched his feet up on the sill. He sat there thinking, trying to ignore the tingling in his spine which was a sure sign that this thing might be bigger than a small-bag favour for a friend. No way was some rookie going to come up smelling sweet on this one. He would start with the four computer centres he'd listed to Al, though he wasn't certain that he'd be able to access military personnel files. Still, worth a shout. He was due some time and Marcia had never been to Georgia. He knew that for sure. And he loved Montana anyhow. Yeah. A few days maybe. He'd tell Marcia tonight. Denotti pulled a fifty from his wallet and shoved it under the blotter.

Alfredo had not moved from his command post behind the bar. He was there waving a dishcloth and shouting instructions to his harried waiters.

'Yo, Bruno. Go OK?'

'Sure.'

'I made you lunch anyways. You looking kinda skinny.'

' 'Ppreciate it, Alfredo.' Denotti reclaimed his barstool. The spaghetti carbonara arrived moments later, studded with chunky pieces of pancetta and draped over with grated English cheddar, just the way he liked it. He reached for his wallet.

'You kiddin' me, Bruno.'

So Denotti returned his money to his back pocket just like he always did whenever he used Scalini's to make the calls he didn't want traced.

'You looking pleased with yourself.' Alfredo slopped Chianti into Bruno's glass.

'It ain't meant to show.'

Alfredo held his hand up. No explanations needed. 'Enjoy.'

And Denotti did, because if he could close the loop on what Alan had told him, it might just be the type of break to see him promoted to ADC.

18

Bernard Levy looked at the two faces across the table. Their expressions were suitably grim. They were in the office of Samuel J. Baxter, Secretary of Energy. Seated next to him was Bart Grunberg, head of the department's counter-intelligence unit. Both men had received a briefing note ahead of the meeting and he noticed that neither of them had their copies. He had kept the note short and to the point, deploying a carefully selected assembly of words so that the message was hard-hitting and though he fell short of apportioning blame, the implication was clear.

'Sam,' he started, his tone genial, 'there's no way we're going to keep the lid on this thing, not with the number of people that need to know.'

Grunberg nodded accompanied by a tiny movement of the lips that had relief stencilled all over it.

'You said that to the President?' Samuel J. Baxter was surprised.

'Sure. Got to be realistic. The downside is, if word gets out then top heads will roll.'

Grunberg's lips retreated back to a tight line and his head dropped a couple of degrees.

'First thing we need to decide is how to find the sender, what tack we're going to take,' Levy said.

The Secretary of Energy arched an eyebrow. 'I'm sure you're going to tell us, Bernard.'

He ignored the secretary for a moment. 'Ideas, Bart?'

Grunberg nodded. 'Sure. Every single employee at every weapons lab will have to be vetted, questioned and eliminated from the inquiry starting with those with security rating access to any part of the Radar Ocean Imaging Programme.'

'Is that what you had in mind, Bernard?'

'Pretty much, Sam. Only problem is we don't have a whole hell of a lot of time.'

Sam Baxter suddenly straightened in his seat. 'There's a deadline? You didn't put that in your note.'

'Twenty-six days,' Bernard said casually.

'Jeezus!' Grunberg hissed, dismay sagging his face.

'His help at this stage would be appreciated, Bart, but don't rely on it. Now let's start with an investigation into the number of foreign scientists allowed to visit Los Alamos, Lawrence Livermore and the other labs. I know Los Alamos had almost three hundred from China alone last year. Could be linkage with the hundred odd China-born employees who work there. I want the same check-out and cross referencing at Livermore, Scandia and Oak Ridge.'

Grunberg started scratching notes and talking at the same time. 'Starting with departments that had anything to do with ROIP?'

'I think that's sensible, Bart, like Department X at Los Alamos for instance and begin with personnel with "Q" clearance, from the director down.'

'Narrows it down a bit, I guess.'

'Don't guess, Bart. Guessing's no good to me. Now, you've both seen the report by Senator Cox. He points out that the Chinese have got twenty-three missiles aimed right at us, all based on our own Titan design. Guy who gave it them was an officer in the US Army. He's now a general in the PLA.'

Sam Baxter prickled at the reminder of the historical security lapses from the laboratories now in his charge. 'I've already taken measures.'

'Want to tell me about them, Sam?'

'Bart.'

'Sure.' Grunberg's small eyes swivelled up to meet Levy's and then returned to the table-top. 'I . . . we've stopped all work on the computers at Los Alamos, Scandia and Lawrence Livermore. We need to put tighter security measures into place. Each laboratory is networked internally and to each other but there is no connection to and therefore no access from the outside world. Test data and the rest has been lifted right out the systems so we're implementing training sessions on computer security.'

'Brings to mind bolting horses and closing stable doors.' Levy smiled with no hint of irony. 'Problem is, and correct me if I'm wrong, but this data can be downloaded on to disk and e-mailed from a non-network desk-top.'

'Not quite,' the Secretary for Energy interrupted with a small shake of his head. 'None of the unclassified computers are linked to the Internet precisely so they will not be vulnerable to hacking. But the idea of the new measures is to prevent data download from any of the classified systems period.'

'What else is happening at the labs that I need to know about?'

'Aside from increasing the cyber-security programme across the computer complex, we've begun polygraphing employees with access to the most sensitive DoE programs. . . .'

'But we'll concentrate on ROIP.'

'Easy to switch the emphasis.'

'And?'

'Doubled the DoE counter-intelligence budget to thirty-nine million dollars.'

'Got a feeling we'll be burning a whole bunch of that cash in the next few weeks. OK. China's now got six hundred supercomputers they can use to run weapons tests. They need the data so cyber-security will cut their feeds from the labs, for a while at least.'

Grunberg looked mystified. 'I thought that intelligence was restricted.'

'What? To DoE. Bart, a CIA guy saw them at the . . . some place in Beijing. . . .'

'Institute of Applied Physics and Computational Mathematics.'

'Thank you, Bart, exactly.' Bernard Levy could not help a smirk.

The secretary spoke. 'There's more to this Bernard than just a breach of computer security at the labs.'

'So help me out here, Sam.'

'There's a whole lot more to weapons development than just the work at the labs. There's design, materials testing, guidance systems, launch vehicles, flight control, evasion mechanisms and so on. A lot of the work is contracted out to commercial outfits. Security measures are phased. There's the internal security of the firms we invite to tender for pieces of work and we do vet these people. But there's also political control. That's where gaps can appear.'

'You've lost me.'

'The six hundred computers China acquired, for example, were subject to export control. Problem is that this administration's moved authority for granting export licences from State to Commerce. State's interested in national security. DoC on the other hand's more interested in making a buck. Anybody'll tell you that the DoC were and are real keen to develop trading links with China, so they relaxed the export laws and Beijing took advantage. Sure, we've got to tighten our end, but Commerce have got to stop giving this stuff away once we've paid for development.'

Bart Grunberg chimed in, 'If we have to check out everyone with classified access, we're also going to have to do the same with every employee of every commercial outfit we ever signed a contract with on ROIP.' Grunberg relaxed back in his chair. It was an impossible task within the time-frame set by the head of the FBI.

Bernard Levy considered what he had heard. 'Sam, you've got to report back to the President's foreign intelligence advisory board.'

'Sure thing.'

'President's also instructed the national counter-intelligence policy board to assess vulnerability at non-government facilities.'

'That's in hand, yes.'

'OK. So I'm going to make life a little bit easier for Bart here.'

'How's that?'

'I have an idea about the perpetrator, from the note sent to the Oval Office.'

'Yeah? What, you sucked an ID out of the soup of say fifty thousand government and non-government defence workers?' Grunberg stammered in disbelief.

'Something like that, Bart. We're looking for a female, fifty plus, probably with "Q" clearance, or maybe honey-trapping someone who has.'

'And is this person Chinese, Mr Levy?'

Bernard Levy shook his head. 'Oh no, Bart. Straight-up American WASP.'

19

The clement weather was continuing in the Tri-Valley area of northern California. Gertrude Ziegle had taken the bus out of town and was now walking slowly along East Avenue. When she arrived at number 7000 she slowed up some more but didn't stop. The main gates to the Lawrence Livermore National Laboratory allowed her a glimpse of the sprawling, square-mile laboratory complex. It had all started at Los Alamos, high in the mountains of northern New Mexico where Robert Oppenheimer had founded the 'secret city' to build the first atomic bomb in 1945 and from where, forty years later, Wen Ho Lee had stolen the legacy codes for W-88 for eventual transfer to China. In so doing he had demonstrated that anything was possible.

Jamie-Jake walked alongside in that shambling gait which he had affected as a slouch teenager. Even the drill sergeants at the US Marine Corps had failed to eliminate it completely. He turned his face to the sun and smiled his toothy grin. Then her mind released its grasp of his memory and the laboratory gates came once more into focus.

Situated three miles east of Livermore City in Alameda County, the site was first used as a naval air station in the 1940s. In 1952 it was transferred to the US Atomic Energy Commission and established as a nuclear weapons and magnetic fusion energy research facility. Ownership then passed to the Department of Energy. The buildings had now escalated into a tangle of blockhouses operated by the University of

California on behalf of the department's energy research and development administration.

'The Republicans will keep on comparing that little Chinaman to Klaus Fuchs. Of course you remember him, Jamie-Jake. I've told you before: the Los Alamos scientist who passed secrets of the A-bomb to the Soviets in the 1940s. Now the Democrats have chimed in. Oh yes! All scumbags, all with personal ambition on the agenda, all castigating those they think are responsible.' Gertrude Ziegle stared through at the blockhouses. She'd make Wen Ho Lee, and Fuchs come to think of it, look like pygmies.

'And you remember the Rosenbergs too, Jamie-Jake?'

She waited for an answer then chided herself for her forgetfulness. 'Of course not. You'd have been too young. Have I spoken about them before? Maybe not.' She looked away to the deep blue of the sky. 'They were executed. When was that . . . 1953. Julius and Ethel Rosenberg. See, they got caught, Jamie-Jake, for passing secrets to Moscow. Just like Fuchs.'

Gertrude Ziegle shook her head and smiled ruefully at the imagined surprise that sounded in her mind.

Someone walked by with a dog, watching the old lady muttering to herself on the street. Had she looked up, Gertrude Ziegle would have seen pity in the stranger's eyes.

'They can't touch me. They have to find me first, Jamie-Jake, so I wouldn't worry. Not just yet. And when they do, if they do, well I'll always have a hold over them. You see I know all about what goes on in there.'

She returned to her house on Fig Tree Drive sitting alone in the familiar bus, following the familiar route back into Livermore. In her basement office, Gertrude Ziegle switched on her Dell desk-top and opened a file entitled *Payback*.

The morning paper lay by her feet. The headline caught her eye. Something about two men being gunned down in New York City. A revenge killing the newspaper called it. Revenge. Those amateurs didn't know the meaning of revenge. And with that thought fresh in her mind, Gertrude Ziegle went back to her keyboard.

20

The old man was kneeling on the rough floor of the hut. Emmanuel Cortez stood in the shadows by the bed.

Cobra watched Cortez dab at the flubber around his mouth with a white handkerchief. The fence had done his job and done it well. The jewels from the yacht had all been moved. The two plants, Cortez had explained, the pink diamond ring and the gold and emerald brooch, had not attracted the interest of the police. Not yet. He had people watching the store. He had suggested more time, perhaps a month, and then he would retrieve the two pieces and sell them outside the country, if they were not already sold, in which case he would collect his cut, Cobra's cut. Cobra had nodded his agreement to the plan.

A plastic shopping bag bearing the logo of a Manila supermarket squatted on the table. It contained bundled banknotes. All used. Almost $200,000. Cortez had offered the money as a penitent might a sacrifice. Supplication. And then his *coup de grâce*. He had brought the old man forward, shoving him to the floor in a pathetic gesture of machismo.

Sharif Mohammed was sixty-eight years old. A frail, stooping intellectual who bore his age with the dignity of the learned. He had devoted his life to the acquisition of knowledge and rejoiced in teaching what he knew. His face was remarkably unlined, his skin pale and delicate. Long strands of wispy, white hair floated on to his shoulders and a thin beard hung limply on to his narrow chest. Chinese features predominated among the mixed blood of his forebears and age had imbued him with a feathery fragility, a translucence akin to the manuscript he had deciphered.

The extent of the high regard in which he was held by the academic community of the Philippines was equalled in intensity by the humiliation he felt kneeling here, wrists bound with hemp so tightly that he could no longer feel any sensation in his hands.

Cobra came forward, standing so close that the old man could not see his face. He stared down, incensed, felt the tremor of rage filter through his core and that strange intoxication brought on by the imminence of death. He swallowed to stay the nausea.

'You have told me everything?' His voice was reasonable, quiet in spite of the turmoil.

'Yes. There is a diary. The diary will show where the treasure is buried. I have told you this.' Sharif Mohammed's delivery was slow, deliberate. The patience of an intellect superior to that of his many past charges.

Cobra felt the implied superiority prickle his veins. The old fool's placid humility enraged him further. With a movement of electric speed, Cobra bought his knee up into the scholar's bony chest, spilling him sideways on to the floor even as his ribs popped free of their cartilage restraints. A mix of blood and spittle dribbled on to the old man's chin. Air rattled in his lungs and the vessels and muscles of his scrawny neck stood out in harsh relief as he fought for breath.

'How much treasure is there?' Cobra was losing control. Demons rising. 'How much!' he screamed.

Sharif Mohammed seemed not to have heard. His puny frame continued juddering in spasmodic efforts to clutch at air. Eyes tightly closed. 'The diary . . . in the . . . diary.' His voice was broken to a hoarse croak.

Cobra kicked the prostrate figure. Like kicking a dog. Bitter-sweet pleasure.

Behind him a grey metal locker of the type found in any high-school corridor stood against the wall, its dented door hanging open. Cobra reached inside, pulled out a Glock 17 and cocked the pistol.

The old man did not seem afraid. Cobra had searched for fear in the man's eyes. He saw only resignation, an acceptance, a quiet finality.

The door burst open. A rush of outside light filled the shadow. Mae-li was staring at him, transfixed by the scene, mouth open. He saw her wide eyes slide down his arm to the gun in his hand, then to the old man curled on the floor, gasping like a landed fish.

She knelt beside him and cradled the man's head. 'You bastard!' She spat the words at Cobra. 'How much more killing? How much more suffering?' She wiped the old man's chin gently. 'You fucking pig!'

Cobra raised his foot and kicked her away, hard, up against the wall. She flew at him, small bunched fists flailing. He slapped her aside like a gnat. The blow was enough to stun her and Mae-li slumped, semi-conscious.

Cobra aimed the Glock and fired. The report fractured the stillness. The old man's body lifted off the floor. His legs twitched then he was still. A neat entry wound above his right ear. It seemed innocuous. And a pool of crimson blood began to seep from underneath him. Cobra spun round, raised his arm, aimed at Mae-li, between her eyes.

'Don't you cross me . . . ever!'

The muscles of his forearm stood out. He clenched and unclenched his jaw, feeling sweat running down his cheeks irritating the scar on his neck. He scratched at it angrily. Then he lowered his arm and hurled the weapon into the steel cabinet.

'Jimmy!' Cobra yelled. His lieutenant had been waiting outside the hut. He came in, glanced down at the corpse. Stood, waiting for instructions.

Cobra walked towards Emmanuel Cortez. 'Shut the door, Jimmy.'

Cortez shrank back, pressed against the wall. Kept his eyes on Cobra, head pushed back so that his chins spread on to his neck.

Cobra stopped very close. He could feel the fat man's heat and the faint ammoniacal smell of urine. 'You are an accomplice. Again.' Cobra's voice was pleasant.

Cortez opened his eyes. 'Yes . . .' he stammered.

'Where was he from?' Cobra palmed the fat man's genitals, groping.

'San Carlos University . . . Cebu City.'

Cobra squeezed, feeling the fat man's balls scoot in his hand. 'Too close.' He squeezed harder. 'Jimmy,' he said without looking round. 'Take our fat friend here and the old man to Manila. Dump the body. Make it look like a robbery. Use a charter plane. Pay cash. Money's on the table.'

He heard Jimmy go to the table, the break in his stride as he stepped over the corpse, the rustle of plastic as he rummaged banknotes. 'And you, Cortez, you know everything I know. But I still need you.' He tightened his grip. Cortez winced. 'You get the emerald, when *all* the pieces are sold.'

Cortez nodded, his head pumping up and down in frantic agreement.

From across the room came the staccato of electronic blips of Jimmy dialling on his mobile phone. In low tones he organized the charter plane. Another blip.

'All arranged.' Jimmy snapped his mobile shut and stuffed it in the back pocket of his jeans.

Cortez was trying to speak. Cobra eased his grip. 'Talk, fat boy!'

'The diary . . . if there is one. Who's going to . . . translate it?' He had to assume it would be written in the same language. Cobra was an animal. Had killed the old man when he still needed him. The irrational act of a madman.

Cortez was right: it had been a mistake. The fury had blinded him. 'Not your problem,' Cobra hissed. 'I'll think of something,' and with that Cobra gave one, final, vicious twist. Cortez screamed and collapsed to the floor, clutching his genitals, knees drawn up.

Cobra turned round. Mae-li whimpered in the far corner. He stepped towards her, then punched her face. A single trail of dark blood snaked out of one nostril, meandered around the side of her mouth and dripped off her chin. The bridge of her nose was already bruising, a sharp, half-diamond of bone pushing out one side. Fucking whore was no good to him now. Not perfect any more.

Cobra looked at Jimmy. 'The fuck you staring at?' He nodded towards the slumped body of the old man. 'Bag him.'

Jimmy opened the door, yelled instructions and stood there until someone threw him a thick, cloth sack and a piece of torn sheeting.

Jimmy quickly bound the old man's head, to stop him leaking, picked the body up easily and dumped it into the sack.

'Cortez, get the fuck out of here.' Cobra barked the order.

Emmanuel Cortez needed no encouragement. With one hand still massaging his injured testicles, he scurried out.

Jimmy heaved the sack on to his shoulder. A vehicle engine revved outside.

'You know the score, Jimmy. Empty wallet on board. Kill a whore, too, if you think it'll look more authentic.'

'Could just dump the body at sea.' Jimmy braved his opinion.

Cobra calmly shook his head. 'No. He'll be missed. Without a body, the police will be suspicious. This way, he'll be another statistic.'

'What about Cortez?'

'Leave him alone for now.'

'I'll see you tonight.'

A thought occurred to Cobra. 'Get that fat fuck back in here.'

Cortez appeared in the doorway.

'Anyone know he was with you?'

Cortez shook his head violently. 'If he said anything, he would have told them he was going to see a rich man in Manila, for whom he was doing some private work.'

'Even better.'

Emmanuel Cortez did not bother with parting pleasantries. He ran out. Car doors slammed, wheels spun in the dirt and the car drove away, headed for the airfield north-east of General Santos City.

21

Far above, seagulls wheeled on a tropical breeze taking turns to plunge shrieking to the surface to pluck small, wriggling, silver fish from the sea. The prisoner sensed their freedom, their speed. He concentrated on the sensation of wind over their wings until he could feel it himself, gliding over his body, fluttering his hair, cooling the heat of the sun burning down on his back. He flew in wide arcs, gazing down at the ruffled water. And then he dipped his head and fell towards the water, the force of his dive pulling tears from his eyes as he raced towards the cold embrace of the sea.

The clang of metal against rock brought him awake. For a brief moment of release he was uncertain of his dark surroundings. Then his eyes focused on the circle of light high above. Tentatively he placed a hand on his head and instead of hair felt the prickle of his bare scalp. He blinked to clear the tears and sat up on the bed just as the bucket came within reach. He gathered the bucket with both hands, lowered it on to his tea-chest and untied the rope. Carefully he reattached the line to the latrine bucket and, remembering his note, tied it to the handle. He needed more paper and matches. This done, the prisoner tugged the rope twice feeling the resistance from the unseen hands high above. Shadows moved in and out of the circle of light and the latrine bucket began its ascent to the surface. He watched it go until it was lost in the gloom, bending over his food while he did so until he was sure that none of his waste would rain down and contaminate the rice.

Before, he used to eat all the food and then defecate into the bucket. Now his routine was different. During the long days he had melted down candle wax. Using broken pencils as reinforcements, he had fashioned a large bowl and a lid to cover it, a smaller bowl from which to eat and a spoon.

He lit two candles and carefully emptied the bucket into the larger of his two bowls. Satisfied that nothing had spilled he set the lid on top. This done he then placed the empty bucket on the ground. Taking the smaller bowl, he tipped a little water into it from the bottle that had come down with the food. Slowly, with deliberate movements, the prisoner washed his teeth, taking his time, enjoying the experience. Finished, he drank the mouthful of water and refilled the bowl. With a rag and a small bar of soap he dampened and lathered his scalp and taking extra care shaved his head. The process took ten minutes. The dirty water went into the bucket and the prisoner sat down to breakfast. He divided the food, rice and fish and today there was a banana, into three portions and spooned the first of these into the smaller bowl. While he performed his ritual, with the same intensity and delicacy as a Japanese might perform a tea ceremony, he recited a chant:

'*My name is Ben and I am well. My home is England where I dwell. The trees around me burst with green. The feel of life forever seen.*'

Sitting on an upturned red plastic pail with his knees spread wide to allow him to get closer to the tea-chest, Ben began to eat.

22

Simon dialled P-Unit. *Come on, come on.* 'Al?'

'Charlie.'

'Charlie, where's Al?'

'Right here.'

'Put him on.'

Seconds ticked by.

'Simon, what's up?'

'Can you get over to the university?'

'Now?'

'Now.' The clock in the hallway showed just after one. 'I've just called Professor Pereda's office. His secretary answered the phone, told me he'd left this morning on a business trip.'

'So?'

'So when I asked if he'd be back later she said no. He's gone to a funeral, some university lecturer, in the Philippines.'

'What!' Alan almost shouted. 'The Philippines?' Christ! Conspiracy theories rampaged through his head. 'Are you *sure* it's the Philippines?'

'Yes, sure!'

'On my way. We'll meet in the car-park.'

'The Philippines!' Alan looked away, one hand on his hip, the other massaging his lips. Agitated. He spun back. 'Where exactly?'

Simon shrugged. 'I didn't think to ask. She just told me the Philippines. I didn't press for any more info.'

Alan agreed. 'Let's hope she's still here.'

They marched into the university building, Alan striding out ahead. Pereda's secretary was at her desk, typing away on her word processor. She looked up as they came in. A brief flicker of recognition illuminated her face.

'Miss Hastings. Is there anyone else here?'

Pereda's secretary made an exaggerated show of looking around the empty waiting room. 'No one that I can see,' she remarked with dry irony.

Alan flashed his badge at her. 'Where is Professor Pereda?'

'Is he in some sort of trouble?'

'No. But you will be if you don't answer my questions.'

Miss Hastings sighed. 'He flew to the Philippines, this morning.'

'Why?'

'There was a message on my machine when I arrived for work.'

'Can you play it back?'

'I'm sorry, I wiped it off.'

'What did it say?'

'That he was flying to Manila to attend the funeral of Dr Sharif Mohammed.'

'Who's Dr Mohammed?'

'He is – was, Professor of Classics at the University of Southern Philippines.'

'Jesus!' Simon gasped.

'There's your starting point,' Alan muttered. He faced Miss Hastings. 'What happened to him?'

Susan Hastings arched her eyebrows. 'He died, would be my guess.'

Alan allowed himself just the tiniest smile.

'And where is the professor staying in Manila, and don't tell me a hotel would be your guess?'

She scribbled the address on a notepad, ripped the sheet off and handed it to Alan.

The car-park was baking. Alan fumbled with the keys and unlocked the driver's door. 'I've come round to your way of thinking.'

'How d'you mean?'

'I don't believe in coincidence either.'

He frisked himself for his Nokia and scrolled its memory for the number that would connect him directly to Filippo Santos in Manila. An eternity passed before the phone was answered.

Alan wanted details on the death of a Dr Sharif Mohammed. It must have happened sometime in the last seventy-two hours was his guess and yes, in response to a question from Santos, it might be critical to his investigation.

They drove back to the office while their apprehension clotted.

'It could be nothing.' Alan did not believe that for a second, but he didn't even want to think about getting ahead of himself.

Simon pointed out through the windshield, squinting skywards. 'See that?'

'What?'

'Thought I saw a flying pig there for a second.'

'OK. I doubt it's nothing.'

'It puts our guy in the Philippines, just like you've always figured.'

Almost an hour went by before Filippo Santos called back. Alan and Simon were on their third coffee, nerves raw. Alan snatched the phone.

'I don't know what's going on with you, Alan. Doctor Sharif Mohammed was murdered.' The crackle of the loudspeaker did nothing to hide the surprise in the Manila police officer's voice. 'How did you know?'

'I'll explain later. Tell me what you've got.'

'You know who he is?'

'Confirm this. Professor of Classics at the University of Southern Philippines in Cebu City.'

'Bull's-eye. OK. He was found late Sunday night in Malate.'

'Where's that?'

'It's a district in the south-east of Manila, wall-to-wall girlie bars mostly. Strange area for an academic to hang out. His body was in an unlit back alley between Mabini Street and Del Pilar Street.'

'Who found him?'

'Tourist. American college kid looking for a lay. Had a bad night.'

'MO?'

'One shot, through the head. Coroner reckons he'd been dead maybe twelve hours before he was found.'

'Midday, Sunday.'

'Around there. Looks like he was robbed. But that's not all, not the motive by the look of things.'

'What d'you mean?'

'There was a girl with him, local tart. Shot as well. Looks like he may have come off worst in a negotiation on price.'

'Twelve hours? Someone would have seen the bodies before, surely?'

'Maybe, maybe not.'

'Could be he was killed elsewhere and dumped.'

'Could be.'

'Have you got a make on the weapon type?'

'Yeah, Small calibre pistol. Glo . . . ck.'

Alan registered Filippo Santos's slight hesitation over the pronunciation.

'Alan . . . you there?'

'Sure, yeah.' Something else was bothering Alan. He was thinking about the timings. It was all too quick. The academic had been killed on Sunday. Yet the funeral was happening within twenty-four hours! And this was a murder. He put the question to Santos.

'He's a Sunni Muslim. Their religion dictates burial within a day of death.'

Alan thanked Santos and replaced the phone in its cradle. He rubbed his eyes and yawned, raising the back of his hand to his mouth. 'The Philippines it is then. No doubt about it.'

Simon flopped into a chair. 'And they've got the manuscript.'

'Yep. But have they got a copy of the diary, because if they haven't, they sure as hell know it exists now.'

'Seems to me like our next move's already been decided.'

'Yeah. Get over to the Philippines. We're going to need help on the ground there. Santos has got to be briefed, thoroughly.' Alan fumbled in his pocket. He smoothed the page from Miss Hastings's notepad. 'Professor Pereda's staying at the Manila Hotel, in a place called Rizal Park.'

'Are you OK leaving Bet for a while, and Betina?'

'No, not really. But needs must and all that.' Alan shook his head slowly. 'There's no shortcut here, I'm afraid. I wish there was.'

'Guess you're right, Al. God! I'm so tired I can hardly see straight.'

'Ring Pereda will you, find out how long he's going to be there.'

Loud rap at the door and Charlie walked in. He gazed at them, one to the other and back again. 'Well, you two look like shit.'

'And nice to see you too, Charlie. What've you got?' Alan asked.

'You had a call. Bloke called Bruno Denotti. Said it was important.'

23

Alan didn't go into work next morning. Instead the family attended the private funeral for the McGoverns. The bodies were cremated and the ashes scattered over the turquoise spread of the ocean beyond the low laurel hedge at the bottom of the garden.

Betina was playing with her mother, chasing a small rubber ball on her little wobbly legs, as if life had only the best of its fruits to offer her.

'We set on this?' Alan asked, sitting across from Simon at the breakfast table. The investigation couldn't move forward, not without a translation of the diary, and that meant waiting for Professor Pereda to return from the Philippines. Simon had spoken to Pereda, at his hotel in Manila, on Monday night.

'Pereda's flight gets in at two. I'll pick him up from the airport and we'll go straight to the university so he can get back to work.'

'OK.' Alan sat back, glancing through the kitchen window. How to put this. 'I've spoken with Santos. Haven't told him much, just that he needs to clear his desk for a while. I'll brief him, then he can start putting the word about. Can't operate from his office or his home for security reasons. We'll hole up in a hotel. I told him to make arrangements.'

'So how do I contact you?'

Alan shook his head. 'Santos is going out on a limb. You don't contact me. Or him.'

'What about your mobile?'

'Oh. Sure, the mobile, yeah. Call me on that. But only if it's vital. I meant no contact via land lines.'

Simon gave a small shrug. 'Whatever you say.'

'Just make sure Pereda works on the diary as fast as he can. The sooner we get our ducks lined up the better. Then we can start dictating and draw this bugger out.'

It all sounded so ridiculously easy. Take a plane, lay a trail, bang-bang you're dead.

'I hope this Santos guy is good.'

'The best.' Alan checked his watch. 'Quarter of one. You'd better get going.'

Simon stood up. 'Take it easy, Al. Don't take risks, you hear me?'

'Loud and clear.' He stood up, shook Simon's hand, walked him to the front door and watched him drive away in the jeep.

God, he hated lying, hated deceit. This wasn't deceit. It was protection. He could justify it, of course. So why did he still feel dirty? He'd made his travel arrangements yesterday afternoon, after Simon had left the office and taken Bet's car home. After his telephone call to Bruno Denotti.

He went out into the garden lost in an overwhelming surge of love for his family. He gathered his daughter in his arms then turned to his wife. 'Bet, what do you think about a little companion for Betina?'

'I think Betina would like that, Al.'

'So do I. I've got an hour before I have to go to the airport.'

What the FBI agent had told him was dynamite. It blew his investigation wide open. His first objective was to get over to Washington for a head to head with Bruno. He reckoned on two or three days in the States before connecting to Manila.

Bet stopped suddenly, her hand on his arm. 'You'll call me tonight from Manila?'

'Ten o'clock. Set your watch by it.'

'Al, this isn't going to be . . . dangerous?'

' 'Course not, love.'

The FBI had come up with a name. As to danger, who could tell what lay ahead?

24

Alan hated flying. Not so much a fear of flying, more a fear of crashing. The plane had crossed the international date line so by the time he landed at Dulles under leaden Washington skies, he was relieved. A cab took him downtown to an innocuous hotel called The Regent. After a wash and a shave he took a walk using a street map to make his way to a restaurant called Scalini's. Bruno was waiting at a small table by the window.

By the second course they had caught up on all the family news. It was Bruno who broached the reason for the meeting. 'So the stuff I gave you on the phone was important, huh?' He slurped a string of spaghetti sending a spray of Bolognese sauce on to the white paper tablecloth.

'Could be, Bruno.' Alan filled in the details of the case between mouthfuls.

'A hit. Jesus. Well, this guy may be able to shed some light. You going to go see him?'

Alan nodded. 'It may be nothing, but I've got to check it out so yes, I'll take a trip down there tomorrow.'

'Thought you might.' Bruno described the man Alan was planning to see according to the service records Frankie's people had unearthed. He reached into his pocket and pulled out a piece of folded paper. 'Details are on there. Address, phone number and directions. Also flight times day and night.'

Alan secreted the paper in his jacket. 'Thanks, Bruno.'

The waiter came and cleared their plates.

'Actually, Alan, I didn't do a whole helluva lot. See I figured on taking some time off with Marcia but all leave's been cancelled. I mean everybody. Friend of mine out of the New Jersey office, Frankie, he got some of his people on it. You owe me, I owe him, way it goes.'

Alan laughed. 'So you've got something big on then?'

'Big's not the word, Alan. This thing's alpha star.'

'Bloody hell! I remember the priority rating system from that time at Quantico. Alpha star's unprecedented.'

'Sure is. I even figured I might've come on your little trip with you but no can do. A pile of dog turds just landed in my in-tray and get this, Al, the goddamned in-tray's starting to slide real fast toward a great, big fan spinning like crazy in the corner.'

'Some serial killer on the rampage?'

'Nah, bit more complicated, serious national security matter. Got a briefing coming up from the director. Thing of it is, the director doesn't give briefings, if you get my meaning!'

'Makes me appreciate this all the more.' Alan tapped his jacket to indicate the note. 'Anyway, lips sealed then.'

'You're a cop, so what are you going to do, go sell the story to the *Australian Daily News* or whatever it is you guys read down there?'

Alan laughed again. 'Only if it's going to make me rich, Bruno.'

So Bruno told the story. 'So you see, Al, the threat states that the blueprint for the country's radar detection system will be released to China. Wacko who's been doing this has been stuffing secrets into their pockets since 1986. And time's ticking by real fast. This asshole's handed us a deadline like it's some kind of ultimatum or something. It's got everyone real spooked from the director down.'

The conversation moved on to other things. Alan ordered a tiramisu and a third bottle of Chianti. They parted outside the restaurant after Alan insisted on paying the tab. He watched Bruno's cab disappear into the traffic then turned and began to walk back to the hotel, thinking about his trip in the morning.

25

George Gabriel Baker had been named after the state in which he'd been born fifty-two years before. He still lived there, in a wooden cabin at the edge of a forest outside Dublin, Georgia. The kids had left, Tom to New York, an actor, and George Jr., a woodsman, to the other side of town.

Alan followed the road due west out of Dublin trying to get used to driving on the right-hand side of the road. It wasn't much of a place. But he guessed that after the horror of Vietnam, it was home to George Gabriel Baker, and that was about as sweet an ambition as any man could want.

The former marine corps sergeant was sitting on the stoop nursing a glass of lemonade as Alan pulled the hire car off the forest track.

George Baker walked towards the car, raising his hand in a casual wave of greeting, but his face held none of the friendliness of the action. Instead, Alan saw misgivings, apprehension, as though Baker was expecting pain from the meeting. He was tall, Alan noticed, and strong-looking. He would have been formidable in his day, war paint and khakis.

'How y'awl. Din have no trouble finding the place?' George Baker asked.

'No. Your directions were perfect.' Alan had telephoned from the motel and listened patiently while the ex-soldier explained how to find the cabin, checking Bruno's instructions as he listened. He followed

Baker up the stoop to a couple of chairs on the porch. There was a jug of lemonade on the table.

'Molly, ma wife, she's left us some refreshment. Gone to town for shoppin'. Reckon we've mebbe an hour to talk.'

'Should be plenty.'

Baker poured lemonade for Alan and sat in his rocker, waiting. Didn't ask questions. No small talk about the weather or what life was like in Australia.

Alan raised his glass, sipped, nodded his approval.

'Sure can cook, can Molly.' Baker paused. 'How d'you find me?'

'MIA association, indirectly. Mister Baker, I'll come straight to the point. There've been some killings. Who, when, where, how, that's not important right now, what is important is my suspicion that the person responsible may be, I stress *may be* someone you once knew.'

George Baker nodded his understanding. 'Ain't no surprise. Figured it must be somethin' of the kind. You gotta understand, mister, see I got no interest in the details. But I'll help you if I can.'

'Thank you.' Alan waited, just long enough to let the weight of George Baker's apprehension settle. 'You were in the marine corps training programme at Fort Jefferson in 1968?'

'Correct. Joined the corps that Fall. Stayed in twenty years.'

Pride and bitterness in equal measure, Alan thought. 'You were in first platoon, training company.'

'Right again. Thirty of us boys started out. Only 'bout twenty or so still standing by th'end.'

Alan set down his lemonade, hunched slightly forwards. 'Do you know what happened to your fellow trainees?'

'Some of them, sure. Real close situation, training. Makes you real dependent on one another. Natural you gonna take an interest in what happens to 'em.'

Alan wondered just how tight Baker's recall would be. A sergeant in the marine corps meant the guy had to be switched on. Everybody knew the NCOs ran the army, any army.

'Like I say, some fell out of training. Din have it, I guess. We started out with thirty boys. Nine fell out. Of the rest, two left after minimum time. One killed in a road crash, two is serving time, nine died in 'Nam. Leaves seven of us. Three of them since gone to the Lord. Two of them boys is MIA in 'Nam. Leaves me and Sam Lewin. Living Atlantic City last I heard.'

'I want to talk about the MIAs, George. Can I call you George?'

'Surely can.'

'The MIAs?'

'Tom Duffy's one. He's on a forward air patrol close to Da Nang. Tet offensive goin' down. On some kinda recce mission. Anyways, seems the plane got shot down by rifle fire. Word comes through from the NVA that two boys walked out the wreck. Description they give, one of them fits Tom Duffy.'

'And the other one, the other MIA, George?'

George Baker shook his head. 'He was always different. Somethin' 'bout that boy never could figure. Good soldier, mind, real hard, real tough. Name's Kepinski, Billy-Ray Kepinski.'

'Tell me about him, George.'

George cast his mind back over the years. 'I remember him comin' into camp one day, arms all bandaged up and blood seepin' through. We all reckoned he been mutilatin' hissell. Then we seen what he done. Had hissell tattooed. Each arm, with mean, ugly-lookin' critters. Snakes. Everone call him Cobra after that. Though he weren't never too fond of communicatin'.'

'Can you remember anything else?'

Baker's eyes became small, crescent moons. 'He your man? Wouldin surprise me none.' He reached over for the jug, poured himself lemonade. 'There was this one time . . .' – he sipped his drink – 'always remember it as a bystander might recall.' He set the drink down, stared out into the forest, puckered his lips to a tight line and slowly let air escape in a hiss. 'The reveille bell went, four-thirty. I get up, still all bleary eyed and that, standin' in line at the end of my bunk, waiting for the head count as usual. Only one's missing, see. I don't pay it no mind, just glad the drilly ain't gonna be chewing my ass. He's hollerin' and yellin.

'The drilly, he come on over to me and says "Baker, you get down to the heads and have a real good look". "Yessir", I says and run on down there. Still dark out, so I put on the light. Nothin' I can see, just a long line of cubicles. I get on my hands and knees, look under the walls, but I don't see nothin'. I stand and look in on each one. Nothin' down the first side. Then I turn to look down the other side and that's when I seen him.

'Virgin mother of God. He's there, strung up and hangin' with his feet restin' on the bowl, tied either end of a broom handle. He been gutted like a rabbit, everthin' fallin' out of him like you wouldn't believe.

'I was on the floor with my back against the cold tiles. Can't say how I got like that. Figured I musta just fell. Couldn't take my eyes offa him. I sicked up. That's when I yelled for the drilly to come.'

'Gutted? Quartered?' Alan was aware of his own breathlessness.

'Yessir. Just like this.' George traced a large cross over his abdomen.

'What was the weapon used?'

'Knife of some kind. Huntin' knife mebbe. Nothin' ever found.'

'Jesus.' Alan leaned back, visualizing the killing. A breeze brought the smell of wet grass from the forest, obfuscating the stench of the dead boy.

'I'll remember his face 'til the day I die. Real surprised look, eyes all wide. Name was Jamie-Jake Mulcahy.' Baker looked down at his feet, rocking gently. 'Happin on the day I turned nineteen. Some kinda way to become a man. Makes you grow up real fast when you see that kinda thing.'

Silence. Pregnant with George Baker's memories. Then Alan asked softly, 'Where's he buried, George, this boy, Mulcahy?'

'Now there's a thin'. Marines din want make no fuss. Buried that day in camp. Died on active duty was the official line. Din want no upset with the family, I guess. Drilly was real insistent that's the way it happin. And I the only one who seen him, so's up to me to keep ma mouth shut, if I want to get on in the marines.'

'You were threatened?'

'Reckon so. But I figure nothin' to be gained by upsettin' Jamie's folks, so I just done what the drilly say. Boy'd gone to the Lord and ain't no ways the Lord gonna give him back.'

'Why did it happen, George?'

'Nothin' ever proved. Only us boys had suspicions. Funny thin'. They was real close at one time, at the beginnin' of the camp, Billy-Ray and Jamie. Din make no sense to us, but we just left well alone. There was a girl too, pretty little thing. Kepinski, he had a thing 'bout her. Name of McCreadie, Elly McCreadie. . . .'

Alan could swear his heart missed a beat. 'Elly McCreadie?'

'Sure thing. Only she was way outa reach. Daughter of the base commander. Billy-Ray had it real bad for her. Seems that Jamie had the same feelin'. Heard him once talkin' 'bout what he'd like to do to her, sex I mean. Kepinski there too. Went real quiet. Then he said to Jamie he ain't never gonna talk 'bout her like that agin. But nothin' proved, not then, not since. McCreadies moved offa the base shortly after that.' A small shrug from Baker to signal that he knew nothing more.

Alan's heart had settled back into some kind of normal rhythm, but he still felt light-headed. 'You wouldn't have a picture, George, an old photograph maybe?'

'Surely do. Someplace.' He lifted himself from the rocker, shuffled into the house. When he came back he was holding an official graduation picture of the training platoon. He handed it to Alan, stooping, a blunt, workman's finger pointing to a slightly blurred face. Billy-Ray Kepinski, aged seventeen.

Alan peered at the image. Computer enhancement techniques would bring the features into focus and tease out more detail. The computer could then age the face, adding weight, thin the hair, drag the skin down, to give him an idea of what the man might look like today if he was still alive.

'George, can I hang on to this for a while? I'll send it back to you as soon as we're done with it.'

Baker inclined his head. 'Sure can. All it's got is sadness for me now.'

'Did you ever hear anything, about Kepinski being MIA?'

'Sure. Word come back, agin NVA informer. Seems Kepinski was in a POW camp.' He pronounced the letters, *pee oh dubbaya*. 'Up for hangin'. They did that sometimes. Hang a man, only din kill 'em. Faked it, just to scare 'em, make 'em talk and that. Anyways, Kepinski had the wire. NVA never said whether the boy killed or not. Don't reckon Kepinski'd ever talk. Mebbe they put him in the rat trap. Who can say? All we ever heard.'

Alan thanked George Baker. He could see the retelling had been an ordeal. That he was still frightened, all these years later, by what he'd seen.

'And you've never told anyone about this, ever?'

'Molly, ma wife knows 'course. Don't want to burden nobody mind.' George Baker ruminated for a while, staring down at the uneven floorboards of the porch, the muscles of his jaw working into tight, stringy balls. 'Someone else knows now. But don't see what it got to do with you, your work and that.'

Alan shrugged.

'Don't mind tellin' you, I want nothin' to do with this no more.'

'Who else knows, George? It might be important.' Like his host, Alan dropped his eyes to the floor, leaned forward, elbows resting on knees. 'On the other hand it might not.'

'I got three boys Mr Bedale. You got kids?'

'Yeah, one, daughter.'

'Real fierce, a father's love.'

Alan thought about Betina. Fierce, yes. He nodded.

'Nothin' like the pain when you lose a child.'

Alan glanced up. The former US Marine was staring out, his thoughts removed, out there somewhere among the trees of the forest. 'I lost a child. My youngest boy.' George Baker began to cry. Silent tears. 'I loved that boy like you wouldn't believe. We was out one day in the woods, cuttin' timber and the boys're all foolin'. Then my young 'un git hissell on the wrong side of a fallin' tree. Ain't nothin' we coulda done. He died there in my arms.'

'I'm sorry, George, truly.'

'Some time ago now, though the pain don't never leave. That's when I git to thinkin' about Jamie-Jake. Same sorta age as my boy when he died. Didn't seem right his folks not knowin' for sure. So I figured on tellin' them what really happin.'

'Was that fair, George?'

'Who can say, 'cept the Lord? Me and Molly we talked about it, but I just figured they got a right.'

'So you called them?'

'Surely did.'

'When was that?'

'I remember exactly. First anniversary of my own boy's dyin': 30th November 1986, though I din speak to his folks. His sister picked up the phone. Took it bad. I tracked her down to one of them big weapons factories, big place out in the New Mexico hills.'

Alan sat in silence. The date, somehow familiar. He tried to remember public holidays, famous events but could not think of any. Instead he stood up. His mind was still too full of the name Elly McCreadie.

'I won't take any more of your time, George.' Alan shuffled his feet. 'I'm sorry if this has been hard for you.' Birds twittered. Beyond the fire break the sound of a diesel engine neared then faded.

'Hope you git whoever done them things. 'Mazing what you boys can do nowadays.'

As he drove away from George Baker's forest cabin a thought struck Alan. What had Bruno said? Submarine detection plans being handed to the Chinese, secrets being stolen since 1986. 1986? And the dead boy's sister worked in a weapons factory. He'd called her back in '86. Alan shook his head and grinned to himself. Crazy thought. He glanced in the rear-view mirror. The former marine sergeant was rocking back and forth on the porch, still haunted by his memories.

Alan drove into Dublin. Close to the motel he found a photographic store offering a one-hour service. He explained what he needed. Thirty minutes and twenty dollars later, he had two copies of George Baker's photograph. The shop assistant gave him directions to the post office and the local FedEx bureau. From the post office, Alan bagged Baker's original photograph and penned a short note thanking the man for his co-operation. At the FedEx bureau, he expressed one copy to Brisbane with written instructions on the computer treatment he wanted made on the picture, ringing Billy-Ray Kepinski's hard, unsmiling face in red.

Then he called Charlie from the motel. Charlie's voice, when he finally answered his phone, was thick with sleep. The picture would arrive at P-Unit HQ on the overnight service. Alan verbalized his instructions and was acknowledged with grunts down the line. He left the motel, returned the car to the Avis lot at Atlanta airport and with less than twenty minutes to spare, caught a plane to LAX.

No such luxury as Aussie lager on the Delta flight, so Alan contented himself with a Bud, settled in his seat and watched the neatly tended fields of the Georgia agriculture belt recede as the plane nosed through a crisp, cloudless sky.

The whole investigation had turned on a casual remark. Young Miss McCreadie. He sipped his Bud and wondered, not for the first time, at the part played by pure chance in cracking murder cases.

Now he had the link. Billy-Ray Kepinski.

Alan slipped his copy of George Baker's photograph from its plastic sleeve. Despite the fuzziness of the picture and its black and white contrast, it was clear that Kepinski had light eyes. Blue or green. His face, even as a teenager, was hollow, expressionless. He reminded Alan of how a clone might look: a body and a mind but no soul. The newly trained soldiers were in two ranks, the front seated, the other standing behind. Kepinski was standing on the right. Alan noticed that he stood away from the others, not bunched or touching shoulders, but isolated. He stowed the photograph.

Time to talk to Bruno again. No time to head for Washington. He'd call from LAX and have Bruno send the stuff over to Manila. Kepinski's military records would flesh in some of the physical details. In the hands of a behavioural psychologist, course reports and army assessments might lead to a personality profile, at least an indication. And there was something else. Needed to pow-wow with Santos first. But perhaps a US passport might come in useful. He thought of a name. How about Albert McCreadie?

They were flying against the spin of the earth so that by the time Alan landed at LAX, dusk was descending on the city. He transferred to the transit lounge and put the call through to Bruno Denotti's home, describing his visit to George Baker's forest cabin.

'OK, so what d'you want me to do?'

'Can your people do a profile?'

'Where are you now?'

'LAX.'

'Gimme the guy's name again.'

Alan spelt it out. 'K-E-P-I-N-S-K-I.'

'Got that.'

'I'm *en route* to Manila. When I get there I'll give you a fax number.'

'No problem, Al. Say, you reckon he might be your guy?'

Alan was circumspect. Nothing was certain. 'Difficult to say, Bruno, but you know how it is, got to chase down every avenue.' He thought about mentioning the date – 1986. Decided against. Bruno would think he was nuts. 30th November? He glanced at his watch. *Twenty days* – less than three weeks. Crazy. Anyway, while there was any chance that Ben might be alive he wouldn't entrust anyone with Billy-Ray Kepinski's location. 'Anyway, according to George Baker it's likely Kepinski was killed in Vietnam.'

'Sure. We'll talk when you get to Manila. You have a good trip, Al.'

An hour later he was boarding the Philippine Airlines flight. His mind was a jumble. As the aircraft headed west, out over the Pacific, chasing the remains of the day Alan settled back and thought about Elly McCreadie. He wondered why she had dropped the abbreviated name of Elly. Maybe it was because her fiancé, a marine corps captain named William Pearson, had been killed in action in Nha Trang. Maybe he was the one who called her by that name. Instead, she had adopted the anglicized abbreviation of Liz, after her father, General Douglas McCreadie, had moved to London in late '68 to take up his post as military attaché at the US Embassy. Or maybe the man she eventually married in a small Hampshire village on 18 October 1970, an aspiring young banker by the name of John McGovern, preferred 'Liz' to 'Elly'.

26

When the message went out from Bernard Levy that there was to be a meeting of senior personnel at the headquarters building in Washington, none of those attending imagined that the entire management hierarchy of the FBI would be together in the same place at the same time. Many of the conversations bubbling round the hall centred on what a great target they all made for some wacko wanting to make a grand statement.

The director's deputy was present as were the assistant-directors who headed up each of the bureau's nine HQ divisions. Cosseted with each of them were their Deputy assistant directors together with their respective section heads. The assistant directors-in-charge of the two largest field offices, New York and Washington, were among the fifty-three senior agents-in-charge of the other smaller mainland field offices. As a senior agent-in-charge at the Washington field office, third strata in the pecking order, Bruno Denotti was at least grateful that while his leave had been cancelled it had taken him less than an hour to get here this morning. Some poor schmucks had flown in from goddamned Alaska.

Denotti turned in his seat. He recognized a few faces from outside the Washington field office, mostly those from New York and a couple of agents from New Orleans with whom he'd had dealings.

The volume of conversation in the hall quickly softened. Denotti could see the director making his way towards a podium at the front.

*

'Ladies and gentlemen, we've got ourselves a problem.' The microphone added a tinny edge to his voice. The residual hubbub of whispered conversation died instantly. Someone dropped a pen. Everyone heard it. The audience represented the most powerful investigative force ever assembled to catch a crook.

'President's received a note. Not a nice note. Defence have analysed it and the comeback is it's the real McCoy. Somewhere out there is a person or persons unknown who is or are threatening the peace and security of the United States and, by association, the peace and security of western Europe. We've got to find him, her or them. And we've got twenty-four days in which to do so. Now, as some of you already know, the deadline's six p.m. 30th November.'

A splutter of bafflement floated towards the vaulted ceiling.

Bernard Levy waited for quiet. 'First I'll explain the problem. Then I'm going to tell you all the way I figure to find the solution.'

His assistant had arranged the slides and showed him the button on the lectern to press to bring them up. Bernard Levy reached for a second button and dimmed the lights. He pressed the first button. An aerial shot of the Lawrence Livermore National Laboratory appeared on the huge screen behind him.

'There are four weapons labs here in the US. Behind me's the Lawrence Livermore – the most important one as far as we're concerned in this investigation. Why'll become clear later on. Here's the background.' He paused, took a sip of water and continued. 'About half of Livermore's annual billion dollar budget goes on weapons research. The other half goes into other fields, lasers, controlled thermonuclear fusion, biomedical research, environmental physics and so on. But the laboratory's main claim to fame is as leader of the scientific development of nuclear weapons and the assessment of their effects.'

Bernard Levy pressed the slide button again and Livermore was replaced by a graphic. A depiction of a satellite occupied the upper right-hand corner of the screen and below the satellite a representative ground receiving station. The main part of the slide showed a cut-away block of ocean containing a diving submarine. The icons were linked by a series of annotated dotted lines.

'There's only so many weapons one nation can have beyond which further development becomes rhetorical. So Livermore turned their hand to finding ways of detecting other nations' nukes. What you see behind me is what they came up with. It's called ROIP which stands for Radar Ocean Imaging Programme. Here's how it works.' The Director of the FBI picked up a laser pointer and flicked it on. Then he turned and looked up at the enormous image.

'As a submarine moves through the water it creates disturbance. Behind the submarine here you can see ever-increasing circles which it leaves behind in its wake as it moves forward.' The red laser point darted about behind the sub. 'It's what the scientists call a cone of disturbance. The pattern is unique to each sub, in effect a fingerprint. When the cone of disturbance breaks the surface it creates a weak interference pattern. In other words waves on the surface of the sea change.

'Satellites scan the surface of the oceans. Their orbits are such that the areas of ocean they scan are at an acute angle, between ten and twenty-five degrees, called the acute grazing angle. This acute angle means the satellites can detect the weak surface wake of a submerged sub. Signals from the satellites are beamed to earth.' The red point of the laser settled on the icon of a ground station. 'And these facilities interpret the signals, identifying the speed and direction of the sub.'

The atmosphere in the hall had palpably altered and the silence hung heavy. Bernard Levy allowed a few seconds to pass while he turned back to the lectern and powered up the lights. 'The ROIP was developed at Livermore.' Another sip of water. 'This radar technology first appeared on the scene as far back as '78. Since then NASA have added to it and, in the early nineties, Britain came on board in a joint development effort sponsored by the US Government. As you can imagine the Pentagon gave it the highest classified security rating. Rules have been applied to commercial satellite capabilities to safeguard these developments by limiting image resolution to five metres. ROIP goes down to less than a metre. Now I'm sure some of you are thinking how deep can this thing probe? Answer's hundreds of feet, but not thousands. Not yet anyway, but the scientists figure that's just a matter of time.' Bernard Levy rested his hands either side of the lectern. 'Now here's the problem. The ROIP technology's been stolen and whoever's stolen it is threatening to give it to China.'

His words had the predictable effect. Consternation boiled among his audience. Bernard Levy waited until the noise quietened. 'Conclusions here are obvious. No doubt you've all figured it out, but just so's there no mistake: China may very shortly possess the information necessary to develop the technology in double quick time which'll in turn let them find our subs. And if they find our subs, they can destroy them. What this means, is that we no longer have the edge. That being the case, we're no longer the world's policeman and, as we all know, without a powerful deterrent the world becomes a very dangerous place.'

Bruno Denotti slouched in his seat, one arm across his body supporting his elbow, the other hand cupping his mouth. 'Holy shit,' he muttered into his hand. 'And we got less 'n four weeks to find the sonofabitch.'

'We know the document sent to the President was genuine because it contained a segment of legacy code relating to the W-88 nuclear warhead which has since been authenticated by the Department of Energy and the Pentagon,' Bernard Levy continued. 'For those of you who read the newspapers, W-88 will mean something. Others of you here, I know, were directly involved in operation Kindred Spirit four years ago. For those of you who do not belong to either of these two groups, let me fill you in on the detail.'

A low rumble of laughter undulated over the darkened heads of the agents.

'The W-88 nuclear warhead was developed at Los Alamos. It has ten times the destructive power of the Hiroshima weapon but is only three feet long miniaturized. Its great advantage is that it can be launched from anywhere, even the reinforced roof of a motor vehicle. We know that technological data relating to this weapon was passed to China beginning 1988. We also know the culprit, a Chinese-born scientist by the name of Wen Ho Lee. He is now under house arrest in the San Francisco bay area. He has been polygraphed and is not, we believe, responsible for the letter to the President. Nor, more importantly, do we believe he knows who is. However, the legacy code in the letter is similar to that which Lee passed to China. So, we have a starting point at Los Alamos.'

Bernard Levy knew that every agent in the room would have heard of Wen Ho Lee. Equally, it would come as no surprise to any of them that that scientist was not implicated in this latest espionage catastrophe.

'Now we come on to a second character, Peter Lee, no relation.' Bernard Levy changed the slide. A potted history of America's most treacherous spy since the end of the cold war appeared on the screen. 'This guy is bad news, but like his countryman, Wen Ho Lee, he's got through the net. Let's take a look.' A rustle of paper filtered through the air as the delegates flipped the pages of their briefing reports.

'Peter Lee was born in China, 1939. The family moved to Taiwan in '59. Lee graduated from CalTech in 1975 with a Ph.D. in aeronautics and then got naturalized. Between '76 and '84 he was at Livermore working on laser detonation. In '85 he relocated to Los Alamos. Now, here it gets interesting. In January of 1985, Peter Lee went to Beijing and handed over details of his work over here. He stayed at Los Alamos until '91 when he went to work for a private defence contractor, TRW, in Redondo Beach. There he began working on radar imaging research. He was a member of the team conducting trials of ROIP in Scotland with the Brits and stayed in the ROIP programme for six years. He was back in China in '97, guest of the Chinese Institute of Applied Physics and Computational Mathematics – these people design nuclear weapons. During that visit he gave the Chinese information about his radar work, everything he had on ROIP. We, the FBI, interviewed him from October of that year through early '98 as part of operation Royal Tourist. A counter-intel report blocked his further participation in the programme but prosecution was stopped by the navy's reluctance to reveal ROIP details in court. With no witness to testify about the classified nature of the information the prosecution case collapsed. That gives you all some idea about how sensitively this technology is viewed by the military.'

The image on the screen changed to a recent portrait photograph of the Chinese spy.

'The problem as you all know is that sometimes our investigations get hampered by other government departments.' A murmur rose from the agents, an acknowledgement that what they sometimes needed was a *carte-blanche* licence to kick ass. 'As a result of the navy's understandable desire not to follow through the Peter Lee case, the President signed PDD-61 for a DoE counter-intelligence programme. Now we have a senior FBI agent at the Department of Energy with a presidential decision directive. That authority is our springboard for this investigation.'

Bernard Levy killed off the image on the screen and scrolled the lights back to full power. 'The government doesn't like catching spies.' Another murmur of amusement from the floor. 'Too many embarrassing questions are raised like, *How much was taken? How are our allies affected?* You get the picture. Now, two points to start from. Whoever it is has got some kind of connection to both Wen Ho Lee and Peter Lee. They have access to the same information and both these characters managed to get it out. Our psych-profile's pointing at a middle-aged female involved in ROIP from '91, who might have worked for DoE, most likely at Livermore, or a private contractor like TRW.' Bernard Levy drained his water glass and lowering his voice to create a more dramatic effect concluded, 'Do not underestimate the seriousness of this situation. What we're talking here is a direct threat to world peace. I do not want information leaks. Your assistant directors will brief you all individually. We have until 30th November.'

The faces of the agents told the director that the message had been received.

27

Alan was among the throng pressing against makeshift barriers in an attempt to get early sightings of relatives and friends at Ninoy Aquino International Airport. He spotted Simon, dressed in shorts, T-shirt and flip-flops in anticipation of the heat.

Simon barged through the crowd. 'Alan!' They eventually managed to link up through the surge and pull of the human tide.

'How's Bet and the kiddie?'

'Great. Much better. Both of them. Very happy.'

'Let's get out of here.' Alan grabbed Simon's arm and they pushed their way through the crowds.

'Where are we staying?' Simon heaved his bag over his shoulder.

'Manila Hotel,' Alan shouted. 'Very comfortable.'

'How long you been there?'

'This morning. I was with Santos before that.'

'That why you were incommunicado?'

'Yep.'

They walked outside where buses and taxis were gathered in a chaotic knot.

'Got a car?'

Alan shook his head. 'Hotel's got a bus somewhere, but I thought we could take one of these.'

Alan came to a rank of jeepneys and inspected the route boards on the sides of the multi-coloured vehicles. The bodies were adorned with mirrors and statues, lights and pictures of religious themes and most were bedecked with ribbons. He found one that would take them past Rizal Park. There were two seats beside the driver. Both were occupied. Two bench seats, facing inwards lined the open-sided rear of the jeepney. He clambered in beside Simon, peeled some pesos and gave the money to the Filipino sitting next to him to pass up to the driver. When the vehicle was full, they set off towards the city centre ten kilometres away. It was impossible to talk above the city sounds of snarling traffic and drivers keen to exercise their authority by sitting on their horns.

Near to their hotel on Bonifacio Drive, Alan banged twice on the roof and yelled, '*Para!*' The driver slowed and they both jumped off the tail-gate before the jeepney picked up speed again and continued on its journey.

They made straight for the bar inside the hotel. Alan ordered and when two long, cool San Miguels arrived, Simon was finally able to ask, 'So, what's been happening, Al?'

A pianist was tinkling away in the corner. 'I'll tell you in a sec. Have you got something for me?'

'Charlie called last night.' Simon reached down for his bag. 'I picked up the package from the office this morning. What is it?'

Alan slit the brown government envelope with his finger and pulled out the enlargement of George Baker's photograph. He studied it for a moment. 'I think this is our guy.' He handed the picture to Simon.

Simon stared at the picture then shook his head. 'I don't understand, Al. Who the hell is this?'

'His name's Billy-Ray Kepinski.' He had rehearsed this, leaving out any mention of Elly McCreadie.

'Our guy? Where did you find him?'

'The States.'

'What do you mean the States? When were you in the States?' And then realization took hold. 'Oh, right! That's why I couldn't bloody call you! Why the fuck didn't you tell me you were going to the States?'

'It was a long shot. May have proved nothing.'

'You fucking lied!'

'I'm sorry. Had no choice.'

'You better tell me what's going on.'

'A few years ago, '92, there was a pirate attack on a Vietnamese junk, carrying boat people, in the Gulf of Siam. Thai marine police had been tipped off; how I don't know. There was a fire fight. All the pirates were taken out. One of them was a white guy. Turns out he was a USAF flyboy, Vietnam MIA.' He stopped, took a breath. 'With the forensic evidence that one of the men who attacked *Clarissa* was over six feet tall, I got to thinking, this guy might be another MIA. So I checked with the MIA Association. If you have a look on the Internet, you'll find pages and pages of the stuff, kids looking for fathers, that kind of thing.'

'Yeah. But how did you find this guy, this Kepinski?'

Alan took the information he had and twisted the chronology. 'A body was fished out of the water here a week or so ago. Not here in Manila, south, off Mindanao. Guy was a known pirate. He'd been gutted, left for the sharks, that was Santos's guess. Anyway, spring tide bought him in further up the coast before the sharks could get to him.'

Simon took a slug of beer. 'Al, that's all very interesting. But so what?'

Alan sighed. He dropped his voice. 'Those burn marks on your mother . . . that's a little trick some US Marine boys developed in Vietnam.'

Simon lit a cigarette. Alan noticed his hands were unsteady.

'Guy's over six foot. We conclude, white man. Uses a trick originally seen among US troops in Vietnam, so we've got an American white man.'

'Or black man.'

'Or black man. Right. This burning thing was unique to the marines. That narrows the field to marine MIAs.'

'So what about the guy who was washed up?'

'I checked for similar MOs in the Marine Corps, pre-'Nam. A long shot like I said, looking for a killing, an evisceration. Turns out there was an incident.'

'You checked all this?' There was disbelief in Simon's voice.

'I didn't: friend of mine did. Bloke called Bruno Denotti, FBI. We met at Quantico some years back. I stayed in touch. You never know.'

Simon whistled. The disbelief had evaporated with the mention of the FBI. Alan related George Baker's tale of the death of Jamie-Jake Mulcahy, omitting the detail that the killing had taken place at Fort Jefferson.

'This guy Baker gave you that?' Simon tapped at the photograph.

'Yeah. Charlie had it blown up and aged.' Alan shuffled the pictures and stared down at how Kepinski might look today. He passed the computer enhancement to Simon. The face was menacing. Two versions, one blue-eyed, the other green. Overlays built increasing thicknesses of grey hair on the bald head. The features were artificially angulated, but the impression was clear.

'See those?' Alan took the enlargement of Baker's photograph and pointed to Kepinski's arms. The pattern was unclear.

'Tattoos?'

'Snakes. According to George Baker, Kepinski had these done while he was a recruit. Insisted on being called Cobra.' Alan gathered the pictures and bagged them. 'So, you're right: could have been a black man, until I heard Baker's story. So we're looking for a forty-nine-year-old, former US Marine with tattooed arms who goes by the name of Cobra.'

'If he's still alive.'

'Right.'

'Jesus.' Simon hailed a waiter, asked for a couple more beers.

'Have a look at this. It's a psychological evaluation, based on Kepinski's service records.'

There was an introductory paragraph, bringing the story up to date. The father had been a suicide. Only known relative, the mother, had died in an old people's home somewhere in the Midwest, three years ago. Bruno had checked with the superintendent of the home. May-Lou Kepinski, née Pateka, had not been in contact with anyone during her five years in the home. Before that – no way to check.

Simon took the paper. It was official FBI stationery. Sweat sprang up on his hands.

Kepinski was a loner, but capable of displaying outstanding leadership qualities. Moody, he could swing from charming and friendly to hostile with minimum provocation. A deep-seated need to hide or mask his true identity, hence the tattoos, the insistence on a nickname. Psychological trauma at an early age, his father's suicide, could have led to psychoses. Displayed classic aberrant behaviour. Independent, yet craved attention. Diagnosed as potential schizophrenic. He'd been suspected of involvement in some particularly brutal killings in Vietnam; nothing indictable, but with hindsight, pointing to possible psychopathic tendencies.

Simon asked for the portrait photograph, the aged version, and stared at it for a long time, absorbing the detail.

'This Kepinski . . . he could have Ben?'

'Yes. He could.'

Alan reached into his shirt pocket and pulled out a single sheet of folded paper.

Simon could make out the heavily embossed logo of the FBI as Alan unfolded the notepaper.

'Read this, Simon.'

Simon took the paper. He slumped in his seat. 'How the fuck many more surprises am I supposed to take in one bloody day?'

Alan was silent, sipping his beer.

'Your FBI friend again?'

Alan nodded.

'You're telling me that my grandfather had it in for this Kepinski and in killing my parents he was acting out some kind of fucking weird revenge fantasy?'

'I'm not telling you that; the FBI are telling you that. I think he was blackmailing them.'

'By using Ben.'

'Yes.'

'As revenge? My grandfather died a long time ago.'

'You've read the profile on Kepinski; he's a psychopath. Who knows how his mind works. It probably all makes perfect sense to him.'

'Jesus wept! And what about Ben now? My parents are dead. . . .'

'I don't know, Simon. But we've got to follow it through while there's still a chance. You know it and I know it.'

Alan had taken a twin room in the hotel and, after they'd finished their beers, they went upstairs, Simon to take a shower and Alan to make a phonecall and read Professor Pereda's translation of the McGovern diary. He waited until he could hear running water from the bathroom before dialling direct to Charlie's number at P-Unit. His instructions were quick and precise. Charlie was to wait until Bet was out of the house at Woody Point.

'You'll find a plain white envelope in the drawer of the night stand on Bet's side, that's the left. Inside'll be a lock of hair. Take some, not all. The pathologist has got some tissue samples from Sir John. Run a DNA test on both samples. We're testing for paternity here.'

Lady Elizabeth had given Bet the lock of Ben's hair, a memento she'd said, when Ben 'disappeared'. When he had finished the phonecall, Alan lay on the bed and began to read Professor Pereda's translation.

Robert McGovern had been a lieutenant in the Royal Navy, a man of high breeding with a promising career ahead of him, until he was assigned to the command of Captain Harold Cummings aboard HMS *Felicity*. The ship was tasked with a three-year patrol of the islands of the West Indies, reporting to the newly established Governor of the Bahamas in Nassau on the island of New Providence. The ship's mission: to assist in suppressing the activities of pirates operating in the area, among them such notorious villains as Benjamin Hornigold, Christopher Winter, Edward England and Charles Vane.

On 3rd September 1717, a decree had been handed down by Mr Secretary Addison on instruction of the King. Composed in three parts, the decree called for a force of His Majesty's Navy to be dispatched to the area, that those pirates who surrendered themselves receive the King's pardon and finally that a governor be appointed to drive the pirates from their haven on New Providence.

Woodes Rogers, the man charged with restoring order to the islands, sailed on 11 April 1718 on board *Delicia*, accompanied by HMS *Milford* and HMS *Rose* and two sloops. HMS *Felicity* would follow the small fleet.

Robert McGovern's journal was written as a record of the appalling events that took place in the early part of 1719, events that branded him a brigand and prevented him ever returning home.

Captain Cummings, a large and foul-tempered man, bullied the men mercilessly. It was not a happy ship. I became afraid of what the men might do. I heard murmurings which left me no alternative but to warn the men not to act foolishly.

As we neared New Providence, HMS *Rose* sailed ahead as vanguard. The next day, 26 July, we saw a French ship on fire in the harbour. A pirate by the name of Charles Vane had set the vessel alight to prevent HMS *Rose* from entering harbour. Vane, hoisting a Jolly Roger in defiance, fled.

Much of our duty in the islands required the officers to entertain dignitaries and prominent merchants. On one such night I overheard a conversation between one merchant and Cummings, saying a Spanish merchantman was making passage towards Carolina. Such a prize was bound to lure a pirate vessel or two and we must act as escort.

In the morning, I ordered the crew to prepare the ship to go outside the reef. After two days' sailing, Cummings ordered me aloft. I sighted the ship standing westward and I reported to the captain my belief that she was the Spanish merchantman. Cummings ordered more sail and we gave chase. It was my opinion that the merchantman suspected our intention, for many pirates will hoist the sovereign flag as deception.

I went below and begged to speak with the captain, fearing that our charge had mistaken us as pirates. Cummings flew into a rage and threatened me with accusations of mutiny.

The men were becoming anxious, since our intention was clearly hostile. They looked to me for guidance. I ordered them to stand firm and catch the merchantman as the captain had commanded.

As we neared, Cummings ordered the men to open fire and a broadside was launched. A boarding party was hastily grouped and set out in the longboat. Cummings ordered me into the boat. His intention was to involve me to prevent me accusing him later. In so doing he cleverly rendered my position as invidious. If I refused, the crew would undoubtedly mutiny and I, as their leader, would be guilty. To obey his order was to make myself accomplice. I could not disobey.

On board the merchantman, Cummings, who had changed out of his uniform, shouted to be taken to the captain's quarters and instructed me to follow. The Spanish captain was wounded, but he led us to the hold and showed us chests of gold coins. Cummings ordered me to arrange for the cargo to be moved to HMS *Felicity*. The Spanish captain pleaded on behalf of his men. His wife was also aboard and clinging to her husband. She wore a green stone set in a gold necklace of such a size that I wondered how she was able to lift her head. Cummings tore the pendant from her. It became clear to me that Cummings would not spare the crew and the sight of the gold had made a pirate of him. Before I could inter-cede on behalf of the Spanish captain, Cummings pulled his pistol and shot the man in the face. His good wife received the same treatment. Cummings ordered me above decks to finish the unloading.

Cummings then ordered the men to open fire on the merchant-man one final time and sink her in deep water. Some of the men had followed the captain's lead. Most were dressed like pirates and others were drunk.

I watched with terrible sadness at the merchantman being bombarded by our guns, splintering to driftwood and sinking.

Cummings ordered course away from New Providence. His thinking was demented. He no longer seemed human. I went to his cabin to plead with him, but Cummings was beside himself with rage. 'You will obey me instantly,' he shouted. I replied that the action had bought disgrace upon me and my family and that I would no longer countenance this madness. 'Mutineer,' he shouted, so loud that I had to retreat. He ordered me bound and lashed to the mainmast. Then he ringed the mast with gunpowder.

Cummings stood on a barrel to address the crew. He proclaimed that he would make rich men of them all. They need never return to grey England but could live in the sun with women and land and wealth. Some men cheered at this and others stayed quiet. Some looked towards me. Those men with families were afraid. I knew he was about to make an example of me to win the compliance of the others, I being an officer and of noble birth.

Cummings asked me a final time, 'Are you with me?' 'No,' I replied. He lit the powder and the explosion nearly killed me. My clothing caught fire and I suffered the most terrible burns. Some men loyal to me rushed forward and put out the flames. I cannot remember what happened then, but when I awoke I was in my bunk.

Some days passed. The cook tended my wounds with salt. I could no longer move and I inspected the damage to my legs. The flesh was burned and in places the jagged bone showed clearly.

I begged the cook to give me his knife, which I stowed beneath the blanket. I ordered the cook to request Cummings to see me. When Cummings strode into my cabin he was in good spirits. He wore the green stone around his neck. I was convinced that he had gone mad. I asked him to come closer. Cummings approached the bunk and bent forward to catch my words. As he stooped, I plunged the knife towards his heart with all the remains of my strength. Cummings gagged and fell. As he fell, I grabbed the stone at his throat. I was in disgrace. Should I return to England, I would be imprisoned at Marshalsea in Southwark and strung up for mutiny. I would be tried as a common murderer.

Most of the men cheered when the cook reported what I had done. Those who had supported Cummings changed their allegiance, all except three. We put these three on a small island with water and food and some of the gold. I ordered the sovereign flag be lowered and the ship renamed to that of my beloved wife, Clarissa, whom I would never see again. I ordered the helm to set a course south-east to round the Cape of Good Hope and then to the island of Madagascar.

I provisioned the ship and set a course for the Seven Sisters *(note: I conferred with one of my colleagues. The Seven Sisters became known as the Three Brothers, then the Séchelles by the French and latterly the Seychelles. PP)* a good place for the men to settle or make their way back to England. I was becoming weaker with each passing day at sea.

For those men who wanted to return home, I told them to share a common story, that HMS *Felicity* had been attacked by pirates whilst going about the King's business, that the ship was lost and that Cummings and myself were dead. If they adhered to the story then no harm would come to them.

Clarissa sailed on and, sighting the islands of the Seychelles, anchored in the bay of the Second Sister *(Isle de Palme, now called Praslin. PP)*. I was close to the end. I ordered the cook to bring some of the gold to the captain's cabin. I marked the position of the ship by taking bearings to three points of land and dropped the treasure over the side. I entrusted the green stone to the cook and begged him to return to England, find my beloved Clarissa and to tell her of my fate. I prayed that God would be merciful to him and protect him on his journey. I could not bear to think of Clarissa and our son Joshua never knowing what became of me. I also gave him this diary with instructions that Clarissa should hide it, together with a letter pointing to this account, for Joshua or some other generation of my family to some day return to this place and recover the gold.

I then ordered to be taken ashore and left high on the side of the hill, to give me a good view of the sea. The cook, who has become my trusted friend, sits with me as I write this account and he will take it from me when I die.

I have become the hapless victim of evil circumstances. To my beloved Clarissa I say that I will hold out after this in wherever place has been ordained by God until we join again. As for Cummings who did these evil deeds, kindness will hunt him down from the four points of the compass.

28

Ben could smell the food. Confined in near darkness his other senses had become heightened, like those of a blind man. But smell especially. Anything new which impregnated the staleness of his dwelling place bounced along his olfactory nerve and into his brain like a star-burst. The bucket descended slowly, careful hands high above anxious not to spill the precious cargo. It happened sometimes like this, a break from the norm, a mind-saving departure from the timelessness and the tedium of his imprisonment. Hell, it was a treat. Ben grinned at the dank walls as he reached up for the bucket and lowered it gently on to his dining table, closed his eyes and breathed in, deeply and evenly, feasting on the joyous aromas of fresh food. Above his head a shadow moved in and out of the circle of light. Ben opened his eyes again and quickly retied the rope around the handle of the latrine bucket, tugged twice and lifted the latrine bucket off the floor.

Chicken with bananas and rice. The chicken was freshly cooked, still warm. The bananas over-ripe and soft. He glanced up watching the skyward progress of his portable lavatory, wondering at the identity of his unseen benefactor. Whoever it was, he thanked, laughing out loud, laughing because the food would taste unbelievably good and laughing that he could feel such gratitude while he was stuck here in this miserable hell-hole. He should feel hate, humiliated that they could manipulate him like this, but grateful was how he felt.

Ben organized the food, carefully arranging some on his plate. He lit two candles, all the more to enjoy the ceremony of quelling his hunger. When he finally set about eating the food he did so ravenously, but not greedily. Standards had to be maintained. The barrier that kept him from hopelessness was a delicate tissue in his mind and it would not take much to break it. So, when a grain of rice dropped from his lip to the floor, he bent carefully to pick it up, chastising himself silently that his clumsiness had left a mark on the carpet.

29

Scarface. It was a trite nickname, but unavoidable, unless he doled out large sums to a plastics man.

He was thirty-eight years old and had two things: number one, he had a score to settle; number two, he had information that Kepinski would pay a lot of money to possess. Locked in his mind the information was useless. And worthless.

Ten years in the merchant marine had taught him many lessons. Most importantly, he knew the sea and seamanship. Second, he figured that piracy paid better. Third, acceptance within pirate ranks was directly proportional to brutality shown.

The young Englishman and the fat man were treading dangerous water. He knew why they were here. To die. These were the thoughts that collided in his mind as Scarface made his way to the airport to go earn his spurs.

Rumours had spread among the girlie bars, which aside from providing entertainment for tourists functioned as an efficient and covert criminal grapevine. The hearsay had reached him, then bounced off him in different directions, information retransmitted as misinformation. He had crossed turf boundaries, different bars controlled by different groups, leaving confusion in his wake so that would-be bounty hunters would finish running up their own arses. In that respect Manila was no different from New York, where the Mafia had carved up the territory then signed agreements and treaties to keep the peace. All that happened was the war went underground. Scarface had changed the rumours. Bunches of thugs would be chasing rainbows, leaving him free to zero in on the prize. Police too, corrupt as hell, most of them. Confuse them, and the thugs and filth would all confuse each other. His advantage was he didn't belong to any group or gang. No rivals after his blood. He could float above the petty fighting like a butterfly and settle where he pleased, fitting with seamless, anonymous integrity into the woven fabric of the criminal fraternity. He was qualified, too. It was all there if anyone cared to check with a crooked police buddy. Good. Excellent.

Scarface flew to General Santos City.

He amused himself thinking about Cobra. Clever fucker to have survived so long. Cobra understood the nature of the game and had picked the right place to play. The Philippines were attractive for several reasons: great climate; easy pickings; bent cops. It was often not the identity of the culprit that left crimes unpunished but the lack of compelling evidence to build a prosecution case. Often too, the lack of resource meant that round-the-clock surveillance was impractical for extended periods. Anyway, a couple of thousand dollars pressed firmly into the ever upturned palms of the police and evidence could change. Easily.

The PAL jet put down in Buayan district, eight clicks north-east of General Santos. It was a place Scarface knew well. He'd been born in a shack not ten miles from here. A taxi took him along the coast road towards Glan, to a street on the outskirts of town.

He walked in the early morning. It was his favourite time. Thirty minutes to the guest house, a rambling wooden building isolated in the midst of an unkempt garden. Backpacker land. Lopsided balconies hung off the side of the house. He pushed through the rusty garden gate which creaked on its hinges. The squeak attracted the attention of the girls draped listlessly in hammocks suspended between beams on the upper floor. A mongrel scratched itself by the open front door. Here you could get a meal, a bed for the night and a girl to warm it for forty bucks. He'd take the food and a bed. For the moment.

The reception area formed part of the bar. Windows were shuttered and the place was dark. Some travellers were lounging on a terrace out back, sipping Coke.

Scarface paid cash. The room was on the top floor. It was large with an old iron bedstead, wooden floorboards which creaked, unwashed sink and above the sink a mirror that had become speckled with age. A narrow bathroom and lavatory led off one side. He pulled the light cord, just to have a looksee, and noticed a family of cockroaches scurrying for cover. Perfect.

Scarface sat on the bed, bare-chested against the mounting heat. The ceiling fan pushed a breeze down on to him. He composed a note. It was short, to the point. He had information. He was here.

He went out of his room. The girls were still on the balcony along the corridor. Their faces blended into a monotonous scroll of apathy. He read the faces, a cigarette dangling from his lips, searching for signs of intelligence. One of the girls stepped forward, jutting her chin, offering business. She seemed assertive, more so than her companions. He looked at her, turned and walked back towards his room, hearing her footsteps shadowing his.

The girl started unbuttoning her tight-fitting blouse.

Scarface shook his head. 'How much?'

'Twenty.'

'How would you like a hundred?'

Fear passed through the girl's eyes. Scarface could almost hear her thinking, what the hell do I have to do for a hundred?

'Can you deliver this?' He held the folded paper between thumb and forefinger under her nose. He saw her relief. She shrugged. He peeled a fifty and shoved it down her cleavage. There was enough threat in his actions to elicit a nod.

'Take it.' Scarface pushed the note into her hand. 'Address is on the front.' It didn't matter if the girl read the note. Wouldn't make sense to her. And if they didn't come, he'd know she was trying it on. Curiosity alone would prompt a response. So he'd know. 'You get the other fifty when my friends show up.'

The girl looked sullen. She pulled the fifty note from between her breasts and stuffed it into the pocket of her tight denim skirt that barely concealed her buttocks.

'You want I say you here?'

'Yeah. You tell them that.' Like they wouldn't have smacked it out of her.

She left the room without another word.

Cobra reread the message. He wandered briefly if Cortez had something to do with this. Then banished the thought as quickly. No way Cortez would try and mess with him. No way. So who then?

The note was signed *Degarda*. And a date of birth. That was it. Just *Degarda*, like he was supposed to guess the first name, or the last. It was a clever trick. Made him want to know. That was on the guy's plus side. He was smart. The downside, Degarda was familiar. He didn't know when or where he'd come across a Degarda. He'd already put a call through to one of his contacts, Sergeant Castella, a fat homosexual policeman with a penchant for little boys. Jimmy Pran had been dispatched to collect the information.

The muffled sound of a distant engine bought Cobra to the present. He ambled across the compound towards the operations room just as Jimmy slewed the camp's Wrangler jeep to a halt in a cloud of dust.

'So? What did you get?' Cobra led the way inside the ops room.

'Castella checked.' Jimmy slouched down into a chair. 'It's all here.' He reached into his back pocket. 'Degarda's got a record, a long one.' He gave the print-out to Cobra.

The various forces that make up the Philippines' police all pool data at central criminal records. Regional squads can tap into the centre and pull information on suspects. All data being entered is time flagged. That meant that no one could create an alias. Back-dated entries would stand out as false by the mismatched time flags.

Degarda's history was impressive. Assault in 1986: he'd been given three months. Robbery the following year: the sentence, nine months. In 1992 and 1994 he had been tried for piracy but was acquitted. The attacks had been up in the north. Three years for handling stolen goods, released twelve months ago.

Cobra flicked the sheet on to the table. He sucked his breath in. 'What d'you reckon, Jimmy?'

Slight shrug from Jimmy. Cobra only rarely asked for opinions so Jimmy was caught a bit off guard. He hesitated. 'Got nothing to lose . . . I mean. . . .'

'Yeah. Right. I think so too. Better get this sap to tell us what he knows.' There could only be two things. Either something to do with the jewels from *Clarissa,* which is why he'd thought of Cortez, or the manuscript. The dead smartass teacher guy.

'You want I should work him over?'

Cobra eyed Jimmy coolly. 'You're being very territorial, Jimmy. Maybe this Degarda really does have something useful to us.'

'I wasn't planning on killing him, just getting the information, then killing him.'

Cobra laughed. Degarda. Something about the name. Not a police op. Castella would have heard and coughed. 'Could be police from outside the region nosing about.'

'Manila?'

Cobra chewed his thumb. 'Could be. Stones are there. The old guy's body was dumped there.'

'Want I should check with Castella?'

'Nah. I'll do it.' No point going local. 'Stick around, Jimmy. If it is a sting, you have my permission to go break this fucker's neck.'

Jimmy grinned.

'Now get me the phone, then fuck off for ten minutes.'

After Jimmy left, Cobra dialled Manila. He negotiated with his informant and agreed a thousand. His informant knew nothing off the top of his head. He said to call him back after he'd made some discreet enquiries.

Cobra was thinking. Degarda was merchant marine. Ex. Second officer. Ticket revoked. But he could still read a map, still navigate. And Cobra's navigator was now shark shit. So he had a gap in his team and there was no one to fill it. And no way Degarda could know that.

Cobra called the informant again. He'd checked. Nothing.

'Jimmy!' Cobra shouted.

Jimmy came in. 'I get to meet him?'

'Tonight. Just go easy, Jimmy. He might be useful to us.'

Scarface was getting a little anxious. Not that he thought they weren't coming. Just the longer he waited the more nervous he became. Predictability was a gauge. They would come just out of curiosity, he knew that much but the longer they made him wait, the less predictable they became and every passing minute was pushing him further and further on to the back foot.

The cassette deck behind the bar was playing some seventies crap, Captain and Teneal. Ironic, seeing as El Capitano had managed to get himself murdered in the Philippines. The salutary lesson, if there was one, was lost on the group of sweaty backpackers talking excitedly in the corner. Scarface finished his beer. Nine o'clock. He was tired. The dope smoke was beginning to bother him. Maybe they wouldn't come today.

The girl was sitting on the top stair staring vacantly into space. Her legs were slightly apart and the shortness of her skirt meant he had a full, eye-level view of her crotch as he went up to his room. He felt himself stiffen. He hadn't given her the other fifty. Maybe she wanted a bit more.

This time he watched her undress in the darkness. He undressed too. No ceremony. Her body was good, young, contours polished by the luminosity of the moon. He laid her on her back, held her wrists and pinned her arms above her head. He made love to her, slowly, tenderly, losing himself briefly from the danger, the risk. When he had finished he was pleased that he seemed to have satisfied her too. He laid his head on the pillow and was instantly asleep.

Stars spangled his vision, then excruciating pain in his kidney. He was groggy with sleep. Another thwack and the pain was repeated, only this time on the other side. He tried to yell but couldn't. Felt like he was being pummelled with a baseball bat. He tried to roll over but there was pressure on him, too great to shift. Someone was sitting astride him.

They were here.

And they were going to kick the living shit out of him.

His vision cleared but the pain was throbbing in his sides.

'You Degarda?' a voice said.

Scarface nodded in the darkness. The weight lifted off his back. He rolled over. Something hard crashed into his jaw. Dizziness sloshed about inside his head. He could taste warm, salty blood leaking inside his mouth. Whoever was beating him moved away. He could tell by the creak of floorboards receding from the bed.

The sound of heavy breathing reached him. He realized it was his own. Objects in the room began to assume shapes as his eyes grew accustomed to the dark, the end of the bed, the washstand. He heard a whoosh of air, another thwack and his left arm caught fire above the elbow. Scarface could have sworn it was broken. He shuffled up to the end of the bed, hugging his knees, hoping for some kind of protection.

The overhead light flicked on, blinding him. He cowered down, holding his arms over his head. Blood was flowing cleanly from a cracked lip and running down his chest. He felt incredibly exposed and vulnerable, sitting there on the bed, huddled in a ball, pain ricocheting around his body. He could see his thighs and his cock and the rumpled bedsheet. Slowly he lifted his head.

There were three of them. One of them was huge and clutching a piece of heavy-duty rubber hose. Could inflict a lot of pain but wouldn't break bone. They were leering at him. They didn't bother guarding the door. No one was going to come in. The girl was gone.

'You Degarda?' The same rasping voice as before. It was the big guy in the middle.

Again Scarface nodded.

'You got information.'

The big one was the leader. Scarface didn't know whether he'd just been asked a question or not, so he nodded.

The leader started slapping the hose against his palm. 'What informa-tion?'

Scarface turned his head to the side of the bed and spat blood on to the floor. 'If I tell you that, I'll be dead in under a minute.'

The three men looked at one another, sniggering.

'You're dead anyway, shithead,' the leader said.

'I'll talk to Cobra—'

Jimmy Pran moved so fast that Scarface had no chance of avoiding the hose. It smashed into the side of his head, pitching him on to the floor. He scurried into the corner. Now there were six men in the room with him. One of the others kicked him in the stomach so hard he puked, fighting for air at the same time. The room darkened. The floor became water moving between the walls. One more impact like that and he was gone.

'Tell . . . Cobra. . . .'

'Yeah?'

'*Santa Maria* . . . I was there . . . saw him . . . never said . . . anything.'

Jimmy Pran watched the figure in the corner lose consciousness, his head lolling forwards and his naked body sliding down the wall.

The sky was ribboned pink, sending an ethereal light into the room through the semi-open shutters when Scarface came to. He clamped his eyes shut while a wave of nausea washed over him. He tried again, this time more slowly, one eye at a time. The room settled and became still. The stench of vomit filled his head. Congealed blood glued his shoulder to the floor. A jack-hammer started up in his brain. He closed his eyes and realized he was tensing every muscle in his body. Breathing deeply, Scarface made an effort to relax. The jack-hammer eased off a bit. He pushed himself up so that his back rested against the cool wall. Very slowly he managed to lean forward, get on to all fours. Gradually, he drew one knee forward, then the other until he was squatting on his haunches. Peeking through one eye, he reached up to the sill and tried to stand. Fire crackled around his kidneys; the nausea came, but he fought it. He stayed like that for a while, rocking gently on the balls of his feet, getting used to the idea of being upright while his body protested. His mind was empty of thought, his will concentrated on remaining on his feet.

The sun's dawn rays warmed his front while the ceiling fan sent draughts of cool air rippling down his back. Finally, he shuffled towards the washstand, leaning heavily on the chipped basin. He raised his head and looked at himself in the mirror.

The left side of his face was caked with drying blood. Saliva and dried vomit clotted his chin and neck. His left arm felt weak, barely able to support the weight of his leaning. Livid welts, purple under the skin, discoloured his arm and his left eye was practically closed from the swelling.

But he was alive! A chuckle escaped his lips and immediately dispatched a spasm of pain rocketing down his spine. He coughed and spat into the sink, a mix of blood and saliva. He steadied himself, reached down and lifted his cock on to the edge of the sink. The cold porcelain pressed against his thighs. He turned the tap and listened to the tinkling sound of running water until he felt a small urge to pee. Looking down, Scarface urinated into the water. The pee was yellow. Looked okay. He cupped his hand, peed into his palm and bought his hand close to his face. No blood. No serious damage to his kidneys.

It took him ten minutes to work his way across the room. Each manoeuvre needed careful planning so that he was always in reach of support. Still didn't trust himself to stand unaided. The bed was a good staging post and bought him to the bathroom door. Clinging to the door-frame, Scarface pulled the light cord so hard the mountings ripped from the ceiling. He managed to get into the bath by sitting on the edge then slowly swinging his legs in, one at a time.

The cold shower revived him. He stood under the weak jets of water, head bent, making occasional sweeps of his hand to remove the blood and sick.

They hadn't killed him. Which meant they weren't going to.

Scarface lay down in the bath with the shower dribbling on to his neck and shoulders like rain. He was in! Then he fainted. He didn't know how long he stayed like that. When he came to, the light filtering into the bathroom was stronger. The shower had reduced to a drip. Gnawing hunger pains hollowed out his stomach. He tried to get out of the bath, but decided against the effort, so he just lay there, summoning strength for the Herculean effort to get to the bed.

30

Angela Ramierez was expecting them. At ten o'clock that morning, when the call came through that two foreigners had just arrived, she told the officer manning the reception desk to send them straight up to the third floor.

Angela Ramierez was twenty-six, smart, a psychology grad and stunningly beautiful. One of those women who can *arrest* men on the street, in a restaurant, anywhere. She could act, too. Couple of years back, she'd done a six-week stint as a lap dancer at the Goodnight Club on Roxas, part of an undercover team busting a drugs ring. A G-string wasn't much of a prop to hide behind. You either had it or you didn't. Angela Ramierez had it, in abundance. Several very good reasons why Santos had chosen her to pose as his wife during the hunt for Elizabeth McGovern's jewels.

The lift doors peeled back on third.

'Miss Ramierez?'

'Alan?'

He stuck out his hand.

She shook it perfunctorily. No smile. Simon, it seemed, was incidental. 'Follow me, please.'

Angela turned and walked briskly down the corridor.

Alan glanced at Simon. 'Tough cookie.'

Simon's eyes slid down her body. 'Pretty tough cookie.'

They followed her through a door stencilled with Filippo Santos's name in peeling white lettering. The blinds were drawn. The desk neat and clear, as if the occupant was away on holiday. Angela sat behind the desk, opened a drawer and took out a piece of paper. Notes were scrawled on its surface.

Not a print-out, Alan noticed, because that would have been timed and therefore traceable.

'Yesterday afternoon at six-fifteen an enquiry was registered at central criminal records from General Santos City.' Angela glanced down at the paper.

Simon and Alan exchanged quick glances. 'Go on.'

'The enquiring officer was a Sergeant Castella, 8365280, enquiry number FF5386H. The enquiry related to the previous convictions of José Luis Degarda.'

'He's in!' Alan exclaimed. He punched a fist into an open palm. 'Bloody good.'

Angela looked at Alan. No emotion on her face. 'He's alive.' She paused, eyes flicking between the two of them. 'For the moment.'

'He's safe,' Alan countered. 'Cobra isn't going to do anything until he's got what Filippo's offering.'

'I don't get it,' Simon said, puzzled. 'Can't Cobra check that Degarda's a fake cover?'

Angela shook her head. 'He has checked.' Then she explained the time flags on data entries to central records. 'Cobra knows this. Filippo has several covers. For example, when a criminal dies say, then an officer can bury any record of death and continue making entries from time to time to keep the alias alive. Not every policeman can do this, only those with special access. Filippo has access.' She didn't elaborate.

'Is that what happened here?'

'Degarda was killed in a car accident five years ago.'

Alan filled in the blanks. 'Degarda was a crew member on board a ship called the *Santa Maria*. It was attacked by pirates. Degarda was the only survivor. Santos investigated the case. Problem was that Filippo never made an arrest. It really bothered him. The *Santa Maria* was one of the ballistics matches to *Clarissa*.'

'I remember,' Simon said.

'Degarda identified one of the attackers as having tattoos of snakes on his arms.'

'Same as the guy in the picture?'

'Same tattoos, right. Santos never got further than that. So when we got the ballistics match, it was pay-dirt as far as Santos was concerned. Kept Degarda alive for the express purpose of maybe one day getting a crack at this bloke.'

'Jesus!' Simon sat back.

'What will you do?' Angela's question was directed at Alan.

'Me and Simon are going to take a little trip down to General Santos City.'

Simon was shaking his head. 'Don't you know what's going on?'

Angela fixed him with an unblinking gaze. 'Yes, I do.'

'Well then. Cobra has the manuscript, for sure, otherwise your boss would be worm's meat by now. Doctor Sharif Mohammed must have translated it for him. Problem is, we need to *prove* he's got the manuscript. But he hasn't got the diary.'

'And you're going to give it to him. I know the plan.' She was aloof, as if she thought the plan was nuts.

'This prick murdered my parents, Miss Ramierez. He gutted one of his henchmen; he placed a lump of lead inside the brain of Dr Mohammed. And we think, Alan and I think that my broth— So yes. I'm going to give him the diary, then I'm going to rip out his heart and eat it.'

'Easy, Simon.' Alan squeezed his shoulder. Then he looked at Angela Ramierez, whose expression hadn't changed. 'Do you have anything else that might be useful?'

She shook her head. 'I've been over the reports on the deaths of Lee Chu and Dr Mohammed. There's no reliable evidence to make a conviction stick at this stage. Maybe if we could get a match on the weapon that killed Dr Mohammed, but then we've got to prove that Cobra pulled the trigger. And we can't get the weapon without infiltrating his camp. There's no point launching an assault on the camp and making arrests—'

'I know. In case the weapon's been chucked.'

Simon added, 'And if we did bust in there and find the manuscript, who's to say this Cobra character didn't pick it up for a couple of bucks at the local market?'

Angela nodded. 'In which case all we'd do is alert Cobra and give him a chance to protect himself. Anyway, an assault is out of the question now that Filippo's infiltrating.'

'Likely to be tipped off by this Sergeant Castella anyway.'

'Yes.'

'That's why I'm going to give him the diary, Miss Ramierez,' Simon interjected. 'So he'll go for the gold. You see, the manuscript is no good on its own. The diary is no good on its own. He needs both to get him to the site. So if he gets to the site, we'll know he's got the manuscript for sure. And if he's got the manuscript, he could only have got it from *Clarissa*. And if he got it from *Clarissa*, we'll know he killed my parents. Then you can launch your assault.' Simon stood up. 'I don't think there's anything else.'

Angela stayed seated, cool, as though she hadn't heard the remonstration. 'I do not agree with Filippo; I think your plan is flawed.' She looked at Alan. 'I was trying to find another way.'

'Believe me, Miss Ramierez, there is no other way.' *And then there's Ben.* Simon had almost let it slip. No one else knew about the possibility that Ben might still be alive. Except for Filippo. He also knew about Elly McCreadie.

Angela sighed. 'I have some equipment for you to take. That bag in the corner.'

An unmarked, black canvas holdall rested on the floor. Alan unzipped the bag and checked the contents. One of the items was a small box enclosed in a waterproof rubberized casing with a magnetized backing plate. He handed it to Simon.

'Should be okay. I can programme this to emit on the hour.' Simon gave the GPS tracker back to Alan.

'Well, let's hope I'm not phoning you with code words,' Alan looked at Angela while he zipped the bag.

'I'm curious about something: how did you find Cobra?'

He slung the bag up on to his shoulder. 'Plain old donkey work,' he said. 'We should be moving.'

31

'Time you told me what the fuck is going on here, Mr Degarda.' Cobra was using his reasonable voice.

Santos had noted every detail of the camp, from the time the car had turned on to the track across the swamp. The armed barricade, the arrangement of huts, the perimeter fencing. They had picked him up at midday. The same thug who'd almost killed him. He guessed they'd given him until midday to recover from the beating. At least enough so that a second going-over wouldn't finish him off. Necessarily.

Cobra inclined his head slightly to one side in the manner of a teacher hiding exasperation at a dim-witted pupil. 'You have information.' A statement. The dome of his head was polished with sweat, shining like a white cannon ball.

Santos was standing in front of a table in what he guessed was the mess hall. He could smell boiled rice coming from somewhere nearby. His entire body ached, reminding him not to overdo the technique of drawing information.

'You say the information you have is important to me. Now, Mr Degarda, how could you possibly know that?'

Santos listened intently. There had been no hesitation at Cobra's use of the name Degarda. No careful pronunciation, no deliberation. Just Degarda. Like he believed it.

Cobra raised his arms behind his head and stretched, arching backwards in his chair. With alarming ferocity, he bought his fist down, smashing the table top.

Santos jumped. Shit scared. He needed to be aware of his true feelings. Had to stay rooted. Interrogation technique. He was trying to draw information. Good. Cobra had an aura, a presence. No doubt about it. Fearful.

'I have information,' Santos stated flatly.

Cobra reverted to reasonable mode. 'And how did you come by this information?'

'In Manila.'

'I didn't ask where. I asked how.'

'Talk. In the bars. Rumours.'

Cobra laughed. It was not an unpleasant sound. Santos wondered what this guy might have done with his life in other circumstances. Maybe a surgeon with weekends at the country club. Or a lawyer. Dark suit, shiny shoes.

'What rumours?'

'Gold. Treasure.' Santos blurted the words as if he didn't believe them himself.

Cobra became more attentive. Placed his hands together, interlacing his fingers. 'What has that got to do with me?'

Santos was thinking, as quickly as he could through the numbing pain in his head. No expression of surprise from Cobra. No denial of the existence of any treasure.

'The Leopard, Lee Chu.'

This time surprise registered. Clearly. Santos was careful to stay impassive. The surprise wasn't to do with Lee Chu blabbing. People talked. He knew the nickname, Leopard. It had been a guess, a wild risk. Lee Chu's body had been washed up. Photographs taken. The man's entire back was one huge tattoo. A leopard.

'What did you hear?'

Relief swept through Santos's body like a cool wave. 'He attacked a yacht. The people were called McGovern.'

No admission from Cobra. No denial either.

'How do you know Lee Chu?'

'I don't. Only heard.'

'So what have you got for me?'

'He is here. . . .'

'Who is here?'

'McGovern, the son, he is here in the Philippines.'

Cobra glanced over Santos's shoulder to Jimmy who was standing behind. He gave an imperceptible nod. The air parted.

Pain exploded in Santos's back. He felt his knees crash to the floor then sand bite into the side of his face.

His breath came quickly. Even, rapid little pumps to try and control the pain. He rolled on his back then his side. Someone heaved him up by his arms and sat him in a chair.

'Why did you come here, to me?'

'I . . . remember . . . you . . . from the . . . *Santa Maria* . . . never saw your . . . face . . . just the . . . tattoos.'

Jimmy was about to smash the guy's head but Cobra stayed him with a raised hand. He remembered the *Santa Maria*. All the crew had been killed. All of them! Except Degarda. Which is why he was still alive. He hadn't shopped Cobra. Now was his chance to get a look-in. He'd remembered the name the instant Jimmy had relayed the message from Degarda about the *Santa Maria*.

Cobra pieced together the puzzle. Of course people knew who he was, knew the camp. Gang members came and went, they had families, the men screwed whores, not everyone could be relied upon to keep their mouths shut.

Even he had failed. One day, when he'd been a dumb kid, held by the VC, they'd put a wire round his neck and said they were going to hang him. He'd lost his shit, hadn't kept his mouth shut. A platoon of marines had got wasted as a result.

'McGovern? Where is he?'

'Manila.' The pain was beginning to recede. 'Knows you're down here, Mindanao. He's coming looking. Says he's got a diary. Wants to kill you.

Says you need the diary to get the gold. . . .' Santos slid off the chair. Crashed to the floor.

From somewhere distant he heard a voice say, 'And what do you want, Mr Degarda?'

His eyes seemed unwilling to open. 'I help you find the gold . . . I get . . . a piece of it.' He relaxed his whole body, pretending to be in a faint.

Strong arms gathered him up. Shouted instructions. He was carried outside. Felt the sun's heat on his body. A step up, then cool shade again. Handcuffs were snapped on to his wrists, his arms embracing some kind of pillar. Then the sound of a door closing and silence.

Santos opened his eyes. It was dark. His eyes gradually became accustomed to the dim interior. He was in a small hut. There was a window but it was boarded. No furniture. A central pillar of palm trunk supported the roof. Cobra had time to think, to figure it out, to understand that Degarda was a good guy. Or a good, bad guy. The joke made him smile. A spasm of pain electrocuted him.

Cobra waited for Jimmy. So much to think about. Had he been compromised? That had been his first thought. When Jimmy had paid Degarda a visit then come back and mentioned the *Santa Maria*, he decided to spare the man's life. For a while. His story checked out. And now the rumours about the McGovern kid. They were true. He'd heard them himself. Dumb fuck. What'd the kid think? That by mouthing off in bars some gook would show him the way?

Jimmy came in still brandishing the rubber hose. He tossed it to one side and sat down opposite Cobra.

'The Leopard had a big mouth,' Jimmy hissed.

Cobra shook his head.

'Degarda said.'

'Degarda's full of shit.'

'We heard about the McGovern kid.'

'Thing that worries me is how the fuck the kid figured I hit the yacht and how come he found out I'm here in Mindanao.' *Waited 2,000 friggin'*

*miles to hit the yacht, just so's to be way away from base. No one going to
peg me. But the kid had.*

Jimmy shook his head. 'You thinking Degarda's a cop?'

Cobra thought about that. 'Story checks out. He saw me on the *Santa
Maria*. He's not a cop. Why bother with all this crap? If the kid knows I'm
here and Degarda knows about the kid and Degarda's a cop, then what
the fuck is he doing here?'

Jimmy grunted, 'Dunno.'

'Degarda says the kid's got the diary. Wants to flush me out. Fucking
prick.' Cobra didn't need Jimmy for this. Guy was an ape brain. 'Jimmy,
go find out what Degarda knows about the kid's movements.'

Jimmy stood up and went to retrieve the hose.

'Don't take that, Jimmy. I've already told you, Degarda's not a cop.
You don't need that. Just go find out by asking.'

Cobra was thinking, kid must either be smart, lucky or got someone
helping him out. Whatever else, he was no dummy.

Jimmy came in. 'Kid's here someplace, on the coast. That's what
Degarda says he heard. Was going to take a boat so he could take a look
at the coastline and pinpoint the camp.'

'Smart, dumb kid. There's a hole someplace, an information leak.
Gotta plug the leak.' Cobra was thinking his only other option was to
pull out. Forget the whole deal. Get rid of the papers, everything. Except
the McGovern kid had found out.

Santos was twisted around the pole. Couldn't get comfortable. The big
gorilla had come in, asked a couple of questions. So Cobra had to be
thinking about things. And he was still alive. His story was holding. Had
to be holding. No beating this time. Just a couple of questions. Good.
Good. So far.

The door cracked open, just an inch or so, enough to let in a wedge of
sunlight. Santos slithered around the pole so he was facing the door.
Maybe this was the end. Maybe they didn't buy it. The door opened a bit
wider. A girl stepped inside the hut. Her face was a silhouette. She

padded over to him. Knelt beside him. Not a word. Up close he could see her face. Beautiful, despite the bruising around the eye and the misshapen nose. She placed a gourd of water then backed away two steps, standing up, looking down on him. Her movements were agile and feminine. Reminded him of a Japanese geisha, all butterfly delicacy.

His training resurfaced. Cobra might be using her. The soft approach. Lull him. Maybe even seduce him.

'Are you hurt?' Her voice, like her body, was willowy.

Yes! And scared. And call Angela Ramierez to get some choppers down here full of armed officers! 'I'm okay.'

'There's water.' She pointed to the gourd.

'Thank you.'

She was quiet for a moment. 'Why have you come?'

A plea. Christ! Did he detect a *plea*? 'Why have you?'

'To help you.' She stared down at him. 'Because I want to get out.'

Careful, Filippo. 'So leave.' He said it as if that was the simplest thing in the world.

In the darkness Mae-li emitted a sad little laugh, a slight agitation of her shoulders. It might have been a sob. 'I wish I could.'

'He will hurt you?' Santos tried to hold himself from travelling too far down this road. A contrary instinct told him to follow it. He had stepped over the boundary.

'He would kill me.'

She seemed calm again. Santos listened to the chilling words, spoken with such ordinariness he was left with little choice but to believe her. Another voice in his mind screamed at him to stop this. He was being led into a trap. He shook his head, denying her in the darkness.

'I can't help you. I'm here on business.' Business! It sounded absurd.

'Then why are you handcuffed in the darkness like an animal?'

Fair question. 'Cobra must be careful.' Stop this. Now! 'You must go. My business is not with you.'

Mae-li turned to go.

'Wait!' What the fuck am I doing. I'm losing it! She's come in here, I don't even know who she is. Information is power. 'Who are you?'

'My name is Mae-li.'

Santos detected hope in her voice, nestling expectantly between her words.

He tried the direct approach. Tease her out. 'You are important to him?'

'I was. I don't think I am, any more.'

'What have you done?' The girl seemed anxious to talk. So let her talk. If this was a trap, he'd already figured a way out.

Mae-li squatted down, bringing her face to the same level as his. He could smell her. A scent of powder, like a baby. 'He saved me once. A long time ago. I was a child. Now, I don't know the outside world.'

This is bullshit! Get her out of here! She sounded scared. Either that or an actress of sublime ability. His instincts waged war.

'You're afraid. . . .'

'I'm beyond afraid. I don't care what happens to me.'

He could see that. Her whole being was somehow slumped. Even here, in the darkness, he could sense that. Quite clearly. His concentration was locked on to Mae-li. Hadn't heard the pad of feet from outside, approaching.

'*The fuck is going on!*' The door smashed back on its hinges so violently, Santos was mildly surprised the carpentry had withstood the impact. He jolted instinctively, making the handcuffs bite painfully into his wrists.

'*The fuck is happening!*'

Painful sunlight flooded in. Cobra marched over to Mae-li who stood, transfixed.

Squinting against the brightness, Santos could see the extent of Mae-li's beauty. He felt strangely overwhelmed by it. At the same moment he felt his heart slide away down into his guts. Apprehension crushed his chest like a slab of concrete. Fucking entrapment.

'She brought water.' It was the only thing Santos could think of. He realized he was trying to save her. The next thing he knew, Mae-li was flying through the air and sprawling across his legs. The sound of the blow followed as thunder follows lightning.

Cobra kicked the gourd away, splashing water against the wall.

Don't save her. Save yourself. Santos moved his legs, rolling Mae-li off. Deny any collusion. He saw a chance to stay in the game. Seized it. His way out. 'Bitch wanted me to help her. I told her no way, man.'

Cobra became very still. Santos could swear the temperature in the hut dropped. 'I'm here to talk business with you, man. Don't want any shit from some woman.' And, as he betrayed her, Santos died a little.

Cobra grabbed Mae-li's ankles and dragged her towards the open door. Her body was limp, but her dark eyes were fixed on Santos. Her arms unfolded and straightened as she was pulled, her fingers creating trails in the sand-covered ground. She made no sound, just stared at him as if she could see straight through.

Santos strained to hear what was happening outside. Blinking in the sunlight. Sounds faded. The camp felt peculiarly deserted. A shadow fell across the floor. Cobra stepped into the hut. Santos could see a handgun tucked into his waistband. His guts turned to water. He developed an incredible urge to shit.

'Unlock the handcuffs.' Cobra lobbed a ring of keys on to the floor.

Santos fumbled. His mind had blanked. No thoughts, no plan, no strategy. Just empty. He unlocked the cuffs and massaged his bruised wrists. There was no one with Cobra and the man made no attempt to draw his weapon. Maybe the ploy had worked. Maybe he had won Cobra's confidence.

'She only brought water.' It seemed safe to say.

'Sure.' Cobra was back to reasonable. The rage of earlier dissolved. 'Follow me.'

Santos, still massaging his wrists, walked to the door. The compound, cordoned by the ring of huts, was full of people. Thirty he guessed. Their silence was shocking. Their stillness reminiscent of ritual. They had assembled like ghosts, formed into a semi-circle. Involuntarily, Santos sank to his knees. The silence thundered. He knew an execution scene when he saw one.

Cobra turned at the sound of his collapse. Surprise showed on his face. He walked back, stooped, placed a hand at Santos's elbow and encouraged him to stand.

'You're here on business, Mr Degarda. Remember?' Cobra seemed amused.

Santos stood with difficulty and walked a few paces with Cobra until they were standing in the centre of the clearing, surrounded.

'Jimmy!' Cobra barked.

A little squirt of urine escaped Santos's bladder. A shuffling reached him from somewhere behind the crowd. Then the men parted, forming a human corridor. Jimmy led Mae-li through the passage.

She was brought into the centre, made to kneel in front of Cobra. Then Jimmy came and stood behind Santos.

'It's such a pleasant day for death,' Cobra said conversationally. 'Hers or yours.'

Santos looked at Cobra. Saw the madness that inhabited his eyes, glinting as he spoke like shards of blue glass.

'Loyalty is paramount.' Cobra was whispering now. None of the men except Jimmy could hear. And Mae-li. She was staring down at the sand. 'Disloyalty cannot be tolerated.'

I haven't been disloyal. The logic came to him through a mist of fear. Fuck. I've killed her!

'You've killed her, you know that, don't you, Mr Degarda?'

The guy was inside his brain, his words dripping like acid as if he'd written his thoughts.

Cobra hefted the pistol from his waist band, cocked it and offered it to Degarda, butt first.

I could kill the fuck right here, right now. He found himself trying to get rid of the thoughts in case they appeared in his eyes. He took the weapon. The gun felt oily in his hand.

'Shoot her.' The order was calm, utterly casual. Then Cobra took one step back and folded his arms, waiting.

Santos scanned the deadpan faces of the pirates gathered round him. They stared back like a collection of statues.

She was, had been, important to Cobra. His consort, perhaps. Surely he would execute her himself. Santos felt his arm rising, controlled by some other power. This is a test. The barrel fell into line with a point between Mae-li's eyes. I kill her, I'm blooded. Is that the game? Began to take trigger pressure. Don't pull the trigger and I'm dead, Simon's dead, Alan's dead. Felt slight resistance at the end of the first trigger pressure. Squeeze and she's dead. One life instead of three. Murderer or innocent. Felt the take up of the second trigger pressure. Want to cry. Want to die.

Squeezed.

32

Gertrude Ziegle stared up at one of the few adornments on her office walls, a picture of the Los Alamos hills. She had liked it there. Enjoyed the tranquillity, the solemnity, the feel of the pulse of the earth. It was raw, undisturbed, unchanged for thousands of years. In her mind's eye it was easy to imagine primitive man lumbering across the barren landscape. Incongruous then that set among such beauty should be the derived wisdom of mankind, the pinnacle of his evolutionary development focused on the creation of weapons of incredible destructive power. And the source of this power? The manipulation of nature, by reconfiguring the very atomic particles that made up life itself. The contrast shadowed her, the monstrous side of man evoked in the clean, sunlit lines of the New Mexico hills. The hypocrisy could not be more apparent, not to her, because she knew. Oh, yes! She knew what it was to feel the deeply embedded blade of betrayal. Beauty and destruction. Order and chaos. Honour and deceit.

'Bastards!' She screamed so loudly her vision blacked and starred. Gertrude Ziegle remained still, breathing deeply until she felt herself regain composure.

'They'll think I'm crazy,' she said to the empty room, to the silent hills. 'I'm not. Oh, no. Dangerous, yes. But not crazy.' A small laugh escaped her dry lips punctuated with flecks of spittle. 'I have become the ultimate hypocrisy.' Her mind bucked off in another direction. What was his name? An English doctor, a serial killer they'd called him, murdering his patients by administering injections of diamorphine. Shipwright. Shipman! Harold Shipman. She'd make the guy look like a pygmy. The thought suddenly struck her that she would very shortly become the biggest killer in history. By a long, long way. She'd single-handedly take out more people than the final death toll of the Second World War.

She jumped at the chime of the doorbell.

Gary Simonsen was bored. His boss had come back from Washington and stirred up a hornets' nest with talk of imminent nuclear doom. The agents at the San Francisco field office had buzzed into activity. A week later the energy had dampened, the routine had been established and now the boredom had taken hold. Simonsen had been allocated Alameda County. He had checked into the Blue Springs motel in Livermore and found the resident agency above a liquor store five blocks east. Special agent Rich McAteer had been assigned as his partner. The two had retired to a coffee house to decide how to execute the orders from Washington. Their plan was simple. The names and addresses supplied on the search list were sorted to geographical area. Rich would drive because he knew the neighbourhoods. They would alternate the house calls, five each then switch. If a person on the list was not home they would return later. If either of them became suspicious, whoever was in the car would radio the agency then come and assist. Simple.

Gary glanced over his shoulder. Number 673 on the list. He could see Rich slouched behind the wheel of the black sedan reading the sports page, munching a doughnut.

The house was like a million other homes spread across America. Gary reached for the doorbell and heard the chimes echo inside. He had a hard-copy print-out of names. He scored a line through this one, folded the print-out and slid it back into his raincoat pocket.

To Simonsen's twenty-six-year-old eyes the woman who answered the door seemed very old and very frail. Spittle glued the corners of her mouth and her breath was laboured. *As though from exertion?*

'Excuse me, ma'am, are you Miss Gertrude Mulcahy?'

'Yes, I am.'

'Ma'am, I need to ask you some questions if I may.'

'Who are you?'

Simonsen palmed his badge and held it close enough for her to read.

'My, my. The FBI. Come in young man.'

'Just for a moment.' Simonsen looked over to the car. He saw Rich turning the page.

The house was as he imagined the other million might be. Plain floorboards covered with a thin rug. Everything neat. The smell of cheap cologne and dust in the air. And slightly too warm.

Simonsen followed her into the lounge. The woman seemed to be waiting expectantly. He noticed the silver frame on the mantel, a young man in Marine uniform.

'We have a situation, ma'am. I am required to check out all personnel who worked at the Lawrence Livermore laboratory within the last fifteen years. You did work there?'

'Yes, I did.'

'When did you start?'

'Let me think. Well it would have been very late in 1986.'

'What work did you do?'

'I was in the catering department.'

'Did you have or know anyone who had access to sensitive material, ma'am?'

'What do you think, young man?'

Simonsen grinned. 'I won't take any more of your time.'

Out in the hall, Gary Simonsen stopped by the open door under the stairs that led down to the basement. He genuflected on to one knee and tied his shoelace. And he couldn't help but glance down the narrow steps to the basement. By the time he made it back to the car Rich had finished the paper and the doughnut.

Gertrude Ziegle was incensed. Her head pounded ferociously and none of the analgesics had made even a dent. Stupid boy! Stupid, stupid boy!

Oh no, not you, Jamie-Jake, that man from the FBI. They're not taking me seriously, Jamie-Jake. They send a silly young man with a stupid grin. Asking impudent questions. I'm an old lady so I couldn't possibly be taken seriously!

Gertrude Ziegle was pacing around her lounge, the silver-framed photograph of Jamie-Jake clutched to her bosom.

'Did you know anyone with clearance?' She talked out loud, bobbing her head from side to side. 'What department did you work in?' Her voice was singsong, patronizing.

'I even gave the moron a hint, Jamie-Jake; I told him the first part of the deadline code, 1986. Fool. *Fool!*' she screamed, and then scurried quickly downstairs to her basement hide in case any passers-by or the neighbours had heard her shout.

She shut the door and placed the frame gently on the desk next to her computer. She looked adoringly at the image it contained and slowly shook her head. You were sacrificed to save some general's career. Behind her, pinned to the cork board in the middle of the American flag was a colour portrait image of the President of the United States torn from the pages of *TIME Magazine*. He was smiling broadly. Protruding from the middle of his forehead was a dart.

When Gary Simonsen filed his report later that afternoon, there had been nothing odd, out of context, unusual or unexpected among the 763 persons he had been assigned to question. None warranted further investigation. There was however one footnote. He entered it beside the name *Mulcahy, Gertrude* of 21 Fig Tree Drive, Livermore. He had noticed it on the way out of the house as he was passing the open door under the stairs that led down to the basement. For a moment he wasn't sure, so he'd ducked down and made a pretence of tying his shoelace. Surreptitiously he glanced down the stairs aware that the old lady was standing right behind him. A dart. On the floor. At the far end, on the wall the bottom of what looked like the Stars and Stripes, another dart protruding from it. Strange. Maybe grandkids. He thought it prudent to add it in. Then he forgot about it. Never mentioned it to Rich or the local resident senior agent. They'd pick it up in the report and follow-up if they felt it necessary. He had a game to go see back in 'Frisco. Just maybe the 49ers were on their way to the Superbowl.

33

The Rajah Muda Beach Resort was perfect. Situated out of town, the resort had a private sandy cove providing direct access to the sea and since the sea was where their work was to be done, this consideration ruled out any of the hotels in General Santos City. Angela Ramierez was a phonecall away and had Alan's mobile number if any new information emerged. Other than Angela, no one knew they were here, not even Santos. Alan had found the place on the Internet, sitting in the business centre of the Manila Hotel.

Simon had spent the first morning in town buying scuba gear – four tanks, four buoyancy vests, four regulators, four weight belts, two masks each and two sets of fins each. Duplicate sets. He bought new wetsuits and two mini pony tanks, each the size and shape of a car fire extinguisher. The ponies would provide either emergency air or increased manoeuvrability, depending on the circumstances.

Back at the hotel, he explained the equipment – fitting the tank to the buoyancy vest, attaching the regulator, opening the air supply, checking pressure. Then he took Alan through the basic procedures of mask-clearing underwater, hand signals for ascent, descent, out of air. In the pool, Simon had demonstrated underwater drills for achieving neutral buoyancy, losing and relocating the regulator, emergency breathing and buddy breathing. Out in the bay, renting a boat, they had gone through the drills again, repeatedly, in deeper water until he was sure that Alan was ready, at least competent.

The fierce sun beat down relentlessly as it had since their arrival. This was their third day out, sitting in the hired speed-boat, a twenty-footer with twin outboards, anchored in thirty metres of water, two miles offshore. Below the surface, the currents moved in a smooth even rhythm. Up top, the sea rolled in a heavy swell, like a marauding army regrouping after its fractured passage around the islands of the Banda Sea.

Simon hoisted a tank on to his back, fitted his mask and fins, checked his air was running then toppled backwards into the cool water. He resurfaced and grabbed the gunwale rail of the speedboat. Alan dropped two complete sets of equipment into the water. Each set comprised a tank, vest, regulator attached, fins and mask all bound together with a weight belt. All the air had been squeezed out of the vests and the belts immediately pulled the kit under. Simon let them fall away then ducked under the water and followed them down, pinching his nose and blowing hard to clear the pressure in his ears as he descended.

On the seabed, he orientated himself to the silhouette of the boat's hull. The two sets of gear had landed on the sandy bottom ten metres apart. He stowed them next to a large boulder directly beneath the boat, checking the air pressure on each tank one final time. They were both at 200 bar. He closed off the valves. A last look round, then a glance up at the surface to make sure no other vessel was approaching. All clear. Ascend.

'Did you open the air?' said Alan, as he hauled Simon over the side.

Simon shook his head. Alan had asked that before, twice. Nerves. 'No. They could roll in the current.'

Alan nodded.

'May press on the regulator, then we'll lose the air.'

'Right. And give ourselves away.'

'That too.'

They sat in silence, staring out over the empty sea towards land. The suck and gurgle of water at the bow sounded hollow and light.

'This is crazy, Al.' Simon suddenly turned to face Alan. He squeezed the rail hard.

Alan continued staring out. 'Only way.'

'Suppose Santos is dead and has told them?'

'Then we won't get the signal and we're over the side.'

Simon squared back to his vigil. 'You sure this is going to work?'

'No.'

'I need a beer.'

'I need about twenty.'

Simon lit a cigarette and puffed away. It tasted sour. But he smoked it down to the butt anyway.

Santos only had the clothes he'd been wearing when Jimmy had collected him from the boarding-house; jeans, red T-shirt, scuffed trainers. After the 'execution', Jimmy had taken him to the mess hall, which he said, in new, friendlier terms, was known as the ops room.

He would remember that empty click booming into the stillness forever. And afterwards, the eruption. Men jeering, laughing, closing in on him. He had looked down at Mac-li lying in the dirt, eyes wide open, staring at his feet, panting with death shock. Two men had picked her up and dragged her away, her eyes transfixed on his face until she'd disappeared behind some bodies. Someone had reached down and disengaged the gun from his fingers. Cobra. Holstered the pistol behind his belt.

'Jimmy'll get you something to eat. We'll talk later.' Then he was marching off, joking with his men.

After a meal of boiled rice and fish, he'd been billeted in a hut with three other men. He learned they all had nicknames. Rule one: never use real names. Security. His hut-mates were *Knifeman*, a kid of eighteen or so who carried no fewer than three knives of various sizes about his person. Another, whose face bore the remains of debilitating acne was called *Pockmark*. *Mickey* was so labelled because a rendition of Mickey Mouse coloured his entire left buttock.

He, predictably, had been christened *Executioner* and, Santos noted, with a feeling of disgust he was careful to shield, that some of the less fortunately labelled showed signs of envy, men known as *Ugly*, *Hippie* and *Shithead* among them.

Cobra summoned him. The ops room was empty. Eating, it seemed was a necessity, not a luxury. Rule number two.

Cobra was relaxed, pleased with the day's work, buoyed by his role as organizer then lascivious spectator at the game of death.

This time he was allowed to sit. He was still in considerable discomfort from the beating administered by Jimmy, or *Big Guy*, the nickname he'd heard Jimmy referred to by some of the others.

Cobra sat astride a simple wooden chair, one arm dangling over the back. He eyeballed the new boy. The Glock which Santos had used on Mae-li rested on the table between them. Cobra's eyes flicked almost rhythmically between the gun and Executioner.

'Tell me again what you know, what this McGovern punk is planning to do?'

Santos desperately wanted to ask about Mae-li. Where is she? How is she? Christ in Heaven. How the fuck does someone go through that and come out the other end with their mind intact?

'They're looking for you. For the camp. . . .'

Cobra braced. 'They? Who the fuck are they? You said there was the kid. Who else?'

'Two. There's two of them.'

'This is new.' Threatening.

Santos wondered why the gun was on the table. 'I saw two. That's all. There's only the other guy with the kid.' He figured Cobra was thinking, *How many more?*

Cobra nodded, slowly, deliberately. 'You certain? Two's all?'

'I followed them out of the hotel in Manila, to a restaurant. No one else was there.'

'Don't prove shit.'

'And they were sharing a room.'

'Which hotel?'

'The Manila.' He knew that would be checked.

'Who's the other guy?'

Santos shook his head. 'Don't know. Friend maybe.'

'He young?'

'No. Older guy. Fifty maybe. Fat shit.'

'White guy, black guy, fuckin' Martian?'

'White guy.'

Cobra looked past him. 'Go check it out, Jimmy. Get the fuck's name.'

Jimmy Big Guy left.

'So the kid and the fat guy, what they gonna do?'

'I heard they had a diary, or the kid had a diary. I heard there was some piece missing and they needed that to find this . . . this . . . gold. It was difficult for me to get close when I found them. Couldn't overhear the conversation. All I heard in the bars was talk of coming down here and smoking you out.'

Cobra chuckled. 'Smoke me out, huh. What . . . they think I'm a fuckin' rabbit?' The chuckle graduated to a laugh.

Santos smiled alongside, a sheepish grin, like an unfunny guy who's finally got someone to laugh at a joke.

'How the fuck they figure I was here?'

Santos wasn't certain he'd been asked. Shrugged. 'Dunno.'

'Smoke me out. Fuckin' prick. Ain't the dumb kid seen what I done to his mammy and his pappy?'

Santos knew he was staring wide-eyed. He looked away, wiped sweat from his lip. It had all been speculation: Alan's deductions, George Baker, Fort Jefferson, Marine MIA, Elly McCreadie, Degarda's witness report about the attack on the *Santa Maria*. Now Cobra had admitted everything.

'How they gonna smoke me out?' Remnants of his amusement were posted on Cobra's lips.

'Come down here, take a boat, find the camp.' Santos spoke in earnest. A co-conspirator.

Cobra clicked his tongue against the roof of his mouth. The identity of the second man was bothering him.

Jimmy came back into the ops room. Took up the same position as before, behind Executioner. Still wary of the new boy. 'McCreadie,

Albert McCreadie,' he said without ceremony. The name was meaningless to him.

For a moment Cobra's face remained the same. Santos could see the smirk hiding in Cobra's cheek muscles. The amusement became a smile, the smile a chuckle, then he was serious again. 'Ain't no police. Just another asshole.' He shook his head at the foolishness of bungling amateurs. 'Coupla assholes and they reckon they gonna smoke me out.' He looked back at Executioner. 'You could recognize these dumbfucks?'

Santos pursed his lips. 'Sure. No sweat. Fat bald guy. Skinny kid. No sweat.'

'They'll be out on the water?'

'That's what I heard.'

'They'll be staying locally someplace?'

Santos feigned boredom. 'Guess so.'

'They here now?'

A trick question, lobbed in. Real smart man Cobra. Santos shook his head. 'Dunno. I guess, maybe.' He saw a chance. 'We can check local places. They stayed in a hotel in Manila. Wasn't no sweat finding them. No reason why they wouldn't do the same here. We find them, take them out.' He held his breath.

Cobra nodded. 'No good. Too messy. No one's got to know. Shedload of gold waiting at the end of the rainbow. If they're here, they'll try and locate the camp from the sea. That's what I'd do.'

Santos breathed again. Murmured a little prayer inside his head.

'We'll patrol and take them out on the water. Make it look like an accident. Can't go near a hotel.' Cobra thought some more. 'Likely to have a local boat driver with them but that's tough shit.' As he spoke, Cobra glanced at Executioner and Jimmy in turn. He was issuing orders.

'I'll ready the boat,' Jimmy said.

Cobra waited for Jimmy to leave and begin the preparations. He would take enough men to act as crew, and issue their weapons. No need to check the fuel. Tanks were always kept topped up. Fight-or-flight response.

'I can ID them.'

'Dead right.' Cobra laughed at his small joke. 'What's your weapon of choice?'

Santos glanced at the Glock. Close-quarter fighting meant a handgun rather than a rifle. Easier to manoeuvre up close. Low calibre. No need to use a hammer to crack a nut.

'Handgun.'

'I thought so.'

Predictable. That's why the Glock was on the table. Make the asshole feel good about himself.

Cobra slid the Glock over. 'Last time was a try-out; this time it's for real.'

Santos picked it up, weighed it like a child might a wrapped Christmas present. Slid out the clip. This time it was fully loaded. Seventeen rounds. Snapped the clip home. Aimed it at the wall. 'Bang, bang, fat man. Bang, bang, dumb kid.' Then grinned, as evil a grin as he could muster.

Cobra began the search in Sarangani Bay. No dice. When the light began to fade, Cobra ordered the boat back to camp. He spoke with Jimmy, instructing him to organize a watch guard on the jetty overnight. 'These two are civilian amateurs. That makes them stupid. Stupidity might get them to thinking they can roll up here, blacked-up, playing at commandos. Keep a watch. Problem with amateurs is they're unpredictable.'

Next day, they extended the search to outside the bay, running five-mile parallels off the coast to a mile offshore. The lookouts on board were briefed on a low-profile target, a three, maybe four-man boat. The parallels had to be tightly spaced because a low-profile target would be below the horizon at a thousand metres. Again, no dice. Another 200 metres further from the shoreline and they would have sighted the target, but instead they came back to camp with only memories of the wide blue ocean for their efforts. On the third day, they continued running the parallel search grid, starting where they'd finished the previous evening, a mile offshore and working progressively seawards. Three lookouts armed with high-powered binos shifted from the port to starboard sides depending on the direction of the run. At 12.43 on that third day, the central lookout, *Mister Willy*, legendary at the local clap-traps, raised his binos, lost the target in a swell, raised them again, then yelled, 'Contact! Contact!' at the top of his lungs.

Alan's mind had wandered, the result of endless hours staring over the interminable blue of the ocean. Simon was suddenly tapping his thigh. Alan came out of his trance, his eyes following in the direction Simon was pointing. A white boat. Maybe 700 metres away, a creamy moustache at its bow.

'Jesus. This is it, Simon. Jesus!'

Adrenalin deluged Alan. Flooded him. His heartbeat was suddenly, painfully palpable in his chest. A white boat, eighty foot, steel hull. That's what the forensic boys reckoned.

'Check your gear!' Alan unzipped the front of his wetsuit. He checked. Zipped himself back up. Neoprene stretching over his girth. Simon did the same.

'Al, the tracker's in one of the pockets of the vest.'

'Which one?'

'I forgot. One of them.'

The white boat was closing fast.

'Look busy,' Alan hissed. 'Just make sure you're facing them all the time. And sitting. Got it?'

'Got it.'

Alan looked across the water. One hundred metres. The white boat was beginning to look awesomely large. From this distance he could see the bow was streaked with rust, heavy lines of it, falling from the anchor chain eyelets, like tears of blood.

The bow of the white boat suddenly settled low in the water and the creamy bow wave diminished. Only powerful engines could push the bow that high out of the water. Escape and evade. Made sense.

'Don't stand up again. Keep your arms by your side.' Alan's face had discoloured to a pasty grey as if his fear had changed the colour of his blood.

'Al, I just want to thank you . . . if anything happens . . . I mean . . .'

Simon blurted. The boat was fifty metres away and nosing towards them.

'It's okay, Simon. Everything will be okay. Just look for the signal.' Alan glanced at Simon's waist. Calmly he said, 'Simon, put your weight belt on.'

'Shit!' He scrambled at his feet, slung the weight belt round his waist and fumbled with the clasp.

'Watch for the signal.'

'Tell Bet I love her.'

'She knows that. Watch for the signal.'

'Al. . . .'

'Slow to half,' Cobra barked at the helm. 'Bring her round, ninety to port.'

'It's them,' Santos yelled. For the first time he was uncomfortably aware of the Glock pressing against the small of his back. 'What do we do?'

Cobra's hand settled on his shoulder like a tired bird.

'Blow 'em away.'

The others in the wheelhouse, Jimmy Big Guy, Spider who had the helm and Rags the engineer, greeted this announcement with loud cheers.

'Bring her in slow, Spider,' Cobra ordered. 'Come alongside, starboard side to.'

'Aye, aye, Skip.'

Cobra popped his head out the door. 'Lookouts inside,' he ordered. Mister Willy, Knifeman and Shithead piled into the wheelhouse.

Santos checked with the binos one more time, just to be certain. 'Looks like just the two of them. Can't see any crew.'

'Check,' Shithead confirmed.

In the confined space, the pirates' smell was thick: sweat, oil, salt and tobacco. Their gene pool was a diverse one. Chinese, Malay, Vietnamese. All of them wore bandannas, except him and Cobra.

'Slow to three knots, Spider.' Then Cobra turned to the group. Final briefing. 'Executioner will go out first. He found them, he gets to snuff them!' Cobra swivelled his steely-blue eyes to Santos. 'You don't go until we're close enough that you can jump the gap. Understood?'

'Yes, Skip.'

'You slot them. Go for whatever shot you favour. Head shots are best, but that boat out there's not very big so it'll be rocking as you land. So, go for whatever shots you're comfortable with. Just make sure you kill them.'

Someone slapped him on the shoulder.

Cobra eyeballed the other members of the crew. 'Rags, you stay on board with Spider. They may be armed. Look out for damage.'

Rags grunted.

'Willy, you keep watch on the port side. You're looking for escort craft. Coastal patrol or police patrol boats.' He flicked his attention back to Rags. 'Make sure we're ready to move if Willy gives the word.'

'No sweat, Skip.'

'If we're compromised, Spider'll take us due south. We'll lose them in the islands and come back under cover of darkness.'

'No fuckin' ways any puke gonna catch me, man.' Spider was grinning behind wrap-round shades, his unshaven jaw working furiously against a ball of chewing gum.

'One fifty,' Spider said.

'Shithead, Knifeman, you two follow Executioner. Finish 'em off if you have to. Then we search the boat.'

Shithead, who suffered the indignity of a weak stomach and a propensity towards diarrhoea, grinned mawkishly at Knifeman, who, in turn, was desperately eager to bury his blade in human flesh. He had the idea he might take a scalp, like the American Indians.

'Seventy-five.'

'Stations!' Cobra commanded. Rags disappeared down the companionway towards the engine-room. Mister Willy ducked out of the port-side door to take up his watch position.

'Assholes're waving,' Spider laughed. He throttled back. The engine noise deepened to a throaty growl.

Santos felt the vibrations rattle up through his feet. He glanced

through the window. Alan and Simon were both waving. A little too frantically, he thought. He pulled the Glock from his waistband, flicked the
safety catch off. He had hollowed the noses of the first two rounds in the
clip, borrowing a pointed commando knife from Knifeman for the task.
'Useful in close quarters, man. Know what I mean? Might only get one
shot. Need to create maximum grief.' Knifeman's face had lit up like a
starburst. 'Grief, yeah. Fuckin' A, man.' And Executioner reckoned the
kid believed he'd found a friend for life.

Knifeman and Shithead had taken up their weapons. AK-47s. Santos
wasn't worried about Knifeman; it was Shithead who bothered him, the
way he was drooling and fingering the trigger. Santos made a mental
note to try and block him on his way out and obstruct any shots if
Shithead felt a need to spray 7.62mm rounds in the general vicinity. He
edged towards the starboard-side door. Ready to spring.

Only the engines sounded in the wheelhouse. Even their breathing
seemed to have ceased.

'That's it! He's there!' Alan hissed between clenched teeth. He had seen
the red T-shirt in the open doorway. The signal. Santos. A wave of nausea
engulfed him and his body rocked in a near faint.

What followed happened so fast Alan had no time to think. His body
was guided by instinct and reflex, yet he saw events in slow motion. And
silence. No soundtrack to accompany the screams of the assailants, no
crack to add dimension to the gunshots.

The white boat loomed over them dissolving the narrow gap between
the two craft. Red T-shirt spun out of the doorway falling forwards in his
haste. Shadows behind him erupted into movement. And then the red T-
shirt was airborne, coming towards them. A raised arm, something black
in a hand, then flame.

He was aware of Simon falling backwards, into the water. Then pain
spreading through his own body. He sensed his chest moving backwards,
whipping his head forwards, his legs stretching out straight in front. He
experienced a curious sensation of flight and suddenly the side of the
speedboat, the side he had been sitting on, was in front of him, away from

him. Cold water and then descending in a blue gloom. The sea filled his mouth and nose, making him want to choke. Crushing pain filled his chest. Blood spiralled slowly about his face like mist. He remembered the pony tank lodged in the back of his weight belt. The pressure of the water was becoming intolerable. He grabbed for the pony tank with his left hand, ripped it free and bit down, desperately sucking air. He pinched his nose, blew hard and heard the squelch of air released inside his ear passages. His body thudded gently on to the seabed while thick, red blood lifted out of his chest like fire smoke.

Santos was looking down, his back to the speedboat. He could see it, a white and blue streak at the rim of his vision. He guessed the gap at two metres. Could feel the soles of his trainers tacky on the rubber grip mats on the beam deck. Bent his knees for the pounce, then began to fall back and sprang upwards and outwards using every ounce of strength in his thighs. He raised his right arm, picked the target on the right, aiming in the centre of the man's chest and fired. He landed with a crunch. His firing arm was already sweeping left to the next target. Then a heavy jolt next to him, on his left. Must be Shithead, too big to be Knifeman. The jolt transmitted across his shoulders, down his right arm, tensioning his trigger finger. The Glock bucked in his hand. He could actually *see* a chunk of flesh lift out the back of Simon's shoulder as he hit the water and a fine, blood mist explode behind. He swivelled his head minutely left. The gun was already lined up on the second, bigger target. Alan. And he was closer now. He fired and watched Alan lift off the side of the speedboat and crash into the water.

The speedboat rocked crazily, taking water in over the side as the gunwale momentarily dipped below the surface before springing back up. Shithead was past him, almost knocking him over in a continuation of the initial jolt. He heard the *rat tat tat tat tat* of rapid fire. High white spikes of water danced on the surface. Then Knifeman was past him, on the right and bent over the side, viciously stabbing the surface of the sea, AK held aloft.

Santos dropped his arm. The firing stopped. Knifeman heaved himself upright, arms, head and chest soaked. Two shadows fell away into the deep. Two lifeless forms, arms and legs spreadeagled like free-fall parachutists. And pink water lapping against the low freeboard of the speedboat.

'Jeeesus!' It was Knifeman. 'That was some hotshit friggin' shootin'!' There was awe in his face. 'Hey! Shithead! You see that or did you blink and miss it? Jeeesus!'

'Them's two dead gooks,' Shithead contributed, slinging his AK.

Santos was standing between them. The speedboat was listing dangerously with their weight. He took a couple of steps back to even the distribution.

'Either of you get them?' Santos looked anxiously from Knifeman to Shithead.

'Nah,' Knifeman muttered with casual regret. 'Couldn't stick 'em.'

Shithead shrugged. 'Maybe. Couldn't tell. Amount of blood, I reckon you done the damage, Execution man.'

A slow clapping from behind. Santos spun round.

Cobra was leaning against the wheelhouse, a steady grin painted on his face. Spider was behind his shoulder, still chewing on his gum. 'Very impressive. Better get back up here. Knifeman, Shithead search the boat.'

Santos heaved himself back aboard the pirate vessel.

Knifeman found a nylon briefcase. He tossed the case to Cobra and disappeared to see what else was worth taking.

Cobra yelled through to the port side, 'Any sign of an escort, Willy?'

'No, Skip.'

'Keep a sharp watch!'

Cobra unzipped the bag. Inside, he found a sheaf of papers, typed and stapled. The pockets of the briefcase were empty.

Santos scoured the top sheet of paper. 'This is it!' he proclaimed with exaggerated jubilation. He was thinking about Simon and Alan. 'Must have copied it.' He was careful to avoid the word *translated*.

Cobra snatched the papers, scanned the cover sheet quickly, then flipped through the rest, getting the gist of the words.

'OK,' he said with cool control. 'Let's go. Willy! Clear?'

'Clear, Skip.'

Shithead and Knifeman clambered aboard.

Cobra was zipping up the briefcase. The anticipation of laying his hands on possibly millions of dollars' worth of gold was clear, putting him into a dead calm.

'We going to blow the boat?' Shithead wanted a display of pyrotechnics.

'No time. Those two are shark meat. Let's go!'

Simon clutched at his injured shoulder with his left hand. He glanced round but couldn't see Alan. The salt water was stinging his eyes. His chest was agony, but he had managed to get some rhythm into his breathing. The boulder was nearby. He reached down to the spare kit. Using his left hand he unclasped one weight belt and felt for a mask. He got the strap over his head, tilted his face up, breathed in and exhaled through his nose into the mask, emptying it of water. He grabbed the fins and slipped them over his heels.

Where the hell is Alan? He waved the wafting blood away from his face. Alan was fifteen metres away. He could see the pony tank in his mouth, arms encircling his chest. The air traces were spasmodic and shallow.

Simon began rummaging through the weight pockets in the buoyancy vests. His fingers closed round the sharp edges of the GPS marine tracker device, an aluminium box the size of a dictaphone with a rubberized seal and a magnetic backing plate. Simon glanced towards the surface. The silhouette of the hull of the pirate's launch dwarfed the speedboat. The props were still. He fed the GPS device into his right hand and kicked towards the surface trailing a great ribbon of blood.

The pain in his chest was worsening. Loss of blood was beginning to make him feel faint.

The pirate boat's keel drew two metres and he came up directly below, handing off against the keel edge. He was positioned four metres forward of the props. Leaving his injured shoulder exposed again, he reached down to his right hand and pulled the GPS unit away from his numb fingers, keeping himself steady with slow fin strokes and clamped the unit in place on one side of the keel.

The pitch of the engines suddenly rose, the vibrations running together into a continuous whine. Simon desperately pushed away from the keel, inverted his body and kicked down to the safety of deep water. The propellers thrashed, churning the water above him. The down draught tugged at his back. The thrashing became a drone, then a faded hum. By the time he reached the boulder the only sound he heard was the escaping air of his breathing.

Alan lay on his back on the seabed, knees bent, rolling passively to and fro in the chill bottom currents. His chest was a mass of pain. He kept his arms wrapped round his sides, squeezing the ribs together. It helped. Squinting his eyes against the sting of sea salt, he watched Cobra's blurred launch speed away over the surface above. And then Simon's silhouette descending slowly towards the boulder.

The red dye from the punctured blood sacs between the inside of his wetsuit and the outside of the Kevlar body armour had leaked away. But he noticed that Simon was still bleeding. Surely Simon's blood sacs should have emptied by now?

He swam towards the boulder, brushing the water aside with one hand. He found the second mask and cleared it. Even at this depth, in the blue filtered light, Simon's face was ashen.

Alan wondered how long it would take before sharks picked up the scent. He squeezed Simon's cheeks between his fingers. Through the mask he could see Simon's eyes were half closed. He tipped Simon forward, placed a full tank against his back and tightened the waist belt. Then he removed the pony from Simon's mouth and pushed the main tank regulator between his teeth. No bubbles. The air! Twisted the valve open. A great flock of bubbles burst from Simon's mouthpiece. Quickly, he shrugged into the second buoyancy device, unclipped his weight belt and inflated his vest. Slowly, they began to lift away from the boulder.

Alan broke surface first. Simon bobbed up beside him. He spat out his regulator. 'Hold on to the rail!' He prised Simon's right hand away from his damaged shoulder and lifted it to the gunwale railing, pressing the fingers closed. He slipped out of his buoyancy jacket and let it float free. Then he heaved himself over the side and, with the remaining vestiges of his rapidly ebbing strength, grabbed Simon's tank and hauled him into the boat.

They both lay there, a jumble of limbs, panting feverishly. He remembered his own kit, crawled to the rail and grabbed his tank before it drifted beyond reach.

Simon's eyes were shut. Must have lost at least a pint, Alan guessed. 'Water. Where the bloody hell did I put the water?'

'Under the seat.'

Alan lifted a deck seat. He pulled out a plastic bottle and pressed it to Simon's lips. A damp T-shirt had been discarded on the deck. He folded the material, pressed it over the wound and tied it off, tight, to stem the bleeding.

'Jesus Christ, Al. What the fuck happened?' Simon murmured.

'You're all right, mate.' Relief coursed through him. 'You had me scared there for a minute.'

The water was helping. Simon tried to sit up. 'I didn't know anything about it. One minute – second – I was sitting there; the next . . . boom.'

'You got the short straw, mate. Old Santos blew off twice at you. Think one of the other blokes knocked him.'

Simon attempted to move his arm. The movement was relatively free.

'How's it feel?'

'OK.'

'I don't think it's broke.'

'No.'

'Flesh wound.'

'Yeah.'

'Something to tell the grandkiddies, eh.'

Simon tried a laugh, but it hurt his chest.

Alan glanced at Simon's chest. A circular divot, three inches in diameter, had been torn out of the Kevlar. He inspected his own body armour. Just a small entry hole.

'You got a hollowed bullet, which spread on impact and distributed the force to a wider area. Santos must have only had two. Your shoulder got the second. I got hit with a normal round. Jesus, but I was winded. I'll have one God almighty bruise.'

Simon looked down at his chest, then at Alan's. 'Still think I came off worse.'

They both laughed which brought on coughing spasms.

'Told you Santos was a good bloke!' Alan slumped against the driver's seat.

'Yeah. Remind me to thank him. Now can we get the hell out of here before that mad bastard decides to come back?'

34

'Alan?'

'Angela! Yes . . . it's me.'

'Thank God . . . I hadn't heard. I was worried.'

'We're fine . . . well . . . Simon was shot.'

'Shot! Is he OK?'

'Yeah! Yeah, he's OK. Took a bullet in the shoulder. Flesh wound. I think the shock of actually being hit did more damage than the injury.' Small laugh. 'Local doctor patched him up and prescribed some antibiotics. He'll survive. Otherwise we've both got bruising on our chests.'

'What about Filippo?' The bruising, evidently, was less important.

'Filippo acted his part a bit too convincingly for my liking!'

He heard Angela laugh. Palpable relief that so far there had been no casualties. And the worst of the danger was past. The laughter ebbed. 'Are you now at the second RV?'

Alan and Simon had not returned to the Rajah Muda Beach Resort. Instead, waiting for darkness to shield them, Alan had guided the boat up on to a deserted beach. The plan, if either Simon or Alan had been badly hurt, called for the survivor to telephone a codeword to Angela Ramierez, who would initiate a co-ordinated air, sea and land assault on Cobra's camp.

The hire car was parked in an isolated spot 400 metres inland from the beach.

'What about the diving gear? Can't just leave it.' Simon had remembered the kit while Alan repacked his wound.

'We take it with us.'

They were both dressed in shorts and T-shirts. The body armour and
wetsuits were packed in the canvas holdall. They abandoned the speedboat, but close enough to the hotel that it would be found.

The second RV was the Fisherman's Inn on the corner of Salazar and
Veteran Street. Alan had checked in using his authentic Australian passport. The fake American passport, issued by the FBI in the name of
Albert McCreadie, was stowed in the canvas bag, together with their
other documents and money.

'Yeah. We're at the second RV, Angela,' Alan confirmed. 'We'll go
take a look at the camp tomorrow night.'

'Be careful.'

'I can assure you, I don't want to go through that again!'

Alan replaced the phone. Simon was lying on his bed. The local doctor
had done a good job patching up his wound. No stitches needed. For one
hundred bucks, the doctor saw no need to record any details of the
patient or his companion. And he pretended to believe the story that
Simon had sustained the injury by swimming in a rocky bay. Simon had
made an excellent recovery. His arm was not disabled. There was no
major nerve damage and no arteries had been severed. The numbness in
the fingers of his right hand had faded and although his shoulder was
stiff and sore, Simon acknowledged that he had been extremely lucky.
Had the dumdum bullet struck an inch to the left it would have blown
his arm off.

The room was a comfortable twin with *en suite* bathroom. Plenty of
tourists staying at the hotel, so they were reasonably anonymous. Alan
sat on the bed opposite Simon. 'Have you got a reading?'

Simon sat up. 'Bingo!' His triumph was undisguised. 'Where's the
chart, Al?'

Simon had programmed the GPS transponder to emit on the hour, so
whatever time zone they might find themselves in they'd know when to
switch on the receiver to get a reading.

Alan rummaged through the bag for the marine navigators' chart they had bought in Manila. He slipped the plastic wrapping off the map and unfurled it on Simon's bed. The chart depicted the southern coast of Mindanao, detailing Sarangani Bay.

Simon read co-ordinates, longitude and latitude, and then committed the reading and the displayed time to a way-point memory slot. The GPS receiver unit was picking up a signal emitted by the transponder on the keel of Cobra's boat via a geo-stationary satellite several hundred miles above the surface of the earth.

Alan plotted the co-ordinates and marked the spot on the map with a small cross. He checked the map's scale and calculated. 'Must be the camp. I reckon about thirty miles south of here.'

35

There were only the two of them. Not even Jimmy was in the hut. Sharif Mohammed's translation of the manuscript and the transcript of Robert McGovern's diary were spread on the table. Adjacent was a marine chart and a world map.

That he had been so quickly absorbed into Cobra's ranks was a worry to Santos. He surmised that maybe Jimmy's role lay more in implementing Cobra's decisions rather than assisting in their formulation. But still, Jimmy's absence was cautionary. He worried too that in despatching Alan and Simon, where training and reflex had taken over, he may have inadvertently demonstrated that his technique with a weapon was conditioned rather than natural, leading Cobra to suspect either a military background, or worse, police training. For the moment, there was nothing in Cobra's behaviour to suggest he was suspicious, but then the guy was psychotic, a consummate performer.

Cobra had allowed him to read the translation. Together, they had pored over the diary, tracing Robert McGovern's escape across the Atlantic Ocean, round the African Cape to Madagascar, then north-east to Mauritius, before finally setting a course north to the Seychelles archipelago.

Santos's attention was now on the landmarks Robert McGovern described in the back of the diary. It was clear that the landmarks were on the island of Praslin, the second largest of the Seychelles group.

Distances were given in the translation of the manuscript. It became a matter of co-ordinating the information and then interpreting the difficult language of Robert McGovern's time to decipher exactly where he had dumped the gold.

Robert McGovern described three fixes. Two were already plotted. Santos reached for a Breton plotter protractor and marked off the angle of the third fix. The first and second fixes formed a triangle, the island's coastline acting as one side. According to the distances Robert McGovern indicated, Santos had marked two points along each fix and joined the marks. The gold lay somewhere along that line. The third fix should pinpoint the position. The first landmark was taken off the highest peak on Praslin, the second from the second highest. Now Santos took the bearing from the third highest peak and ruled in the bearing line. It bisected the tangent joining the first two positions almost exactly in the middle.

Cobra ringed the spot. 'Gold aplenty!' he mimicked the latter day impression of a pirate accent.

'Depends.'

'On what?'

'That Robert McGovern got it right and what he describes as the highest peak actually is, and the second and the third. Otherwise the bearing could be off any peak.'

'Mister Executioner, you are a pessimist!'

And you're a fucking murderer and I'm going to nail your ass. Santos grinned. 'We'll see when we get there!'

'We will.'

Cobra, ecstatic at yesterday's capture of the precious diary, had placed his men on high alert as soon as the boat had docked, with lookouts posted round the camp's perimeter for the rest of the day and night. Just in case of follow-up activity. By morning, he stood them down, reckoning that the danger had passed. Then he had allowed his men to leave the camp, if they wanted. Most had, to visit the nearest whorehouse. Some had stayed behind and got drunk. Outside, twilight was beginning to close in.

There was a commotion just outside the hut. A girl's high-pitched whimper. Santos immediately recognized Mae-li's cries. His body stiffened. He was suddenly afraid for her. Events immediately after the 'execution' had swept him along, without any suitable respite for enquiry, however guarded, about Mae-li. No one spoke about her or, it seemed, to her. She lived solely in his mind, her face of cold stone, her dark eyes drilling through him, her disbelief as evident as her hatred.

Santos pretended to concentrate on the plotted position of the gold. Cobra seemed not to have heard.

'Right!' Cobra banged the table. 'We make the boat ready.' He began rolling up the charts. 'We'll leave at dawn.'

Jimmy burst into the hut. He towered over Mae-li, gripping her arm, like a child clutching a rag-doll. Defiance was etched in her face.

'What're you doing, Jimmy?' Cobra asked.

Santos made a huge effort not to look at her immediately. It was clear to him that Cobra's interest in the girl had waned. It was now only a matter of time.

'Found these.' Jimmy held some papers out towards him. Santos stepped forward, eyes locking momentarily with Mae-li. He took the papers. Dread crashed through him. He glanced at Mae-li again. She stared back.

'You are a pig like the rest of them,' Mae-li hissed.

Santos turned his back on her and gave the papers to Cobra. 'She's copied the translation of the manuscript.'

'Naughty girl.' Cobra's voice was low, calm. Deeply menacing. 'What were you planning to do with these?' Cobra rustled the papers in the air. His face reddened, eyes bulged as his fury gathered. He walked towards her and crashed his fist across her face. She slumped and would have fallen had Jimmy not held her up.

He knew, this time it was over. Cobra's face, his aura, was like ice. Whatever happened he had to get her the hell out of here and fast.

'You are all pigs!' Mae-li screamed. 'I cannot live as the whore to a pig! I would rather die.'

'Oh, my dear, but you are going to die.'

Santos listened to Cobra's chilling insanity. The psychopath meant it. Mae-li was going to die unless he did something, anything to buy some time.

Cobra realized that he had never been in love. He had thought about that before, but never dwelt on it, never assumed he had a right to expect love. He felt no need for dependence. The tune of an old Simon and Garfunkel song played in his head, *I Am A Rock*. His song. Written specially for him. His soul was encased in an impenetrable bunker, secured underground in the darkness, while his body and his mind roamed free above, free of constraint, free of compromise. He enjoyed the concept of detachment, of control. No complexity. And yet he thought he might have come close to love. Once. When he had first seen Mae-li as a child, small and timid and afraid. And he had taken her purity and guarded her and made her his own. He wanted love in the way a poor man dreams of impossible riches. At the end of the dream, isolation always seemed the preferable option. So he destroyed love. She could have brought love out of him. His love! No other man on earth could give of himself as he could and he had offered her the key. But she had squandered the opportunity. Thrown away the best chance life would ever offer her. Rejected him and everything he could have given her. Betrayed him! Betrayed me! Bitch!

'Give me your gun.' Cobra looked directly at Mae-li as he spoke, but held his hand out towards Executioner.

'Loyalty is the ability to maintain an objective despite the obstacles.' He felt Executioner fit the handle of the Glock into his palm. He offered the gun to Jimmy. 'Loyalty. Well, Jimmy, I suppose this is the ultimate test. Shoot her.'

Jimmy took the gun. Flicked the safety catch. Pressed the muzzle to Mae-li's temple.

'Cobra!'

The noise irritated him. He turned to look at Executioner. It seemed to him that Degarda was having second thoughts. His movement had slowed as if the hut was filled with water, movement hampered by the resistance of finality.

'Have you got something to say?'

'She has betrayed you?'

'Betrayed me?' He considered the question, then nodded. 'Yes. Betrayed me many times.'

'Then make her suffer.'

'Make her suffer?' Cobra glanced at Mae-li. The delicate perfection of her beauty was corrupted by tears and blood.

'A bullet is too quick.'

Cobra noticed Jimmy lower the gun, until it rested by his side, pointing at the floor.

'Make it slow. Make her suffer.'

Executioner's voice drifted into him like a faint smell. But he was right, she had betrayed him. Underestimated his compassion so profoundly, his essential humanity. This whore refused to redeem him. *Make her suffer for the sacrifices I have made*. He felt strangely exalted. 'Yes.'

'The river out the back there, it's narrow and tidal. There's a mooring stake in the mud, exposed at low tide and completely submerged at high tide. Drown her.'

'Drown her?' Cobra repeated.

'Let her think about what she's done.'

'Let her repent.'

'Repent. Yes. See the error of her ways.'

Cobra lifted his eyes to the ceiling. She was confining him now, becoming a burden, a nuisance. 'Let nature take her. I like that Mr Executioner.'

'You control nature to do your bidding. Let her scream her sorrow and beg forgiveness.'

'I will not forgive.'

'But let her beg.'

'Bitch! I gave her everything.'

Jimmy looked confused. Mae-li had evaporated, transformed to a topic.

'Then make her pay.'

'Tie her to the stake and the waters will rise up and consume her.' Cobra shook his head, a slight, sudden movement. He felt himself coming awake. 'It is in my power.'

'You control death.'

Heat began to slither and rise in the pit of his stomach. A faint, uncomfortable twinge of nausea. He placed his hand on top of Mae-li's head feeling the small undulations of her skull. 'Give me the gun, Jimmy. Take her to the river. Get the men there, all of them. Let them see.'

From beyond the hut, Santos heard Jimmy yelling to the others. Cobra marched out. The others, in a tight group, began moving towards the exit of the camp. His hut was across the compound. Knifeman was standing at the door. He raced across.

'Knifeman, inside!' Santos hissed.

The boy stepped back, obeying blindly.

Santos slammed the door shut. 'They're going to kill Mae-li.'

'So what? Let's go see the action.'

'I need a knife, a small one. Have you got a small knife?' Santos was hoping the kid's awe of yesterday's killings would persuade him.

'Sure.' Knifeman reached under the pillow on his bunk and pulled out a switch-blade.

Santos tested the blade. 'Let's go.'

'What you gonna do with that?'

'Come on. I'll show you.'

They walked through the deserted camp to the barrier and on to the track that cut over the swamp. Santos held the switch-blade and let Knifeman get a pace ahead. He judged his moment, reached up and slashed sideways across Knifeman's throat. The flesh peeled back. Santos felt the blade bite through the cartilage rings of the trachea and bury itself deep in the soft structures either side. Two fountains erupted from Knifeman's neck. He sank to his knees, soundless, clutching at his severed throat. Santos kicked him sideways off the track and into the swamp. He jumped down, on to Knifeman's back, pushing the body beneath the mud. Then he climbed back to the track and ran in the dark to join the killing party.

36

'Boat hasn't moved,' Alan whispered in the darkness. They were lying on their bellies, due north of the camp, on the banks of a river estuary. The dense bush obliterated the canopy of stars shimmering overhead. The boat, moored at its jetty, was in view, as was the northern perimeter of the camp and beyond the wall, the roofs of the huts in the compound.

At dusk, they had driven along the coast road south of the city, spotting a narrow track leading off the road, through the bush. Simon, reading the map with a torch, guessed it was the camp's access. No guards. No one at all. They drove a couple of miles past then turned round and headed back.

'We'll have to go through the trees.' Alan had figured it was the only way. 'There's a lay-by up ahead.'

Alan had turned off the road and concealed the car behind some trees, half a mile up from the track. The walk to the shore had taken over an hour and in that time Simon estimated they'd covered maybe 400 metres, forced to negotiate the thick scrub, sometimes wading waist deep through the swamp. The mosquitoes had had a feast. Finally they had broken through the treeline on to the river-bank. The cuttings through the estuary were like giant fingers, wide spread and deeply veined, clawing tentatively at the sea.

'What's happening over there?' Simon squinted in the dark. 'Thought

I saw some movement.'

'I see them.' Alan had the binoculars clamped to his eyes.

'Cobra's men?'

'Don't know. I guess so.' Alan studied the small figures across the estuary. 'One, two, three . . . four . . . five . . . six. . . .' He counted eleven. 'One of them's a girl. I think it's a girl. You have a look.' He handed the binoculars to Simon.

Simon was counting. 'I got eleven too. They seem to be taking someone down into the river. Anyone on the jetty?'

Alan shifted his weight. 'No.' The sky was blooded purple by the dying sun. Thin strands of laughter flecked the air. He listened to the sounds. The ground was wet and spongy, but still uncomfortable pressing against the bruising on his ribs. He rolled over. Closed his eyes. Insects vibrated all around. The air was laden with the musty smell of rotting vegetation. A whine sounded loudly in his ear then stopped. Alan slapped his cheek.

'When it's completely dark we'll go take a look.'

He heard a grunt from Simon. 'Al, they're moving.'

Alan rolled back on to his front, wincing as his body adapted to the new position. He took the binoculars from Simon and focused on the dark, distant figures.

'They're walking away, along a ridge or maybe on top of the river-bank. Anyway, they're silhouetted. Ten? One, two, three. . . .' He stopped at ten. 'Looks like we lost one. Let me see.' It was difficult to make out details of the figures. He started counting again. 'Seven . . . eight . . . nine . . . ten. The girl's missing. They're going back into the trees.' He waited, watching, then lowered the binoculars. 'They've gone.'

Simon nudged his arm. 'Lights on the jetty. They've floodlit the boat.'

Bodies began shifting sacks and barrels on to the jetty. Alan swivelled the binoculars. 'Looks like they're stocking the boat up. And if I'm not very much mistaken, those are fuel drums.'

'Going someplace, our friends!'

'Could be. We can go a bit closer and see what they were doing on the river-bank.'

The water in the estuary was beginning to rise, running gently in over the sandy bottom of the river, shimmering in the moonlight. Alan padded across the water and scrambled up the far bank. He waited for Simon at the top.

'Al, I've got an idea. We're a bit exposed on these ridges. Why don't we stay in the shallow water? We can walk upstream to the road. I remember we crossed the river. Then cut across to the far side and follow the tributary down to where those people were.'

'Okay. Let's go.' Alan was already slithering down the bank.

By the time they made it to the road, the water had risen two feet. The convergence of the estuary's tributaries passed through a semi-circle of concrete supporting the road surface. From within the tunnel, Simon could hear the scuttling sound of sand crabs jumping into their holes.

Going against the tide towards the bay was more difficult and the slosh of water too noisy. Alan led the way halfway up the bank and continued forward in a crouch, keeping his head down, below the ridge. At the treeline he stopped.

'Stay here. I'm just going to have a little look.'

Alan crawled forward, round a shallow bend so he was looking along the tributary, out into the bay. The treeline was forty metres behind him. At first his eyes deceived him. He blinked. Looked again. Someone was tied to a stake in the river. The water was at mid-chest and rising. He was about to start forward when he heard voices behind. Very slowly he climbed up the bank then raised himself just enough to see over the edge. The glowing ends of two cigarettes moved in the dark like fireflies. He slid back down into the water and let the tide take him back to where Simon was waiting.

'Guards,' he whispered, pointing above the bank. 'Twenty, thirty metres from here.'

'What're they doing?' Simon hissed back.

'Watching. And waiting, I guess.'

'For what?'

'You know we counted eleven of them out and only ten back.'

'Like aeroplanes during the war, yes.'

'You're not going to believe this, Simon.'

*

Mae-li was very afraid. She had long resigned herself to a wasted life and in that resignation had accepted death as the only relief. Thoughts of escape had collapsed long ago beneath the weight of apathy and the desolation of believing that she might have loved. Instead she had become a whore. Death had never held fear. Death was part of life. Death was the bedfellow of the damned and she had been damned from the day of her birth.

But the reality was different. The reality crushed the delusion of painlessness. Reality was cold water rising to her breasts, of loneliness in a dark place, the knowledge that she had only hours left and the certainty that her mind would die before her body.

So why had he done it, the one called by Cobra, Executioner, whom she had heard called Degarda? She had heard, too, from others in the camp, that he had killed two Europeans, shot them from point-blank range and become a hero. A hero? Shot them to earn Cobra's trust? And why had he stopped Jimmy from killing her and led her instead to this? And why, after Jimmy had bound her to the stake, had she dropped the knife Degarda had placed in her hands while uttering the words, '*Be free.*'

The soft silt of the river-bed was claiming her. Already her feet were buried below her ankles. Try as she might to pull a foot free and search the riverbed around the stake with her toes, its hold on her was too strong. The knife was near, but the cold had drained her strength. Water lapped at her chin now. Mocking her. How long had she been here waiting for death? Hours. It seemed like only seconds. A tiny wavelet slapped her cheek, fractured water spilling into her mouth. She tilted her chin up, tried to kick her feet free from their muddy tomb, tried to lift herself an inch. The silt held her. One final attempt. Mae-li sucked in a great breath, as much air as she could squeeze into her lungs, hoping that if she made herself buoyant, the air would lift her. She plunged her face into the river-water. The mud would not release her. The rope binding her wrists had become fattened on water. Her arms fought an unequal battle with the rope, but she struggled and pulled and tugged until she felt her wrists would dislocate. Burning began in her chest. She heaved her head out of the water, gasping and spluttering, dragging desperately at the fresh air. Wet strands of hair clung to her face. No choice now but to keep her head back. The river had risen so that now her face was a piece of the surface mosaic. Mae-li strained up, teasing half a centimetre out of her body, stretching for air. Can't keep this up. Standing on tiptoe in the mud. The sharp point of her contact with the river-bed made her sink.

Something brushed her thigh. A fish? A rat!

Mae-li closed her eyes against the salty water. She took her breath in little, staccato sections, filtering air from the undulating surface of the river.

A large, flat pressure on her belly.

She wanted to scream. But that would be the end. She craned upwards, but the water was above her now, sealing her from life. Mae-li slumped against the stake. Her mind was clear. Strangely no panic. Her last breath was turning sour in her chest. Bad air dribbled from her mouth. She could feel desperation imploding her lungs.

A hand gripped her leg. A hand! Mae-li looked down into the black. A yellow fish was eating her. Her chest was heaving. Any second and she would start breathing water.

Moving up her legs! Climbing her! Something hard at her mouth, trying to force itself into her. She turned her head away. The demon was trying to enter her. Mae-li began to thrash her head from side to side. She weakened. She saw herself as a child, a black and white snapshot. She opened her mouth. Cold water streamed in.

Then she was breathing. *Breathing!*

She was biting on a soft bung. A great rush of bubbles as she expelled air. She sucked, blew, sucked, blew, felt giddy. Mae-li opened her eyes. A shadow danced in front of her. There was pressure on her mouth, holding the bit between her teeth. Slowly the pressure eased. She bit hard on the rubber, breathing until her body had quietened, until the suck of air and gurgle of bubbles was metronomic. The shadow moved behind her. A rope of some kind tightened against her arm tugging at the bit between her teeth. She turned her head to create some slack. She felt hands on her hands, feeling blindly in the darkness, orientating the rope around her wrists like a blind man feeling a face. The knife was at her feet. Somewhere! She grabbed a finger, tugged it downwards. The finger broke free, the hands still feeling. Mae-li clutched at water, grabbed hold, tugged down again.

Alan tried to understand the message. He was sure the girl was trying to tell him something. Downwards. Towards the river-bed. The stake was slimy. He squeezed her hand to tell her he understood. Maybe her feet were tied as well? He moved down the pole until he was lying almost flat on the river-bed. The air hose on the buddy regulator became taut. Not enough slack for him to go any further. The problem was he couldn't untie the rope around the girl's wrists. And he couldn't talk to her. Worse, he couldn't break the surface to save air for fear of the guards. They were both breathing off the same tank.

When he had told Simon there was a girl tied to a stake in the rising waters of the river, they both knew instantly that an attempt would have to be made to save her. No way either of them would be able to live with the knowledge that they had let her die. As far as their mission was concerned, the girl might be an asset. Then again, if Cobra returned at low water and found her missing, he might put two and two together and reckon that Santos was an infiltrator. It had been a tough call. One life in exchange for another. The conclusion: Santos was better able to look after himself. And the girl *might* be able to tell them something about Ben.

'Haven't got long,' Alan guessed. 'Water's rising fast.' He'd remembered the diving kit in the trunk of the car. Only ten minutes of air had been used from each tank, the time it had taken for Simon to get them both back to the surface after the attack.

'I'll go get her, Al. You bring the kit.'

Alan rested his hand on Simon's shoulder. 'I'll go. Your arm's buggered.'

Twenty minutes later, Alan waded into the river and slipped his fins on to his feet. 'Ready!' He signalled Simon with a thumb and forefinger sign. 'You go along the bank. Listen for the guards. I'll swim.'

'Okay,' Simon whispered back. 'If the guards spring us, I'll dive in the river, take the second regulator and we'll let the current drift us back. She's got thirty minutes maybe. No more.'

'OK.' Alan gauged the water level. It took twenty minutes to get back to the bend in the tributary. The girl's face was barely above water. They could both see in the moonlight that she was straining for breath. He would have to negotiate by dead reckoning. No way he could break surface in sight of the guards.

Alan's hands slithered back up the pole. He hoisted himself round, wrapping his legs round the girl's thighs. He reached up and stroked her cheek to reassure her then slid his fingers across her face and tried gently to ease the regulator from her mouth. He sensed her resistance. He stroked her face again and tried once more. This time he felt her take a big breath then the regulator was free in his hand. He had to be quick. He lowered himself down her body until he hit the soft, muddy bottom. His hands worked frantically around the base of the stake, ploughing the mud. He felt her ankles. They were not tied. Her feet were immersed in the mud. He pulled them free one at a time. Was this what she had been trying to tell him? He was about to go up again when his finger snagged on something sharp. For an instant he thought he had been bitten. He felt in the mud again, tentatively. Something solid. His fingers closed around a handle. A knife! Alan pulled the knife free and climbed back up the front of the girl's body. He locked his ankles behind the pole and reached downstream where the current would have blown the second regulator. He reeled it in and fed it to the girl. As before, he could feel her taking great breaths, her body filling and emptying. Reaching behind her, Alan worked the blade between the ropes and cut. Her arms came free and were suddenly encircling his chest, clinging with a ferocious strength. Alan dropped the knife.

They began to fall to the river-bed, clinging like lovers, tumbling over in the current in a bizarre dance. Alan tried to measure their drift downstream. 'One elephant . . . two elephant . . . three elephant. . . .' Until he counted fifty metres.

Alan reached for the inflator valve, pumped up his jacket. As he broke surface, he was completely disoriented. Facing backwards, towards the road. He flipped round in the water. Simon was ten metres upstream, on his haunches, looking out to sea. Alan spat out his regulator and hissed in the darkness as the current swept him further inland. She was clinging, head turned to one side, buried in his chest. He saw Simon spin round, and then a great grin split his face and he was running in a crouch along the river-bank, trailing them.

The dark wall of the tunnel running beneath the road loomed. Alan worked his way over to the bank and heaved the girl up beside him. She still had the regulator in her mouth, her breathing noisy now she was out of the water. Alan pulled the regulator out and immediately clamped his hand over her mouth.

'Do you speak English?' he hissed.

The girl nodded, her eyes wide with fright and surprise as the river-water lapped around her shoulders.

'I'm going to take my hand away. There are guards close by. Do not make a sound. Do you understand?'

The girl nodded again. Simon dropped down beside them and placed his hands under the girl's arms, leaned back and pulled her on to the bank.

'I'm going to dump this,' Alan whispered, wiggling out of his buoyancy vest.

Simon shook his head. The girl was panting, trying to sit up. 'They'll find it at low tide.'

'Okay. You take it. I'll look after her.' Alan floated the tank over to the bank and crawled out of the water. He bent over the girl. 'You ready to move?'

Mae-li nodded and waited for instructions.

Simon pulled the tank out of the river, careful to avoid the clank of metal on metal. Alan helped the girl over the slippery bank while Simon checked the road.

'Let's go,' Simon whispered. He clambered up then turned to help the girl and finally Alan. In single file they darted back behind the trees just as a lorry turned a corner piercing the night with twin conical beams of yellow light. The truck trundled by leaving a smear of diesel on the humid night air.

They reached the car. The girl was clasping her arms around her shoulders. Alan opened the back door for her, ushered her in, then closed the door gently.

The bright flare of the match illuminated the inside of the car. Simon drew deeply on his cigarette and blew smoke out of the open window with a sigh as he drove away from the river.

Alan turned in his seat. The girl was shaking, though not he suspected from cold. The night was hot and sultry. Blood seeped from his hand where he had nicked it on the knife in the river. He sucked at the cut.

'What is your name?' he asked. The girl was staring at him and even though he had just plucked her from the jaws of death, she was wary. Frightened. 'We're not going to hurt you.' He smiled.

Simon glanced round to get a look at her. 'She speak English?'

'My name is Mae-li.'

Simon twisted back. 'Mae-li,' he repeated. 'Are you OK, Mae-li?'

She didn't answer. 'Who are you?' she asked in a tremulous voice.

'My name's Simon. And this is Alan.' He flicked his cigarette out the window.

Mae-li stared out at the dark brush rushing past the window. 'I have not been outside the camp for three years.' She looked back at Alan. 'I thought I was going to die tonight.'

'You're safe now. Why were you in the river? Who put you there?'

'You were not at the river tonight by chance. You were watching the camp.' She hugged her arms round her shoulders.

'Yes. We were watching the camp. Who put you in the river?'

'Cobra ordered it.'

Alan glanced at Simon. 'He has women pirates?'

'Only me. I am not a pirate; I am his woman.'

'You were his woman. I am not a betting man, but if I was I'd say he doesn't want you around any more.'

'You know of Cobra?' Mae-li frowned.

Alan could see she was trying to fit the pieces together. 'We know about Cobra.'

'You may have heard of me. McGovern,' Simon said.

Mae-li's mouth dropped open. 'They were your mother and your father?'

'Yes. You hear that, Al?' He looked back at her. 'How do you know their names?'

'From their passports.'

'You saw their passports?'

'Yes. He has them.'

Alan needed more answers. 'Why did he put you in the river?'

'I told him that I would no longer be his whore. He could not free me because I know too much.'

Alan reached out and touched her arm. She pulled away. He could see that it was instinctive. Self protection.

'Why did you save me?'

'Mae-li, is there a prisoner, someone in the camp, a white man like me?'

Alan noticed Mae-li's fingers scratching nervously at her elbows. Her shoulders were hunched with tension. She brushed away strands of wet hair from her face with jittery fingers.

Simon barked, 'Is there a prisoner!'

'Easy, Simon.'

'No goddam prisoner, Al.'

'She may not know. Santos will find out.'

'This whole thing was about Ben. Now there's no Ben. Christ!'

'You're pumped up, Simon. If he's there we'll get him. If he's there.' Alan turned to look at Mae-li. 'How did you end up being with Cobra?'

'My mother and father were both teachers in Vietnam. My father was a teacher of English. When the war came, he worked with the Americans, in Saigon. Towards the end of the war when it became clear that the Americans would leave, my father became afraid. We travelled by night to the coast to get passage on a small boat to Thailand. There were many others on the boat. One night, out at sea, the captain killed all the men. He killed my father. I was six years old and I saw them cut my father's throat. The bodies of the men were thrown over the side. Then they raped the women. My mother died two days later. After two weeks at sea, with only women and children on board, another boat rescued us. They killed the crew. It was Cobra and his men. He said the currents would take the boat into the Gulf of Siam. But he took me and a boy called Jimmy. He left food and water for the others. I have been with Cobra since that day. When I was thirteen, he took me as his woman.'

Alan whistled softly. 'What happened tonight?'

'Cobra would have killed me himself, but one of the others stopped him.'

'Why did one of the others stop him?'

'I do not know. When I was tied in the river, it was he who placed the knife in my hand.'

Alan said, 'This man who tried to help you, what is his name?'

'He is called Executioner.'

'Executioner?'

'Yes.'

'Does he have a scar on his face?'

'Yes!' Surprise registered. 'You know him?'

'He is a police officer.' Alan sensed Simon slow the car. 'Mae-li, is Cobra a white man, like us?'

Mae-li nodded. 'He is an American.'

'Do you know his name, his real name?'

'Yes. His name is Billy-Ray Kepinski.'

'You hear that, Simon!'

Simon twisted round in his seat. 'Mae-li, please tell me. Is there a prisoner, *please*?'

37

The one thing Ben knew for certain was that his prison was near a road. Occasionally at night, he would hear an engine, a minute and distant sound. The sound would grow imperceptibly, hold steady then fade. The infrequency of the sounds suggested the road was not well used. But tonight he had heard a different sound. It was his habit to sleep with the fading of the light and to wake as the circle high above filled with the dawn. But tonight he had heard a cry, a plaintive, haunting sound carried to him on the breeze. It had been a woman's cry. He knew that sensory deprivation had heightened his awareness, but equally he wondered whether his mind had not finally capitulated to the incipient creep of madness. He had not slept. Not since he had heard the screams. Then quiet. He guessed an hour had passed between the screams and the sound of the engine. It had sounded like a truck. And then only moments later another engine, closer than the first and somehow lighter, a car. It was the most activity he had witnessed in all his long captivity and the proximity of people kept him motionless on his bed. That or his reason had descended into fantasy.

Ben blinked up into the blackness. He had wanted to shout out, but fear had gripped him, silenced him. Now the noises were gone and with them the stillness crushed him, squeezing hot tears from his eyes.

38

'How's she doing?' Alan nodded towards the bathroom door. He had come down from his room on the floor above.

Simon shrugged. 'OK, I guess. I mean, it's difficult to say. Looks like she's taken quite a beating. I asked her about it, but she wouldn't say.'

'Police are going to want to interrogate her, eventually.'

'She's too scared, Al. I don't think we can just hand her over.'

'I said *eventually*.'

'OK. I asked her. . . .' He tried again. 'I spoke to her about Ben, told her about him.'

'And?'

Simon shook his head. 'Either she's not saying, or there's nothing to say.'

'Simon, she's scared, like you say. She'll need a little time before she trusts us.'

'Trusts us? You . . . *we* . . . saved her bloody life!'

'Keep your voice down.' Alan looked over his shoulder at the bathroom door. It was shut, the sound of running water seeping from underneath. 'Look, I know we saved her, but shock, trauma, whatever you want to call it, is a funny thing. Affects different people differently.'

'We bust our balls to get here, because of Ben, because of the possibilities. Now we've got her, our key to what's going on in the camp, and you want to give her time. We haven't got *time*.'

'What d'you want to do, drill her bloody kneecaps?'

' 'Course not.'

'Simon, Ben is either a prisoner, or he's not. If he is, he's either alive, or he's not. If he's alive, and it's been some time since the attack on *Clarissa*, then they'll keep him alive. Now don't rush her.'

'OK, Al. All right.'

'OK. Now, she's probably got the key, as you put it to the murders. Your mother's jewels – she can identify them. Then there's Dr Mohammed. She may have seen him.'

Simon sat on the bed. The curtains were drawn and a blue fug of cigarette smoke hung limply in the air.

'You hungry?'

'Starving, now you mention it. Bet Mae-li is too.'

He called down to room service and ordered a plate of chicken mayonnaise sandwiches and a jug of coffee.

Simon waited until Alan had put the phone down. 'Santos is in the camp. He's got the diary, a copy anyway. Mae-li identified Kepinski, just like you did. If she's prepared to tell us, why not a court? She knows he killed Mum and Dad.'

Alan simply nodded agreement. 'Nothing I can refute there. So?'

'So what's the point of tracking this guy to the Seychelles?'

'If he's going there.'

'Come on, Al. What are the chances? Pretty high I'd say. They were getting their boat ready to go someplace.'

'Suppose you're right.'

'Then what are we going to gain? Maybe we'll just be endangering ourselves again for no reason. He leaves and we're free to go look for Ben.'

'If Mae-li knows anything.'

'Even if she doesn't, one of the others is bound to know something.'

'What others?'

'Pirates, the ones left behind, in the camp.'

'You think you're just going to walk in and ask them?'

'Police. Angela can organize that. Hell, you said they were on standby anyhow.'

'And supposing Santos is on the boat. . . .'

'Yeah?'

'And they radio the boat and tell Kepinski the police are crawling all over the place; you want to compromise him, Santos?'

Alan was right. 'But—'

'No buts. It's not an option. And if Ben *is* alive, I don't think we'd be helping him by blasting in there.'

'It just seems . . . crazy, that we can't do something.' Simon stood up, went to the window, peered out. 'Are we just going to hang around for two weeks while Kepinski takes a cruise to the Seychelles, or wherever the hell he decides to go?'

A polite knock at the door. A waiter came in with a tray and deposited it on the table while Alan signed the chit.

Just as the waiter left, the bathroom door opened and Mae-li came out dressed in a towel robe.

'How're you feeling?' Alan asked.

'Better now, thank you.'

'I've got some food here.'

Mae-li went to the tray and immediately started to eat. She sat down in a chair, chewing, stuffing food into her mouth with embarrassed looks at the two men who had saved her life.

Alan watched her for a moment. 'I don't know how much time we've got, Mae-li, but we need your help.'

'I must help Degarda.' She swallowed a mouthful of food. 'He tried to save me. I knew when I saw him that first time in the camp that he was different.'

'Good thing Cobra didn't notice.'

'I am a woman. Women can see things that men are blind to.' She bit into another sandwich.

'His name is Filippo Santos.'

'Santos.' She fed his name through her lips like a child savouring a sweet.

'I want you to write a statement. Everything you know about Billy-Ray Kepinski, the camp, and the attack on John McGovern's boat. And the jewels that belonged to Elizabeth McGovern, have you seen those too?'

Mae-li nodded. 'Yes. Cobra gave them to a man to sell.'

'Did you see a paper, a document, a very old document?'

She thought for a moment then nodded emphatically. 'Yes. Cobra brought an old man to the camp to read it.'

'Sharif Mohammed?'

'Perhaps. I do not know his name.'

'And what happened to him?'

'Cobra killed him. Jimmy took the man's body to Manila.'

'You need to write all this down, Mae-li. Everything, dates, times, everything.'

'I will do this.'

'Now, Simon's already asked you, but I must ask you again. . . .'

'Listen to me very carefully, Simon. Mae-li may genuinely not know anything about a prisoner, Ben or any other.'

'She was the fucker's girlfriend for Chris'sake.'

They were back in their room. The girl was asleep downstairs. If she ran, she ran. They both thought it unlikely.

'She's bargaining.'

'What are you talking about, Alan? She said there was no prisoner.'

'I'll offer her immunity from prosecution if it comes to that and residency in Australia.'

Simon shook his head. 'Am I really that naive?'

'Your parents were being blackmailed.'

'We don't know that.' He rummaged in his pockets for a cigarette.

Alan stepped forward, placed a hand on each his shoulders. The pressure of his fingers was light, a dusting. 'I do,' he said quietly. In the same quiet voice, Alan said, 'You remember Santos had a report about a body being fished out the water. Lee Chu. . . .'

'Yes . . . and the burn marks on my mother; I know all this, Al.'

'The boy Cobra killed was called Jamie-Jake Mulcahy. Same MO.'

'I'm very sorry. So what?'

The weight of his frown pressed against his eyes. 'At Fort Jefferson.'

Simon's body froze. '*Fort Jefferson*? My grandfather. . . .'

'Yes, I know. He was the commander at the time of the killing.'

Simon collapsed into a chair. 'There's a connection, is that what you're saying? Alan! For Chris'sake! Did Cobra and my mother know each other?'

'Your mother and Jamie-Jake Mulcahy were having an affair.'

Simon ran his hands through his hair, stood up and began to pace around the room.

'Kepinski had a thing about the commander's daughter. When he found out about Mulcahy, he killed him. Your grandfather was transferred to avoid the scandal and the whole thing was covered up.'

'Jesus Christ.'

'But there was something else, something that happened a long time ago.'

'At the camp?'

'Yes.'

'What – what happened?'

'Your mother . . . she kept a secret . . . maybe not from your father, I don't know, it's difficult to tell.'

Simon spun back to face Alan. 'A secret?'

'Simon, this is going to be tough. I think . . . *we* think, that is George Baker thinks and who am I to disagree with him—'

'Alan, just spit it out will you!'

'Your mother . . . she was. . . .'

'What, Alan! She was what?'

'Raped.'

'Jesus, we know that, Al.'

'No. No, not on *Clarissa*. Before, at the camp. At Fort Jefferson. At or about the time Jamie-Jake Mulcahy was murdered.'

His hands were working against one another, his fingers knotting and unknotting. 'Who, Al? Who raped her?'

'I couldn't be sure. I'm still not, not absolutely certain.'

'Alan!'

'When Ben died . . . when we all thought Ben had died, your mother sent Bet a lock of his hair, from when he was a baby.'

'She gave me some too, so?'

'I had Charlie take samples to the lab for a DNA analysis.'

Simon felt blood drain from his face. 'This is unbelievable.'

'The hit on *Clarissa* was planned. I knew that from the beginning, I just couldn't figure out why, until I went to the States and met George Baker. Cobra found out who Ben was when he was travelling in the Philippines. How. . . .' Alan shrugged. 'The kidnap would have been child's play and the blackmail started soon after, that'd be my guess.'

'But you don't know for sure?'

'About the blackmail? And the rest is just coincidence? I don't think so.'

Simon went to the window. At the edge of the circles of light the fleshy leaves of jungle vegetation appeared as highly polished green glass. 'Ben's out there, somewhere, maybe even close.' He turned to face Alan. 'Is that why you used my mother's maiden name, Alan, on that fake American passport of yours? I never asked you. I thought it was some kind of statement; revenge for Bet; private stuff, so I left it alone. But you used my mother's maiden name because you figured Cobra would recognize it, if he checked the hotels.'

'That's right, Simon.'

'Did he check?'

Alan nodded. 'Yes, he did. I had Angela make some calls the evening before we were attacked. That way Cobra would believe I was some kind of relative on a revenge kick, just like you, a brother maybe, or a cousin. There would be no suspicion that I was a police officer. I'm sorry, Simon.'

Simon lit a Bensons, pulled hard on the cigarette, pulled hard again and blew smoke towards the ceiling.

'He killed my parents. Where's the incentive in keeping Ben alive?'

'The gold?'

'Oh, come on, Alan, that's bullshit and you know it! There's something going on here!'

'This is hard as hell, Simon, I know that, but you've got to think.

Filippo's in the camp. He knows the score. If Ben's there, believe me, he'll be protected. Angela's in Manila; it'll take time for her to get down here.'

'Call her.'

'I will.'

'When?'

'As soon as I've got a plan.'

'Alan!'

'It's dark out. That gives us a little time. There's nothing we can do until daylight anyway and there's no way you or I or anybody else is going near that camp until Angela's organized some fire-power.'

'I feel so bloody useless.'

'Simon, there's nothing we can do yet. We saw them making the boat ready, at least that's what it looked like. We'll know soon enough if Cobra's making a run for it.'

'You still haven't answered my question. You know bloody well he didn't kill Mum and Dad for the gold, if there is any.'

'Sit down, Simon.' Alan walked to the bed and slumped down.

'What the hell is it, Alan?'

'Sit down.'

Simon perched on the edge of a chair. 'Well?'

'Downstairs, you said something, just before the guy brought the sandwiches.'

'About hanging around, I remember.'

'Two weeks you said, while Cobra heads for the Seychelles. You're right. I'm pretty certain that's where Kepinski's going. Everything points that way.' *Bloody hell! If I'm right about this, the FBI's got twelve days. Twelve days!* 'So, we wait. I'm sorry, Simon. I have to tell you we can't look for Ben while Kepinski is out there, while he can still get to him. We can't attack, approach or even apprehend him while Santos is still exposed. We *have* to wait around 'til we know where Kepinski's going, for sure. And we have to do this because this thing is much, much bigger than just Ben. I couldn't tell you the real reason before.'

'So what is the real reason, Alan? What are you not telling me?'

39

The steel prow dug deep into the swell then tore itself free, juddering in anticipation of the next onslaught. Spray smashed against the wheel-house. Spider, at the helm, fought the wheel, steering the boat obliquely against the regimented waves to minimize the impacts. Rags was below, in the engine-room coaxing his turbines to maximum effort. They had long since broken clear of the islands of Indonesia, and Cobra's instructions were to make full speed due west towards the Chagos Archipelago and beyond them the Seychelles.

Cobra had barely ceased his ranting about the treachery of one of his men, Knifeman, for freeing Mae-li. Worse, Cobra tormented himself with images of the girl, limbs entwined with those of her rescuer in sexual rapture at her freedom. The images never failed to whip him to a frenzy.

At dawn, following Mae-li's execution, Santos had returned to the stake in the river, passing along the swamp road. The place where he had dumped Knifeman's body was still in sight of the guard-house, so he had to be careful. The muddy water was unblemished by human debris. For the moment. By the time he reached the river-bank, he could barely contain himself from running to the edge, but he cautioned himself, for fear of anyone lingering by the water. He did not trust any of the men not to rape the corpse. Any show of eagerness at her possible survival could only implicate him. So he had casually wandered over, a terrible feeling of dread choking his throat, until he had breached the ridge and peered down at the stake. There was no body, no limp form slumped over. No body, no rope, no evidence at all that a young girl had been left to die only hours before. His apprehension dispersed like smoke in a breeze, his heart sang. Now he had to act. Santos searched the mud around the base of the stake, sinking to his knees in the quagmire. He found the knife after fifteen minutes.

Santos had shouted, desperately flavouring his voice with panic. He had raced back to the camp, bursting past the guards and taking a surreptitious look in the swamp on his way back. Still no sign of Knifeman. He had arrived at Cobra's hut, drenched in sweat, panting so he could hardly speak and announced that Mae-li was gone.

Cobra had spun round, his eyes blazing with fury. 'Get Jimmy to gather the camp. I want a roll-call.'

'Is the boat ready?'

'Boat's ready.'

Executioner shook his head. 'We need to get the hell out of here.'

'I said I want a roll-call. Do it!'

'I found this.' Executioner held out the knife, wiping away the mud against his trouser leg.

The camp gathered, shuffling nervously from foot to foot, murmuring in low tones. The news had spread. What retribution awaited them?

All were present except one: Knifeman. Cobra held the knife aloft. 'Does anyone recognize this?'

Several of the men stepped forward for a closer inspection and in unison and with audible relief identified the weapon as belonging to Knifeman.

Santos felt his heart thump when Cobra ordered a search around the camp. After half an hour the men drifted back, shaking their heads, shrugging. No sign of Knifeman and Santos knew there was no heart for the search. He sensed that somehow Mae-li's escape had undermined Cobra's authority with his men.

Back in his hut, Cobra issued orders to the assembled crew; Rags, Spider, Jimmy and Executioner, plus two deck hands. Other than these men, who had also resupplied the boat, the rest of the camp was unaware of Cobra's impending departure. Mae-li's escape added urgency to get underway.

'We have a long voyage ahead of us,' Cobra had said in his briefing. 'We will be sailing nine thousand miles. At the end of the voyage, we will all be rich. The McGovern punk is dead. Only Mae-li knows anything, but even she does not know the details, or where we're going. You are to board now. I do not want any contact with the others.'

The men had obeyed dutifully, except Jimmy, who lingered until the others had gone down to the jetty.

'We should take the prisoner with us.'

'The prisoner? What prisoner?' Executioner was wary. He knew of Alan's suspicions, but this was the first he had heard the pirate talk of any prisoner.

'Only you and I know about the prisoner, Jimmy.' Cobra shook his head. He ignored Executioner. 'No time to do anything now. We need to leave fast.'

'We should take him,' Jimmy repeated.

'As security?' Cobra laughed. 'The little fucker's been our guest for nearly a year. Why do I need him now? I know where the treasure is. It'll mean dumping his body later. Leave him here to die. He's not our problem any more.'

Santos guessed by Cobra's words that there would be no contact with the camp. It seemed he was abandoning the others to their fate, now that Mae-li was free.

Santos was standing in the bridge. There was little to do except to watch the endless mauve of the sea and keep a lookout for passing ships. The radar was sweeping. Whenever another vessel was detected, Spider would take a circuitous route to avoid visual contact and they would all crowd around the screen waiting to see whether the other vessel changed course in pursuit. So far their run had been free of intrusion.

Since leaving the camp, they had already covered more than half the distance to the Seychelles. Santos reckoned less than six days, providing the boat maintained its speed. I wonder where she's gone, Santos thought to himself. I wonder whether I will ever see her again, and the thought that he might not lowered him into a pool of melancholy. Six more days with these animals, and then how long to locate the treasure. Then what? Would Alan and Simon be there? That was the plan, but plans, he knew, had a habit of changing course unexpectedly. Where were Alan and Simon now? And he wondered about the prisoner. About whether it had been Ben.

40

Bruno Denotti made it to Scalini's inside of ten minutes. Alfredo was there counting money in the upstairs office.

'Yo, Bruno. You got me in *cash flagrante*.' Alfredo checked himself and frowned. 'You OK, Bruno? Looks like you just seen a ghost or some-thin'.'

'Got to use the phone, Alfredo.'

'Sure. Be down in the bar.' Alfredo left the banknotes in piles on the desk.

Bruno waited for the door to close, sat behind the desk and dialled. Across the other side of the world a mobile phone started to ring.

'Come on, come on,' Bruno muttered into the empty room, drumming his fingers rapidly. 'Al? Yeah, it's Bruno. Got here as fast as I could.' He listened. 'Yeah, yeah, at Scalini's. It's OK. Shoot.' He listened some more. 'The investigation? How's it going? Like shit is like how.'

'Bruno, this may be nothing. The deadline on this thing – you mentioned there was a deadline, when we met, when I was in Washington.'

'Sure. Al, what's going on here?'

'I'm going to give you a date. You tell me if it's the deadline.'

Bruno became very still. He felt like he might faint.

'Bruno, you still there?'

'Sure, yeah, Al.'

'30th November.'

'Jesus H. Christ, Al, how the fuck you know that? It's the deadline sure. Nine days from now!'

Static crackled across 12,000 miles for what seemed like a long while.

'Listen carefully, Bruno. There's some things I can tell you and there's some things I can't, not yet.'

For fifteen minutes Bruno listened, brushing aside the piles of banknotes and scrabbling for pieces of paper on which he was making copious notes.

'So where's this freak going?'

'That's one of the things I can't tell you, Bruno. Just be ready to go as soon as I say.'

'*Capice*. Stay with me on this one, Al. I'll give you my mobile comms number, goes through the FBI satellite so you can call me any time, anywhere.'

Alan asked Bruno who he thought might be assigned to the case.

'You kiddin' me, Al? I'm going to assign myself – got to protect my asset. My SAC is at HQ acting as data co-ordinator for all the stuff being filed from the field offices and resident agencies. He'll want in on this.'

'OK, Bruno. That's good. I'd prefer to deal with people I know.'

'That's what I'll tell them. I'll talk at you, Al. And thanks.'

'Hey, you put me on to the guy.'

Bruno charged down the stairs into the restaurant area.

'Life's been good to you?' Alfredo pulled a bottle of grappa from under the bar. 'You come in here lookin' like shit; next minute you look like the kid's been given the key to the candy store.'

Bruno grinned. 'I made a mess of your desk, Alfredo. I'll make it up to you.' And then he was gone out the door.

Traffic snarled the ride back to the Washington office. Bruno paid off the cab with a twenty which meant a hundred per cent tip and sprinted the last 400 metres. By the time he made it to his third-floor office he was sweating and could barely talk for panting.

Within fifteen minutes, Bruno was being shuttled across to the FBI HQ building in an agency sedan. He was shown into a conference room on the seventh floor. The assistant director-in-charge, Washington field-office, Brett Golding was there. He came forward and pumped Bruno's hand effusively. Golding's deputy assistant director, Harry Grometz was also present as well as a posse of administrative functionaries who, Bruno presumed, would be responsible for making all the arrangements.

Bruno spoke, standing for ten minutes, aware that his voice was breathless with the magnitude of the break-through.

He focused on Brett Golding and Harry Grometz in turn. 'He won't deal with anybody 'cept me.'

Brett Golding didn't bother conferring with his deputy. 'I got no problem with that, Agent Denotti. As of now you are officially in charge of this case as field officer.' The ADIC turned to Grometz. 'Harry, organize a 4D21 clearance for Agent Denotti and see if that name, Mulcahy, has appeared in any of the field reports. Do it now.'

Harry Grometz left the conference room.

'Sir.' Bruno fixed Brett Golding with an unblinking stare. 'I'll need a plane down to Georgia. I want to go talk to George Baker. We should put a cordon around the Mulcahy house in Livermore, then the plane can take me up there.'

'And what about the contact RV, Agent Denotti?'

'I'll need an assault team standing by. We can mobilize to Nairobi just as soon as we've concluded business in Georgia and California.'

Brett Golding nodded affirmation. He fired instructions round the table. Three people gathered papers and left in a bustle.

Harry Grometz burst through the door. 'We got her! Came in this morning from the San Francisco office.' He thrust a piece of paper at ADIC Golding. 'Special Agent Gary Simonsen was assigned Livermore working with the local residency. Seems he went to the house. Noticed something odd. We would have picked it up and followed through, sir.'

'That's good work.' Brett Golding swivelled his chair round so he was facing Bruno. 'I'll get 'Frisco to tie-up with Livermore and section the house off. We'll get Agent Simonsen to head up the team seeing as he found her too.'

'Sure.' Bruno was acutely aware that ADIC Golding wanted as much credit as he could get for the internal operation that had pinpointed Gertrude Mulcahy as a suspect. 'I'll liaise with Agent Simonsen on the ground.'

'Good. I'll inform Director Levy of this, Agent Denotti.' He paused. 'One question: how did your source know to call you with the deadline date?'

Bruno Denotti took his career in his hands and offered it up to be blown away. 'That's on a need-to-know basis, sir.'

Brett Golding considered the response from his subordinate. Then he smiled and spoke collectively to the remaining agents in the room, 'Right gentlemen, let's go to work.'

As soon as Alan cut the connection on his mobile phone, he opened the back, pulled out the SIM card and destroyed it. Then he called Charlie and ordered him to arrange cancellation of the line with the air-time supplier. He was not sure how they could do it, but he was certain that the FBI could get positional fixes on his location if he used his mobile phone anywhere in the world. And the last thing he needed now was to find an FBI capture team crashing in on his party before he was ready to send the invite.

Within two hours of the conference meeting at FBI HQ, ADIC Brett Golding was in New York briefing FBI Director Levy who was there checking progress with the New York ADIC. Forty-seven minutes later, Bernard Levy was patched through to Air Force One and the President who was *en route* to the Sunshine State to press flesh with those of his citizens who, thanks to Hurricane Blossom, no longer had anywhere to call home. His conversation was to the point. Details were sketchy, but a prime suspect had been identified and was, at this time, being apprehended.

'I'll be back in the White House this evening, Bernard. I want a full report in the Oval Office eight p.m. And Bernard, good work.'

41

A convoy of seven cars was waiting for Bruno Denotti at an airfield outside of Dublin, Georgia. They sped, sirens blaring, through the town and on to the interstate, before turning off for the cabin in the forest in which George Baker was getting round to the weekly task he enjoyed most – baking bread.

The cabin was pretty much as Alan had described. Bruno had instructed that the sirens be switched off as they approached the house and that all cars except the one he was travelling in, stay back while the agents made their way on foot to surround the cabin.

George Baker looked frightened. He came out on to the stoop wearing an apron and wiping his hands on a chequered dishcloth. Flashes of flour whitened the sleeves of his lumberjack shirt. Hard to think of the guy as a former special forces sergeant in the stultifying heat of the Vietnamese jungle. Still, age had a way of hunkering a man down, age and the death of a child.

Bruno bounced up on to the stoop and flashed his badge.

'Reckoned you folks might show up.' George's voice was as resigned as the hung expression on his face. 'This ma wife, Molly.' He held the door open for Denotti.

Bruno went in. Molly was a small woman. Her face was worried. The inside of the cabin smelt comfortingly of fresh baked bread. Easy chairs by the hearth beckoned and Bruno could imagine grandchildren listening to bedtime stories.

'Better take a seat.' George sat down in one of the easy chairs and motioned Denotti to the other, Molly's, Denotti guessed.

'I'll brew some coffee,' Molly said, her eyes skimming between the faces of her husband and the cop.

Denotti forgot about any comfortable preamble. 'Someone came to see you a few weeks back.'

'Surely did; nice fella.'

'Yeah. Alan Bedale.'

'He a friend of yours?'

'You could say that.'

'What can I do for you?'

'Tell me what you told him.'

'This about Kepinski, huh. He find the guy?'

'We think so.'

'So he made it outa there.'

George Baker recounted his nightmare while Molly brought in the coffee and cookies and stared hard at Denotti for making her husband suffer this all over again. She went back and busied herself in the kitchen.

'When we was in 'Nam we get a special order come through. Word had it that the order come straight from the top, from General McCreadie hissell. He only just come into theatre after time in England. Anyways, seems the VC were mobilizing units near to Da Nang. Our mission, me and my men was to set up an ambush down this track. Other marine boys were involved at different points. Idea was to pincer some of the VC and take some live ones for intelligence gathering.'

'Where was Kepinski in all this?'

'He was a good soldier, I told that to the other fella, but reckless, like he had no fear. Problem was, my lieutenant figured he was a risk to other men. Kepinski liked to scout, by hissell, out there among the gooks. Anyways, he was doing just that, feeding back intel to HQ so's the officers'd know where best to deploy us. Well, Kepinski's out there, living like an animal in the trees and such. We get choppered in to the Dee Zee. Heavy fire's pouring in. Mystery how that happin and no one ever figured it out. Seems we had no choice. We get the order to withdraw.

Only Kepinski's stuck in the combat zone on his lonesome.'

'And he was captured?'

'That's what we heard.'

'And what else did you hear, back at base I mean?'

'Same old. General McCreadie decided the intel were no good and pulled us all back.'

'But you reckon differently?'

'It's difficult for me to say, mister. I weren't privy to no O-group with the general. But the word was that the operation was to isolate Kepinski and abandon him to the VC. Various rumours went around, that he had become a liability. But that ain't no good 'cause they coulda withdrawn him and sent him back Stateside.'

'I asked you what you thought.'

'Mister, I ain't in no place to question no general. But it seems to me there weren't no good military reason for us to withdraw. The Dee Zee come under fire sure, but we'd have lost them in the jungle quick time. I figured the VC were tipped. I figure the general was paying his respects to Kepinski for what he done to Jamie-Jake at Fort Jefferson, seeing as how that wrecked the general's career and all. That and what happin to his daughter.'

'That was the word.'

'Yes, sir.'

'Whose?'

'Mister, I ain't—'

'Whose, George?'

George Baker looked down. Betrayal was not in his nature. But the man was dead now. 'Major Thomas, sir. He told me that how it were done.'

'Major Thomas?'

'Commanding Officer Freedom Company, sir.'

'You told this to Alan?'

'Only I didn't mention the CO.'

Bruno sat back, stared up at the beamed ceiling. 'Jesus, that's why he wanted the papers in McCreadie's name.'

'Excuse me?'

'Nothing, George. Just explains something that happened. So, Mulcahy got the general's daughter pregnant, Kepinski killed him and raped her and the general handed Kepinski to the VC for dogmeat. That about the size of it?'

George Baker nodded slowly.

'When you spoke with Gertrude Mulcahy, how did she seem to you?'

'Long time now, coming on fifteen years.'

'I guess I'll find out soon enough.'

'This thing gonna end now, mister, 'cause I'm real tired?'

'It'll end, George. I promise you that.'

On the way back to the airfield Bruno punched a number into the mobile in the back of his car.

'ADIC Golding, now please.'

His boss came on the line. 'Revenge, sir, just like my source said. Seems that General McCreadie was killing the guy for what he'd done to his daughter. Gertrude Mulcahy's beef is that her brother's death was covered up to protect the general's career, sir.'

Bruno listened for a moment.

'I'm on my way to Livermore now, sir.'

'Call me when you've spoken to her. We'll need to brief the President.'

The President. Jesus. One minute I'm sitting in my office trying to decide between pastrami or salt cod and the next thing, they're waiting for me so they can brief the President. Bruno Denotti put a call through to Marcia. Maybe if she told him what she'd found on special at the store, things would regain some kind of perspective.

It was late afternoon when Bruno Denotti's motorcade pulled up outside the house on Fig Tree Drive in Livermore, Alameda County. The routine was the same as he had observed in Georgia. The cars and men had been waiting on the tarmac at the airfield and whisked him in a snaking black line towards the showdown with the woman who was making the President tremble. So, the clapboard house came as something of an anti-climax even though he'd read Special Agent Gary Simonsen's report and had spoken with him by phone from the air.

The road had been sealed with access for the residents of Fig Tree Drive and no one else. An agent was waiting at the check-point. Bruno exited his vehicle.

'You Simonsen?'

'Yes, sir.'

'What's been happening here?' Bruno reckoned he'd already counted twenty agents milling around.

'As soon as we got the call from Washington, local residency agents were on the ground in ten minutes. The suspect was in the house. The agents covered the exits front and back. Special Agent Rich McAteer entered the premises and cautioned the occupant. He's stayed inside with her. I came up from the city with a second team. Arrived three hours ago.'

Bruno was striding towards the house. He stopped at the garden gates. 'How many agents you got here?'

'Twenty-six.'

'You spoken to Agent McAteer?'

'Yes, sir, briefly, when I arrived. My orders were to wait for you. Agent McAteer's still with her, sir.'

Bruno nodded and pushed the gate open. 'That was good work you did, filing that report.'

Simonsen beamed.

'Anything you need to tell me before I go in there?'

Simonsen shrugged. 'One thing, sir: seems she's quite pleased to see us, like it was she's been expecting us.'

'She has been. OK, Agent Simonsen.' Then Bruno hopped up the steps to the stoop and disappeared inside the house.

He found them in the main room. The woman stood by the fireplace. She seemed transfixed. Bruno couldn't see past her. He moved to the side. She appeared to be staring at a photograph.

'You McAteer?'

'Yes, sir.'

'Go check the paintwork on the front door.'

Rich McAteer frowned then bobbed his head in understanding. Bruno didn't hear the door.

'Paintwork inside looks OK to me.'

He heard the door.

'Miss Mulcahy.' He waited, then louder, 'Miss Mulcahy.'

'I'm so sorry.' She turned to face him. 'I'm not used to being addressed by my maiden name.'

'What are you used to being addressed as?'

'Won't you sit?'

'Sure.'

'Mrs Ziegle, of course.'

'You know why we're here, Mrs Ziegle, don't you.'

'I'm only surprised you took so long to find me.'

'Why didn't you just tell us who you were?'

'But then the President would have taken no notice, now, would he?'

Damn but those psychological profilers were good. OK, so they'd said middle-aged, but hell, the rest was bull's eye.

'I'm Agent Bruno Denotti, Mrs Ziegle, and I'm in charge of this case.'

'Who found me?'

Bruno was taken aback. 'I did.'

'That young man who came before. . . .'

'He also filed a report citing you as a suspect.'

She smiled kindly and came away from the mantel.

'Who's that?'

Gertrude turned back, retrieved the frame and walked across to where Denotti was sitting. 'Why that's Jamie-Jake, of course, Agent Denotti. He's the one they sacrificed.'

Bruno studied the toothy recruit. Shook his head and set the frame down. Sons of bitches should never have done that to him.

'Your husband, Professor Ziegle, tell me about him.'

The man's full history had been faxed to his car while he'd been inside George Baker's cabin. Still, he wanted to hear it from her.

'A fine man in his way.'

'In his way?'

'My husband was murdered, killed on the roadside giving help to someone he thought needed help. He was shot in the face.'

'Yeah. I know. He was also a professor specializing in radio wave refraction.'

'Yes.'

'You worked in the catering department.'

'Yes.'

'So?'

Gertrude Ziegle sat down heavily, wincing at the stiffness in her knees. 'Why would a professor marry a cook, is that what you're thinking? Of course, I did not have classified access. Raymond did, however.'

'Which is why you married him?'

'After I received that call from Mr Baker telling me what really happened to Jamie-Jake, I could see no other way.'

'Your husband was committing treason, he must have known that.'

'Of course he knew that. Raymond was a lonely man, Agent Denotti.'

'Come again?'

'Sex, Agent Denotti. I gave him sex, he gave me the ROIP.'

Bruno looked nonplussed. 'Sex?'

'Don't look so surprised, Agent Denotti, I was younger then.'

'But *sex*?'

'Not just sex, ordinary sex. Raymond was really quite deviant. I obliged him; he obliged me. It was a trade.'

'Jesus wept. So you reckon to threaten the President?'

'Isn't that why you are here, Agent Denotti?'

'And what do you want exactly?'

'Justice for my poor, dead brother.' Gertrude Ziegle's voice began to climb. 'They buried my Jamie-Jake and lied to us. They made me into a fucking whore!' she screeched. Then, just as quickly, she composed herself dabbing delicately at her eyes. 'I want the man who killed my Jamie-Jake to be put on trial and then I want to watch him fry in the chair.'

'We don't know who killed your brother.'

'*Liar!*'

'He may be dead.'

'Then China gets the codes. I want Billy-Ray Kepinski telling me he's sorry about Jamie-Jake.'

Bruno picked up his radio from the seat. 'Simonsen, get two guys in here.' He flicked the radio off. 'Mrs Ziegle, we're going to move you to a secure unit. . . .'

'Then they get the codes. It's all in place. Should anything happen to me, there are instructions to release the codes.'

'You don't have them?'

'No.'

'It's for your own protection. Either that, or I'll have to leave men here with you, all the time.'

'I'm not leaving.'

Agents Simonsen and McAteer came in. Bruno ushered them back into the hallway. 'The psychologist here yet?'

'Outside,' Simonsen said.

'Get him in here.'

'Her.'

'Whatever. Agent McAteer, you stay with the old lady. I'm going to take a look in the basement. I've got to see this.'

42

The White House was eerily quiet at eight o'clock that evening. After his exhaustive schedule in Florida the President was glad of the stillness.

'Great news, Bernard. Great news!' The President shrugged out of his winter coat and flung it over the back of a sofa. 'So now, is everything set?'

Bernard Levy allowed himself the luxury of a rare smile. 'A-OK, sir.'

The President settled behind his desk. Bernard sat in front of the desk in one of the high-backed carvers.

'Give me the full low-down, Bernard.'

The Director of the FBI had given the President sketchy details earlier in the day. 'I was waiting for Agent Denotti to report in, sir, after I called Air Force One. The situation is this: Gertrude Ziegle has been placed under house arrest and the premises searched. We've found nothing at this time and she's not saying.'

'House arrest?'

'She threatened to release the information if she was detained at another location. Agent Denotti used his judgement. Six men are with her twenty-four hours, two inside the house, one up, one down and four outside. She's never out of their sight. Each team will run four-hour watches. Phone's been tapped and the computer's checked for e-mails every thirty minutes. She ain't going no place.'

The President nodded. 'Who found her?'

Bernard hesitated a fraction. 'Well, Agent Denotti, sir. Seems he was working on a case with the Australian Queensland police. Turns out the guy they were tracking is the same guy who killed Ziegle's brother, Jamie-Jake Mulcahy.'

'And that's her beef?'

'That's it.' Bernard handed a sheet of paper across the President's desk. 'Details are all down there. Justice Department's files indicate the boy's death in 1968 was covered up. The general commanding the training camp was relocated to Britain then deployed to 'Nam. A Billy-Ray Kepinski was believed responsible but never charged. General McCreadie appears to have set the guy up for a fall in 'Nam. Kepinski was registered MIA.'

The President devoured the document then flicked it back across the desk. 'She wants retribution?'

'Justice was how she described it to Agent Denotti. I've prepared a résumé of the key points.' A second sheet typed on one side, double-spaced was passed to the President.

He read then reread the sheet, sat back, breathed out. 'Sex. A honey-trap, that's how she got the ROIP data.'

Bernard Levy inclined his head to one side.

'Amazing. A man will turn traitor for sex.'

'According to Agent Denotti's initial report it was pretty deviant stuff, sir. She blames the government for turning her into a whore, was how she put it.'

'This boy's death, Mulcahy, George Baker confirmed all this to Agent Denotti?'

'Yes, sir. He says it was just as he told it to Gertrude Ziegle in 1986. Well, she was Gertrude Mulcahy then, of course.'

'That's why the deadline?'

'George Baker says he remembers the date he called her exactly. It's the day his son was killed.'

'30th November. That's eight days. Where's Agent Denotti now?'

Bernard Levy checked his watch. Twenty past eight. 'Airborne, sir, with the apprehension team *en route*. to Nairobi, Kenya. Those were the instructions from Alan Bedale. The apprehension location is obviously near there somewhere abouts. My people have tried analysis but there's not much to go on. Chances are Kepinski's turned mercenary so any one of a number of African countries is a possibility. Other than that are countries off Africa's eastern seaboard, Seychelles, Madagascar, Mauritius. We've taken a lead on this one and contacted the governments in all those places considered a possibility for permission to execute an emergency criminal apprehension and repatriation.'

'Any problems?'

'Some of the Africans are kicking up.'

'Get State to intercede.'

'Will do.'

'This guy, this Australian, where is he now?'

'We do not know at this time, sir. We tried location through a cellular number he was using but it's since been cancelled.'

'So he doesn't want us to find him.'

'The plan is he'll pass the word to Agent Denotti in Nairobi when he's ready to make the arrest. Apparently there are people involved in his investigation whose lives will be endangered if we go now or go too soon. That's all he would tell Agent Denotti.'

'So our mission is clear. We've got to get Kepinski back here before six p.m. on the 30th November or we lose ROIP. But we can't do anything until this guy, – the President glanced at the typewritten sheet – 'Alan Bedale tells us.'

'That's it in a nutshell, Mr President.'

'What do we know about the investigation Alan Bedale is running?'

'He's married to the general's granddaughter.'

'McCreadie?'

'Yes, sir. Her mother, McCreadie's daughter, was murdered. He's investigating the case. He called in a favour from Agent Denotti, seems that they go back some. FBI led him to George Baker and from Baker he tracked down Kepinski.'

'Where'd he find Kepinski?'

'Unknown, sir.'

The President tapped the précis. 'Says here Kepinski raped the girl at Fort Jefferson.'

'It's why McCreadie handed Kepinski to the Viet Cong.'

'So your Agent Denotti must have told his pal the deadline.'

Statement, not a question. 'Apparently not, sir. The guy figured it out.' Bernard Levy considered the FBI case. 'We had her bagged, sir. Report was filed from San Francisco raising suspicions.'

'Would you have followed up in time?'

'I believe so, Mr President.' Bernard Levy dropped his eyes to hide the lie.

'Thank God Italians like to talk.'

'Agent Denotti will be fully debriefed once this thing is over.'

'Do we have any idea of the whereabouts of the ROIP data this woman claims to have?'

Bernard Levy shook his head. 'Not at this time, sir.'

'How do we know she's not lying?'

'Polygraph, sir. She was examined this afternoon, three hours, same questions asked every which way. Came up clean. She's telling the truth.'

The President stood up and leaned on his desk, fingers arched like a sprinter at the start line. 'Do whatever you need to do, Bernard, but above all tell Agent Denotti to tell his friend to make damn certain that Kepinski stays alive.'

43

Santos noted down the co-ordinates from the GPS navigator and plotted their position. The chart table was behind the helm, facing the stern. They had been at sea for six days and in all that time he had not sighted another vessel. Out here, in the open ocean, avoidance was easy. Several passing ships, visible only on the radar, had made radio contact to give weather warnings, but Cobra had not responded, just listened. The fuel levels were constantly monitored. The long-range fuel tanks would get them to the Seychelles, just.

Cobra's mood had continued to swing wildly, but for the last three days he had been calmer and increasingly excited at the prospect of arriving in the Seychelles and getting on with the business of scooping buckets of gold off the sea bed. The crew were similarly buoyed with every passing mile. Quite what fate awaited them once Cobra had the gold, if there was any gold, remained to be seen. Santos's guess was that a bullet in the back of the head would be their reward. No way a nutcase like Cobra was going to share a dime, far less a bar of gold, with any of them. Of that he was certain.

Of the crew, Jimmy had withdrawn into self-imposed exile, rarely speaking, unless to bark an order, or more often, a threat. Perhaps he was thinking about Mae-li. Perhaps regretting that he hadn't killed her himself. Or maybe he understood his master better than the others and, like Santos, reckoned it was only a matter of time before he was floating face down in the sea. And if that was to be their fate, then sure as hell Jimmy would be the first to go. After Cobra, he was their leader. Without him, the rest would be unable to rally. There was also the consideration of his physical strength. The last thing Cobra would relish would be a hand-to-hand with the Big Guy.

Still, seeing Jimmy Pran dead would be one of the highlights of his police career. Santos used a pair of dividers to estimate the distance they had yet to travel. The engines had never faltered and Rags, who had taken to sleeping down in the engine-room assured Cobra, in response to repeated questions, that he could not foresee any problems developing, at least not ones for which he would not be able to apply a prompt remedy.

Santos calculated. Three days.

Cobra clambered up the companionway. 'Where're we at?' He leaned over the chart table.

The smell of stale whiskey dribbled over Santos. 'Here.' He tapped the chart table.

'Wonder if that fucker can give us more speed?' He ripped open a door next to the chart table. The deep throb of the engines boomed into the wheelhouse. '*Rags!*'

Rags appeared, wiping his hands on a greasy cloth. 'Yeah?'

'Can't you go any faster? Exec says we're still three days away. I want to get this done.'

'A few more knots maybe.'

'Then do it.'

Rags disappeared.

'The fuck you looking at!'

Santos redirected his gaze back to the chart. Cobra was drunk. He'd been in a stupor for the past twenty-four hours.

'*Jimmy!*' Cobra looked round the wheelhouse, staggering as the boat lurched. 'Where the fuck. . . .'

Jimmy appeared in the companionway.

'Where those other two?'

Aside from Cobra and himself, Spider was in the wheelhouse and

Rags had gone below to tend to his beloved turbines. Santos supposed then that Cobra meant the deckhands.

'In their bunks.' Jimmy muttered.

'Get 'em.'

Jimmy ducked back down. A few minutes later the deckhands came up, followed by Jimmy. Cobra whispered something to Jimmy, then went below.

'You two. Outside,' Jimmy barked. The deckhands glanced at one another. One of them shrugged. They were both Malays. Tough, squat brutes.

From the rear of the wheelhouse, Santos watched their progress over the bucking deck, treading carefully towards the stern. Cobra re-emerged in the wheelhouse. This time he was carrying his AK-47. Santos swivelled back to watch what was happening outside. The two deckhands were coiling ropes. Jimmy suddenly lashed out with his foot. The guy he was aiming for didn't have a prayer. He was suddenly airborne, a look of startled surprise freezing on his face. Then he fell away into the boat's creamed wake. The second Malay tried to make a run along the side deck. Jimmy blocked him easily, crashed a huge fist into the guy's face and literally picked him up and tipped him over the side.

Santos watched in fascinated horror. No way he was going to protest. Absently he wondered which was worse: drowning or a bullet. Cobra joined Jimmy on the stern deck, leaning back into the breeze, his shirt pressing against his back and his shorts flapping furiously in the wind. Both of them were soon drenched with spray breaking over the wheelhouse.

Spider had locked the wheel and was now leaning against the chart table to watch the sport. Two heads bobbed in the widening wake. Cobra raised his weapon and let off sharp bursts of fire. The fuckwit was using humans as target practice! The phut-phut-phut of detonating rounds reached into the wheelhouse. The head of one of the Malay's exploded in a red vapour cloud. Several more bursts and the second Malay threw his arms wide to the sky, then slumped back to the water.

Santos watched Cobra slap Jimmy on the back. He was mouthing words, but the wind ripped them from his mouth and Santos had no way of overhearing what was said.

Bullets it would be then. He wondered where Alan was right now, right this second. He prayed he was in the Seychelles, standing by with a reception committee and a very strong pair of handcuffs.

44

Privacy was important. They found it at L'Archipel, on Praslin, the second largest of the Seychelles island group, a collection of chalets dispersed among a tropical garden, fringed by a beach of dazzling coral sands. The main building housing the bar and restaurant was set further up the hill, commanding a sweeping panorama of Volbert beach. On the seaward side, a rocky promontory jutted into the placid waters of the bay. One mile out, the flat, turquoise of the lagoon turned a dramatic, deep indigo, the colours separated by a thin white line of breaking surf where the sea sacrificed itself on the jagged teeth of the reef.

Simon sat on the small veranda of their chalet. The hydrographic office's international chart series number 742 was spread on the rattan table. The chart had been folded down to isolate Praslin and her smaller sister, La Digue, to the south-east.

'Al, I can't figure this!' Simon called over his shoulder. He looked out over the balustrade where red-feathered Cardinal birds flocked and squeaked in a desperate scrum to get to the crumbs with which he had littered the earth.

Alan came out of the chalet and handed Simon a cold Seybrew from the minibar.

'We've been over it so many times, mate.' Alan slumped into a chair. 'I'm beginning to think maybe old Robert McGovern got his bearings wrong. We've been here for seven bloody days and how many dives?'

'Sixteen.'

'Where's Cobra now?'

Simon picked up a second chart from the tiled floor, on which he'd been plotting Cobra's inexorable approach. 'Last reading put him four hundred miles away.'

'This is too tight, too damn tight.' Alan gulped beer from the bottle, gasping as the carbonated fluid hit the back of his throat.

'Four hundred miles is ten hours' sailing minimum. You said when you spoke with your FBI contact that they're on the ground in Kenya.'

'Correct.'

'Nairobi's seventeen hundred miles from here, four hours' flying time. That gives us six hours. Tight, I agree but not impossible.'

'But there's the deadline to think about from Bruno's end.' Alan gulped again. 'I mean this thing's been handed down by the President for Chris'sake.'

'They've got to get Kepinski back to the States, right?'

'Deadline's six p.m. tomorrow, San Francisco time.'

'OK, let's figure this out. Twenty-four hours from here to San Francisco, give or take. We're twelve hours ahead of San Francisco.' Simon glanced at his watch. 'It's midday here, so it's midnight last night there, so to speak. So they've got eighteen hours from now to six p.m. on the 29th and twenty-four hours from then to six p.m. on the 30th. Eighteen plus twenty-four, forty-two hours in total.'

'Twenty-four for the flight which leaves eighteen.'

'Right. Kepinski'll be here in ten. You'll have called Bruno in by then, so they'll be here to provide a reception committee. That allows eight hours' fuck-up time.'

Alan grunted. 'Like I said, too damn tight.'

Simon leaned forwards, set his bottle of Seybrew on the table and flipped the chart round. 'Let's go over this again. We've got less than ten hours to find the bloody gold.'

Alan looked away to the sea then back again. 'Tell me what you've got.'

'OK, the first bearing is thirty degrees from the highest mountain,

Mount Praslin, here.' Simon stabbed the map with his finger and traced the bearing line.

'We've checked this a million times.'

'The second bearing is fifty-one degrees from Grand Fon, the second highest mountain.' Simon ran his fingertip along the second bearing.

'I've checked that one, too,' Alan sighed.

'These bearings meet at a point four nautical miles north-east of the island. Right. The distance Robert McGovern gives along the second bearing is two point seven miles. . . .'

'Which puts it on Point Rouge on the island of Curieuse. The other distance he gives is three point one miles along the first bearing. Join 'em up and the treasure's somewhere along that line, between the two bearings.'

'Except it isn't. We've looked!' Simon started fiddling with a pencil. 'The third bearing is thirty-four degrees from Mount Takamaka and bisects the joining line here.' Simon jabbed the map with a pencil. 'I've extended the joining line between the first two bearings. It runs from Point Rouge on Curieuse to the highest point on La Digue. Robert McGovern seemed pretty keen on high points as landmarks, so that would appear to make sense.'

'Only it doesn't.'

'The only thing I can think is that his bearings are out. Let's face it, he was doing this two hundred and fifty years ago, and he was almost dead from his injuries by the time he got here!'

Alan studied the chart. 'Maybe he's deliberately misleading us.'

Simon sipped his beer. 'In that case we could be here for years searching the area.'

'Not with Cobra only a few hundred miles away.'

'Why the hell didn't we just falsify the bearings in the translation he pinched from us! That way we could have got him to go where we wanted, exactly where we wanted, without any chance of him finding the gold, and not us!'

'We should have done. Bloody right. But that was then, this is now. No good belly-aching about hindsight.'

'I'll get the translation. I practically know it by heart, but we'll read it again.' Simon got up, was about to go inside when Alan suddenly clapped his hands.

'I've got it!'

Simon spun round. 'Where?'

'Robert McGovern's ship, what was it called?'

'She. Ships are feminine. *Clarissa*. . . .'

'No! The other one, the one he sailed from England.'

'HMS *Felicity*. Why?'

'Look here.' Alan was tapping his finger at the chart. 'The bearings are correct, except one and that's the bisecting line!'

Simon stooped and gripped the edge of the map. A short distance northeast of La Digue was a small island with a peak at its south western edge. The island was called Félicité.

'It was there all along!'

'Mark it in.'

Simon sat down quickly, pulled the chart over and, using a Breton plotter, drew in the line from Point Rouge on Curieuse through the peak on Félicité. He measured the angle. 'It's bearing one, one, two degrees,' Simon felt breathless. The new line shifted the position of the treasure 500 metres north-east of where they'd been searching. 'We've been looking in the wrong place!'

'We think! One, one, two. One hundred and twelve. Is there any reference to that number in the diary?'

Thirty minutes later they found it, Simon found it.

I have become the hapless victim of an evil circumstance. To my beloved Clarissa I say that I will hold out after this in wherever place has been ordained by God until we join again. As for Cummings who did these evil deeds, kindness will hunt him down from the four Points of the compass.

'Kindness will hunt him down! Felicity is kindness. Jesus! He's using the man's own ship, HMS *Felicity,* to point the finger of guilt.'

'Now is this a long shot, Simon? The four points of the compass. . . .'

'Anywhere in the world?'

'The bearing line is one, one, two. Right?'

'Yes.'

'One plus one plus two is four. The four points on the compass!' exclaimed Alan.

Simon slumped back. 'Bit far fetched, I mean he was dying for God's sake.'

'Only one way to find out. Let's get those tanks refilled and go have a looksee.'

The equipment had come from Brisbane, to obviate reliance on the local dive school. The Seychelles was becoming an increasingly affordable holiday destination for Europeans, and many visitors came for the diving. The last thing they needed was to be told that all equipment was out on loan. But they used the dive school's air compressor to refill their bottles.

The boat was easier. Beach shacks advertising visits to outlying islands and sea tours abounded. Nine hundred dollars in hard currency had bought them a twenty-three-foot fisher for three days. No crew, no questions. The boat was bobbing at a mooring just off the private beach at L'Archipel. The ride across the wide mouth of the bay to the dive school near Volbert village took five minutes. Simon refilled the tanks, wading through the bath-warm surf. Ten minutes later, they were zipping over the aquamarine glaze towards the new position taken off the bearing line to Félicité. Simon followed their course on a GPS plotter towards the keyed-in destination of 54 degrees 45 minutes 06 seconds north, 03 degrees 17 minutes 06 seconds east.

'OK! Cut it, Al,' Simon yelled over the buzz of the outboard when the readings on his handheld unit matched. 'This is the spot.'

Alan killed the engine and slung an anchor line over the side. 'How deep?'

Simon consulted the chart. 'Twenty-one metres.'

'Fingers crossed, eh.' Alan felt the anchor hit, tensed the line and tied it off on a cleat. 'You know, I've often wondered what it would be like. . . .'

'What?'

'Finding treasure.'

'Who hasn't?'

Alan pulled on his tank and tightened the weight belt, scrunched his feet in the soft rubber of his fins and spat on to the inside of his mask. Cobra and the incipient threat of his arrival here, in Eden, receded. His thoughts became focused. His hands tingled with the rampaging excitement that precedes the imminence of long-hoped-for discovery. That excitement had been there the first time they'd dived, at the first site. He swam through the blue light, over the snow sand, climbed the steep thrill. But the ocean was dressed in rags, not gold. He had crested and tumbled down into the deep trough of anti-climax. Now the spark of new hope rekindled desire. He felt on fire.

'Ready, Simon.' But even as he spoke, Alan fell backwards into the promising sea. He ducked his head down, could see the misty mirage of the bottom, and the great, blocking triangles of his fins magnified by the water. Simon splashed down beside him in a furious fizz of salted bubbles.

They followed the anchor line down. The routine was practised. As he touched bottom, Alan peered up, taking a positional reference off the boat. They would swim in ever-increasing circles, around the boat, until they found the treasure, or ran out of air. Already, the naked sand had leeched some of his exquisite euphoria. Simon would swim the same route, only in reverse. Their technique would save time and air, especially if they were swimming larger diameter circles. They could cover more ground. The tapping of a knife against the tank would be the signal of discovery. Simon set off, left side to the centre. Alan, right side in.

The seabed was strewn with boulders, thrown off by the angry earth in the manufacture of the islands. Spears of bright sunlight played over the rocks and sand, pirouetting into dark crevices and reflecting brilliantly off the backs of wandering fish. Alan glided two metres above the landscape, conscious that any treasure would, by now, be camouflaged by centuries of marine colonization.

They had been sweeping the area now for nearly half an hour and concern that Robert McGovern may have been wildly out in his estimation of bearing angles was beginning to gnaw again at Simon's confidence. A huge, irregular boulder loomed in front. Over or round the side? Simon debated. Over, he decided.

No amount of dreaming, no extent of imagining nor any prediction of emotion could have adequately prepared him as he glided up and over the rock, then slid down its far side. Thirty ancient chests, each the size of a child's toy box, squatted in a sandy glade, some on their sides, others end up. At first, his conscious mind had assumed them as yet more haphazard rocks. Deep in his subconscious alarm bells sounded. There was too much uniformity about the dark objects. In an infinitesimal fraction of time, his sub-conscious mind catapulted the information to the present. The effect of his realization was stunning. Breathing ceased as he hovered. The soundlessness was deafening. Time regressed, scrolling back 250 years, and Simon floated down into a world beyond dreams. He was back, in the year 1719.

With the utmost reverence, Simon reached fingertips to an ancient chest furred with coral growth. The wood disintegrated under the pressure of his fingers in a small explosion of dust. Immediately the rich, yellow gleam of gold beckoned. Momentarily panicked by the magnitude of the discovery, Simon kicked away, then reached for his knife and started hammering the blade frantically against his tank.

Through the dulling effect of water, Alan heard the deep clunks. He spun round, unsure from which direction the sounds were coming. It was impossible to tell. He stroked upwards, hovering three metres above the sandy seabed. A column of air bubbles forty metres away pinpointed Simon's position. Alan kicked towards the column. His breathing was quick and shallow. The aquamarine of the shallows turned a darker, colder blue where the sea floor fell away to deeper water and the eddying currents became suddenly chill. An enormous boulder obscured the source of the air column. Alan walked the pitted surface of the rock with his hands until he levered himself over its crest. And beyond, in a clearing was Simon, on his knees, both hands out in front, offering a pile of gold.

45

'Charlie, Charlie, wait up! We have got to know what's happening!'
Bruno shifted the phone to his other side and made a scratching motion
in the air for pen and paper. 'Don't he trust me no more?'

'He thought you might try a trace via the mobile.'

'Mobile? Right, cell phone. Jesus. You know how big this thing is?'

'You told me before, several times. It's come from the President.'

'The President, that's right. Not any president, *the* President, like in
the President of the United States. And guess what, Charlie, he's chewing my ass. We been stuck here in this shit-hole for five fuckin' days now.
We've got to get laughing boy Stateside. You told Alan that, right?'

'I've told Alan everything you asked me to pass on. He's keenly aware
of the situation.'

'Keenly aware. Keenly aware? We got maybe twelve hours, sixteen
max from now, to go in, arrest playmate of the month and get out. So
what I need to know, Charlie, is where the fuck is Alan and when the fuck
is he going to give us the green light, otherwise we're in the brown stuff
if you catch my drift?'

'You wouldn't be much good at chess. . . .'

'What the—'

'Too impatient.'

'Charlie, stop jerking—'

'I'm calling, Agent Denotti, to give you the location.'

Bruno waved his hand at the group of Navy Seals gathered in the confined space of the stripped-out Gulfstream. He meant for them to shut-up talking.

'Shoot.'

'The Seychelles.'

Bruno lowered the phone. 'Seychelles!' He eyeballed Novak, the officer in charge. 'Go tell the pilot. Start the friggin' engines and let's go, now!' He spoke back into the phone. 'Thank Christ. What else you got for me, Charlie?'

The co-pilot pulled up the integral stairs and sealed the door.

'The target will be in the location in approximately eight hours' time, I repeat eight hours.'

'Got that, Charlie.'

'Presumably you'll be landing on the main island of Mahé?'

'Wait.' Bruno lowered the phone. 'Novak! Ask the pilot what strip we've got to set down on.' He lifted the phone. 'Charlie, you there?'

'Still here.'

'Pilot's checking.'

Novak ducked out of the flight deck. 'International airport, only runway's long enough.'

'I heard that,' Charlie said. 'Right, you'll need to transfer to Praslin.'

'That another island?'

'Yeah, about twenty minutes by air.'

'OK.'

'I can arrange for the transfer. . . .'

'My people'll do it.'

The Gulfstream's engines whined into life and they were rolling, gathering speed. Then a sharp turn on to the runway, sudden acceleration.

'You'll have three hours on the ground before the target is close enough.'

'Where's Alan at, where's he staying?'

'That's a negative, Agent Denotti. Transfer from Mahé to the airfield on Praslin. Alan will rendezvous with you there.'

The juddering of the undercarriage ceased and they were airborne, the scattered city of Nairobi receding rapidly under the fierce onslaught of the African noonday sun. By the time they hit the cloud base, Bruno, strapped into a single seat at the rear of the fuselage had cut the connection to Charlie in Queensland and was dialling the secure number of the co-ordination and control centre for Operation Snakepit at FBI HQ in Washington.

46

Crimson and pink slashed the evening sky beyond the palm trees fringing the beach. A warm breeze rustled the palm fronds blending the sound with the whispering surf of the lagoon.

'OK everyone, final briefing. Let's do this inside.' Alan spoke the command softly, his instinct for secrecy heightened by the press of night.

The flight crew who had ferried the team from Nairobi were still with the plane on the tarmac at Mahé. Two helicopters from a local air tour company, chartered by Washington, had been awaiting their arrival and shuttled Denotti and the navy men to the smaller island of Praslin. They had found Alan waiting with three taxis for the thirty-minute drive to the hotel on the other side of the island.

Bruno had clambered down from one helicopter as its skids settled on to the concrete apron on Praslin and rushed over, ducking out of the chopper's down draught.

'How're you doing, Al? Where's our guy?'

Alan had to shout above the noise of the rotors. 'He's slowed down. Simon's at the hotel. He's been tracking the boat. Looks to us like Kepinski's judging it so he's on site at first light tomorrow morning.'

'On site?'

'The gold.'

'Right. You found it!' Bruno exclaimed. Behind him the commandos were pulling gear out of the choppers.

'Yep. One cask, small.'

Bruno slapped Alan on the back. 'Let's just hope. The best laid plans and all that. This is going to be real tight, Al.'

They waited until Novak had organized his troops into two taxis. Alan and Bruno got into the lead car and the ramshackle convoy set off along the narrow road that twisted chaotically between the tin-roofed shacks that studded the coast.

'Charlie tells me the heat is coming from the top.'

'Charlie's right.'

'You found Gertrude Mulcahy?'

'And George Baker. What a pair. But the Ziegle woman, that's her married name, it's what threw us off the scent – maybe's she just a fuckin' loopo.' Bruno pointed a forefinger at his temple. 'But I tell you this, Al, the old bag's got El Presidente sweating, that's for sure. We have to get macho man home and his chest must still be moving up and down all by itself.'

The taxi trundled past the entrance of the Vallée de Mae National Park, the boundaries of which protected a forest of prehistoric Coco de Mer palms. The thickness of the forest canopy blotted the evening light to murky grey.

Alan shook his head, staring out the window at the ancient trees. It was the first time they had talked directly since he'd revealed his knowledge of the ROIP deadline. 'It was just a hunch, but Bruno, you understand why I couldn't say anything?'

'Understand? Oh, sure. Anxious time. You heard anything more?'

'No. We've left the camp alone. I've been keeping in touch with Angela Ramierez. She's on stand-by in Manila.'

'Sure. And your guy, Degarda?'

'Santos.'

'Right.'

'Presumably on the boat. If he's not he's dead. He freed the girl. My feeling is it'll probably have cost him his life. If he is on the boat, I guess he'll be looking for us or waiting for something to happen.'

'And what about the girl, where's she?'

'Manila. Safe-house.'

Bruno grunted. 'Makes sense I guess. Great about the gold, huh! Makes your case stand up for sure.'

At L'Archipel the new arrivals were billeted in three similar chalets dispersed in the grounds. The chartered helicopters would remain at the airfield with instructions to fly into L'Archipel if so ordered.

The group of men gathered on the small veranda of Alan's chalet filed into the dim interior, some sitting, others standing. Two of the Navy Seals chewed gum. No one spoke.

Bruno Denotti dumped himself into a sling-back chair. A representative of the Seychelles police sat on one of the beds. His presence was a condition of the Seychelles Government in response to the earlier request from Washington to land armed men on their territory.

Alan closed the French doors and turned the key in the lock. 'Simon, you want to give us the low-down on Cobra's location?'

Simon stood in front of the men. He held up the chart. 'I took a reading on Cobra's position at seven o'clock.' He checked his Rolex. 'Ten minutes ago. He's one hundred and forty miles from here. By my calculation, he'll be on site at six tomorrow morning.'

Bruno interjected. 'Al says he's slowed up some.'

'That's right. He's making about fifteen knots. I think what he's planning is to be in sight of land for the shortest possible time. His speed will put him in the location of the gold at first light.'

'Nothing much he can do until then anyways,' Bruno commented.

'OK. As you know there's not that much, one chest. We've left it there, spread it about a bit so it'll take him longer to gather it all up. That was Alan's idea, to keep him in the vicinity. We did bring a couple of pieces back with us.'

Alan flicked a doubloon to Bruno who examined it and handed it to François René, the Seychellois.

'The gold is here.' Simon tapped the map. 'Right where Robert McGovern said it would be.'

Alan stepped forward. 'Thanks, Simon. OK. We'll keep the area under observation starting at three a.m.'

'Fine by me,' Bruno said, looking around for dissenters.

'As soon as we see the diver or divers go down, we launch the inflatables and make the arrests. That's assuming they dive at first light.'

'They'll be armed,' Bruno confirmed.

'Sure. But they'll be within sight of land, so they'll be careful about blasting us. We should be close enough in to fire first if it comes to a firefight.'

'If your man's on board, I hope he's good,' Bruno said.

'If he's on board, he's good, Bruno. He'll twig what's happening and if necessary take them from the inside.'

Lieutenant Novak spoke for his men who were all clutching M16s. 'I think we'll assume that there are no friendlies on board. If he is on board and we open up, he'll just have to keep his head down.'

'Fair enough. I had these copied. This is Filippo Santos.' Alan handed enlarged portraits to the Americans. 'If that face appears in your gunsights, try to miss.'

'What about Kepinski?'

'Here,' Alan took another portrait, the one Charlie had blown up and aged from George Baker's original, and handed it round. 'That's how we think Billy-Ray Kepinski might look today.'

The men studied the picture intently, stowing the image in their memories.

'You got anything, Bruno?'

'Lieutenant Novak?'

'Surprise is our best weapon. It's light at 0630 hours.' Novak stood and went to the chart Simon had been using. 'We'll exit this location at 0530. That gives us thirty minutes to get into position here.' He stabbed the map with his finger. 'The divers, namely myself, Farr, Henson and Squires, will drop off and make our way underwater to the gold, a distance of approximately five hundred metres. We'll be using Nitrox air mix which'll give us two hours down time at thirty metres. One of two events will occur when we reach the contact location: either we'll encounter the target in the water, or the target will be on-board his vessel. Murray will be on the inflatable with Cusack. Cusack will spot for us relaying information on the radio.' Novak went back to where he'd been sitting. 'I'll go through a detailed brief with my men at 2000 hours in my hut. Any questions?'

'Tide'll be coming in,' Simon pointed out. 'You'll have a job swimming out to Cobra's position.'

Novak nodded. 'Correct. We'll have thirty minutes. That'll be sufficient. Anyone else?' He looked around the room. 'Alan?'

'When the boat's secure, Kepinski's boat I mean, we'll come out in our speedboat. We've got our own diving gear.'

'OK. I'll give you one of our radios. You'll get a call when it's OK to move.'

'We should organize the watch rota,' Alan suggested. He looked at Novak. 'When will you have your equipment set out?'

'By 2200 hours.'

'Ten o'clock. OK. The watch will have to guard the kit and plot Kepinski's approach on the hour, every hour.'

Novak did not want his men going without sleep for too long. 'Each man will stand watch for one hour commencing 2200.'

'Agreed.'

'I'll go first, 2200 to 2300, then Henson, Squires, Farr, Cusack and Murray who'll take 0300 to 0400.'

Simon calculated timings. 'Alan, why don't you take watch from four to five. I'll do five to five-thirty?'

'Fine by me. Lieutenant Novak, you want a final briefing?'

'Yep. We'll meet back here at five.'

No one had anything else to add, so Simon then demonstrated the use of the GPS tracker. The main job on watch besides guarding equipment was to track and plot Cobra's approach using the GPS receiver.

Alan ended the briefing. 'I suggest we all get something to eat and some kip.'

Bruno nodded his head. 'Sure thing. OK, I've got to go call Washington.'

When the others had gone, Simon turned to Alan. He threw his arms wide and yelled with delight.

'Keep it down.' Alan pressed a finger to his lips, but even he had trouble containing himself.

'God! Telling them there was only one chest, Jesus, I was almost biting my tongue off.'

'And that Seychelles cop. We'd be slung in the bloody nick if he knew we'd moved some gold back to where we thought it'd been dropped.'

'Wow! I'm still staggered by it!' Simon exclaimed. He studied the chart. 'Are you sure Kepinski will go there, to the first spot, I mean?'

Alan interrupted. 'Not one hundred per cent, but hopefully he won't figure out the Félicité connection.'

47

The first lights of Praslin punctured the dark cloak of night. Cobra, watching from the wheelhouse, saw them first. He glanced at the console clock. Almost five o'clock. Unseen, Félicité and the 'Sister' islands, Grand Soeur and Petit Soeur, slid by on their port side.

Cobra saw more lights dancing in the distance off the port bow. He bent over the chart. 'Must be La Digue,' he muttered. He straightened, standing just behind Spider. Much of the epic passage from Sarangani Bay had been directed by the auto-pilot, with permanent watches stationed to monitor the radar and radio. For the approach to Praslin, Cobra wanted Spider at the helm. Until they saw the lights.

'Where are we now?' Cobra asked.

Spider pointed to a place on the chart.

'No hurry. Be dark for an hour yet. Throttle back. We'll approach slow, get into position ready for daylight.'

Spider glanced round quickly. Something in his eyes betrayed weariness. 'What position?'

'Stay on course. I'll tell you when we're closer.'

Down below, Jimmy and Rags slept. Santos too was in his bunk, but awake. He heard the engines slow and the boat begin to pitch more deeply with the loss of momentum.

Cobra fingered the handle of his knife. His hand closed round the grip. In a quick and simultaneous action, he plunged the blade into

Spider's back, clapping his other hand over the helmsman's mouth, yank-ing him backwards, using the man's body weight to force the blade deeper.

Spider's strength ebbed immediately. No thrashing, just a stifled moan. Then he slumped backwards into his assassin's waiting arms. Cobra dragged the dead man out of the wheelhouse and tipped the body into the oily water.

Santos heard the splash through the steel skin of the hull, a sound distinct from the pattern of slapping water which had characterized their passage. He stiffened. Soft footfalls down the companionway. Why soft? Someone treading carefully, not wanting to make a noise, not wanting to alert the others. Predatory footsteps. Santos sat up. The firearms were locked in a steel cabinet. Only Cobra had the key. Not even Jimmy was permitted a firearm onboard ship. The footfalls passed the closed door of his cabin. Jimmy had a similar cabin on the starboard side. Except for Cobra, the rest of the crew slept in hammocks in an open area below the wheelhouse, by the galley and the heads.

Cobra felt his way in the dark without hesitation, the way a blind man knows his own home. He reached behind and pulled the Glock from the waistband of his cut-away denim shorts. Sweat ran down his face. He braced himself against a bulkhead, facing Jimmy's cabin door, legs apart to augment the boat's rolling movement. The Glock model 17 was his preferred weapon of choice. A 9mm calibre, short recoil, semi-automatic, the weapon did not rely on a hammer but on a self-cocking striker system. Much more dependable. The seventeen-round magazine also meant he had plenty in reserve.

'Jimmy! Quick!' he hissed in the dark. He was rewarded with the rustle of movement from inside Jimmy's cabin. Cobra raised the Glock in a two-handed grip.

Jimmy opened the door.

Cobra's finger jabbed twice at the trigger. The second round followed the first, more or less exactly, smashing though Jimmy's forehead and ploughing through the soft matter of his brain.

Santos jumped at the crash of the shots and cracked his head on the steelwork above his bunk. Nowhere he could go from here. Open the door and he'd run into Cobra. And a child wouldn't be able to squeeze through the porthole above his bunk. Play it cool, he cautioned himself. He's either going to kill you or he isn't. You choose.

From the bowels of the ship, Rags screamed, 'What the fuck!'

Cobra pivoted round, facing the companionway below. Rags bounded up the steps. As soon as he appeared, Cobra released three bullets in split second succession. Rag's face imploded.

The echoes thundered around Santos. Then he heard the soft clatter of a dead body falling and the brittle snap of breaking crockery. Somewhere deep inside, his fear gave way to panic. The door of his cabin burst open.

'Mister Executioner, seems like you and me are the only ones left.' Cobra's voice held a jocular note. His smile flashed bright in the dimness.

'Jesus H! What a fuckin' racket!'

Cobra flicked the light switch flooding the cabin with harsh fluorescence. 'Can't share all that gold with a bunch of morons and fuckwits.' He slipped the Glock back into his waistband. 'So I took care of them.'

'Can't a man get some sleep round here!'

'Give me a hand. We'll chuck 'em over the side.'

And then he turned and was gone. Santos realized he was shaking, his body sheened in sweat. Dear God, he prayed, I hope I can hold on until daybreak.

They flung Jimmy and Rags over the side.

'Where's Spider? You turn him into fish food, too?' Santos leaned on the railing of the side deck, panting.

'He always did like the water.' Cobra's mirthless laugh hung in the breeze. The lights of Praslin were closer now. 'I need you to navigate us into position,' Cobra shouted from the wheelhouse.

Santos followed him inside. Whatever the lunatic's intentions, he didn't plan any more killing. Not just yet. Cobra had the wheel.

'You got the co-ordinates?'

Santos knew them by heart. He punched them into the GPS. The navigator would take a fix of their current position and direct a course to the gold.

48

Simon couldn't sleep. The ceiling fan pressed hot air into his face. He reached across to the bedside table and picked up his Rolex. Its luminous face glowed in the dark. Ten to five. He threw back the bedsheet. He'd heard Alan leave the chalet at four to stand his watch. He pulled on shorts and a T-shirt.

On the beach, Novak's team's equipment was arranged on the sand. Some of the soldiers were there making final checks, talking to Alan in low voices.

Two Scorpion inflatables each fitted with a Mercury outboard were laid out side by side in front of Bruno's chalet. Three full sets of scuba kit rested on the planked flooring of each boat, each set comprising twin tanks. Attached to the left tank of each apparatus was a black mask and a pair of black fins.

Next to the boats, on a piece of canvas, were four spear guns, night vision aids, powerful binoculars, pony tanks and the radios which would allow Cusack to feed information to the divers about the activity on Cobra's launch. The men each carried their personal weapon.

Simon went over to Alan. 'Got the chart?'

Alan spread it on the floor of Bruno's veranda. Simon activated the GPS receiver. At exactly five o'clock the boat's new co-ordinates flashed on to the display screen. He carefully plotted the position.

'Jesus. He's here,' Simon muttered. 'I mean, I knew he was coming, but now he's actually just out there . . . in the bay.' His expression was stony. as he refolded the chart and switched off the receiver.

'You ready for this, Simon?'

Simon breathed deeply, closed his eyes. Opened his eyes. 'Yeah! Let's go.'

They went back to whcrc Novak was standing by the equipment.

'Kepinski's here.' Simon pointed out over the black waters of the bay.

Lieutenant Novak followed Simon's outstretched hand but could not see anything. 'Where's Denotti?'

Alan answered. 'Calling Washington again.'

The rest of the commandos came out of their chalets. All the men were dressed in full-length, black neoprene wetsuits with balaclava hoods pulled back.

At five minutes past five the men collected in Bruno's chalet for the last time leaving Simon alone to stand watch.

The briefing was conducted by Lieutenant Novak who went over timings and roles. The meeting lasted twenty-five minutes and with each passing minute the tension in the chalet became more palpable. At 5.30 Novak's team, looking menacing in their skin-tight neoprene, left the chalet for the last time followed closely by Bruno Denotti. The plan called for Alan and Simon to stand by for the call from Cusack once the target was secure. Alan was about to make his way to the beach to watch the US Navy Seals commence the operation when he heard the slap, slap, slap of running feet bouncing into the room. Then Bruno burst through the door, his chest heaving for breath.

Alan spun round. Bruno's face was bleached of colour. 'Jesus, what's happened?'

'Simon with you?' Bruno gasped.

'On watch. He's with the boats.'

'Wrong!'

'What d'you mean?' Alan dropped the chart and started towards the door. 'I'll find him. Maybe he's—'

Bruno held out an arm. 'One of the inflatable's gone.'

The implication hit Alan immediately. 'Christ! He's gone out on his own!'

'Looks that way.'

Alan raced out of the chalet, through the garden and on to the beach. He hit the water running and waded out to the fisher. He clambered up, into the cockpit well. Both regulator air feeds had been cut through. He could see Bruno, in the shadows, waiting on the beach. Alan waded back to shore. 'The lines on our kit have been cut. I'm going after him.'

Lieutenant Novak ran over. 'The fuck's going on here?'

Alan ignored him, making fast decisions. 'Right, Lieutenant Novak, take two of your men in the other inflatable. Bruno, me and François René will follow in the fisher.'

Alan felt hopelessness engulf him. He thought about Bet. 'Why, for Christ sake?'

'He's going to try and take Cobra out himself? It's going to be no fucking contest!' Bruno muttered.

'He may have blown the element of surprise, but we've still got darkness to cover our approach.'

'We've got to airlift Kepinski out of here within the hour if we're going to make it back Stateside by the deadline!'

'We can do it!' Alan didn't want to waste another second. 'Okay! Simon's got a half-hour headstart. Let's go!'

49

Simon cut the engine of the Scorpion. Cobra's boat was 400 metres away, edging forwards tentatively. Simon guessed he was manoeuvring into an exact position. Calmly, he zipped his wetsuit. He stood up, balancing carefully, confident that the grey rubber hull and black engine would be indistinguishable against the oil-black sea. Cobra couldn't be expecting trouble. He believed his adversaries were dead and who else was left to threaten him? The thought brought a grin to Simon's lips. He felt bad about Alan, but what could he do? Couldn't have spoken to him. And while this Kepinski bastard still breathed God's sweet air, then he would remain dead inside. Ben incarcerated like a fucking animal! Probably dead by now. Two dead parents! And the hell he'd put Bet and Alan through. So what was the plan? Arrest Cobra. Then what? Try him for murder, while some scummy lawyer lies to the court to defend the animal on the premise that some nutcase may or may not have stolen some defence secrets.

Simon reached down, picked up a pot of petroleum jelly and began smearing the grease over the outside of his wetsuit. He kitted up, taking the chain he'd purchased the day before and wrapped it round his waist. Finally, he dropped a padlock into one of the weight pockets in his buoyancy vest and checked he had the set of handcuffs stolen from Angela Ramierez's office in Manila when he and Alan had put Mae-li into the custody of the Manila police. Then he slipped over the side and lowered

himself into the water, reaching inside to get the pony tank before letting
the Scorpion drift away on the current.

Simon swam on the surface, shielded by the dark. At one hundred
metres, Cobra's boat throttled back. The rattle of the anchor chain
belched into the dawn. Thin strips of purple emerged from the inky
blackness of the sky. The low throb of the pirate boat's engines floated
over the water. Suddenly, the engines stopped and the immediate, heavy
silence smothered him like a fog. Simon lined himself up with the boat's
stern, swimming so gently that he hardly made a ripple. He tried to think
of nothing else but what he must do. The US Navy mask was full-face
with an integral regulator. The radio was built in to the moulding, the
earpiece on the right side, the microphone grille in front of his mouth.
Simon fitted the mask over his face, took a last look at the looming stern
of the pirate launch and slid below the surface.

A school of Jackfish slipped through the tropical blue, as oblivious to the
loathings and desires of humankind as was possible for any living things
to be. The stream of air bubbles rising from the diver thirty feet below
posed a minor inconvenience, otherwise they paid him no heed nor bothered their collective consciousness with thoughts of why he might be
there. Had they known of the devils which ran amok in his mind, or the
hatred which clogged his throat, or the terror in his heart, they wouldn't
have cared. Only he cared because only he demanded retribution for the
hurt which had been done to him.

Simon spun round at their shadows, banging his tank against the
smooth side of the granite boulder from where he was keeping watch.
His panicked breathing escaped his regulator, bubbling incoherently
upwards through the turquoise haze.

'*Fuck!*' He screamed the word through the rubber bit clamped
between his teeth. That made him feel better. The Jackfish passed silently
overhead, disappearing as quickly as they had come in the sealed stillness of the sea. The black neoprene of his wetsuit merged with the rock
contours providing some camouflage. He started to laugh, burning
precious air. *Jesus Christ. How the fuck had it come to this?* He looked

down. His fins were causing tiny sandstorms to erupt on the seabed. He stopped laughing, acutely aware that he was in danger of becoming hysterical with fright.

Sixty metres away, the silhouette of Cobra's long, white, rusty boat rode a shallow swell, soaked in the thirty degree heat of early morning. He checked his watch. Twenty minutes had elapsed. The trap was set. The chain was wrapped tightly round the base of the boulder, secured with a padlock and covered with sand. The ancient treasure taken from the chest that had lain hidden for nearly three centuries was scattered over the shifting carpet of white sand. He gripped the trailing end of the steel chain. One bracelet of the set of handcuffs was locked through the last link in the chain. The second bracelet was open, the free chain falling heavily against his leg.

'You wait here.' Cobra casually removed the keys from the ignition and hung the string which attached the keys round his neck. 'Just in case you fancy taking off while I'm down there.'

'Where the hell exactly, do you think I'd go?'

'Pretty place, the Seychelles, so I'm told.' Cobra was already dressed in a full length wetsuit, torn, frayed and faded with use. He heaved a tank on to his back and tested his air flow by breathing through the regulator several times. 'Time to go get us some gold.' Cobra picked up a torch and a spear gun, feeding the rubber handle loop over his wrist.

'I'll be right here,' Santos said. 'At least he'd have a little time to think and he was thankful for that.

The sun erased the remainder of the night. The high dome of the sky was coloured a deep purple, lightening to blue in the east. Over the water, towards land, there was no sign of life. Alan had to be here somewhere, close.

'Wish me luck.' Cobra pulled his mask over his face and stepped over the gunwale into the water.

'I wish you were dead,' Santos muttered, watching Cobra shimmer beneath the surface then gradually blend into the deep.

*

Simon stared into the miasma with only the ponderous burden of revenge as company. It was reckless facing the danger alone but danger had become his accomplice.

The distant splash of a diver entering the water stopped the breath in his throat. He was out here, isolated in the wild with a maddened, predatory animal. Anxiety and fear rampaged through him, buckling him so that he had to lean against the boulder to stop himself from collapsing to his knees.

He pressed the deflator valve on his buoyancy vest. A rush of air escaped. The tank immediately felt heavier and his heels settled into the powdery sand. He kept the deflator valve depressed and raised the hose above the level of his shoulders squeezing out the last of the air trapped in his vest. Adrenalin forced the pace of his breathing to a rapid, shallow rhythm. He felt for the harness, aware of the tremor in his fingers. He snapped the clasp open and shrugged the tank from his back, disconnecting the regulator. Using his hands he scraped a shallow grave and buried the tank. Only the black vest showed, its straps wafting like the spines of a giant urchin. Grease from the harness had found its way on to his hands. He scooped sand and rubbed it away. Old air dribbled from the corners of his mouth. The comforting bulge of the emergency pony tank pressed into his stomach. He slipped it out from under his weight belt and snapped it on to the docking ring on the underside of his mask. Five minutes emergency air. He needed to concentrate on his breathing, to oxygenate his body. When it came to the fight he wouldn't have the luxury of air.

Simon settled back against the boulder, light and manoeuvrable. An eighteen-inch overhang protruding from the western face of the rock made him invisible from above. He strained his eyes eastwards into the blue-grey gloom. A rivulet of seawater sneaked into his mask and ran down the side of his nose.

He guessed about a minute to contact. Too late to abort. He glanced at his dive computer. Less than two minutes of air remained in the pony tank. He refocused on his vigil, squinting through his mask.

A shadow? His heart thumped, his skin prickled. A faint form evolved out of the gloom. A conical beam swept back and forth over the sea floor like a stage light.

He sucked air deeply into his lungs, once, twice, three times. The air became harder to draw as the supply depleted. He removed the pony tank and dropped it to the seabed. Above his head, his final breath agitated its way upwards to the surface. His fingers tightened around the handcuff. One chance was all he would get. He poked his head around the side of the boulder. If there were others following, he would die here in this strange, aquatic world.

For the final time Simon pulled back behind the boulder. Air dribbled from his nose and mouth. Almost a minute without oxygen. He felt the pressure beginning to mount in his brain, a mild burning took hold in his chest. Despite the cool water his palms felt sticky. He couldn't afford movement. Even the clinking of the chain would resound like an alarm.

In a clear patch of sand beyond the boulder, the metal framework of the chest, gnarled by marine growth, lay dormant like the skeleton of some long dead animal. Inside, a mound of doubloons beckoned like a siren.

He glanced up. The overhanging rock was directly above his head. He saw the torchlight splay over the ledge. His lungs gave an involuntary heave for air. Only seconds now. Then it would be over. Either way.

Billy-Ray Kepinski floated down in the gloom. He hoped Executioner enjoyed the morning. It would be his last. The thought made him chuckle. And all those assholes at the camp near Glan. There was over $300,000 in his safe on the boat. The exquisite necklace he'd promised to that fat slug Cortez was also nestling comfortably in the safe. Some time or other, he'd steal back into the Philippines and collect the rest of his money from Cortez. His bowels contracted as the sandy bottom of the ocean rose up towards him. He landed with a dusty puff of sand and flicked on his torch. Which way? Circles, swim in circles, that was the only sure way. An image of Mae-li drifted into his mind's eye. Dumb bitch shoulda stuck with me, he thought. She'd have been rich beyond imagining. He'd disappear, forget about Mae-li. Maybe go to Mexico or Brazil. Yeah! Brazil. No extradition, not that anyone would know. The McGovern kid was dog meat so was that fat McCreadie fuck. As for Ben, well he'd rot at the bottom of the well shaft for all eternity.

Cobra played the torch beam over the sand. Just up ahead the fluorescent pinks and greens of a fish caught the light and dazzled him. But something else dazzling, not moving. His heart leapt. He finned forward. Shone the light. Gold winked through a thin covering of sand. An invisible current, like the hand of a ghost brushed the sand aside. A round, yellow glint. Cobra dived down, scrabbled the seabed and pulled a Spanish doubloon from the grip of the sea. He felt panicked, excited and agitated all at once. He dropped the coin and wafted sand with his hand. More gold! Not bad for a farm boy from Clear Lake, Iowa!

Cobra followed the trail. The stuff was probably all around. Jesus! He came up against a tall boulder. He splayed the light over the top. More coins! He swam up to retrieve them. The torch beam spread to a wide arc, capturing something beyond the rock. Cobra directed the beam. Three metres away, the metal ribs of an ancient chest guarded a mound of gold. Cobra hovered, staring. He couldn't believe what he was seeing. This is it! The beginning of the rest of my life!

Simon lunged up, dragging the chain with both hands. He focused on Kepinski's naked ankle. That's all he saw, concentrated on nothing else. He snapped the open bracelet round the white flesh and pressed it closed, feeling the ratchets lock until he could squeeze no more. Simon kicked away, but not before Cobra turned and grabbed at him. Tight hands closed around his leg, but the petroleum jelly made him slippery as an eel and the hands slid away. Simon kicked forward colliding with Cobra. He reached down and ripped Cobra's knife from his leg holster. He slithered up through a bear hug and slashed Cobra's air line. A frantic stream of bubbles erupted from the severed end of the regulator tubing. Cobra spun round crazily, suddenly unable to breathe. He released his attacker, reaching up for the damaged line.

Simon took his opportunity, circled behind Cobra and cut the speargun from his wrist. He could feel dizziness swamp his brain. He dived down, towards the base of the rock, yanked his tank free from its sandy hiding place and kicked violently away from the rock to a safe distance, beyond the length of chain which tethered Cobra.

Simon fumbled for the air hose, felt it into place and snapped it home. He drew massive breaths, heaving the precious air into his body. The dizziness faded. Another huge breath. His pulse thundered in his ears. His chest was working independently, expanding and collapsing until his blood gases fell into equilibrium. He slipped his arms through the shoulder slings of the vest, still clutching Cobra's knife. No way for Kepinski to escape now, not even by cutting through his own leg. Going for the knife had been a massive risk. But when he had seen it strapped to Kepinski's leg, he knew he'd had no choice.

Cobra tried breathing from the tube, but the pressure of air was too great for him to control its flow. By placing the severed end in front of his nose, he was able to draw off some of the escaping gas. He had two minutes, three at most. He looked down at his anchored leg. The handcuff was biting into his flesh. He tugged and yanked, drawing blood. The chain was never going to break. He pulled himself down, following the chain to the base of the rock. His fingers reached the padlock. He tore at it. Reaching up, Cobra grabbed the air line and breathed. Who had attacked him? Here!

Cobra held the air hose to his mouth. The stream of bubbles was beginning to slow as his tank pressure dwindled. He yanked his leg viciously, trying to break the chain. Blood swirled as the steel cuff bit deeper, to the bone. His captor hovered just out of range of the chain. Something familiar about the face behind the mask. Like his mother. No! The boy! *The McGovern kid!* They'd trailed him across the world! They'd played him for a fool! He began to take in water, breathing it deep into his lungs. Should've killed him . . . should. . . .

Simon watched. He felt nothing, not triumph, not sadness. Nothing. He watched Cobra become still and look towards him. Watched the horror of recognition transform the face of his tormentor to stone.

Above, wake trails cut the surface. He recognized the outline of the other Scorpion buzzing around the bigger boat like an agitated hornet. A larger hull approached from the west. Alan, he guessed.

Billy-Ray Kepinski's body wafted in the gentle breeze of the current three metres above the seabed, pulling the chain taut. Air bubbles trickled from the severed air line. Kepinski's mouth was open and his eyes staring vacantly. The muscles of the dead man's hand relaxed. His fingers uncurled. A golden doubloon dropped free, glinting in the shifting rays of the sun.

50

The thud-rush, thud-rush of helicopter rotors penetrated the blackness of the ancient well shaft. The prisoner was immediately alert, looking upwards towards the tiny ring of light 200 feet above and he cocked his head to listen to the sound filtering through the canopy of leaves. He didn't shout out, or jump, or scream, or wave his arms because he was sane and his sanity prevented him from needlessly forfeiting his energy.

The sound of the helicopter faded until it impinged only on the very edge of his hearing. Then it grew louder, passing close overhead, then faded across the other side. The prisoner deduced a pattern. The helicopter was flying a search grid, back and forth over the forest and his heart began to beat faster until he felt it as a fluttering in his throat and the blood pounding though his veins as a tingling in his hands. Through the thud-rush of the rotors came another sound, closer. The prisoner recognized his own voice, the peace chant, to calm himself, to keep himself from tipping into hopeless hopefulness.

> '... I am the wind and I kiss you, yellow fields
> I am the water and I soothe you, brown earth
> I am the sun and I warm you, my heart. . . .'

And as he recited the chant over and over, the tiny ring of light blurred and misted. The prisoner blinked and for a moment the light became clear as hot tears streamed down his gaunt, blackened cheeks.

Simon hung out of the open door of the Sea King helicopter, the rotors' down draught flattening his hair. On the bench seat opposite, Mae-li stared down at the forest canopy. Alan, sitting next to Simon, leaned across to get a view.

Beyond the abrupt treeline, Simon could see the flat plain of the river delta and he imagined, in the harsh sunlight of late afternoon, that he could see the stake from which they had rescued Mae-li. He glanced across at her and tried to yell over the thudding roar of cut air.

'Do you recognize any of this?'

Mae-li leaned forwards and Simon yelled the question again. When she shook her head, Simon unhooked the headphones from a cradle above his head and motioned her to do the same.

She held the headphones over her ears with both hands, listening. The forest canopy was a dense bubbling green. Suddenly, Mae-li pointed out the door. Simon followed with his eyes. Several hundred feet below a path had been hacked from the woods and beyond it a clearing.

'See that, Al?'

'Seen.' Alan peered down at the forest canopy. 'What's down there?'

Simon heard Alan's voice clearly though the headphones. He was talking to Mae-li.

'A village. Nobody lives there now.'

'You recognize it?' Simon asked.

'Yes,' Mae-li nodded.

Alan stood up and leaned against the pilot's seat. He tapped his shoulder and pointed towards the clearing. The pilot looked down, saw the break in the trees and acknowledged with a thumbs-up sign before swinging the helicopter round in a tight manoeuvre.

Beyond the delta, the coastline faded to silver. Simon flicked his eyes up towards the horizon. Three coastal patrol craft were stationed in the bay, close to shore, facing what he guessed was the location of Cobra's camp. Inland, above the camp, two helicopters, tiny from this distance, like flies, hovered. He imagined the ground troops closing in, sealing the perimeter and the entrance road over the swamp. Somewhere down there, Filippo Santos would be directing operations. Any escapees would be herded by the boats or the choppers. By any reckoning the operation appeared efficient, from this distance anyway.

Mae-li had flown down from Manila with Angela Ramierez. Alan had been in contact with her on and off during the night and she had confirmed, finally, what Santos had learned from Kepinski about the location of the prisoner. Since news of her lover's death, she had been free of her fear, free to give Alan and Simon the information they desperately sought.

Simon returned his attention to the clearing. Two hundred feet below he could see the village huts were neglected. Their palm-thatched roofs had fallen in and the sandy ground was littered with dead wood from the crumbling buildings. The pilot made a slow sweep but the place seemed deserted.

'Can we land in the village?' Alan yelled into his microphone. The pilot nodded, checking the trees below for any loose branches that might clip his rotor blades. Slowly the canopy began to rise up towards them. The down draught hit the clearing, tossing up great orange dust clouds.

They had been airborne for over an hour, surveying the forest in east-west parallels running south.

Mae-li only knew the prisoners were kept away from the camp, some-where in the forest, but she had not been able to be more specific. From the air she had become disoriented, unable to locate the village until she'd seen the disturbance in the forest canopy.

The Sea King settled unevenly, coming to earth with a jolt, before the nose wheel bit. Simon was already out and running, ducking beneath the rotors and shielding his eyes against the dust. The police escort who was riding with them came up beside him, armed, just in case. Simon waited for Alan, whose arm was around Mae-li's shoulder, her hair flapping furiously in the wind blast. Alan looked towards the cockpit and moved a pointed finger in a circle to indicate the engines should be kept running. The pilot, eyes hidden behind aviator shades, gave a nonchalant wave.

'Let's look in the huts,' Simon shouted, bent almost double against the down draught. He figured that if anyone was going to take a pot shot at them they would have done it by now. 'I'll take this side. Al, why don't you take the other side? We'll meet in the middle. Mae-li, you stay here with the guard.'

The huts were empty. Discarded belongings and cooking utensils spilled on the wooded floors.

Simon shook his head when he saw Alan. 'Nothing!'

'Me neither. What about the track?'

'Let's take a look.'

They went back to where Mae-li and the guard waited, seeking protection from the dust behind the last hut. They walked away from the village, down the track into the forest. Above their heads a strip of sky aimed a rectangle of sunlight to the ground. Either side of the track, the air was cool and the light faded to a gloomy green.

Simon noticed it first: eighty metres down the track, the air turned sour.

'Smell that?'

Alan sniffed the air then screwed his face to a grimace. 'Stinks!'

'What's that, over there?' Simon could see a rope coiled against the base of a tree. A discarded newspaper fluttered in the breeze.

'Wait a sec.' They all stopped. Alan bent down, picked up a cigarette butt. 'This is recent, not discoloured by rain.' He tossed the butt aside. 'Someone's been here.'

A massive iron grid squatted incongruously among the trees. The ground around the grid had been trampled flat. More cigarette butts littered the sand. Some old, some newer. Simon pressed a foot on to the grate, to test its strength. The iron was thick and clean of rust.

'What the hell is this?'

Alan stood by the side of the grid. 'A well shaft maybe ... or a mine. . . .'

'That rope must be a couple of hundred feet long. You think maybe it's used to lower stuff down there?' Simon bent over the well, but only blackness greeted him. He walked over the grate and squatted down next to the hatch. His heart began to pick up speed.

'Al, check this out.'

Alan came up beside him and fingered the padlock. 'Big enough for a man. Now why the hell would someone cover a well or a mine, then leave an access hatch?'

Mae-li and the guard were standing by the edge of the grate.

Alan went to the edge and walked around the outside of the grate. No retaining bolts. 'Simon, get off a sec. There's nothing holding this thing down. Give me a hand, see if we can shift it.'

Simon joined Alan and together they tried to lift the grid.

'No bloody way to move this,' Simon grimaced. He glanced at Alan. The weight of hope was too much. Alan's suspicions were crazy, surely. But Mae-li said there were prisoners, different ones at different times. The line between belief and fantasy had blurred. He would never have dared hope he might see his brother alive . . . and yet. He kneeled over the abyss.

With desperation he could not hide, Simon called his brother's name.

> '. . . I am the wind and I kiss you, yellow fields
> I am the water and I soothe you, brown earth
> I am the sun and I warm you, my heart. . . .'

The thud-rush became muffled and distant. The prisoner strained his hearing. Somewhere, at the reaches of his senses he could hear the noise settle to a murmur. He waited for the murmur to cease. But it persisted. A constant whisper. The prisoner started chanting again, this time slowly, still staring up at the ring of light.

Presently, voices drifted down to him. The words were indistinguishable but the voices seemed near. The prisoner became silent. He listened. Watching the light. He listened to the voices, for the harsh banter of his captors, the evil laughter, the staccato language. But the voices were different. The voices were smooth, questioning, timid, afraid, weary. The voices spilled on to him like the voices of angels.

The ring of light was broken. The prisoner blinked and squinted to sharpen his focus. Shadows above moved in and out of the light like moths. He reached his arm upwards, fingers spread, to touch the silhouettes. He tried to shout, but his throat had become constricted and the noise he emitted was a croak which bounced against the walls and disintegrated. He felt his face crumple. He felt the rough floor crunch into his knees as he collapsed, still reaching upwards. The shadows moved and were gone and the voices were still.

The prisoner tried to shout again, but no sound came. He bent his head. He tried to calm himself. He summoned his fear and his hate and his strength and he called to the monster that lived within him. He knew he was close to madness now. He knew that he could not survive this, not if the shadows were only the impressions of his mind, made alive with voices. Not if he was still alone. Not if the helicopter was a figment to add credence to his dream. Not if his rescue was only in his mind, fuelled by the impossibility of it.

'*Ben! Ben!*'

His name exploded in his brain. And the monster came and spilled out of him and the prisoner screamed at the demons, screamed so that his vision became spangled with bursts of light, screamed so that he felt fire in his throat, screamed because he was on the very abyss of madness.

The noise erupted from the mouth of the well and drenched Simon so that his flesh burned and his stomach crawled.

Alan came and bent over the grid. 'Ben!'

And the scream came again. A tormented wail from the depths of hell. Then silence.

'Simon . . Simon!'

Alan was shaking his shoulder.

'Someone's down there. It may be Ben, it may not. We've got to shift this grid.' He spun round to the guard. 'Is there a rescue line in the helicopter?'

The guard nodded.

'Right. Go back to the chopper. Secure the safety line to the underside, then get the pilot to hover over us and drop the line to me. We need to pull this thing off.'

The guard turned and ran.

Simon bent over the hole. 'Hang on, Ben!' he yelled. He wanted so much to believe it was Ben, so much to believe that Alan was right and that Ben was still alive. So much. . . .

He could not control the sobs. They blurted out of him, racking his body. 'Hang on, Ben!' But his words had become crumpled helpless things that reached only Alan, whose arms were suddenly around his shoulders, squeezing him, whose broad chest was a comfortable place for him to rest and pray that his brother was down there.

The trees began to sway and the wind beat the leaves apart and showered them with dirt. Alan looked up and waved. The steel cable fell into the clearing. Alan grabbed the end and looped it several times around one of the grid's bars. Then he motioned for the chopper to slowly advance. The cable tightened and with a grinding of iron on earth, pulled the grid over the ground until a two-foot slice of the mouth of the well was exposed. He waved up at the pilot to stop and the cable slackened.

'Simon, get me that rope.'

Simon raced to the tree and hauled the rope back. Alan tied one end to the cable then kicked the coiled rope into the well.

Alan kneeled and bowed his head to the void. He cupped his hands around his mouth and screamed above the noise of the hovering chopper, 'Grab the rope, Ben! Pull on it when you are ready!' He held the rope waiting for the tug. It jerked twice in his hand. Alan glanced up. He could see the guard looking down, hanging out of the open side of the chopper. Alan spread his arms wide, palms up and raised his hands.

The message was understood and slowly the helicopter began to lift.

Simon waited at the edge of the well, watching the rope regurgitate out of its mouth.

A bony hand appeared, clutching the rope. A shaven head, blue eyes appeared enormous in the chiselled contours of his white, pallid face, a skull-like face from which the flesh had dissolved away. The body, stripped of fat, was ridged and knotted with stringy muscle. Ribs poked through. The eyes were wide and staring. The prisoner stepped from the rope ring he had tied, on to the ground at the edge of the well. And there he stood, a filthy sarong wrapped around his bony pelvis. The prisoner's skin was blackened with encrusted dirt and the smell of him was almost overpowering.

The prisoner stood and glanced around, his eyes blinking rapidly against the white brilliance of daylight, resting on each of their faces for only a moment. Simon was the last. The eyes stared into his from the hollowed face whose cheeks were streaked with the white remnants of tears.

Simon searched the face. 'Ben?' he whispered as if in prayer.

The prisoner's eyes watered. His mouth pulled back in a rictus and he whispered, '*I am the sun.*' And from the edge of infinity he rushed to the sanity of his brother's arms.

Epilogue

The final tally of the number killed by the bloody hand of Billy-Ray Kepinski remains a mystery, despite the best efforts of the Federal Bureau of Investigation and the United States Maritime Administration.

When Simon drifted to the surface after his self-directed exorcism, he pressed a small key into Bruno Denotti's palm. It was only later that morning when he dived to recover the body, with his colleague, Lieutenant Novak, did Bruno fully appreciate the magnitude of what Simon McGovern had suffered. That realization was sufficient to quell some of his chagrin at the unscheduled death of his quarry and the catastrophic consequences it might unleash.

Billy-Ray Kepinski's body was flown back to the United States in company with Lieutenant Novak's team of US Navy Seals and Special Agent Bruno Denotti. At exactly seventeen minutes to six on the evening of 30th November, just before the expiry of the deadline imposed on the White House for the safe return of the ROIP data, Gertrude Ziegle was shown into a windowless room in the basement of the Livermore Hospital. There, in the presence of Bruno Denotti she met a man who introduced himself as George Gabriel Baker, formerly of Freedom Company, United States Marine Corps. He identified the body on the steel gurney as Billy-Ray Kepinski, supporting the identification with a photograph of his training platoon taken at Fort Jefferson in the summer of 1968. Standing next to Kepinski in the back line was Jamie-Jake Mulcahy, crew-cut and smiling for the camera.

Shortly afterwards, the US Marine Corps successfully applied for an exhumation order on the remains of Jamie-Jake Mulcahy. He was rein-terred with full military honours.

Bruno Denotti continued to work on the case. Armed with a warrant from the US Supreme Court requiring any persons served to submit all materials in their possession held on behalf of Gertrude Janet Ziegle née Mulcahy, he spearheaded a nation-wide search of US attorneys.

No such material was found.

At the conclusion of Bruno Denotti's unsuccessful operation, FBI Director Bernard Levy met with his counterpart at the CIA, Howard Cheney. They agreed to execute an action within Department F of the CIA's Clandestine Operations Division. Three days later, Gertrude Ziegle was killed, the victim of a 'hit and run' incident not far from her home on Fig Tree Drive.

The US Senate Intelligence Committee dismissed the threats from Gertrude Ziegle as a hoax, despite evidence which the chairman of the joint chiefs of staff had previously accredited. The incident never received a public airing. The Virginia-class submarine project, a $30 billion programme to design and build a new generation of super-subs, is still on schedule for launch sometime in 2004. Stolen data relating to the Radar Ocean Imaging Programme has never been recovered.

François René supervised the salvage of Robert McGovern's treasure from the spot where Billy-Ray Kepinski died. He never voiced his disap-pointment that only one half-full chest of gold was recovered. He did nonetheless receive the thanks of his superiors and a promotion. His superiors held on to sixty per cent of the gold, some of which appeared briefly in a local museum.

Simon, Ben and Alan returned to Australia. On their first evening home, Bet announced that she was pregnant. Eight months later she gave birth to a little boy. Alan and Bet named their son, John, in honour of his grandfather.

Ben was hospitalized and fed a controlled, high-protein diet. He received trauma counselling and underwent a physical rehabilitation programme. He was also deloused. A bed was put into his room so Simon could spend the nights with his brother and be there for him when he woke screaming from his nightmares.

After five weeks, Simon and Ben returned to England. Simon spent his time in England disposing of his apartment and his parents' Kensington residence. As executor of his father's estate, Simon sought the agreement of his siblings and became their treasurer.

Simon and Ben flew back to Brisbane. Ben opened a bar, close to the beach at Deception Bay. He still finds it difficult to be alone.

Alan did manage to get Mae-li a residency permit but she decided to return to Manila. Filippo Santos telephones Alan regularly. He is always coy whenever Mae-li's name is mentioned. Alan plans to spring a surprise visit on him one day.

As for the gold, Simon has bought a seventy-foot, ocean-going launch which he is having refitted with a small crane, a compressor and a secret hold. The boat is named *Clarissa III*. He is planning to sail to the Seychelles with Ben, Alan and Bet sometime soon.

One task remained for Alan to perform before he could finally close the file on the murders of Sir John and Lady Elizabeth McGovern. He requisitioned all of the DNA evidence concerning the issue of Ben's paternity. Then he destroyed it. Charlie was the only other person who knew the truth.